EURIPIDES AND DIONYSUS

An Interpretation of the Bacchae

R.P. Winnington-Ingram

Second Edition
Foreword and Bibliography by P.E. Easterling

This impression 2003
This edition published, with permission, in 1997 by
Bristol Classical Press
an imprint of
Gerald Duckworth & Co. Ltd.
61 Frith Street, London W1D 3JL
Tel: 020 7434 4242
Fax: 020 7434 4420
inquiries@duckworth-publishers.co.uk
www.ducknet.co.uk

First published in 1948 by Cambridge University Press

A catalogue record for this book is available from the British Library

ISBN 1 85399 524 X

CONTENTS

FOREWORD

Euripides and Dionysus is in every way an unusual book. Between writing and publication there was a long wartime gap: although it was essentially complete by 1938, the work was not even sent to a publisher till 1946. When it came out two years later it was politely reviewed but made little immediate impact: Winnington-Ingram himself at the end of his life recalled that it 'dropped like a stone'. But by the late sixties there was enough demand for a reprint to be issued (Hakkert, 1969) and nearly thirty years later its classic status has become self-evident. Monographs on single plays are liable to fall out of fashion quite quickly, yet here is a book that goes on being read and cited as if it were a contemporary contribution to the critical debate.

Winnington-Ingram's unpublished memoir tells the story of its origin. He had been appointed to a Readership at Birkbeck College in London in 1933, when he was barely thirty. Up to that point his research had largely been on Greek music, but he now began to spend more time on Greek drama, linking his research more directly with his teaching, and he began by working closely on Aeschylus. Then in 1937 he gave a course of lectures on the *Bacchae*,

> which excited me so much that I laid aside all other work with the intention of writing one or two articles on the play – and discovered that I was writing a book. This was the only time I found myself able to work late in the evening after teaching at Birkbeck [where teaching ran from 6 to 9 p.m.]. I wrote the first chapter in a week and most of the subsequent chapters in a fortnight apiece. Only the last chapter remained to be written when I became involved in the process of getting married, and that chapter I wrote, with great difficulty, on the return from our honeymoon in 1938. The draft was shown to various people, laid aside during the war, then revised and published as *Euripides and Dionysus* (1948). I think I can claim that it is still read.

He goes on to sketch in the background of public events at the time he was writing:

> I was not – and could not be – indifferent. Since my time in Italy in 1928 [he had spent a summer vacation working as a tutor for an English family who were strongly opposed to the prevailing ideology] I had been passionately anti-Fascist, anti-totalitarian, undeceived by those well-meaning conservatives who would

> persist in looking at Nazism in terms of colonies! (*Euripides and Dionysus* was haunted by the Nuremberg rallies.) I was anti-Franco, though not too happy about the Communist supporters of the legitimate government, being the kind of 'liberal' for whom Communists have the greatest contempt. I was restive about our slowness to rearm; I was against appeasement (though, humanly, relieved when Chamberlain returned from Munich with his scrap of paper)...

Some passages in the book become more pointed if they are read with this contemporary experience in mind: the paragraph on peace, for example ('...“peace”, like “wisdom” and “sanity”, is a word to play with; and what stands as peace must be judged by its quality and by its fruits' [p.67]), or the discussion of the dangerous group organisation and mentality of Dionysiac worshippers (p.97), or the comment on Pentheus' language at *Bacchae* 778-86: 'Thus not only does he meet force with force, but counters one intoxicating emotion with another; for an army on the march, an army with banners, is a Dionysiac drug, and not least for the general who commands it' (p.101).

There must have been plenty of other more typically academic factors shaping the formation of *Euripides and Dionysus*. The reviewers, who (with one interesting exception, mentioned below) made no comment on the possible links with recent events, were certainly sensitive to the book's scholarly agenda – though they did not necessarily single out what now seem its most distinctive qualities. Of the colleagues named in the Preface the most influential for the development of Winnington-Ingram's thinking was E.R. Dodds, who was working at the same period on the first edition of his commentary on the *Bacchae*. This appeared in 1944, in time to be used for the revision of the typescript of *Euripides and Dionysus*, of which Dodds had seen an earlier version in 1939 (he acknowledges a debt to it in his Preface and quotes it from time to time). The books reflect the friendly interaction between two scholars who in important, though very different, ways were ahead of their time. Both are clearly influenced by Gilbert Murray, who had been a pioneer in *his* time; all three had the kind of imaginativeness and critical agility which resists type-casting in the conventional philological mould. The other scholars thanked by Winnington-Ingram, two friends from King's College Cambridge whom he must have known when he was at Trinity, Donald Lucas and Patrick Wilkinson, and his old tutor F.M. Cornford, were all sensitive readers and good judges of critical writing, but none was as close as Dodds to his project.

Euripides and Dionysus offers a systematic reading of *Bacchae* in twelve chapters, of which two-thirds are devoted to running commentary paying close attention to form and language. This scrupulous attentiveness, a feature of all Winnington-Ingram's work, is one of the qualities that have given it staying power. It was not common in 1948, still less in the pre-war period when the book was written, for Classical scholars to look as closely and systematically as this at the complex interplay of language in the texts that they studied with such minuteness. Winnington-Ingram insisted that his primary concern was 'with the text of the play, and with the whole text' (p.10); there was no question of picking out a few key themes if one was to do full justice to the whole. J.S. Morrison, in a slightly quizzical review (*CR* 63 [1949] 96-7) calculated that this worked out at nearly a page to each ten lines of the text, which by the standards of a modern monograph would not seem over-lavish, but Morrison wondered if there was all that much more to be said 'after Professor Dodds' exhaustive edition'. Only a couple of reviewers (H.H. Huxley in *Greece & Rome* 18 [1949] 90-1 and W.B. Stanford in *Hermathena* 73 [1949] 104) saw that in providing translations of the passages he discussed Winnington-Ingram had made it possible for non-classical or Greekless readers to use the book.

One or two examples will point the contrast between the two sorts of commentary. On Pentheus' threatening outburst against Teiresias (*Bacchae* 343-51) which includes the command to his servants to

> go to his seat where he watches birds, lever it up and overturn it;
> mix everything together topsy-turvy and cast his holy ribbands
> to the winds and tempests,

Winnington-Ingram remarks that Pentheus' paroxysm of rage is

> behaviour comparable to that of the king's antagonists. When worshippers of Dionysus are opposed, then there is an outbreak of violence. It happens with our Bacchanals upon the mountains, when they fall upon flocks and villages; it is symbolised by the earthquake which follows the imprisonment of Dionysus.

To which he adds the footnote, 'Nor is it, I think, coincidence that an identical expression links together these three passages (349, 602, 741, 753) "topsy-turvy" is the Greek ἄνω κάτω, which, if not uncommon, is sufficiently arresting to be recalled by repetition' (p.55, with n.4; cf. pp.85, 97 n.1); he goes on to give the statistics for the use of the phrase in surviving tragedy. This phrase and its prominent repetition are not mentioned by Dodds. In another instance, where Winnington-Ingram illuminatingly discusses the ambiguous resonance of the word περισσός (*Bacchae* 429, 1197; pp.67-9 and 137), Dodds half-acknowledges the word play, but in very austere terms (on 1197). It was not only particular words and phrases that Winnington-Ingram explored in this detailed way; some of his finest analyses are of patterns of thought in a whole lyric, as in his remarks on the Third Stasimon (pp.105-16; such passages foreshadow his influential later articles on Aeschylean and Sophoclean odes). Dodds's rich discussion covers some, but not much, of the same ground.

This habit of seeing every word of a dramatic text as potentially significant, not only in its immediate context but in its complex links with other passages, looks entirely familiar and 'natural' these days, but Winnington-Ingram wrote his book long before even New Criticism started to exert its influence (Cleanth Brooks's *The Well-Wrought Urn* was published in 1947). Bernard Knox's *Oedipus at Thebes* (1957), and W.B. Stanford's commentary on *Ajax* (1963) are examples of the way things were to go; it is interesting that *Euripides and Dionysus* captured the new mood so early, and it would be good to know where the impetus came from. Winnington-Ingram was a person of great independence: his own fastidious reading of the text must account for a good deal. Another of his publications from the same year as *Euripides and Dionysus* was the article 'Clytemnestra and the Vote of Athena' (*JHS* 68 [1948] 130-47), which many years later was hailed as a feminist critique *avant la lettre*. But it would be surprising if he had not been responding to changing intellectual and artistic currents, and I.A. Richards's *Practical Criticism* had after all been published in 1927, when he was working in Cambridge. During his Editorship of the *Cambridge Review* in 1926-7 Winnington-Ingram had written book reviews across quite a wide range (including one [11 February, 1927] in which he expressed intense excitement at David Garnett's use of language and recurrent motifs in the novel *Go She Must*); he was certainly in closer touch with modern culture than some Classical scholars, and keenly followed theatre and ballet as well as being himself a serious musician. It is also possible that the friend whose help he acknowledges in the Preface, E.O. Symonds, had a part to play: Winnington-Ingram describes him in the memoir as having 'one of the most brilliant and original minds I have ever encountered. Beginning as a scientist and inventor, he became totally absorbed in the philosophy of Whitehead and in the study of Shakespeare. Together we had long discussions into the small hours.' Symonds died young and had no wider intellectual influence, but he may have contributed significantly to the development of this book.

Whatever may have been true of his sources, there is no doubt that he was quite self-conscious about his methodology, little as he makes of it in *Euripides and Dionysus*. This is clear from some of his reviews written around the same period. On F.R. Earp's *The Style of Aeschylus* (Cambridge, 1948) the main criticism he makes is of Earp's mechanical listing of images: 'What E. fails to take into account is something which might be called the structural use of metaphor. This cannot be brought out by counting occurrences...' [he illustrates the point by reference to the naval imagery of *Septem* and the language of light and darkness in the *Oresteia*]. 'Considerations of style lead into considerations of form which would greatly extend the scope of the book but cannot safely be neglected in the treatment of metaphor' (*CR* 63 [1949] 95-6). On Fraenkel's *Agamemnon* he has this to say: 'Verbal ambiguities he tends to reject; and those who regard this means of conveying irony as particularly characteristic of the poet will feel here a limitation in Fraenkel's criticism. The presence of verbal ambiguity can seldom be proved or disproved, and it is not always very important one way or the other...' [then follows a detailed and telling discussion of its importance in the Herald scene] (*CR* n.s.1 [1951] 147-51).

Not surprisingly, there are plenty of ways in which *Euripides and Dionysus* shows its age, beginning with the treatment of Dionysus himself. When Winnington-Ingram wrote on p.1 'Dionysus was relatively a newcomer to Olympus. His worship had been introduced into Greece at an unknown date from Thrace or Asia or perhaps from both, since Thracians and Phrygians were closely akin in blood and culture', he was expressing the generally held view of the time, which despite the challenge of Walter Otto (*Dionysos: Mythos und Kultus* [Frankfurt, 1933]) remained dominant until the discovery of the name of Dionysus in Linear B tablets from Pylos (later confirmed by discoveries on Kea and at Khania in Crete; see Bibliographical Note). Scholars nowadays are more likely to explain the ancient stories in which Dionysus was represented as an outsider from Thrace or Asia as mythical ways of articulating his role as a god of epiphany, not as any kind of historical narrative; but it is worth noting that Winnington-Ingram's reading of the god's dangerous doubleness can still be found illuminating in the context of these discussions (Edith Hall, for example, makes use of it in her account of the 'barbarization' of Dionysus, *Inventing the Barbarian* [Oxford, 1989] 151-3).

More broadly, the whole framework within which Dionysus is viewed has changed as perceptions of religious practice have changed, with the emphasis shifting from theology and ethics to the analysis of cult and ritual as phenomena of social structure (in this area it was Dodds who was the pioneer). Now that the Greek gods and their myths in general are commonly understood as less orderly, more wild and raw, but also more functional within the life of the polis than when terms like 'Hellenic spirit' were current, and now that so much more is known about the prevalence of mystery cult, it is easier to read the *Bacchae* without having to choose between the sort of models that had dominated earlier debate. Winnington-Ingram was influenced by, and felt obliged to enter into dialogue with, a broadly rationalist reading of Euripides (though he was sufficiently independent of it to put his critique of Verrall on the 'palace miracles' in an Appendix). This led him to make a rather uncomfortable distinction between the 'mythological' Dionysus, the object of the poet's satire, and Dionysus as a mighty force of nature which the poet understood and feared. At all points he is concerned to show how the play works as a whole, but this admirable concern leads him to make claims about Euripides' own position that in their confident intentionality are hard for late twentieth-century readers to share, particularly the terms he uses in his concluding paragraphs (pp.178-9):

> Euripides recognised Dionysus for the danger that he was, publicly in the societies of men, when he works at full strength through the group, and privately in the lives of individuals. The worship of such a god he could not commend; and the anthropomorphic god upon the stage is treated with a satire which is essentially consistent with the treatment accorded to his subtler manifestations throughout the length and breadth of the play. Euripides recognised, but hated Dionysus. He recognised his power, and saw that there was only one weapon to employ against him, which was to understand him and to propagate understanding of him.

In the end Winnington-Ingram found it hard to allow for a genuinely religious dimension: like Murray and Wilamowitz, he was suspicious of religious establishments, and in his remarks on Teiresias ('something of a ritualist', p.55) there is a whiff of his contemporary world (he came from a clerical family). So he looked elsewhere for explanations, and found them in what he saw as the political and psychological constants in human society (e.g. p.152).

What is still attractive is the intensity and coherence of the reading: in his understanding of 'the Dionysiac' as unrestrained emotionalism of a very distinctive kind (as an individual psychological phenomenon and particularly as a feature of group mentality: 'all history is full of the Dionysiac reaction of the crowd', p.178) Winnington-Ingram is drawing on powerful recent experience, just as Ronald Syme wrote *The Roman Revolution* with modern fascism as an explanatory model. The only review that picked up the contemporary resonance of *Euripides and Dionysus* criticised him for attributing to Euripides and his audience the concern felt by modern readers about 'the danger of mass movements, "reaching for the stars" and suppressing opposition with fanatical cruelty' (L.A. Post, *CPh* 46 [1951] 130-1), but quaintly enough the reviewer went on to describe an experience of his own which illustrates the way the play could appeal to contemporary sensibility: 'Certainly Dionysus is an ironical character, a smiling tormenter. His face, as made up for a performance at Bryn Mawr in 1935, in which I played Teiresias, gave me a horrid dream of being in the clutches of a servant of Hitler, who had the face of Dionysus, as I recognised when I woke'. Post used the story as part of a critique of Winnington-Ingram's view of Euripides as *engagé*: 'As an artist, Euripides, I suggest, was ironical in that he was...detached from his own work when it was done. He created an imaginary horror that moves most the spectator who has in himself most fear of the irrational'.

It could certainly be argued in criticism of *Euripides and Dionysus*, as indeed of many other later discussions, that it does not make enough allowance for the 'imaginary' nature of the action – that neither the women of the chorus nor any of the characters are best understood as representing human beings in some more or less naturalistically conceived situation. (So there is some awkwardness in his emphasis on the identity of the chorus as 'actual human Bacchanals', while Dionysus is both the 'personal adversary' of Pentheus with 'human traits which develop unpleasantly' and at the same time 'an impersonal power too strong for him', p.73.) Just as the complexity of Dionysus is best grasped if he is taken as a symbolic figure, as Winnington-Ingram saw – despite the distracting complications introduced by the satiric interpretation – so it helps to take the chorus or Teiresias or Pentheus as having an emblematic function in addition to evoking a more directly emotional response. Like Dodds, Winnington-Ingram argued strongly for a Pentheus who is 'betrayed by enemies from within' (p.58), though he was by no means satisfied with a reading that stopped at character-portrayal for its own sake (p.58):

> To regard Pentheus merely as the central figure of a drama, hero or villain, whose personal attractiveness or unattractiveness matters for his own sake, is to misread the part. He belongs to a

> wider pattern, of which he is a subordinate, if important, element – a pattern which reveals by similarity and contrast the operations of Dionysus in the world of men. Pentheus appears as the persecutor of Dionysus and his followers; Teiresias is their advocate. But, to the discerning eye, Teiresias has little in common with them, Pentheus all too much. He thinks he is rational and prudent, but really, like them, he is at the mercy of irrational impulse, and, like them, he expresses himself through violence. But in his isolation he is no match for them. No force that he commands can compete with theirs, while his unrealised sexual impulses and his lust for power – traitors within his own heart – will deliver him, bound and helpless, into the hands of his enemies.

This eloquent passage well illustrates the writer's tact: he is in fact very sure of his reading of Pentheus, surer than many more recent critics might be. They might want to allow a greater indeterminacy in the construction of Pentheus' inner desires, or to make room for intertextual evocations of other Pentheuses in other plays or other figures matching Pentheus in the role of Dionysiac initiand, or to see aspects of Dionysiac ritual embodied in the action and performance. But he does not close the text down, because he always candidly exposes the workings of his interpretations, and these are always based on close scrutiny of language. And in the process he is not afraid to find contradictions at the deepest level.

For the student of reception this is fascinating evidence of the way in which some works of literature are repeatedly found to have a new kind of relevance. Of the plays in the surviving Greek tragic canon *Bacchae* above all has proved to have special meaning for readers and audiences in the second half of the twentieth century. If Winnington-Ingram had been writing now he might have found the idea of the 'Dionysiac drug', which he uses often as a metaphor, more literally instantiated in contemporary society, and he might well have wanted to shape his argument differently, attracted by the diversity of postmodern readings and by new approaches to the study of performance in cultures ancient and modern. But it is hard to imagine him surrendering the independence of his judgement or the fastidiousness of his writing, qualities which have given his work its continuing vitality.

BIBLIOGRAPHICAL NOTE

R.P. Winnington-Ingram

For an appreciation of his life and work see M.L.West, 'Reginald Pepys Winnington-Ingram 1904-1993', *ProcBritAcad* 84 (1994) 570-97. There are brief comments on *Euripides and Dionysus* in A.N. Michelini, *Euripides and the Tragic Tradition* (Madison, 1987) ch.1.

Bacchae

Work on the play over the last fifty years has been intensive:

(i) Text:

Diggle, J., in Vol III of the OCT of Euripides (Oxford, 1994); with textual discussion in *Euripidea: Collected Essays* (Oxford, 1994)

Kopff, C., (Leipzig, 1973)

(ii) Commentaries:

Dodds, E.R., 2nd edition (Oxford, 1960)

Roux, J., 2 vols (Paris, 1970-2).

Kirk, G.S., translation with notes (repr. Cambridge, 1979)

Seaford, R., text, translation and commentary (Warminster, 1996)

(iii) Studies:

Arthur, M., 'The Choral Odes of the *Bacchae* of Euripides', *YCS* 22 (1972) 145-79

Burnett, A.P., 'Pentheus and Dionysus: Host and Guest', *CP* 65 (1970) 15-29

Buxton, R., 'News from Cithaeron: Narrators and Narratives in the *Bacchae*', *Pallas* 37 (1991) 39-48

Devereux, G., 'The Psychotherapy Scene in Euripides' *Bacchae*', *JHS* 90 (1970) 35-48

Foley, H.P., *Ritual Irony. Poetry and Sacrifice in Euripides* (Cornell, 1985) ch.5

Goldhill, S., *Reading Greek Tragedy* (Cambridge 1986) ch.11

Gould, J., 'Mothers' Day: a note on Euripides' *Bacchae*', in L. Rodley (ed.), Papers given at a Colloquium on Greek Drama in honour of R.P. Winnington-Ingram = Hellenic Society Suppl. Paper 15 (London, 1987) 32-9

Gregory, J., 'Some aspects of seeing in Euripides' *Bacchae*', *G&R* 32 (1985) 23-31

Kovacs, D., 'Notes on the *Bacchae*', *CQ* 41 (1991) 340-5

March, J., 'Euripides' *Bakchai*: A Reconsideration in the Light of the Vase Paintings', *BICS* 36 (1989) 33-65

Oranje, H., *Euripides' Bacchae. The Play and its Audience* (Leiden, 1984)

Philippart, H., 'Iconographie des "Bacchantes" d'Euripide', *Revue Belge de Philologie et d'Histoire* 9 (1930) 5-72

Scott, W.C., 'Two Suns over Thebes: Imagery and Stage Effects in the *Bacchae, TAPA* 105 (1975) 333-46

Seaford, R., 'Dionysiac Drama and the Dionysiac Mysteries', *CQ* 31 (1981) 252-75

Segal, C., *Dionysiac Poetics and Euripides' Bacchae* (Princeton, 1982)

———*Interpreting Greek Tragedy: Myth, Poetry, Text* (Cornell, 1986) ch.9

Seidensticker, B., 'Comic elements in Euripides' *Bacchae*', *AJP* 99 (1978) 303-320

———'Sacrificial Ritual in the *Bacchae*' in G.W. Bowersock et al. (eds) *Arktouros. Hellenic Studies presented to Bernard M.W. Knox* (Berlin and New York, 1979) 181-90

Vernant, J-P., *Myth and Tragedy in Ancient Greece*, 2nd ed. (New York, 1988) ch.xvii 'The Masked Dionysus of Euripides' *Bacchae*'

Versnel, H.S., *Inconsistencies in Greek and Roman Religion, Vol.1 Ter Unus* (Leiden, 1990) ch.II

Willink, C., 'Some problems of text and interpretation in the Bacchae', *CQ* 16 (1966) 27-50 and 220-42

Dionysus

(i) For helpful overviews of the vast bibliography, including references to newly found evidence, see the entry 'Dionysus' by A. Henrichs in the *Oxford Classical Dictionary* 3rd edition (Oxford, 1996) and J. Bremmer, *Greek Religion* (=*Greek & Rome New Surveys in the Classics 24*) (1994), 19-26

Iconography: C. Gasparri, 'Dionysos' *LIMC* III.1, 414-566 and III.2. 296-456

(ii) Recent work on Dionysus and theatre:

Bierl, A.F.H., *Dionysus und die griechische Tragödie* (Tübingen, 1991)

Carpenter, T.H., and Faraone, C.A. (eds), *Masks of Dionysus* (Ithaca and London, 1993)

Easterling, P.E. (ed.), *The Cambridge Companion to Greek Tragedy* (Cambridge, 1997) ch.2

Friedrich, R., 'Everything to do with Dionysos?', with R. Seaford's reply, in M.S. Silk (ed.), *Tragedy and the Tragic* (Oxford, 1996) 257-94

Henrichs, A., '"Why should I dance?" Choral Self-Referentiality in Greek Tragedy', *Arion* 3 (1995) 56-111

Seaford, R., *Reciprocity and Ritual* (Oxford, 1994)

Sourvinou-Inwood, C., 'Something to do with Athens: Tragedy and Ritual' in R. Osborne, and S. Hornblower (eds), *Ritual, Finance, Politics* (Oxford, 1994) 269-89

Winkler, J.J., and Zeitlin, F.I. (eds), *Nothing to do with Dionysos?* (Princeton, 1990)

Zeitlin, F.I., *Playing the Other* (Chicago, 1996) ch.8

(iii) The religious background:

Three particularly influential books to have appeared since the publication of *Euripides and Dionysus*:

Burkert, R., *Greek Religion* (Oxford, 1985) [German original 1977]

Dodds, E.R., *The Greeks and the Irrational* (Berkeley and Los Angeles, 1951)

Girard, R., *Violence and the Sacred* (Baltimore and London, 1977) [French original 1972]

PREFACE

I do not know whether any excuse is needed for devoting an entire book, though a short one, to the *Bacchae*. If so, it must be found in the great diversity of interpretations to which the play has given rise. 'En regardant attentivement la pièce,' remarks a distinguished French scholar, 'il est aisé de découvrir la pensée de celui qui l'a faite.' So the individual interpreters may think: but their discoveries are not identical. The same justification must serve for the method I have adopted, which, apart from two chapters in introduction and two in conclusion, is that of a running commentary following the course of the play, and following it in great detail. By selective quotation it is not difficult to give a colour of plausibility to almost any theory. It is a harder test to show, if it can be shown, that an interpretation illuminates and is consistent with the whole of the play, doing justice both to the wood and to the trees. That the subjective and the speculative have been entirely eliminated, I would not dare or wish to claim, but I have endeavoured to discipline speculation by the closest attention to the text and, above all, to matters of form. For it is form—the fact that the dramatist has shaped his play, his scene, his sentence, in this way rather than that—which provides perhaps the most objective criterion available to the literary critic.

This method has involved the quotation of a large proportion of the play; and, since I hope that some Greek-less readers may be interested, I have quoted in translation and have banished Greek in the main to footnotes. It was my first intention to ask permission to use the prose translation of Mr D. W. Lucas. I found, however, that, though for so eloquent and poetic a version it is remarkably literal, it was not quite literal enough for my purposes; so I have made my own construe, for which no positive literary merit is claimed, though I hope it is readable. I have gratefully borrowed turns of phrase from Mr Lucas, from Prof. E. R. Dodds, and from other sources.

It is a pleasure to acknowledge even more substantial debts which I owe to these scholars and to others. A first draft of this book, completed in the summer of 1939, was read in typescript by Prof. Dodds, by the late Prof. F. M. Cornford, and by Mr L. P. Wilkinson: as I was heartened by their encouragement, so I hope that I have profited by their criticisms. Mr Lucas has been kind enough to read the proofs and make a number of valuable suggestions. I have discussed every chapter with my friend Mr E. O. Symonds. Finally, I count myself fortunate that Prof. Dodds's edition of the play appeared before my book was in final shape. Not only have I learnt much from it, but on many difficult and disputed points I have been enabled simply to refer my readers to this edition. There are questions of interpretation, major and minor, on which I venture to disagree with Prof. Dodds, and these naturally receive some prominence. I should be sorry if such polemics concealed my admiration for his work and my gratitude for his assistance.

The conclusion to which I come—that the *Bacchae* is in some sort a play against Dionysus—will perhaps be thought reactionary. I cannot find in the play that impartiality or that acceptance with which Euripides is sometimes credited to-day, and I believe that critics of the last generation, who found his drama permeated with a spirit of protest, won territory which should not lightly be surrendered, though the frontiers need to be re-drawn. Since those critics wrote, we have lived through events which have demonstrated, tragically, the dangers of group emotion. Though contemporary history can be a fallible guide to antiquity, our own experience may help us to understand how Dionysus appeared to Euripides when his world also was troubled by the god.

BIRKBECK COLLEGE
LONDON
July, 1947

Note

The titles of modern works quoted are, in general, given in full upon the first occasion of reference, but the following abbreviations are used:

Dodds: *Euripides' Bacchae*, edited with introduction and commentary by E. R. Dodds (1944).
Dodds, *Maenadism*: E. R. Dodds, 'Maenadism in the Bacchae', *Harvard Theological Review*, XXXIII, no. 3 (1940), pp. 155–76.
Farnell, *Cults*: L. R. Farnell, *Cults of the Greek States* (1896–1909).
Grube: G. M. A. Grube, *The Drama of Euripides* (1941).
Kitto: H. D. F. Kitto, *Greek Tragedy* (1939).

The text translated is that of Murray, unless other readings are specified.

CHAPTER I

INTRODUCTORY

Euripides was more than seventy years old when he accepted an invitation from King Archelaus to visit the court of Macedonia. There he died, but not before he had completed the play which, most perhaps of all his works, has captured the imagination of later generations. It is a play which has been very variously interpreted. It has been felt, whether rightly or wrongly, to stand apart from his other extant plays; and although this impression may be deceptive, it will be well to understand how it arose.

The subject-matter of the *Bacchae* is a legend of the coming of Dionysus to Greece: a historical event, but placed in that setting of myth and saga which provided Greek tragedy with the great majority of its themes. For Dionysus was relatively a newcomer to Olympus. His worship had been introduced into Greece at an unknown date from Thrace or from Asia or perhaps from both, since Thracians and Phrygians were closely akin in blood and culture. This Thraco-Phrygian god, known under various names, was a spirit of vegetation, of the fertility of nature and the excitement attendant upon it; wine was one of his gifts, but his sphere was far wider than that of a mere god of wine. His worship included wild rites, devoted to the production of ecstasy by music and dancing, by bloody sacrifice, by the sheer intoxication of being one of a band of worshippers, a *thiasos*. For as Dionysus was pictured as attended by a group of followers, divine or human, nymphs satyrs or Sileni, Maenads or Bacchanals, so the worshippers felt him among them and within them, till they became themselves Bakchoi or Bakchai, incarnations of the god. Such a religion, so novel, so attractive, and so obviously dangerous, could not but meet with opposition when it attempted to proselytise a land which had already attained a sober habit of worship.

The gods of Greece lived a life upon Olympus that was no less (if no more) orderly than that of human society and, though they might appear to men and women in human form and bestow their patronage in the form of counsel, of love, or of aid in battle, they knew their place and kept their distance: the religion of Dionysus blurred the distinction between god and man. The Olympian gods were worshipped with song and dance and sacrifice, but in the heart of civilised communities with due order, and (mainly) by day: their worshippers did not roam the mountains in frenzied bands by night. Naturally Dionysus was opposed, and this opposition may be reflected in legend by the stories of those who, like the daughters of Minyas and the daughters of Proetus, resisted the god and suffered for it. Most famous of such stories was that of Pentheus, king of Thebes, who was torn limb from limb by the Bacchanals whose worship he was trying to restrain.[1] Euripides was not the first to put this story on the Attic stage. Aeschylus before him had written a *Pentheus*, a play which formed part of a trilogy now lost, dealing with the introduction of Dionysiac worship; and we know that the theme had been handled by other dramatists.

There is, then, no novelty in the subject-matter of the *Bacchae*. In method it is distinguished from other extant plays of Euripides in at least one respect. The Chorus was a legacy from the origins of Attic drama, and during the fifth century its role in the action and the sheer bulk of its songs had shown a broad tendency to diminish. In Euripides the choral odes are seldom, if ever, quite irrelevant to the action, but the Chorus tends not to be deeply involved in that action and its presence is sometimes a positive embarrassment. Far different is it in the *Bacchae*. In no other extant Greek play since Aeschylus, and in Aeschylus only in the *Supplices* and *Eumenides*, is the Chorus so prominent. For it is formed of a band of Asiatic Bacchanals who have followed the god, in his human disguise, to Greece. Not only are they passionate adherents of the new religion, but their own fate is closely bound up with the god's success at Thebes; and Euripides does not allow us to forget that they, a band of women in a foreign land, are in danger of bonds or death.[2] Though they have little part in the dialogue, their songs are clearly of fundamental importance for an understanding of the play.

In this, and in other respects, Euripides was returning to older

[1] These stories were greatly influenced by ritual (see p. 24 n. 3), but may nevertheless reflect historical events. 'Pentheus may be a figure compounded (like Guy Fawkes) of historical *and* ritual elements—at once the god's historical adversary and his ritual victim' (Dodds, p. xxiv).

[2] There is a certain dramatic awkwardness in that they must be allowed to remain at large, a vocal opposition at the palace gates.

artistic methods, perhaps deliberately to the Aeschylean model.[1] But in a dramatist as versatile as he had shown himself to be, such a departure does not necessarily demand a recondite explanation, nor does it account for the impression—right or wrong—that here is something different from most or all of his plays and rather puzzling. This impression was caused by the treatment of religion in the play. It has been said that there is no novelty in the subject-matter of this play. The statement demands qualification. It is true that gods figure in many of the plays of Euripides, but in most of these they merely appear at the beginning or the end of the play, to speak a prologue or to announce *ex machina* the destinies of the human characters. If the gods play little direct part in the action, miracle (with one exception) plays less. In the *Hercules Furens* two minor divinities make an appearance half-way through the play, and a sensational event occurs.[2] But the *Bacchae* is pervaded by the miraculous. Miracles were believed to be a regular accompaniment of the worship of Dionysus, and miracles are here adduced as evidence of his divinity and employed to assist his vengeance. Not only do the audience hear of miracles, of doors that unlock and bonds that loose themselves, of milk, honey and wine that flow spontaneously from the earth, of deeds impossible to mortal powers performed by Dionysus and his Bacchanals, but a miracle of fire and earthquake invades the very stage. Again, Dionysus himself, instead of making a solitary appearance in superhuman grandeur, dominates in human shape the central scenes of the play. Few Euripidean gods cut impressive figures, but Dionysus directs the action of this play towards his own triumph.[3] Mere man has doubted his godhead and suffers for this presumption a terrible fate, which the god himself supervises. Meanwhile the glories of his worship are sung in superb lyrics or told in thrilling narrative. That a god should play such a role amid miraculous circumstances—this certainly differentiates the *Bacchae* from the other extant plays of Euripides. What is to be made of it?

[1] Dodds, pp. xxxiii sqq. See also p. 164 for the use of an Aeschylean technique.

[2] There are minor miraculous elements in several other plays. One may mention the sea-beast that Poseidon sent to destroy Hippolytus, the great waves in the *Iphigeneia in Tauris*, and (particularly) the appearance at the end of the *Medea* of the human heroine in the chariot of the Sun.

[3] Thus the word τύχη which haunts the later plays of Euripides is not to be found in the *Bacchae*, where nothing is left to 'chance'.

'The Bacchae is a most glorious play...', wrote Macaulay. 'It is often very obscure; and I am not sure that I understand its general scope. But, as a piece of language, it is hardly equalled in the world. And whether it was intended to encourage or discourage fanaticism, the picture of fanatical excitement which it exhibits has never been rivalled.' But few writers (if many readers) have been content with such a non-committal judgement, and many diverse interpretations of the play have been advanced. A view which once prevailed is that the *Bacchae* is a kind of recantation. Nearing the end of his life, Euripides had repented of his earlier scepticism and returned to religious orthodoxy, and, in an attempt, perhaps, to counteract the influence of his earlier plays, had put upon the stage a picture of scepticism dreadfully punished, of religion wonderfully vindicated. In a generation which was shocked by scepticism, horrified by atheism, and which accepted miracle as the primary evidence for its own religion, such an attitude is comprehensible. Dionysus was, after all, a god; and much of the expression that faith finds in the play might rouse echoes in the mind of a pious Christian reader, who was used to being reminded that only in religion was true happiness to be found, that God in heaven was watchful to punish offenders, and that a cleverness that led to a denial of His existence was but the folly of the Psalmist's fool. By the figure of Dionysus before Pentheus he might even—half-afraid of blasphemy—be reminded of Christ before Pilate.[1]

But does not such a parallel stultify itself? The meekness of Dionysus—if meekness is the word—was not the prelude to *his* crucifixion, and it was Pentheus, not Dionysus, whose end provided the author of *Christus Patiens* with material. This god may attempt to convince by miracle, but he punishes by craft, and, when he has his victim in his power, he plays with him as a cat plays with a mouse, before delivering him over to be torn in pieces by his own mother. Is not this the epiphany of a fiend rather than of a god? And when, towards the end of the play, a human character protests that gods should not be like in temper to mortals (1348), do we not feel that the protest has been, if anything, too mildly phrased? According to this view, which gained currency towards the end of the nineteenth century, Euripides is doing in the *Bacchae* precisely what he had been doing all his life; he is exposing the inadequate conception of

[1] On the history of this comparison see Weinreich, *Genethliakon für W. Schmid*, pp. 338 sqq.

divinity inherent in the legendary theology of Greece and proclaiming that such gods are worthy neither of worship nor of imitation.

Nor of credence. For this view assumes that Euripides did not believe in the real existence of such anthropomorphic deities; they and their doings are, to use a phrase of his own, 'unfortunate tales of the poets'. Verrall indeed went farther. He argued that Euripides not only denied the existence of these gods, but sought to explain the apparent operation of superhuman agencies by natural causes: he was a 'rationalist'. In the case of the *Bacchae*, where to all appearance a god takes a direct part in the central action and the element of miracle is continually obtruding, he held that the character who is known to our manuscripts as Dionysus is, to the discerning eye, merely an oriental adept and prophet of the god, as indeed he describes himself; the miracles are, when closely examined, not miraculous at all, the palace-earthquake being an entirely subjective phenomenon, visible only to the Chorus, while the strange deeds of Dionysus and the Bacchanals come to us upon authority which the poet deliberately makes suspect.

But if Euripides has portrayed the mythological Dionysus as a fiend or even explained him away as a young Asiatic, the religion of Dionysus remains. It is upon the religion rather than the god that interpreters now tend to concentrate attention. This religion is compounded of beauty and terror, and on both Euripides has lavished his lyrical and descriptive powers. The poet who wrote the Entrance Song of the Bacchanals had a deep imaginative appreciation of the beauty of such worship; the poet who described the end of Pentheus was not unaware of the dangers of an orgiastic cult. Did he intend to represent the beauty as fatal illusion, bound to issue in disaster? Or to represent the danger as arising simply from the obstinate rejection of the beauty? Perhaps there is no 'moral', but merely a dramatist taking the facts as he found them and making an exciting play, or, less crudely, a poet presenting with a poet's fidelity the stark tragic contradiction which he saw. These questions are further complicated by reference to the psychology of the poet. The religion of Dionysus is a religion of unreason. What response did it evoke in one whose theatre owed so much to the intellectual life of his age? That Euripides yearned in his own spirit after the untrammelled emotionalism of the Bacchanals has been held alike by some who see in this yearning the ultimate revolt of a philosophic rationalist and by others who regard the poet as having been consistently sceptical of the validity of reason in human life.

Confused with such a welter of divergent interpretations,[1] the reader may perhaps prefer to enjoy the play in the spirit of Macaulay. But he may also think it odd that a dramatist of such manifest power should have failed to make his intention clearer. He may, indeed, recollect the slightly patronising tone that can sometimes be discerned in discussions of Euripides, as of one who had great emotional force and vivid intellectual curiosity, but who lacked the stability and control which alone can create great drama, so that any uncertainty of effect in his work can be ascribed to the disharmony of a brilliant, many-sided, but unstable personality.

Such an explanation might be true. Yet to adopt it too readily shows a disrespect for genius which may damage the critic more than his subject. Least of all should we be ready to adopt it in dealing with the *Bacchae*, which is by common consent an artistic success. In other plays of Euripides we may find halting action, dubious characterisation, apparent irrelevancies, to be admitted or explained, but not in the *Bacchae*, where a vigorous rhythm runs without break from end to end of the play, and where the problems of criticism concern final aims rather than defective methods. This study is undertaken in the conviction that Euripides saw his aims clearly and controlled them firmly, and that by careful scrutiny of his methods we can understand his aims.

It will perhaps help to clarify the issues if we make the reasonable supposition that Euripides wrote a play which could carry effect at different levels of approach. This assumption is necessarily made by all who hold that the play contains religious criticism. For, while such criticism is addressed to an intelligent minority, the groundlings also must have their play. And an exciting play it is, if events and speeches are taken at their face-value and only the most obvious and superficial judgements passed.

It is not easy at this date—or perhaps very important—to enter into the mind of an average member of the original audience, but we may suppose that he found the play exciting but terrible, a blend of the familiar and the exotic. It was familiar in that it showed the doom of a tyrant who had offended against the Greek ideal of moderation and had set himself in opposition to a god. This god,

[1] The preceding account is indeed over-simplified, as will be seen on reference to Nihard, *Problème des Bacchantes d'Euripide*, pp. 9–14.

however, in the sensual beauty of his human disguise, might stir curious emotions. No less strange, no less in contrast with the ceremonies, grave or genial, of the Attic cult of Dionysus, were the rites described in the course of the play. There was nothing surprising in the idea that a god should take ruthless vengeance, but to a man of human feeling the extravagance of this god's revenge may have seemed somehow shocking. He would, however, remind himself that the gods are self-justified and must not be judged by human standards.

But an Athenian of intelligence and sensibility, whose social position had allowed him to come in contact with the sophists and to hear Socrates talk, who had seen or read earlier plays of Euripides, might not be satisfied with such an uncritical acceptance. Not only would the idea of protest against such stories of the gods be familiar to him and find a response in his own conscience, but Euripides himself had already encouraged him to judge the gods by human standards. If he discerned in the *Bacchae* the same satirical methods which Euripides had employed in other plays, he might draw the conclusion that the Dionysus who was portrayed in this play as a malignant person had no title to respect and that the manifestation of his Olympian deity was the implicit denial of it, though he would doubtless feel that issues had been raised transcending the simple acceptance or rejection of conventional theology.

Assuming the presence of such criticism, we have, then, two plays for two different audiences. This was also Verrall's contention. But for Verrall the superficial assumptions as to miracle and the personal agency of Dionysus which held good upon the one level were abandoned on the other. He believed that it was a major purpose of Euripides to show how natural fact might have grown into supernatural legend, how normal happenings inaccurately seen and even more inaccurately reported by simple credulous people might attain the status of miracle. This view can be criticised upon many grounds: one will suffice here.[1] Euripides cannot have written his plays with the primary purpose of providing 'rationalistic' explanations of myth, because—to put it simply—he had more interesting things to say, which would be hopelessly prejudiced and obscured by such ingenious constructions.

Let us consider briefly two episodes. Early in the play, a soldier comes to Pentheus, leading the Stranger captive. He tells the king

[1] See Appendix for a further discussion of this question.

of this capture, but also of the miraculous escape of those Bacchanals who had already been imprisoned. In this narrative Verrall finds 'every circumstance which, according to the habits of rational mankind, would naturally invite disbelief', and concludes that Euripides has deliberately presented the miracle upon bad authority. Leaving aside the question whether a theatrical audience weighs evidence like a High Court judge, this interpretation misses the whole point of the speech, which falls into two parts. The first is dominated by the motif of the θὴρ πρᾶος, 'the tame, gentle beast': Dionysus submits to bonds with confidence and with a smile. The second part gives us a companion and complementary picture. Dionysus is bound (δεῖν, 439): 'but the Bacchanals that you *imprisoned*, that you *seized* and *bound*...are gone'. The reiteration is significant. Dionysus is for the moment bound, but simultaneously we are given an indication of the feeble power of prisons, bolts and bonds upon this disruptive spirit. Surely the question that we most readily ask is not 'how did the Bacchanals really get away?' but 'what will happen when Dionysus himself is under lock and key?' Perhaps he has reason to smile.

What in fact happened was the 'palace-miracle', whose dramatic function will be considered in due course. Pentheus takes his captive into the palace to imprison him in a dark place (509 sqq.). After a choral ode, a voice is heard calling on earthquake and fire to destroy the house of Pentheus; and the Chorus sees the palace-front shaken and fire blaze up in Semele's tomb. Then Dionysus comes out and describes the scene which has taken place within. Pentheus, he says, had been mocked; thinking to bind the Stranger, he had struggled and sweated to bind—a bull; then the Bacchic god had shaken the palace and fire was seen; Pentheus had rushed to and fro and had pursued, sword in hand, a phantom which he took for his adversary—and all to no purpose. On the level of simple acceptance, this is plain fact: Dionysus the wonder-worker has worked a wonder, and it is sufficiently exciting. On the level of theological criticism, everything will depend upon the conduct and motives of the god and on the general tone. 'Rationalism', however, will find suspicious features in the story and will deny that the Stranger's account of events is a true one. But, by so doing, it will distract attention from something which is more important than the immediate excitement of the story, more important than the motives of an Olympian, infinitely more important than a piece of ingenious rationalisation—

it will distract attention from the symbolism of the events described. For Dionysus symbolises the power of blind, instinctive emotion. Seek to take him by force and imprison him in the dark, and the result is, inevitably, catastrophic. Similarly with the binding of the bull. Its appropriateness has always been recognised, for the bull is an avatar of Dionysus. Here it represents Dionysus as animal (a motif that runs throughout the play) and perhaps especially as sexual animal; and Pentheus, as he sweats and grimaces and pants out his heart, is a symbol of crude asceticism, engaged upon a hopeless task. For the true, the essential Dionysus is sitting quietly close at hand, biding his time (618 sqq.).

That a Greek dramatist should take Dionysus as symbol and base upon symbolism the main content of his play is less surprising than at first sight it might seem. It was not really a difficult movement of mind for Greeks to make. For it is something of a paradox that a people whose myth-making impulse clothed the gods in such concrete anthropomorphism was, at the same time, prone, as every reader of Hesiod and Pindar knows, to deify abstractions; and in the case of deities who had a clearly defined province in natural or social life, the passage was easy from a concrete to an abstract view of them. Thus, if Aphrodite was a person who might appear and be represented artistically in human form, she was also a power working in the human heart, so that if a Greek were to lose his literal belief in her, he might still see in the personification a symbol of the force. If Dionysus was no god in the accepted sense, yet he stood for something of supreme interest and importance in the world. To us, thousands of years after, it is the symbolical aspect of Dionysus that counts. That a mysterious legend about him had been explained away by common-sense would matter little, merely stirring in us a passing appreciation of the ingenuity. That a Greek poet, with sharp irony, dissected the current conceptions of divinity is an event of some interest in the moral history of mankind. But Dionysus as a universal power does not belong to any particular age or generation. It is not merely that emotional forms of religion are still known to-day; for such religions tend to be but a particular direction of forces which are active also in other than religious groups and even in the isolated individual. So when Dionysus is manifested in the play as the purveyor of drugs of many kinds, as the source of ecstasies and disasters, as the enemy of intellect and individuality and the defence of man against his isolation, as a power that can make him feel like a god while acting like a beast, as a spirit that partakes of the beauty and the callousness of man's natural environment, this is a god whom all can recognise.

These are levels at which the play may be approached. But if the consideration of these levels helps to clarify the issues, a mass of divergent interpretations still remains. Dionysus may, at the deepest level, be a symbol of wide generality: but to what end and purpose did Euripides use this symbol? When so many views have been advanced with persuasive argument under the authority of well-known names, it may be that a fresh interpretation will appear to be no more than a personal reaction which will convince only those of a similar idiosyncrasy to the author's. In literary criticism there are obvious limits to the degree of objectivity which can be attained; indeed the attempt to attain complete objectivity involves its own dangers. Much has already been done to elucidate the background of thought and cult; in the foreground is the play itself—and it is with the text of the play, and with the whole text, that this study will be primarily concerned. By observing what Euripides has done we should be able to frame a reasonable judgement of why he did it. By studying methods we should be able to discover aims. Form, in the widest sense, should throw light on content. Without anticipating the detailed analysis of later chapters, let us point to certain elements in the play for which the critic must account and which are, within the limits of the subject-matter, objective tests of the validity of his conclusions.

The critic must recognise and account for the way in which Euripides has contrived the general effect of his play. The dramatist has under his control the sympathies of an audience: how does he manipulate them? A marked shift of sympathy can be discerned as the play proceeds, affecting particularly our attitude towards the principal characters and towards the Chorus. Pentheus has been variously judged, but it is perverse to deny that in the earlier scenes he is—he puts himself—in the wrong, with his intolerance and his high-handed impatience (to quote only defects which not even his advocates can disregard). As his grim fate overtakes him, feeling is gradually turned in his favour, till finally the lament of Cadmus over his heir reveals a more sympathetic aspect of Pentheus than has yet appeared in the play (1305 sqq.). Conversely, his adversary the god, whose conduct at first does not belie the beauty of his outward form, rouses our distaste, if nothing more, when he mocks a deluded

Pentheus before conveying him to a horrible death. (We must, of course, be on our guard against ascribing our own modes of thought and feeling, without consideration, to ancient Greeks. One may doubt, however, whether the reaction of civilised beings to the rending in pieces of a son by his mother has changed much in the passage of the centuries.) So also with the Chorus of Bacchanals who have attended Dionysus on his travels. At first their songs are full of beauty and—what is more remarkable—full of peace (though with hints of violence in the Entrance Song); they persuade, they attract. Then, as the play develops, their tone changes; they pray for vengeance with a dreadful concentration and gloat over the vengeance when it is achieved.

This shift of sympathy is dictated to some extent by the given plot and might be ascribed merely to competent dramatic technique. It must be considered, however, whether Euripides has not given it a significant emphasis. He has presented both the peace and terror of Dionysiac religion; the peace comes first, the terror afterwards, and it is the terror that is left uppermost in our minds. Here again, the plot dictates the order; the question is whether the poet has not emphasised this contrast in this order more than the plot required him to do. How beautiful—but how dangerous! If this is the final impression of the play, we may be misreading it if we say—dangerous perhaps, but how beautiful![1]

We must account not only for the broad impression, but for the detail of the play in respect of form and characterisation. If we cannot do so coherently and satisfactorily, we may argue that the failure is that of the poet, but we must hold that argument in the last reserve. Here are a number of questions to which answers should be given; and answers—correct or incorrect—are given in the course of the ensuing chapters.

Why does Euripides give to Dionysus, the patron-god of an emotional religion, the characteristics of rationality and control? Why is he σοφός and σώφρων, and how do his 'wisdom' and 'moderation' relate to those of his followers? Why, on the other hand, is Pentheus, so far from being a rationalist, portrayed with an unstable emotionalism? Why is Cadmus given a motive ulterior

[1] On the shift of sympathy see Murray, *Essays and Addresses*, p. 78; Dodds, pp. xliii and 186 (*ad* 973–6); A. R. Bellinger, *Yale Classical Studies*, VI (1939), p. 25. I am also indebted to Mr L. P. Wilkinson for interesting observations on this topic.

to his piety? How is Teiresias treated? For Teiresias—the representative of the old religion who defends the new—was the spokesman if Euripides wished to champion a regulated Dionysiac cult. But if Teiresias is treated, as many have thought, with satire, one possible interpretation of the play is rendered difficult, if not untenable.

There are also questions of form, particularly in connection with the choral odes. Why, for instance, and to what effect does Euripides repeat the doctrines of the second chorus in the fourth and fifth? In the fourth and fifth choruses he introduces refrains at the end of strophe and antistrophe. A feature, evidently, of cult hymns; but what use, if any, does he make of the unusual formal arrangement which results when a single strophe and antistrophe, with refrains, are followed by an epode? Again, in this play Euripides employs the Aeschylean technique of recurrent motifs, and such words and ideas as σοφός, καλός, νόμος, are constantly and emphatically repeated. We shall have failed to interpret the play unless we can give them due significance. Like an Aeschylean play, the *Bacchae* is dominated by a key-metaphor—the image of the hunt which turns into dreadful reality. Our interpretation must give full value to this most persistent theme, which runs from the Entrance Song, through the great Messenger speeches, to the final scene with Agave. The Messenger speeches themselves, like the choral odes, must be analysed in form and content; and in the course of the analysis it will be well to remember that it is with poetry we are dealing and, consequently, we should not attend exclusively to logical meaning and sequence of thought, but should examine the aesthetic aspects of speech and chorus, listening for the overtones of word and phrase and for the harmonies or discords that are engendered.

The relation of the Messenger speeches to the choral odes is itself a question of fundamental importance, which can be put in several forms. What is the relation between the rite described in the Entrance Song and the rites carried out on Cithaeron? What bearing has the practice of the Theban women upon the creed of the Asiatic missionaries? What is the relationship between the two sets of Bacchanals, who, seen and unseen respectively, dominate the play? The Chorus are devotees who have accompanied their god upon his mission; the Theban women have been driven mad and made into worshippers perforce. Are the actions of the latter then determined by the creed they now follow or by the circumstances of their 'conversion'? Is the similarity or the difference between Theban and Asiatic Bacchanals the more significant? It is only in the songs of the Bacchanals of the Chorus that we can find the answer. It will, however, later be argued that Euripides has characterised both sets of Bacchanals by the same combination of peace and fury, has preferred to leave their difference of status upon the surface, and is thus enabled to use the choral odes to expound the theory of which the Messenger speeches describe the practical exemplification.

Dionysus speaks through the Chorus, acts through the Theban women. But he also speaks and acts in person upon the stage—a strangely rational Dionysus, calm, collected, clever. In many plays Euripides had introduced divine personages; in none (of which we know) had a god played such a striking role. It will be convenient, before we proceed to our main analysis, to study the treatment of this god upon the stage. It may not be through the Stranger who confronts Pentheus, still less through the Olympian who appears *ex machina*, that the profoundest revelation of Dionysiac religion is conveyed. Yet the impression made by the god and by the god's triumph cannot, if the play is to count as a complete artistic success, fail to be consistent with and to contribute to the total impression which the dramatist intended to produce.

CHAPTER II

EURIPIDES AND DIONYSUS (I)

The attitude of Euripides towards the gods his fellow-Greeks worshipped was not simple, and an adequate discussion of it is beyond the scope of this book. It was not simple partly because the gods themselves were not simple in nature. In their origins most, if not all, of them represented powers of nature or phenomena of human life: realities of which mankind is bound to stand in awe. Their cult was for the most part dignified and beautiful, free from the grossness of magical superstition. It was a triumph of Greek taste and sanity and reason. But the Greek mind had also worked upon them in a different way. The same reasonableness that had banished or suppressed magic had imposed clarity and distinctness of form upon the gods, and had done it in the most obvious, the most intelligible way: by making or re-making them in the image of man and attributing to them a social organisation analogous to that of man. Thus was satisfied not merely the reason of the Greeks but their lively, concrete imagination; for about these glorified human beings that were their gods they wove the fabric of a mythology so various and so vivid that it has captivated all succeeding generations.

There is, however, a moral disadvantage in anthropomorphism, even apart from the trivialities which it may involve. If you turn a power of nature into a quasi-human being, you are in a dilemma. 'Either you have to admit that you are worshipping and flattering a being with no moral sense, because he happens to be dangerous, or else you have to invent reasons for his wrath....And they are pretty sure to be bad reasons.'[1] This dilemma faced the Greeks when art and poetry had perfected the Olympian system, and it was in part responsible for its ultimate decay. The myth had authority, yet its moral level was often deplorably low. To estimate from generation to generation how much authority the myth held in matters of belief and conduct is a subtle and difficult task for the historical imagination. The Greeks were not tied to a literal acceptance of every single detail, and the pious could without penalty reject and remould. Homer himself, the chief exponent of the myth,

[1] Murray, *Five Stages of Greek Religion*, p. 90.

made fun of the gods; and, if the mainland was more serious than Ionia in these matters, so did the comic poets of the Attic stage, and on a sacred occasion. Yet the myth did provide not only a definitive statement about the nature of deity, but also standards of moral conduct. At least Plato thought so, and gave that reason, among others, for banishing Homer and the tragedians from his ideal state.[1]

Plato was not the first to protest against grotesque and immoral myths. Over a hundred years before, Xenophanes had criticised anthropomorphism; and between Xenophanes and Plato stands Euripides. All three were in spirit rejectors of the myth; but, while the two former could reject it openly, Euripides must, by tradition of his calling, use it, and so provides the paradoxical spectacle of the sacred dramatist using the myth to destroy the myth.

It is a commonplace of criticism that Euripides satirised the Olympian gods, treating them and their motives with the same realism which he applied to his human characters. When we turn to ask in what spirit he did so the answer may not be so simple. We must, no doubt, beware of finding a serious moral or religious purpose where the poet intended a *divertissement*. The tone of the satire is clearly relative to the tone of the whole play in which it operates; and in a play of melodramatic or tragi-comic type[2] the treatment of the gods will itself be of a less than tragic seriousness—it may even be fun as innocuous, or nearly (from an orthodox Greek point of view), as that of Aristophanes. But satire (or whatever we should call it) at the expense of the gods is not confined to the *Helen*s, the *Ion*s and the *Electra*s. It is present also in plays of the most serious intention. It is satire, for instance, in the *Hercules Furens*, which reiterates the theme of justice to prepare the vengeance of jealous Hera, a vengeance which (and this also is satire) revolts even the divine underling who carries it out.[3] 'If the gods do what is base, they are no gods', said a character in a lost play of Euripides. In what context the line was spoken we do not know, but this is a case where good currency drives out bad, and we can be sure that the criticism which the words imply came no less from the heart of Euripides than when the Huntsman in the *Hippolytus* (120) prayed Cypris to have pity, for 'gods should be wiser than mortals'.

[1] *Rep.* 391e.
[2] To adopt Professor Kitto's convenient classifications.
[3] See p. 24 n. 1. For the express conclusion see *H.F.* 1307 sqq.

But Cypris did not listen, perhaps because she 'was not a god after all, but something greater than a god if such there be' (359 sq.). The matter becomes less simple. For, if Euripides rejected the attribution to gods of the worst passions of men, as a poet he was concerned with a world of tragedy resulting from the interplay of mighty forces. The forces that govern human life cannot be denied; nor could the gods of Greece be denied, when, and in so far as, they represented real forces operating in the world.

We can perhaps make a distinction which is helpful. Apollo, for instance, plays a part in more than one play. But what reality was there for Euripides in Apollo? In origin he may have been a god of shepherds, but for the later Greeks he was essentially a patron-god, patron of medicine, of music, of archery; he was also a true prophet, through his oracle at Delphi, and expounder of the will of Zeus. But it is not these attributes which dictate the part he plays in the *Ion*,[1] which is that of a seducer anxious to make some satisfactory arrangement for his victim and their illegitimate son. In the *Electra* and *Orestes* he appears as an instigator to murder, and here he does represent a force working upon the murderers—not the passions in their own hearts, but an external convention which, whatever usefulness it once had, has become obsolete and evil. In the *Ion* there may be, as Professor Kitto has suggested, more ridicule than criticism; in the *Electra* and the *Orestes* Apollo is subjected to the satire which plays impartially over god and man. But in the *Andromache*, a play with some tragic content, Apollo is virtually himself the murderer of Neoptolemus.[2] The criticism of Apollo may well derive from his position as a high moral authority throughout Greece and the fact that the limited codes of Delphi were backed by the prestige of healer and musician represented in the perfect athlete's form. Apollo was σοφός: but how wise in fact was he?[3] Here was unreality to be attacked, exposed and ridiculed.

With Apollo contrast the goddesses of the *Hippolytus*. They too are personages of mythology and, as such, act meanly out of petty jealousy. The clash of their personal interests is satirised by Euripides, and they are drawn as the only kind of persons who could be deliberately responsible for the events they cause. But at

[1] Though his attributes may be brought into ironic contrast with his role (cf. 881 sqq.).

[2] 1161 sqq. Cf. *Or.* 1656 sq. (where δίκας is satirical).

[3] *Andr.* 1165, *I.T.* 570 sqq., *Or.* 417.

the same time they represent the real forces of sexual passion and uncompromising chastity, which in their conflict make the tragedy, about which there is nothing petty, and whose cruelty is completely impersonal. Thus, while Apollo (or Hermes or the Dioscuri or even Hera) is mainly a figure of mythology and a butt of satire, other gods have both real and mythological aspects, both valid and necessary to the understanding of the plays.[1]

So we come to Dionysus in the *Bacchae*, a figure of mythology, complete with parentage, legend and personality, but also representative of a real force at work in the world. How does Euripides treat this paradox of the impersonal force of emotionalism swayed by personal emotions? In his other plays which have come down to us we hardly find one god or goddess appearing upon the stage or represented as personally affecting the action who, if not the object of direct criticism, is free from all degree of satirical treatment.[2] But Dionysus is a special case. Unlike the goddesses of the *Hippolytus*, Dionysus, in human guise, plays a leading part in the action. Nevertheless, he is an Olympian god and as such appears in glory, like many another in Euripides, at the end of the play. As a god and as a person, how is he treated by Euripides? When he appears in triumph, what response does his triumph evoke?

As in most Euripidean prologues, the opening speech of Dionysus in the *Bacchae* is a more or less undramatic recital of the necessary facts. It resembles the soliloquy of Aphrodite in the *Hippolytus* in substance—for she also proclaimed a slighted divinity and a design for vengeance—and to some degree in tone. But there is perhaps less of the *odium mythologicum* in the *Bacchae*, and for good reason. Unlike Aphrodite, Dionysus does not disappear from the action after speaking his prologue, and the role which he plays thereafter is, as we shall see, enigmatic in its earlier stages and would be prejudiced if too strong a reaction, favourable or unfavourable, were provoked in the audience at the outset. The tone, therefore, is more

[1] Cf. Dodds, *C.R.* XLIII (1929), p. 102.

[2] The Prologue of the *Troades* has a serious function (*v.* Kitto, pp. 210 sq.), but its divine politics are not untouched by satire. The rape of Cassandra is not worth mentioning (41 sqq.), except as an insult to Athena and her temple (69 sq.). 'Go to Olympus', says Poseidon to Athena (92); and that is where they belong. Hecuba is then made to expostulate, not against the gods, but against the vague realities of δαίμων and τύχαι (98, 101, 102, 104, 112).

neutral than in the *Hippolytus*. The god has come, it is true, to punish and avenge, but words of punishment and vengeance are absent.[1] The emphasis is upon the idea of manifestation,[2] the proof of his divinity which is also the vindication of his mother Semele. Though he has already inflicted a 'punishment' upon the Theban women, it is in the form of unwilled participation in the blessings of his cult, to be sung so eloquently by the Bacchanals in the succeeding Entrance Song.[3] How he will prove himself to Pentheus we do not yet know, but when he speaks of the threat of war between the government of Thebes and the Maenads led by himself, it is apprehension we feel rather than horror.[4] Dionysus is here an anthropomorphic god and his motives are personal, but there is no strong impression of vindictiveness. To reveal himself is the natural desire, even the function, of a god: all turns on what he reveals himself to be and how he brings about the revelation. How do gods reveal themselves? How did Hera?

For in his first sentence Dionysus speaks of Semele who bore him 'with the lightning-flash for midwife' (3). The cruel myth is but touched upon, but every member of the audience knew how the pregnant Semele, tempted by jealous Hera, had begged that her lover would visit her in his true form and how Zeus, coming with lightning and thunderbolt, had blasted her. Dionysus refers to 'the immortal *hubris* of Hera against my mother'.[5] *Hubris*—cruel and violent outrage—is (with its cognates) a word of frequent occurrence in this play; and it occurs first of an immortal.

This discord is quite in the Euripidean manner, and further references to the divine birth will be in keeping.[6] At the outset of the play, it receives some prominence. After a jealous Hera, what kind of Dionysus shall we see? But the Prologue leaves the question open. For the dramatist did not wish, at this stage in the play, to turn the sympathies of the audience against the god, who is at least

[1] Contrast *Hipp.* 21 (τιμωρήσομαι), 50 (δίκην). Dionysus does not use these words in the *Bacchae* till 847 (δώσει δίκην), 1081 (τιμωρεῖσθε).

[2] 22, 42, 47, 50; cf. 39 (ἐκμαθεῖν).

[3] N.B. ἧνται (38): the peaceful phase.

[4] Cf. Grube, p. 401.

[5] ἀθάνατον Ἥρας μητέρ' εἰς ἐμὴν ὕβριν (9): ἀθάνατον because the flame on Semele's tomb is its undying memorial, but the expression is also intended to suggest 'outrage from an immortal'. On ὕβρις see further p. 60, p. 83 n. 1, p. 146 n. 2.

[6] See p. 33 and p. 78.

as sympathetic as the gloating sisters who traduced his mother, or as Pentheus, the fighter against his deity. More than by his words, the spectator will perhaps be influenced by his appearance. He is beautiful, but in an effeminate style, and as such might well arouse conflicting emotions in a male Greek audience. His mask is set in an unvarying smile.

At the end of the Prologue he departs to join the Bacchanals upon Cithaeron, and nearly four hundred lines are spoken or sung before he reappears on the stage. Meanwhile we hear much about the nature of his religion, something about the mysterious Stranger who leads the Asiatic band, but nothing that is decisive about the dramatic role which he is to play.

It is with a smile that he returns, led captive by the pleased, yet puzzled soldier, who tells, in a speech which has already been discussed,[1] of the prey that refused to run for his life, the prisoner who never changed colour but held out his hands to be bound, smiling. It is a smile of confidence, a smile at the folly of those who believed that bonds could hold him. Immediately, to reinforce this impression, comes the story of the loosing of the Bacchanals, those other prisoners of Pentheus whom bonds and prison had been unable to hold. In the ensuing dialogue, Dionysus answers the questions of Pentheus with complete self-assurance. His tone is never deferential, but ranges from the polite to the superior; and on occasion his rebuke is not veiled. 'That was a clever evasion too,' says Pentheus, 'though you give but an empty answer.' 'To a fool (ἀμαθεῖ),' comes the reply, 'a man may speak wisely (σοφὰ λέγων) and seem to have no sense' (479 sq.). And later to Pentheus's 'You must be punished for your wicked sophistries (σοφισμάτων κακῶν)' Dionysus retorts, 'And you for your folly (ἀμαθίας) and impiety towards the god' (489 sq.). Pentheus's anger, which he has deliberately roused, he meets with unruffled calm, as he asks for the details of his punishment (492), and with consciousness of his own power, as he ironically comments upon them. When Pentheus's scanty patience is finally exhausted and he orders his prisoner to be bound again, the retort is significant. 'I say "bind me not"—I who am master of my senses (σωφρονῶν) say it to you who have lost yours (οὐ σώφροσιν)' (504).

It is significant because Dionysus here lays claim to *sophrosyne* (sanity or self-control), as in an earlier line to *sophia* (wisdom or

[1] See p. 8.

cleverness). Now these are words bandied about throughout the play. In particular, the Bacchanals of the Chorus also claim both virtues. This claim of theirs will be examined at a later stage; here it is enough to say that upon both they place a characteristic interpretation of their own. But Dionysus is σοφός and σώφρων in normal connotations of those terms. He is σοφός as a master of tactics for whom Pentheus is no match, whose superior cleverness, indeed, Pentheus himself is later to admit. He is σώφρων because, by contrast with the confused and excitable Pentheus, he is calm, collected, in control of the situation; because he knows what he is doing, as Pentheus does not. What claims Dionysus, as represented by his human followers, may have to wisdom and sanity is a fundamental issue of the play. But in this scene the mythological Dionysus is clever and calm with a psychology which is more Olympian than Dionysiac, but Olympian with a characteristic Euripidean twist.

For Dionysus in this scene is also the calm and clever 'intellectual', and by these qualities infuriates the hasty-tempered 'man of action' Pentheus, just as Hippolytus, by a somewhat similar bearing, infuriated Theseus.[1] The parallel is perhaps instructive if we would know what Dionysus intends with Pentheus. This remains ambiguous, and was bound to be ambiguous at this stage of the play. The audience must not sympathise with Pentheus; the god must still be an enigma capable of more than one solution. Yet his way of dealing with Pentheus is not calculated to save a sinner. It has been well remarked by a recent writer that 'the allusions of the Stranger to his true nature are in no way an attempt to instruct Pentheus, but take his unteachability for granted'.[2] Provided his power is manifested, the fate of Pentheus is a matter of complete indifference to him; what he will do with Pentheus is still concealed behind the smiling mask. At present he is merely concerned to establish an ascendancy over him.

The episode of the palace-miracle follows. It will be shown in a later chapter that this episode is vague in detail, rich in symbolism, and on a plane of reality which is not quite that of the main action

[1] *Hipp.* 1038 sqq.; note especially εὐοργησία (cf. *Bacch.* 641). Hippolytus is σώφρων not only in point of chastity (80). He is also σοφός (987), and his 1034 sq. shows the same kind of verbal subtlety in which Dionysus indulges. Theseus's reaction is similar to that of Pentheus: he considers it trickery (ἐπῳδὸς καὶ γόης, cf. *Bacch.* 234).

[2] Wassermann, *Neue Jahrb.* N.F. v (1929), p. 277.

of the drama. In it the role of Dionysus is that of wonder-worker. Pentheus had accused the Stranger of being a trickster and a magician, and such the god will show himself to be. The tone of his narrative, when he comes out to reassure the Chorus, is light, almost humorous.[1] For this is an interlude, if a profoundly significant interlude, before the main contest of wills between god and king is resumed. Yet it is itself a part of the cumulative process, and there is no real discontinuity between the Stranger who faces Pentheus on the stage and the magician god who played tricks with his palace and cast illusion upon him in the dark stables. For the keynote of the episode is the calm and easy exercise of power on the one side, the flurry and futility on the other.[2] The last words of Dionysus, before the re-entry of Pentheus, run as follows: 'Calmly will I bear with him, however high his rage; for it is a wise man's part to practise an even-tempered self-control' (640 sq.). Still σοφός, still σώφρων, in contrast with the foolish, flustered Pentheus.

And so it continues during the ensuing scene, after the Messenger from the mountain has told his story. This is a climax of the play, and the dialogue between Dionysus and Pentheus falls into two parts. In the first Dionysus offers to settle the matter peaceably, to bring the women home to Thebes without the use of arms (804). It is a specious offer, and as sincere perhaps as any offer which is made in the knowledge that it will not be accepted. For Dionysus knows that Pentheus is unteachable and untaught. And Pentheus duly rejects the offer and continues to speak of armed force. Therefore new methods must be tried, and the conflict enters a new phase in which Dionysus seems to exercise a kind of psychic power over his adversary. The scene will be examined in detail in a later chapter, where it will be shown how the god plays with Pentheus in the full consciousness of power; extorting from him a confession of his desire to see the Bacchanals together upon the mountains (811); feigning a shocked surprise (813); raising difficulties and suggesting as the one solution a female disguise (821); interesting a reluctant Pentheus in the details of the costume.[3] He indulges in a fiendish irony (837, 839); he lies to him (841); then, when Pentheus, gathering together the remnants of his sanity, postpones the decision, 'So be it,' says the god, 'I am prepared for all' (844): Dionysus

[1] Dodds, p. 144; Grube, p. 411.

[2] 614, 622, 636; 620, 625, 634, 647.

[3] And eliciting a tribute to his own σοφία (824)!

can deal with either situation. Yet he knows that Pentheus will in fact fall into the trap which he has set, and that he will 'come to the Bacchanals, where he will suffer the just punishment of death' (847). 'Dionysus,' he continues, when Pentheus has left the stage, 'now the task is thine, for thou art not far away. Let us take vengeance upon him' (849 sq.).

It was with a fiendish irony that he hinted at the blood which will be shed when Pentheus joins issue with the Bacchanals (839). For now the enigma is at least partially resolved and the methods of the god made manifest. Pentheus is to die (847), a punishment which will also be the vengeance of Dionysus (850). The mode of his death, the final details of the intrigue, are now expounded to the Chorus. The king is to be filled with 'an inconstant frenzy', dressed in woman's costume, led in mockery through Thebes[1] and taken to be killed by his own mother (850–9). Thus will he 'learn how Dionysus, son of Zeus, is very god most terrible, yet most kindly to men' (859–61).[2] 'Killed by his mother'—'son of Zeus'—'god': the discord is in characteristic Euripidean technique. Louder and more insistent, it recalls the discord that intruded even in the Prologue.[3] This is how Dionysus will prove his divinity upon the king; this will be the epiphany of the kindly god, who still smiles as he enters the palace.

From now onward the play is dominated by the note of vengeance. Struck by Dionysus, it echoes in the following chorus. Vengeance is a gift from the gods, honourable in the sight of men (877 sqq.). The chastisement of the gods is slow but sure; cunningly they conceal it, but all the time they are on the track of the impious man (882 sqq.). The doctrine is orthodox and a main pillar of the singers' faith, which is now to be vindicated by a loathsome act that they will acclaim as divine justice. Certainly, whatever moral ambiguity may attach to the motives of a jealous and vindictive deity, there is nothing equivocal about Dionysus's method.

Nor, when once that method is revealed, is there anything equivocal in the character of the god upon the stage. The Pentheus who

[1] This point is not subsequently referred to, because by the time the Messenger makes his speech it has ceased to be relevant: but it makes its effect here—Dionysus will break his promise of 841 (cf. Kitto, *C.R.* LX (1946), p. 66).

[2] 860: ὡς (Dobree). The sense of ἐν τέλει is uncertain (see Dodds)—'a god with a god's authority' (Brodeau), or perhaps we should read ἐντελής (Hirzel): 'complete, perfect'.

[3] See p. 18.

now issues from the palace in Bacchic costume, drunk with Dionysus, sees him in the shape of a bull. There is insight in his apparent illusion, for Dionysus is now revealed as bestial.[1] Yet bestial is here an inadequate term, so much human malice seems to intrude. Pentheus has been deprived of will and reason, and Dionysus shows off his paces, parades him before an audience, to whom he talks over Pentheus's head. We listen with that tribute of amusement over-mastered by disgust which we give to the trainer of performing animals upon the music-hall stage.[2] But, while the animal trainer may be affectionate in his contempt, here there is cruelty in every line, up to the concluding apostrophe: 'Stretch out your hands, Agave and her sisters, daughters of Cadmus; I bring the young man to a great contest, wherein I shall be the victor—I and Bromius. The rest the event will show' (973 sqq.).

The event will show, for these are the Stranger's last words. When next we see Dionysus, he is in glory, Pentheus dead, and Agave aware of what she has done. The intervening scenes are too intricately patterned for detailed exposition here, and it must suffice to point to some of the recurrent motifs with which Euripides elucidates his satire. Each of them has been introduced already; now they are to be reiterated and interwoven with one another.

First the motif of *justice*. The vengeance of heaven is *ex hypothesi* a just punishment. And, when the common Greek phrase for punishment (δίκην διδόναι) occurs in the god's speech before the robing of Pentheus (847), the word 'justice' may leap from its conventional context and link itself to the theme of vengeance (850) and the revelation of that vengeance's nature (857 sqq.). But in the main it is reserved for the immediate neighbourhood of its accomplishment. In the chorus that follows the departure of god and victim to the mountain and precedes the arrival of the Messenger, it sounds out clearly. 'Let Justice come, manifest and sword in hand, stabbing through the throat and killing the godless, the lawless, the unjust man, earth-born of Echion's breed' (991–6=1011–16);

[1] See p. 29.

[2] The handling of the mad Ajax by Athena (Sophocles, *Ajax* 71 sqq.) is not dissimilar, but it is more impersonal and her justice is tempered with mercy (cf. 753–7). See Bowra, *Sophoclean Tragedy*, pp. 33–7. Perhaps the most striking feature of the scene is, however, the pity of Odysseus. If Sophocles does not apply human standards to his gods, Euripides does so constantly.

and the brief verse is given emphasis by repetition.[1] When the Messenger's brief announcement elicits from the Bacchanals the query, 'Say to me, tell me, by what death perished the unjust man that worked injustice?' (1041 sq.), it cannot but remind us of the questionable morality of his punishment. Later still, the accomplished vengeance is to be greeted as an act of justice by the Chorus (1327 sq.) and—with a qualm—by Cadmus (1249).

The vengeance is not only just, it is *fair, honourable, glorious* (καλόν). 'What gift from the gods is fairer in the sight of men than to hold the hand of mastery over the head of foes? That which is fair is ever dear.' So sang the Bacchanals (877 sqq.), while waiting for the robing of Pentheus. 'Fair is the contest—to clasp a child with a hand dripping with his blood!' they sing when the whole story has been told to them (1163 sq.). 'What is there here that is not fairly done?' asks Agave (1263).[2]

It is not only glorious, but it has the special glory that attends upon *success in an athletic contest*.[3] The victor in such was greeted as καλλίνικος, glorious in triumph; and as καλλίνικος Dionysus was hailed by Agave, and the Chorus pick up the word (1147, 1161). 'Contest' and 'victor': these themes were given out by Dionysus, as he left the stage, in words recently quoted: 'I bring the young man

[1] Cf. also ἀδίκῳ (997), δίκας (1010). A similar technique is employed in the *Hercules Furens*, where the entry of Iris and Lyssa to effect the jealous spite of Hera is prepared by the reiteration of δίκη, ἄδικος (733, 739, 740, 756, 772, 776, 813; contrast 842), and the idea of divine justice.

[2] And (by contrast) οὐ καλόν, says the Messenger to the triumphing Bacchanals (1040); καλὸν τὸ θῦμα, says Cadmus with bitter sarcasm (1246).

[3] Professor George Thomson (*Aeschylus and Athens*, pp. 139 sqq., 166 sqq.) calls attention to the sequence πομπή—ἀγών—κῶμος in the treatment of the death of Pentheus. I do not feel competent to criticise his general theory that this is a ritual pattern, derived from tribal initiation ceremonies, which can be traced in the organisation of the Olympic festival and in the City Dionysia at Athens. It may be that the ritual upon which the story of Pentheus is based (elucidated by A. G. Bather in *J.H.S.* XIV (1894), p. 244) exemplified such a pattern. It does not follow that Euripides in using these themes had such a ritual in mind. It seems to me more probable that they were intended by him, and would have been taken by the audience, to refer metaphorically to the Olympic games, Pentheus being thought of as the champion of his state (963), Dionysus as the escort of the state mission to the festival (πομπὸς σωτήριος, 965; πομπὸς θεωρίας, 1047—see p. 128 n. 2). The association of καλλίνικος with the games is well marked, if not exclusive.

to a great contest, wherein I shall be the victor—I and Bromius' (974 sqq.). For victory in the coming struggle was for neither of the participants, but for the unconquerable god (1001). Nevertheless, the god triumphed in the person of the mad Agave (1200 sq.).[1] Now the return of the victorious athlete was celebrated by a κῶμος, a revel or revel-band, wherein his friends dance and sing the song of glorious triumph (ὁ καλλίνικος ὕμνος, cf. 1161); and to the return of Agave the Bacchanals give the hideous semblance of such a celebration, receiving as they say, the κῶμος of the Bacchic god, receiving Agave as their fellow-reveller (1167, 1172). But the celebration demands a feast; and here the theme of victorious athlete blends with that of successful hunter.[2] For what should provide the banquet but the prey? Thus Agave invites the Bacchanals to partake of the feast (1184), and bids her father invite his friends to it (1242). 'A fair victim have you offered to the gods, that you bid Thebes and me to the feast!' replies Cadmus. For the feast follows a sacrifice, in which Agave, as priestess, has already done her office (1114).

The death of Pentheus, then, is a just and honourable vengeance; it is a glorious victory for the god; it is a sacrifice to him. But all these aspects are subordinate to one: it is a manifestation of his divinity, such as he promised in the Prologue he would make.[3] 'Lord Bromius,' cry the Bacchanals, when they hear that Pentheus is dead, 'thou art manifested as a great god' (θεὸς φαίνῃ μέγας, 1031). So far the manifestation is only to the mind. Soon the eyes will have something to see—Agave displaying her son's head in triumph and making the ground of her joy that 'great things, great and manifest, have I wrought by this hunting' (1199).[4] Finally there comes the visible epiphany of the great god himself, no longer moving in human disguise upon the stage, but elevated in glorious robes above it, to deal out destinies and underline the moral. 'This say I, son of no mortal father, but of Zeus. If you had known moderation (σωφρονεῖν), when you would not, you would have had the son of Zeus for ally and been happy!' (1340 sqq.). Thus Dionysus, the moderate god, to the Thebans who have offended

[1] Cf. 1239 (τἀριστεῖα).

[2] See p. 30.

[3] See p. 18.

[4] The visual manifestation has already been stressed by her ὡς ὁρᾷν πάρα (1175). In fact the whole scene is full of words of 'sight', partly no doubt because she alone can *not* see what she holds in her hands. For further discussion see pp. 135, 164.

against moderation. For the Dionysus of the 'machine' is not merely a mythological appendage, not merely a reappearance, to round off the play, of the Dionysus of the Prologue: calm, controlled, superior, he is still the person who moved amid the action as an Asiatic stranger. Then, working out his purposes, he was vital and vivid. Now he is flat, perfunctory and impatient, for his vengeance is achieved and his godhead recognised.[1]

This flatness, if it furthers the poet's aim to cheapen the epiphany, is also designed to give the interest of the play's close to the human characters; and their reactions to Dionysus are now more important than Dionysus himself. Cadmus finds the divine vengeance just, if excessive (1249); and, as he surveys the indiscriminate suffering which the god has inflicted, he is forced to one conclusion only. 'Wretched am I,' he says, apostrophising his dead son, 'and unhappy you, piteous your mother and her sisters. If there is anyone who scorns the gods, let him look upon this man's fate and believe in them' (1323–6). Acceptance can be as effective as protest for the Euripidean satire. Yet towards the end of the play, one of the human characters—Cadmus or Agave, for this remains uncertain[2]—speaks with the voice of humanity in tones of protest against a god who had returned *hubris* for *hubris*. 'Gods should not be like in temper to mortals' (1348). It is hard to believe that this protest evoked no response in the hearts of the Greek audience, incredible that it should not represent the final comment of Euripides upon the personal deity who was about to quit the stage.[3]

Dionysus in this play claims his place upon Olympus (554); and establishes it, in that he proves himself worthy to be associated with a lustful Zeus, a sexually jealous Hera, a vain and vindictive Artemis,[4] a callous Apollo. Beauty and wisdom and the calm

[1] 'What for his human opponent is fate and destruction, for the god is an episode between coming and going' (Wassermann, *op. cit.* p. 273). Cf. 48 sq.

[2] See p. 146 n. 1.

[3] Cf. Bellinger, *Yale Classical Studies*, VI (1939), p. 24. On mutual ὕβρις see p. 83 n. 1 and p. 146 n. 2.

[4] The reference to Artemis at 337 sqq. illustrates the satirical method of Euripides. Actaeon, like Pentheus, was a grandson of Cadmus, and had already met a terrible death. Cadmus, who was always preoccupied with family, points—as a final warning to Pentheus—to his cousin's end. 'You see the miserable fate of Actaeon. He was torn to pieces by the ravening hounds he had reared himself, because he boasted in the mountain

exercise of power were conventional attributes of deity, with which the reported actions of the gods were in conflict. So Euripides makes the beauty of Dionysus skin-deep, turns his wisdom into cleverness and his calm control into the calculating pursuit of a personal vendetta.

If the foregoing analysis is correct, Dionysus, regarded as an individual, as a personal agent, as an Olympian god, does not emerge with more credit from the *Bacchae* than other gods from other plays, despite the preponderating rôle he plays. Euripides the satirist has been at work on him; and though the treatment of the personal Dionysus is far from being the whole of the play, this fact (if fact it is) must contribute to our final judgement.

This satire is of a piece with the other work of Euripides; it was a part of his mind. Whether we should call him a religious reformer is a matter which could only be determined by a complete review of his surviving plays. It is indeed probable that he felt intensely antagonistic to a view which saw gods as men, attributed to them human motives and, at the same time, responsibility for events, and then worshipped them as not only powerful but wise and beautiful. It was dangerous that a commonplace mind could cite extenuating precedents from the divine mythology, as the Nurse in the *Hippolytus* cites the amours of Zeus and of the Dawn goddess (451–8). But in the preceding lines she had spoken eloquently of Cypris as a universal power in nature, thus illustrating within a short compass the contrast between real and mythological aspects of deity. Neither Aphrodite nor Dionysus is adequately accounted for as a person. Perhaps, however, the satire with which Dionysus is treated in the *Bacchae* does not derive wholly from his mythological status.

glades that he was better at hunting than Artemis. Let that not be your fate.' Artemis, like Dionysus, takes a cruel revenge for a slight. The parallel is all too close. The scene is Cithaeron (1291); not only does διεσπάσαντο (339) relate to the *sparagmos* of Pentheus, but ὠμόσιτοι (338) suggests the omophagy of 138 (a motif which for sufficient reasons subsequently recurs only in the imaginary banquet of Agave). With ἐν ὀργάσιν (340), compare 445. Both Artemis and Dionysus are associated with the beauty of wild nature, and both, to gratify revenge, foul their own nests (cf. 1137 sq.). Yet Dionysus does not come well out of a comparison. Actaeon was torn in pieces by the hounds which he had reared; Pentheus will be torn by a human pack (731, 977) led by the mother that reared him.

It was suggested in the first chapter that the play could usefully be considered upon more than one level. There is the level of superficial melodrama; there is the satire directed against a crude mythology; and—clearly of the profoundest importance—there is the permanent significance of Dionysiac religion. It may well be asked whether the concurrence of satire upon an Olympian god with the wider exhibition of real Dionysiac phenomena is not distracting and dangerous to the artistic success of the play. The spectator or reader must judge; and if the 'levels' were watertight compartments, and if the bitterness of the satire derived merely from the indignation of a reforming moralist, the judgement might necessarily be unfavourable. But this is not the case.

The calm and detachment which the god exhibits upon the stage are not merely a presentation of Olympian serenity and wisdom applied to an ignoble end. For Pentheus is pitting himself, not merely against a personal adversary whose coolness and cunning are a foil to his own excitable simplicity, but against a great impersonal force, which, like flood or fire, seems, despite its crude violence, to be moving unhurried towards an end. Is the god calm, controlled, serene? The force moves with no less relentless calm over trivial opposition.[1] Is the god cruel, and indiscriminate in his cruelty? Nor has the force either pity or discrimination. It is because they have these common characteristics that the personal god, petty and immoral though he may be when judged by human standards, can serve as a symbol of the impersonal force, which is beyond good and evil. And the satire which attends this god, in whom jealousy leads through cunning and intrigue to malicious cruelty, perhaps derives its venom less from the moralist than from the sensitive poet confronted with the conditions of humanity. The powers which govern human life cannot be denied but they may be hated. 'I am wroth with the gods', sang the singer in the *Hippolytus* (1146), when she did not yet know how great was the cause for anger. The dying Hippolytus longed to curse the gods (1415). Pentheus, like Hippolytus, was broken by the forces within and around him, and Euripides found it odious that such things can happen, and inexorably do happen, with little justice and no mercy. At least, he says, let us not pretend that this is the work of a worshipful divinity.

[1] Murray (*Ancient Greek Lit.* p. 272) speaks in this connection of 'things utterly non-human and non-moral, which bring man bliss or tear his life to shreds without a break in their own serenity'.

How much else he had to say about Dionysus and his religion will be seen when we now proceed to examine the play in detail. For the god who speaks, and whose role we have just considered, is mainly, though not entirely, a figure of mythology. But there is also the god who works and is manifested by events and by the human beings who are filled with him, so that it is primarily to the action and to the human characters that we must look for a revelation of the nature and quality of his religion. It is through them also that we shall see the god Dionysus in an aspect which has not yet been considered in this chapter. This aspect will serve as a transition to the fuller analysis.

Dionysus, like the other Olympians, was an anthropomorphic deity. But, if legend makes him so, belief and cult did not, or not entirely. Nor does the play; and in the preceding account one important element has been left out, and, in particular, one important strand in the fabric of the closing scene has been left out. If Dionysus was an Olympian, he was not quite as the other Olympians; if he was anthropomorphic, he was also theriomorphic.

The status of Dionysus in the Greek pantheon was anomalous. Though a late-comer, he had found his way to Olympus, had achieved sonship to Zeus, had collected a nimbus of legend. But, though he had come to be an Olympian god, he had not ceased to be a beast. In whatever relation other major Greek deities had once stood to the animal world, to the snake, the owl, the bear, that play a part in their story or worship, they had become as persons wholly distinct from them; if legend transformed Zeus into a bull, it was a mere convenience for the lover. It was different with Dionysus, who found in bull or goat a veritable incarnation.[1] In the *Bacchae* this aspect of him is interwoven with the Olympian, from the Entrance Song onwards. The Chorus sang of him as son of Zeus, but it was a god with bull's horns that Zeus bore from his thigh (100). To Pentheus, in the last stages of his obsession, those horns were visible (920 sq.). Again, the final epiphany of Dionysus was of an Olympian in glory; but the Chorus prayed him to manifest himself as bull or snake or lion (1017 sqq.). The prayer is not answered by a metamorphosis visible to the audience. It is answered by Agave and her ravening pack, and (obliquely) by the illusion that makes for her a lion of Pentheus; it is answered, that is to say, by Agave the

[1] Cf. Farnell, *Cults*, v, pp. 126 sq. In other cases (e.g. bull-headed river-gods) animal form goes along with feeble personification.

huntress and Pentheus the hunted. In listing the themes that form the fabric of the closing scenes one was omitted (for it serves far wider purposes than merely to make horrible the god's immediate epiphany); yet it is the one that impresses itself most forcibly upon the hearer. 'Hunt, prey, beast': the words fall again and again with battering effect upon his sensibility.[1] 'Our lord is a hunter', cry the Bacchanals (1192), but he is also a beast, for in nature the roles are doubled. This too is a revelation of Dionysus, and one which comes close indeed to his essential nature.

Yet it is made through the human characters. It is a link binding the mythological god of legend to the real god at work; but it does not invalidate the principle that it is in the action and in the human characters that we must seek the true Dionysus. We may conclude this chapter by admiring the tact with which Euripides has handled this aspect of the god. Dionysus is manifested as beast, but not upon the stage. Still the god who speaks and who is seen is essentially the Olympian. The soldiers of Pentheus catch a 'tame, gentle beast'; but their captive talks like a god, or a sophist, or both at once. Pentheus in the palace may wrestle with a bull; but it is the sophist-god who tells us the story. Finally, in the last scene between the two adversaries, it is Pentheus that to all appearances is brute-beast, Dionysus his inhuman tormentor. Pentheus alone can see him in animal shape; and this is right, for Pentheus is now one in guise and mind with the Bacchanals, who know that their god has horns like a bull and may at their prayer appear as bull or snake or lion.

[1] Cf. 1188–204. In these 17 lines ἀγρεύς, ἄγρα, ἀγρεύειν occur six times, θήρ three times.

CHAPTER III

INTRODUCTION TO BACCHANALS

The preceding chapter has been in a sense preliminary to the main investigation. In examining the treatment of Dionysus as a stage-god, it reached certain conclusions: that, as a person, Dionysus is not handled in a way essentially different from gods in other Euripidean plays; that he is as odious at the end of the play as he was enigmatic at the beginning; that his triumph is attended with cumulative satire. If these conclusions are correct, we can hardly be blamed for thinking that Euripides was not entirely favourable towards this deity and his religion. But it is not as satire upon a crude theology that the *Bacchae* lives; and, if the satire has, as was suggested, a wider reference, then this wider theme demands an examination that will go far more deeply into the play and will take cognisance of scenes and songs to which the anthropomorphic Dionysus is almost if not quite irrelevant. Henceforward, therefore, we will follow the course of the play and trace in full detail how Euripides composes his picture of Dionysiac religion.

The Prologue, so far as it concerns the mythological Dionysus, has already been discussed: the myth of the birth, the 'immortal *hubris*' of Hera, the design for self-revelation and the hint of vengeance. But Dionysus there speaks, not merely of himself and of his motives, but of his worship and of his effects. And it is first to be noted that, though Theban-born, he brings his worship to Greece from Asia. All the East has accepted it, Lydia and Phrygia, Persia and Bactria, Media and Arabia; so have the coasts of Asia Minor, where Greeks live in contact with orientals. But now, at Thebes, it impinges upon Greece (13–22). What success will attend this god, returning to his birthplace, yet as an alien? Can Greeks accept what comes to them from antipathetic Asia?[1] Or is there that about this worship which, being universal, transcends such differences? What is its nature? It involves rites and dances (21 sq.), but of their quality we still know nothing.

But Dionysus has turned the women of Thebes into Bacchanals; and line by line the picture is filled out. The worship has its characteristic cry (24), its characteristic costume—fawn-skin and ivy-tipped

[1] Pure Greeks unsullied by contact with the barbarian (18).

wand or thyrsus (24 sq.). It is akin to madness, to the frenzy induced by a gadfly's sting (32 sq.). The worshippers are women. The worship takes place on the mountains, amid green pines and 'roofless rocks' (38). These rites the city of Thebes must learn. How will they comport with the civilisation of the *polis*? How will these women of the city behave upon the mountain? Time and the play will show. Meanwhile Dionysus calls forward another band of Bacchanals.[1] 'You who have come leaving Tmolus, the bulwark of Lydia, my sacred band, my women, whom I have brought to be my comrades in rest and march—rouse the drums native to the city of the Phrygians, which Rhea the great mother and I invented; come and beat them about the royal palace of Pentheus, that the city of Cadmus may see'[2] (55–61). The *thiasos* of Dionysus, a band of Asiatic women, comes to beat the drums of Phrygia in the middle of a Greek city.

The drums make a ground-bass to the end of the god's speech; and, as he leaves the stage, the Chorus enter singing the prelude to a hymn.[3] It is a hymn, and not a rite; and, though towards the end the emotional tension increases, it remains essentially a hymn; not itself ecstatic, it is full of the contemplation of ecstasy, and of a nostalgic yearning after it. For these devotees, these missionaries, are far from the land which is to them the natural setting of their rites. But they will sing the songs of their god in a strange land; though they have left Asia and holy Tmolus, to cry 'Evoe' to the Bacchic god is a 'sweet labour' (πόνον ἡδύν) and a 'toil that is not toilsome' (66). Thus the note of joy and ease, the antithesis of painful effort, is struck early; and it is important. Their next words are the familiar prohibition to the uninitiated, the *procul este profani*, and carry, as such exclusions do, an aura of spiritual pride. 'Who is in the road, who is in the road? Who is in the house? Let him make way;

[1] Pentheus being introduced between the two sets of Bacchanals in a way that foreshadows his future predicament. On the relationship between the Theban and Asiatic Bacchanals see pp. 153 sqq. Note that, as Masqueray (*Euripide et ses idées*, p. 146) points out, the offenders were the sisters of Semele, the 'punishment' is shared by all the women of Thebes, a first illustration of the indiscriminateness of Dionysus (cf. 1303 sqq., 1323 sq.). This may explain the emphatic ὅσαι γυναῖκες ἦσαν (the sequence being: ἐπεί μ' ἀδελφαὶ μητρός... τοιγάρ νιν αὐτάς... καὶ πᾶν τὸ θῆλυ σπέρμα... ὅσαι γυναῖκες ἦσαν).

[2] On ὁρᾷ (which can be explained as 'come and see', but may have a deeper meaning) see pp. 164 sq.

[3] See Deichgräber, *Hermes*, LXX (1935), pp. 323 sqq.; Dodds, pp. 68 sq.

let every man make holy his lips in silence; for I am about to sing to Dionysus the hymns that were ever customary'[1] (68–71).

The first stanza (*Strophe* 1) is devoted to dogma, to the praise of holiness and the promise of blessing. 'Blessed is he, who having the happiness to know the sacraments of the gods, consecrates his life and enters with his soul into the *thiasos*, as he worships on the mountains with holy purifications. Practising the rites of the great mother Cybele, shaking the thyrsus on high, crowned with ivy, he serves Dionysus' (72–82). It is a promise of blessing and well-being[2] to those who are made and kept pure by certain rites. The promise of happiness and the demand for purity are characteristic of all mystery-religions. But of the quality of this happiness and this purity we still know nothing. All we learn here is that they are attained through the group and exercised upon the mountains. The stanza concludes with an appeal: 'Come, ye Bacchanals, ye who escort Bromius, god and son of god, Dionysus, from the mountains of Phrygia to the spacious streets of Greece' (83–7). Once more the contrast of environments —the mountains of Phrygia, the streets and squares of a Greek *polis*.

In the answering stanza (*Antistrophe* 1) they pass to the myth of the divine birth. Such myths are a staple feature of cult-songs, and they sing the story in a glow of receptive piety. It is easy to read and re-read the stanza in the singers' own spirit of acceptance, such a glaze of uniform religious emotion do they spread over the whole song. They sing of Bromius, how 'while his mother was carrying him, the lightning of Zeus took wing, and in forced pangs of labour she bore him, struck out untimely from her womb, and died from the stroke of the thunderbolt. But straightway there received him, in secret recesses of birth, Zeus, son of Cronus, and covered him up in his thigh and fastened him in with golden clasps, safe hid from Hera' (88–98). The petty Olympian intrigue, like the cruelty of the blasting, belongs to the myth and could be treated in this way or in that, as the poet willed. Here, by the order and choice of words,[3] Euripides

[1] 71: τὰ νομισθέντα ἀεί. The first hint of an important theme: see p. 111.

[2] On μάκαρ and εὐδαίμων ('blessed' and 'happy') see p. 156.

[3] The logical sense is given in the translation: the aesthetic sequence is as follows. Pregnancy (ἔχουσα); normal birth (ἐν ὠδίνων λοχίαις ἀνάγκαισι—the common lot of women); the thunderbolt; abortion (νηδύος ἔκβολον... ἔτεκεν). The word ἐκβάλλειν is used by Greek medical writers

has momentarily brought the myth to earth and made of the act of Zeus the violence of a lover who has caused his mistress to miscarry and to die. Such satire might appear intrusive were it not also relevant to the nature of Bacchanals. There is a harsh discord between the callousness of Zeus, the jealousy of Hera in this stanza, and the suggestions of blessedness and purity in the last, which makes a moral and aesthetic anti-climax. But the singers in their uncritical acceptance are unaware of any such descent.

At the close of the stanza a new and important theme is introduced. The god that Zeus in due time bore had horns like a bull, and Zeus 'garlanded' him with snakes; 'whence it is that Maenads entwine in their hair the beasts their prey' (99–104). It is an explanation, an αἴτιον, of the practice of the Maenads. But it is also the first hint of the bestial in Dionysus and the first reference to hunting. Who will do the hunting in this play? Who will be the prey?

Now (*Strophe* 2) the metre becomes more rapid, the style more vigorous, as the singers appeal to Thebes to share their worship. 'Nurse of Semele, Thebes, put on a garland of ivy; abound, abound in green, fair-fruited bryony; be very Bacchanal with boughs of oak or pine; gird your garments of dappled fawnskin with white curls of braided wool, and in handling the violent wands be holy' (105–14). The lines are full of immediate visual appeal. Vegetable and animal nature alike are laid under tribute to provide a strangely decorative garb. Such is the innocent beauty that follows immediately upon the more sinister themes with which the last stanza closed. But they are not forgotten, or meant to be forgotten. The word 'garland' acts as a link—the garland of ivy, the garland of snakes, both equally characteristic of the Bacchanal; and Thebes, if she wears one, must surely wear the other. The pretty dappled fawnskin—how was it come by? There can only be one answer now: the Maenads wear the skins of their prey.[1] Finally, the wands, the *thyrsi*, are—*hubristic*.

The word (ὑβριστάς) is unexpected and desperately hard to translate. It is applied to the wands perhaps because these are the symbols and instruments of their magical power, and the underlying

of abortion and miscarriage (*v.* L.S. *s.v.* VI and on ἐκβόλιον). Since this *is* a premature birth, can ἔκβολον here fail to carry this suggestion? See also p. 78 on 519 sqq. For an entirely different aesthetic treatment of the story see *Phoen.* 649 sqq.

[1] On the complicated relationship between fawn and Bacchanal see p. 107.

notion is partly that of power, partly that of pride—the spiritual pride they feel in that they are superior to ordinary mortals, are 'holy' (ὅσιοι). Thus for the singers *hubris* and holiness are complementary conceptions, for the sense of power which the thyrsus gives is altogether in harmony with their sense of consecration.[1] Yet there is an aesthetic discord also. It is impossible to separate any cognate of *hubris* entirely from the normal connotations of the word: wanton violence and cruelty.[2] In fact, in the course of the play, the wands are used not merely for the working of beneficent miracles (704 sqq.), but for injurious attacks (733, 762, 1099). The word suggests then not merely the power and pride of initiates, but also a potential cruelty. The song continues: 'Straightway the whole land will dance, when Bromius leads the bands[3]—to the mountain, to the mountain, where waits the throng of women driven wild from beside their looms and shuttles by Dionysus' (114–19). For the appeal to Thebes is, thanks to the compulsion of the god, already in part answered. The women of the city have exchanged the humdrum tasks of their normal life for the 'sweet toil' of Dionysus upon the mountain. We begin to understand the fascination of this cult for women;[4] we continue to wonder how it will prove consistent with civilised life at all.

After the birthplace of the god's mother they address the birthplace of his father (*Antistrophe* 2). The moral is perhaps that Thebes should not be less eager to celebrate the son with Bacchic revelry than

[1] The translation of the phrase (ἀμφὶ δὲ νάρθηκας ὑβριστὰς ὁσιοῦσθε) is based on Dodds. The only possible sense for ἀμφί seems to be 'in respect of', 'in relation to', 'in dealing with'. My difficulty about his interpretation is that the general tenour of the stanza is 'be Bacchanals' and not 'be careful' and that the use of the thyrsus is part of what makes the Bacchanal ὅσιος (cf. 80 after 77). I doubt, therefore, if the sense is precisely that of a warning that the thyrsi are dangerous *unless* the handlers are ὅσιοι.

[2] The sense in which the word has already occurred—of Hera (9)—and will occur again and again in the play. See p. 18. Note specially the relation between ὁσία and ὕβρις in 370 sqq., where the holiness is all on one side, the *hubris* on the other.

[3] 115: εὖτ' ἄν (Elmsley); *v.* Dodds *ad loc.*

[4] Doubtless Euripides was familiar with the Boeotian myth of the daughters of Minyas 'who stayed at home over their weaving and disdained to accompany the other women to the orgies, until suddenly ivy and vine-runners twined themselves about their looms, and milk and honey dropped from the ceiling; they caught up one of their little sons, tore him to pieces, and hurried to the mountains and joined the Maenads' (Nilsson, *A History of Greek Religion*, p. 207).

Crete the father. For it is of the circumstances of the latter's birth that the stanza treats. 'O Chamber of the Curetes, and holy secret places of Crete that saw the birth of Zeus, when the Corybants with triple helm devised for me in the cave this circle of stretched hide; and in tense worship (βακχείᾳ) mingled it with the sweet-voiced breath of Phrygian pipes and gave it into the hand of mother Rhea—to beat time for the cries of Bacchanals; and from the goddess mother the mad (μαινόμενοι) satyrs won it and wedded it to the dances of the second-year festivals, wherein Dionysus rejoices' (120–34). So the history of their drums is bound up with the birth of Zeus, as that of their snakes with the birth of his son. This pious archaeology, however, implies a doctrinal point of some importance, if a Bacchic type of worship, so far from originating with Dionysus, was already associated with Zeus. It was in fact true that the systematisation of Greek theology (as, for instance, in the Hesiodic *Theogony*) had incorporated elements oddly out of keeping with the Olympian, the Homeric, Zeus. The legend of the birth of Zeus and his tendance by the Curetes was a legacy from the pre-Hellenic religion of Crete, an orgiastic religion which worshipped a chthonic god under a serpent emblem and included in its rites the slaying, dismemberment and eating of a bull and a noisy dance by young warriors. The child-god of Crete, whom the Greeks incongruously identified with Zeus and whose goddess-mother Rhea was mythologised as consort of Cronus, they also identified, at other times and with better reason, with the Thraco-Phrygian Dionysus. Knowledge of the rites of Cybele, the great Anatolian goddess, and her devotees the Corybants added another equation; and the rational minds of Greek mythologists imposed clarity and order. As Rhea was identified with Cybele, so the Cretan Curetes were identified with the Anatolian Corybants and both regarded as forerunners of the satyrs and Maenads of Dionysus. Euripides accepts these equations, nay more, insists upon them;[1] and they are important for him in more than one way. For, if in the myth Dionysus is a new god revealing a new religion (new to Greece, comparatively new to Asia), yet essentially that religion is as old as the human race, the god as old as nature itself. By carrying the Dionysiac behind Dionysus and in particular by associating it with Zeus, Euripides is stressing its fundamental importance in the scheme of things. At the same time he is insisting upon the connection of the worship of Dionysus in Greece with wilder worships elsewhere, in

[1] Cf. 59, 79.

Crete, in Phrygia. He has been leading his Athenian listener by gradual steps towards a realisation of what the Dionysiac in full measure means.[1] Between the Attic cult and the ecstatic rite of Asia or Crete a link is provided by the 'trieteric' festivals of Thebes and Delphi. It is a *trieteris* he is now to describe, but a *trieteris* in Asia and in the heyday of Bacchic vitality.[2]

For still we know little of actual Bacchic worship. We know that there are rites with dancing and music which bring purity; we know that Bacchanals are mad, and that they hunt; we know that they are close to nature. But so far both detail and strong emotion are lacking; the tone is contemplative or expository or exhortatory. Now in the final stanza (*Epode*) there enters a more intimate excitement, as the singers picture vividly and with an obvious nostalgia a scene of Bacchic ecstasy in their native land. A creed, an orthodoxy, is suddenly clothed in personal emotion.

The emotion is personal, and it is concentrated upon a person, upon their leader, who has brought them, a band of missionaries, from Asia; who is the god himself, though to them he is god only in the sense that 'he who leads the cry of Evoe is Bromius'. It was inevitable that they should sing of one who must have dominated their lives, and they do so with admiration and love: indeed they are more than half in love with him as he tosses his long sensual locks in the air and bids them join him in the Bacchic dance. 'Pleasant (ἡδύς) is he[3] upon the mountains when out from the running bands he falls to the ground, clad in his sacred garment of fawnskin, hunting the blood of the slain goat, the delight of raw flesh devoured (ὠμοφάγον χάριν), as he hastens to the mountains of Phrygia, of Lydia. Bromius is he who leads the cry of Evoe!' (135–40).

So we return to the Bacchic hunt, in which a goat is torn in pieces and eaten raw. The hunt is led by the incarnation of the god, and the Bacchanals joy to see him, joy too themselves to join in the chase.

[1] A point well made by Deichgräber, *op. cit.*

[2] See p. 154.

[3] The subject is not the god, but the ἔξαρχος, the celebrant, or rather the god in the person of the celebrant, who dominates the stanza from the beginning as he does from 144 on. The only plausible emendation (ἡδύ γ'... ὃς ἄν) is unimpeachable Greek, but the use of the masculine and the succession of masculine participles offend, not indeed against the grammatical usage, but against the desired picture, unless they refer to the celebrant. 136 (πέσῃ πεδόσε): 'the celebrant falls unconscious and the god enters into him' (Dodds). The goat has not yet been killed.

With one of those abrupt transitions which are characteristic of the artistic method of Euripides (and no less characteristic of the Bacchic mind) we pass to words of peace and plenty: 'and the ground flows with milk, flows with wine, flows with the nectar of the bees' (142). The clash is staggering; yet both elements are part of the Bacchic experience, for both are part of nature. We shall do well to remember that the ground which flows with milk and honey will flow also with blood, as we return to the picture of the 'Bacchic One' (145) shaking his smoky torch, exciting his followers with his running and dancing and cries, and tossing his luxuriant locks.[1] 'And amid the cries of Evoe he shouts: "Come, Bacchanals, come, pride of Tmolus that flows with gold, hymn Dionysus to the rumbling drums, honouring with Evoe the Evian god, with Phrygian cries and clamour, when the sacred flute melodious rumbles out its sacred sportive music in apt accord with those who roam to the mountain, to the mountain"' (152–65).

A final sentence is the conclusion of the whole matter. 'In joy then (ἡδομένα), like a foal beside its grazing mother, does the Bacchanal leap as she speeds swift-footed' (165–9). Joy begins and ends the stanza; joy begins and ends the ode (66, 135, 165). The Bacchanal has joy, and she has it in everything, in the dancing and music and torches, in the milk, honey and wine, in the leader, and no less in the hunting, in the tearing and eating of the prey. The Dionysiac promise of blessedness and demand for purity have begun to acquire a context.

Our analysis of this choral ode has revealed something of its aesthetic complexity; and, since the method of Euripides here is his method elsewhere, it may be well to comment upon it as a footnote to this chapter. The complexity lies in the fact that the poetry has almost throughout two aspects. One is towards the singers, for the ode is an adequate and beautiful expression of what is immediately in their minds. Of the other aspect they are entirely unconscious; not so the poet and the audience. It is not a matter of the familiar dramatic irony, by which the speaker or singer uses in all innocence phrases of ambiguous import. It is rather that the poetry is so written

[1] See Dodds on the text of 144–50, which is disordered, though the main details of the picture are clear. 151: ἐπιβρέμει, for he *is* Bromius, the roaring-god (cf. 156, 164).

154: χλιδά (Victorius).

as to involve wider relationships than the singers have in mind, to invoke standards, emotional, moral or intellectual, which are not their standards. So it may happen that the song contains a comment upon or criticism of the singers themselves, of their thoughts or emotions or way of life. Both aspects are valid, and both must be borne in mind, if the full content of the poetry is to be appreciated. It is indeed possible for the hearer (or reader) to surrender himself entirely to the singers and share their limited lyricism. But this is not, it will be observed, simply a matter of primary emotional impact modified by subsequent reflection. The method is essentially aesthetic; and the better attuned the hearer is to the overtones of words, the more sensitive to their flavours and associations, the less easy will such facile surrender be to him. Commentary and criticism are the result, not of conscious judgement (though such a judgement may follow), but of contrast of emotions, even to the point of discord. Thus, the cruelty of Semele's fate emerges from the associations of νηδύος ἔκβολον; the holiness of the wand-bearing Bacchanals is complicated by the ambiguous flavour of ὑβριστάς.[1] Joy and terror, the innocent and the sinister are enigmatically juxtaposed; they are linked by verbal repetitions (as στεφάνωσεν, στεφανοῦσθε at 101, 106; or πεδόσε, πέδον at 136, 142), so that memory, conscious or unconscious, may insist upon their being held together in the sensibility of the hearer. We may put it in another way. The mood of the singers is integral; but the poet has so written their song as deliberately to leave certain elements in it unintegrated and inharmonious. Now harmony and integration may be achieved upon different levels and with different values. Is the harmony of the Bacchanals valuable, is it worth the cost? That is a fundamental issue of the play.

[1] M. R. Glover, *J.H.S.* XLIX (1929), p. 86, rightly draws attention to such discords.

CHAPTER IV

THREE MEN

The cue is 'Bacchanal' (169)—foal-like and nimble; the entry is that of a figure, wearing Bacchic costume indeed, but male and old and blind. In a few moments he will be joined by another old man, similarly clad. The scene between them is full of humour.[1]

If there was a contrast of tone between Prologue and Entrance Song, between the utterances of a mythological personage and the warm emotions of real women, there is more than contrast here, there is anti-climax. Whatever may be true of the other Greek dramatists, Euripides was not afraid to demand versatility of response from his audience. But this is no mere *tour de force*. In point of immediate dramatic effect, the scene is justified by surprise and suspense: we expect, if not the reappearance of the Leader, the appearance of the Persecutor, and this is deferred. It is justified, however, on more fundamental grounds than that.

The preceding song has told us something of the character of the new religion that had come from Asia to Greece. There is a myth, fantastic and, in its implications, cruel. There is a worship in which 'holiness' and 'madness', bloodshed and the beauty and bounty of nature, are enigmatically combined. The song ended with the picture of the happy Bacchanal, indiscriminately happy in all of it. To the listening Athenian it must indeed have seemed a curious mixture of the familiar and the exotic. Of its stranger features he might know something, if only from the stage,[2] but he was bound to be struck by the difference between this wild abandonment and the regulated cult into which it had developed.[3] The scene before us supplies in part an explanation of the change. To the Asiatic missionaries succeed representatives of the Greece that they have come to proselytise; in particular, Teiresias, prophet of the Delphic

[1] The presence of humour cannot be argued; it can only be felt. The critics who can feel the humour here do not agree as to the extent and significance of the comedy. Cf. Kitto, p. 379; Grube, p. 402; Dodds, p. 86.

[2] Xenocles had produced a Βάκχαι in 415.

[3] He may, however, also have been reminded of orgiastic cults of recent introduction, and the controversy between Teiresias and Pentheus may, as Dodds has suggested, reflect contemporary arguments about Sabazius and other oriental deities. See p. 151.

god. For it was Apollo and his people who, it appears, had taken the wild immigrant god in hand, civilised him and made him fit to join the Greek community. Teiresias represents the subtle 'ecclesiastical' wisdom that had achieved this triumph.[1]

But there is more to Dionysus than a historical cult, Asiatic or Hellenic. His is a religion in a wider sense; his worship symbolises a whole attitude towards life. The present scene will widen and deepen our knowledge of this also. The Chorus is of real women, but they are not normal women. They are detached from any normal human environment and set apart. Juxtaposed to them are two figures of ordinary life, prosaic against this background of lyrical exaltation and a reminder that the actual world is full of such human beings, organised in humdrum societies and unapt to mystical excitement, a factor which a religion claiming to be universal must take into consideration. Further, while the Chorus is of women, these new characters are men, such as pretend to organise the world upon a basis of reason. Finally, these men are old. What can Dionysus do for the old? One answer is that he can make them ridiculous.

Teiresias speaks: 'Who is at the gate? Call Cadmus from the palace, Agenor's son, he who left the city of Sidon and founded this walled town of Thebes' (170–2). A sounding introduction, equivalent in its effect to a string of titles and recalling to us that Cadmus is a famous figure of saga.[2] The Cadmus who answers this summons is senile, and clearly dependent on the stronger personality of his companion, whose suggestion it had surely been that they should put on Bacchic costume and join in the worship upon the mountain. Why had he suggested it? Why had Cadmus agreed? 'My dear friend,' says Cadmus,—'for I recognised you by your

[1] On this process see Nilsson, *op. cit.* pp. 208 sq. (also Farnell, *Cults*, v, p. 113). The word 'ecclesiastical' here and later demands some justification. Admittedly, the differences between Delphi and a modern 'church' are great and obvious (see Nilsson, p. 200). It was, however, the only religious organisation in Greece that approximated to one; it had its representatives or 'exegetes' in the various cities, and a central priesthood at Delphi, which could frame a policy and influence affairs; it gave advice on major and minor matters; it was on the whole conservative, standing for institutionalism and ritualism. It would not be surprising if an 'ecclesiastical' type had developed in connection with it. One might use the portrait of Teiresias here as evidence that it had.

[2] For a comparable effect see *Or.* 352 sq., introducing the dapper sophist Menelaus.

voice from within the house, the wise voice of a wise man! Here I come all ready in the god's equipment. He is my daughter's son, and we must enhance his greatness as far as in us lies' (178–83).[1] For Cadmus's guiding emotion was care for the interests of his house; he liked having a god in the family; and if this involved putting on strange clothes and staggering a step or two in the dance, Cadmus was willing to find it enjoyable. 'Where must I go and dance? Where plant my foot and shake my grey head? You who are old, Teiresias, explain it to me, who am old also; for you are wise. I shall never grow tired, night or day, of smiting the earth with my thyrsus. Joyfully (ἡδέως) have I forgotten that I am old!' (184–9).[2]

Joyfully, like the Bacchanals; and old Cadmus is perhaps for the moment intoxicated with the novelty of it. But is it altogether to be commended that old men should forget that they are old, to the extent of thyrsus, fawnskin and dance? Teiresias is quick to answer: 'Then you feel as I do; I too am young and will attempt the dance.' 'We shall take a chariot to the mountain?' asks Cadmus, who feels that a line must be drawn somewhere. 'No,' says Teiresias, 'that would not do the same honour to the god.' Cadmus readily gives in, and Teiresias promises that the god will bring them on their way without weariness (194). This is Bacchic orthodoxy, for the toil of Dionysus is sweet (66). Teiresias will always say the proper thing. When Cadmus asks with somewhat puerile eagerness if they alone of the city's men will dance to Bacchus,[3] he replies: 'We alone are in our senses.' Εὖ φρονεῖν, φρονεῖν, νοῦν ἔχειν, σωφρονεῖν: the Greek terms are of very similar import, suggesting soundness, sanity, balance; a right, a salutary attitude towards things. There is competition throughout the play for the right to claim this quality. Here it is claimed by Teiresias for Cadmus and himself on the grounds of their piety towards Dionysus. Cadmus, too, preens himself: 'I, a mortal, do not contemn the gods' (199). The matter is, however, slightly complicated by the fact that the god most in question is the son of his mortal daughter. We already suspect—

[1] With some hesitation I follow those editors who omit 182 (Διόνυσον ὃς πέφυκεν ἀνθρώποις θεός). But see Dodds *ad loc.*

[2] ἐξηγοῦ (185) may have special reference to the Delphic ἐξηγηταί (cf. Verrall, *The Bacchants of Euripides*, p. 47 n. 4). Note the stress on old age (175, 186, 193) and the paradoxical παιδαγωγήσω in 193.

[3] μόνοι—alas no; Pentheus also will do so (962) and the irony is pointed by the fact that they clearly have Pentheus in mind here (as at 199 sq.).

later it becomes more than a suspicion—that family policy has something to do with the 'pious acceptance' of Cadmus. We may even suspect that ecclesiastical statesmanship weighs more with Teiresias than simple faith. But Teiresias is the cleverer man and does not give himself away.

Teiresias is a clever man. Clever or wise, for σοφός cloaks an ambiguity. Perhaps both. Σοφία, 'wisdom', is a virtue allied to *sophrosyne*; and both are claimed by Dionysus, both by the Bacchanals (though the latter put their own interpretation upon the terms); to Teiresias's σοφία Cadmus has twice already paid a tribute. But it is a dangerous one for the pious to accept, cleverness being under suspicion in religious circles.[1] Accordingly, the prophet quickly caps Cadmus with: 'Nor do we play the sophist with the gods'.[2] Then, in sonorous terms: 'The traditions which we have received from our fathers, coeval with time itself, no reasoning shall overthrow, no matter what cleverness subtle minds achieve' (200–3). But, well though it sounds, this sermon (if we may use the word)[3] has two weaknesses. In the first place, it is superficially inappropriate to the situation; for Dionysus's claim is new, is even revolutionary. Secondly, it is, as we shall soon see, far from the preacher's real intention to abdicate from σοφία. In Greek thought the acceptance of tradition is generally opposed to cleverness, to the critical intellect. This relationship will be taken up again in an important context in which the Bacchanals claim a special wisdom of their own.[4] So far as this scene is concerned, the truth is that

[1] Mr L. . Wilkinson suggests that it is a sign that Cadmus is no true believer that he will call Teiresias σοφός, to the latter's embarrassment!

[2] οὐδ' ἐνσοφιζόμεσθα (Musgrave). See Dodds *ad loc.* I do not see the necessity for Fraenkel's οὐκ. Teiresias does not break off the stichomythia till 201; 200 caps 199, and the connective is in place. But 200 suggests to him sentiments which he has probably expressed many a time before; he clears his throat and delivers them. The beginning of this sentence may possibly be lost (*v.* Dodds), but the general sense cannot be affected thereby.

[3] Since there were no sermons in Greek worship, whence did Teiresias derive his pulpit style? Presumably from the sophists, who, though not traditionalists, were preachers. There is something of the sophist, as well as of the ecclesiastic, about Teiresias, and doubtless if we knew more about the personalities and cross-currents of the sophistic movement the humours of this scene, if not its general significance, would be enhanced for us.

[4] See p. 65.

Teiresias is at once a traditionalist and an exceedingly clever man; and he is faced with a situation in which all his cleverness will be needed to defend the tradition. He represents, we may say without distortion, the established religion, being the prophet of Apollo, the interpreter of Delphi. To such persons the impact of 'revivalism' in any form presents a problem. Unqualified rejection or acceptance is dangerous; and compromise with the uncompromising is difficult. But if in some way the wild forces can be brought under constraint, the enthusiasm canalised? It was such a triumph that Teiresias sought; it was such a triumph that Delphi was, as a matter of historical fact, to win.

The cleverness of Teiresias is given an immediate illustration. Unlike the slightly senile Cadmus, Teiresias is self-conscious about the ridiculous aspect he is now presenting. 'Will anyone say', he breaks off abruptly, 'that I have no shame for my age, since I have bound my head with ivy and mean to dance?' His verbal subtlety is equal to the occasion. 'The god has not defined whether the young or the old should dance, he wishes to have honour alike from all, and in his will for glory he rules none out' (204–9).[1] It is an ingenious defence, but essentially a sophistry. If the god is no respecter of the dignity of grey hairs, so much the worse for him; and Teiresias knows it.

At this moment Cadmus catches sight of his grandson and announces his approach to the blind prophet. The principal human personage of the drama is about to enter, the persecutor and victim of the god. His character has been as variously interpreted as the play itself. For those who have accepted the play at its face-value, he has been the typical atheist and blasphemer, whose fate, if pitiable, is a salutary example. With the swing of the pendulum, other critics, relieved of the need to regard him as a sinner against god, have found instead a tragic figure of real dignity and worth; the emphasis is laid upon the conscientious king, the dutiful grandson, while his final degradation is ruled out of court as the product of an external force. It would seem that the pendulum has swung too far.

Up to the time of his entrance we know little enough about him. We have the partial statement of the Prologue that he is a 'fighter against god'.[2] More than that we know only that he is 'tyrant' (and,

[1] On the text see Dodds *ad loc.*

[2] Though not, it will be noted, against all gods (45 sq.).

after all, there are tyrants and tyrants upon the Greek stage), that he is young and has succeeded (presumably recently) to the power of his aged grandfather. This situation in itself may not have been easy, when the palace contained a senile ex-ruler, a princess-mother and two royal aunts. Then the blow fell: mother and aunts and all the women of his city suddenly quitted their household tasks and went to the mountains, asserting that they were worshipping Dionysus, divine child of Cadmus's daughter Semele, and did so at the bidding of a young Asiatic who had come to Thebes with a band of female attendants. What was he to think? What was he to do? It was an awkward problem to face a young ruler, and a stern test of his quality. So much we can read from the situation itself.

First impressions in drama are important. See then how Pentheus is introduced. 'Here is Pentheus', says Cadmus, 'coming to the palace in a hurry—Echion's son, to whom I have given rule over the land. How excited he is! Does he bring bad news?' (212 sqq.). Indeed, Pentheus has reason to be in a hurry, reason to be excited. However, the latter word is a strong one (ἐπτόηται), strong enough to be used later of the Bacchic distraction of Agave.[1]

By a convention of the Greek stage, Pentheus is at first unaware of the presence of Cadmus and Teiresias, and his address is in effect to the audience. In a speech of some length he attacks the new religion and its new adherents. It is answered by a still longer speech from Teiresias in their defence.

'During an absence from this land I have heard of strange evils abroad in the city: that our women have left our homes on a pretence of Bacchic rites, and gad about in the dark mountain woods, honouring with dances this upstart divinity Dionysus, whoever he may be; that full mixing-bowls stand in the middle of their bands (θιάσοις), and that they creep, one here, one there, to solitude, to serve the lusts of males—pretending, indeed, to be inspired Maenads, but really ranking Aphrodite before the Bacchic god' (215–25). No wonder Pentheus attacks this topic at once and with vigour. It is the behaviour of the women that has brought him in hot haste to Thebes: and yet is he too sensitive upon this point, too deeply interested, too curious? There is no charge against Pentheus that his modern advocates[2] are keener to rebut than that of prurience. Nor should we hurriedly condemn him. He is reporting what others have

[1] 1268. Cf. *Or.* 1505 (after 1492).

[2] E.g. Verrall, Pohlenz, Deichgräber.

told him, and this is what it was inevitable that people would say. True, neither would Pentheus be reluctant to accept the suggestion of insincerity. Agave and her sisters had been foremost in throwing scorn on Semele's story of a divine lover, and Pentheus, as he grew up, was of their party (242 sqq.). Now they have gone back upon him. Naturally he suspects there is something behind it, and, for a man—and a man without sensibility—can it be other than one thing? Devoid of sensibility he may be; devoid of imagination he is not. There is one subject upon which even the most insensitive 'man of the world' will use his imagination. Is not this the case against Pentheus, that he has not only heard evil rumours, he has dwelt on them with loving curiosity? The picture is far too vivid and detailed. The dark woods, the wine bowls, the women slinking off, one by one, to find a lover in the thickets. If Pentheus is obsessed with curiosity and desire, the victory of Dionysus is half won already.

At all events it is a scandal; and Pentheus has taken energetic measures to deal with it. Some of the women he has caught and imprisoned, the rest he will 'hunt from the mountain' and 'putting them in iron toils will quickly stay them from this pernicious revelry' (βακχείας) (226–32). He continues: 'They say there has come hither a stranger, a charlatan magician from the Lydian land, with long golden scented locks, wine-flushed and with the charms of Aphrodite in his eyes, who day and night associates with the young women under pretence of Bacchic (εὐίους) rites. If I get him within this house, I will stop him from making his thyrsus ring and shaking his locks, by severing his head from his body!' (233–41).[1]

Again it is but hearsay, and again Pentheus is only too willing to accept it. For the stranger as described is not at all the person of whom Pentheus, full of Hellenic prejudice, can approve. Yet when the two are confronted we must remember the young king's preoccupation with what he thinks the stranger does. Is there a touch of envy—of envy and fascination as well as disproval? Meanwhile, however, he knows what to do, for physical force is his panacea.

A few more words to emphasise the stranger's insolence. 'It is he that says Dionysus is a god, he that says he was stitched in the thigh of Zeus!' It is on the evidence of a long-haired Asiatic that Pentheus is asked to accept such a story, though the truth was (he goes on)

[1] Reading οἰνωπός (236); *v.* Dodds *ad loc.* συγγίγνεται (237) is a common euphemism. προτείνων may mean 'dangling before them' (Dodds), but in view of 218 I prefer to translate as above.

that Semele's child perished with his mother in the lightning-flash because she lied that Zeus was her lover. It is indeed a monstrous insult, whoever the stranger may be (242–7).[1]

At this moment Pentheus at last catches sight of the others—of the prophet and his own grandfather in dappled fawnskins. 'A very laughable sight', he says; but if Pentheus laughs it is without mirth. A young ruler must be insistent upon dignity. In terms of mingled indignation and affection he begs the old man to respect his age. 'Come, shake off the ivy wreath, free your hand from the thyrsus, you who are my mother's father.' There is affection here, and our sympathy is with Pentheus. But since human motives are ever mixed, there is also injured pride.[2] Cadmus has made Pentheus ridiculous.

He turns on Teiresias. Now, within his own range, Pentheus is no fool; at least he can realise that the prophet holds an ascendancy over the senile Cadmus. More than that, he can penetrate the prophet's motives, in so far as they are discreditable. 'You instigated this, Teiresias. You want, by introducing one more new deity to men, to have the watching of birds and the fees of burnt sacrifice' (255 sqq.). It is the traditional charge against seers, and too crudely put. But does not Teiresias realise that a religious revival, if it can be brought under control, will redound to the good of religion in general and of Teiresias in particular? Pentheus continues: 'If your grey hairs did not save you, you should have been set in bonds among the Bacchanals for introducing evil rites. For with women, when the sparkling juice of the grape is present at the feast, there, I say, is the end of all wholesomeness about their ceremonies.' Thus the speech of Pentheus returns upon itself and ends as it began.[3] Alas for the 'wholesomeness' of Pentheus's mind. His poet is determined that last impressions of him, like first, shall be of unrealised sexual preoccupation, of dark forces working in the dark.

Meanwhile Teiresias has been gathering together his arguments, which he now brings to bear with a calm confidence in his superior

[1] ὕβρεις ὑβρίζειν; a recurrent theme (see p. 18 n. 5). ὅστις ἔστιν (247) is ironical after 220, since god and stranger are in fact the same.

[2] '*My* mother's father.' It is ἐμῆς (254) that takes stress from the word-order, aided by the unusual rhythm of the line.

[3] This form is familiar to readers of Aeschylus and Sophocles (T. B. L. Webster, *An Introduction to Sophocles*, p. 135). Instances in this play are in the Prologue (4, 53 sq.) and in the Entrance Song (66, 135, 165—cf. p. 38). It is a mode of emphasis as well as a formal device of symmetry.

cleverness that perhaps masks no small degree of irritation. As an extempore defence it is a good speech, and he knows it; and, though lack of preparation, and the necessity of answering Pentheus point by point, cause it to ramble a little, he has done his best to give it shape.[1] The speech deserves careful analysis: it is a minor masterpiece of satire.

First a prelude. 'When a clever man finds an honest case to argue, it is no great feat to speak well. But though you have the fluent tongue of apparent sense, there is no real sense in what you say. And the ready speaker who depends on impudence proves a bad citizen by reason of his lack of sense' (266–71).[2] Teiresias knows that he is the clever man who is going to speak well to a good brief; that he is the good citizen who is showing sound sense in a matter of great political importance. By contrast, he also knows the limits of Pentheus's intelligence and the instability of his character. He is also aware that no insult could hurt Pentheus, the conscientious ruler, more than the implication of 'bad citizenship'.

Pentheus has denied the very existence of the god (220, 242 sqq.). He must first be answered upon this score. 'This new deity at whom you scoff—I cannot tell you how great he will be in Greece. There are two primary things, young man, among mankind. There is the goddess Demeter (she is earth—call her by which name you please): *she* feeds men upon *dry* foods, while he who has come after, *Semele's son*, has discovered, for his part, and introduced to mortals the *moist* draught of the grape' (272–80). Where is now the simple faith of Teiresias, the abjuring of 'sophistry'? For, though his language is guarded and does not rule out personal deities, it is clear that he is in fact equating Demeter and Dionysus with their gifts as the great 'primary things'—an equation made (as his lecture-room manner would remind the audience) by a famous fifth-century sophist.[3] To

[1] See Deichgräber, *op. cit.* It is good to find this speech greeted as a 'brilliant piece of characterisation' by Grube, *Trans. Amer. Ph. Ass.* LXVI (1935), p. 41.

[2] On the uncertain text of 270 sq. see Dodds *ad loc.* θράσει (or θρασύς) suggests absence of σωφροσύνη, of φρένες, of νοῦς, which combined with fluent speech constitutes the danger. Dodds points out that such an exordium—'a denunciation of the opposing speaker's abuse of professional skill'—is much favoured by the orators.

[3] Cf. Sextus Empiricus, *adv. math.* IX, 18. Prodicus was, in fact, returning to a primitive concept that had been overlaid by the more powerful Greek tendency to anthropomorphism; cf. Farnell, *Cults*, V, p. 121.

make it may be sound 'comparative religion', but it is surely rather dangerous to the mythology. Again, Teiresias slides over the difficulty that, while Dionysus is a new god, the gift he brings is the time-honoured gift of wine.[1] In fact, the doctrine appeals to Teiresias, not only because it is neat and clever, but also because it enables him to accommodate the new to the old, to represent Dionysus as no mere upstart, but old upon earth as the vine itself.

Thus Teiresias makes Dionysus primarily a god of wine (though he will suggest other aspects of him later in his speech). This he is not, exclusively, either in origin or in the play, where the intoxicating power of wine is an element of fluctuating importance. We may, indeed, say that he is a god of all intoxication, and as such he appears to different persons in the aspect appropriate to them. Perhaps it is fitting that to the old men he should be the bringer of forgetfulness and sleep, rather than of ecstasy; Teiresias, like Cadmus, would forget that he is old. For observe how he continues.

'...the moist draught of the grape, which gives to unhappy mortals ease from grief, when they are filled with the juice of the vine, and gives them sleep, which is the forgetfulness of each day's ills, nor is there any other medicine for sorrow' (280–3). He says it with such unction that we are convinced, until reflection shows the sleight of hand that has been practised upon us. Wine is a deliverer from grief, but can it remove the causes of grief, or can man exist perpetually intoxicated?[2] Then sleep—what is the sleep that Dionysus sends except a drunken stupor? We see what Teiresias has done: he has enlisted, unscrupulously, in the service of Dionysus all the associations of normal sleep ('the death of each day's life, sore labour's bath, balm of hurt minds').[3] Finally, wine is 'the only drug, the only medicine for sorrow'. Actually, wine is only one of the many drugs which Dionysus has at his disposal; were it not so, there would be no play. But when the sober rationalist, Teiresias, asserts that only by the opiates of Dionysus can grief be treated, we hardly know whether to be amused or shocked. The Bacchanals in the next

[1] So does Euripides, for throughout the play the properties and uses of wine are assumed to be familiar (cf. esp. 284 sq.).

[2] It is interesting to note that in fr. 1079 the speaker attacks the use of wine as λύπης φάρμακον.

[3] Shakespeare is not evidence, but Homer is (*Il.* XXIII, 62 ὕπνος... λύων μελεδήματα θυμοῦ). The best parallels of all come from the *Orestes*: 159, 174 sq. (νὺξ ὑπνοδότειρα τῶν πολυπόνων βροτῶν), 211 sqq. (ὦ φίλον ὕπνου θέλγητρον, ἐπίκουρον νόσου...ὦ πότνια Λήθη τῶν κακῶν).

Chorus will pick up these themes and develop them in all sincerity; for they are essentially 'escapists'. But Teiresias!

He closes this section of his speech with an ingenious argument. 'He, a god born, is poured in libation to the gods, so that to him men owe all their blessings' (284 sq.). Thus men bribe the gods by offering up a god to them. It is a *reductio ad absurdum* of his equation of the god with the element of wine, a farcical demonstration of its repugnance to the mythology. As an argument it is ridiculous and (one feels) beneath the intellectual level of Teiresias. But it sounds well enough (θεοῖσι...θεός), and he slips it in: it may save a soul.

Pentheus has scoffed at the story of Dionysus's second birth (243). Here too Teiresias has an answer. He welcomes the harder test, and rationalises even more ingeniously: 'You jeer that he was stitched up in the thigh of Zeus? I will instruct you how this is rightly to be taken. When Zeus snatched him from the lightning flash and carried the infant up to Olympus as a god, Hera wished to cast him out of heaven. But Zeus, like a god, devised a plan to thwart her.[1] He broke off a bit of the ether that encircles the earth, and made of it a "hostage"...' (286–93). Here the text becomes uncertain but clearly in some way Zeus deceived his spouse with a counterfeit Dionysus formed of 'ether'. But men got the words confused: ὅμηρος ('hostage') and μηρός ('thigh'), and so came to believe that Dionysus was 'stitched in the thigh of Zeus'. Doubtless Teiresias was pleased with his punning sophistry. It is, however, a little surprising to find a modern writer describing it as 'a rationalism which, holding to the substance of faith, seeks to purge it of gross accidents'.[2] It rather exemplifies a futile attempt at reason and refinement, which leaves the myth no better than it was before. It is instructive to observe what parts of it remain untouched. The violent fate of Semele remains, as do the jealousy of Hera and the trickery of Zeus. But the theologian's intellectual conscience must somehow be satisfied. So the physically grotesque must go, and for it shall be substituted a vague, plausible and refined explanation, bringing theology into harmony with 'modern science'; for 'ether', then as in more recent times, was a word to conjure with.

[1] On βρέφος see p. 78 n. 2: the embryo god. In 291 οἷα δὴ θεός has an ironic ambiguity—'with god-like ingenuity and skill' or 'just as a god [this god] would'.

[2] See Sandys, p. 141, quoting 'Mr Jebb, in the *Dark Blue* for July 1871'.

Having answered, to his own complete satisfaction, the scepticism of Pentheus, Teiresias now makes certain further claims for Dionysus. Not only is the god the giver of wine, he is an inspirer of prophecy and, in some sense, a god of war, since 'sometimes fear strikes with panic an army under arms and in its ranks, before a spear is touched: this too is a madness from Dionysus' (302–4). It was a sound intuition which saw in Dionysus 'the cause of two unaccountable modes of behaviour, second-sight and panic, two μανίαι whose common characteristic is that in both of them human will and reason are submerged by a mysterious impulse coming from outside the individual consciousness'.[1] But Teiresias has, as usual, his politic motive. He sees that he can relate Dionysus's functions to those of Phoebus and of Ares and so build yet another bridge for the new god peaceably to enter the Hellenic pantheon. Ares, being a great god at Thebes, was a particularly strong card to play. But, since Teiresias is a prophet, prophecy comes first and receives the greater emphasis. 'And this god is a prophet; for the mad Bacchic frenzy has in it much prophecy. For when the god enters in strong force into men's bodies, he makes his maddened votaries speak what is to be' (298–301). What an odd contrast there is between the words spoken and the speaker! There was surely little *mania* in the discreet bird-watching of Teiresias; and, if for politic reasons he accepts ecstatic diviners as his fellow-professionals, in his heart he probably felt they did the profession no credit.[2] Yet it was Delphi that would welcome and civilise Dionysus.

[1] Dodds (*ad loc.*). The threat of panic fear is relevant not merely to 761–4, but also to the hint of armed conflict in the Prologue and to the subsequent martial threats of Pentheus. But the connection between Dionysus and war is superficially tenuous, even paradoxical (cf. *Phoen.*, 784 sqq., where Dionysus and Ares are elaborately contrasted).

[2] It is partly for the sake of this contrast that the subject is introduced by Euripides. In the Greek cult of Dionysus, as contrasted with its Thracian original (Farnell, *Cults*, v, pp. 100, 132 sq.), prophecy played a small part, and, though Dionysus was welcomed at Delphi, it was Apollo who inspired the prophetess. The fact that it was inspirational or ecstatic prophecy, in strong contrast to the *art* of omen-interpretation (as practised by Teiresias and other prophets in the epic period), may indicate a Dionysiac influence (cf. Rohde, *Psyche* [Eng. transl.], pp. 289 sqq.). No doubt Euripides suspected that the Teiresias-element bulked larger than the *mania* in the Delphi of his own day. (The supposed etymological connection between μανία and μαντική was doubtless stressed by a pedantic delivery of 299.)

'Hereafter shall you see the god himself even upon the rocks of Delphi, leaping over the twin-peaked plateau, torch in hand, poising and shaking the Bacchic branch—and great throughout Hellas' (306 sqq.). With this impressive prediction he returns to his opening theme (272 sqq.). But, lest in this burst of prophecy we should forget the sophist, he adds a neat piece of verbal play, with which he is as pleased as Polonius. 'Be persuaded by me, Pentheus; do not be too sure that might is what dominates human affairs; and do not, if you have a thought and your thought is sick, think you are wise therein; but receive the god into the land and pour libation and partake in his rites and garland your head' (309–13).

Here doubtless he meant to stop, having returned to political wisdom, the subject-matter of his exordium. But a mention of the rites reminds him of the charges Pentheus has brought against them. These he answers with a half-truth—'It is not for Dionysus to compel women to be chaste in love, but this is what you must consider, whether chastity is by nature within them in all respects and always; for in Bacchic rites also she who is truly chaste shall not be corrupted' (314–18).[1] The last statement is doubtless true for what it is worth. But the relation of sexual extravagance to Dionysiac religion, a matter of some little importance to the play, will be discussed later.[2]

It is now necessary for Teiresias to perorate again; and he is made, in his peroration, to return to the personality of Pentheus. But if the speech opened by hinting at the latter's instability and lack of wisdom, it ends by touching his deepest springs of motive. 'You see', says Teiresias, '*you* are glad when crowds stand at the gate, and the city magnifies the name of Pentheus. So He, too, surely, delights to be honoured' (319 sqq.). Such an appeal—to a kinship of emotion between god and worshipper—is beloved of preachers. But the connection of thought with what precedes is perhaps in the mind of the poet rather than in that of the speaker. Is Pentheus, who brings such charges, himself *sophron*—in all respects and always? To the suspicion, already implanted, that his mind is not pure in sexual matters, comes now a suggestion of the pride and vanity of the ruler in him. A time will come when suspicion and suggestion give place to a clearer revelation, when inhibition is relaxed in Pentheus and

[1] Retaining 316 and adopting εἰ for ἐν (Porson) in 315.

[2] See p. 91.

submerged motives frankly avowed. Meanwhile, Teiresias has still something to say upon the subject.

'So I and Cadmus, at whom you mock,[1] will wreathe our heads with ivy and will dance, a grey-haired couple, yet dance we must; and I will not be persuaded by your words to fight against a god. For you are mad most sorely, and neither are you curable with drugs, nor has your sickness come on you without them' (322–7). A strange remark, which has exercised the commentators. Perhaps Teiresias himself did not mean very much by it. He is an easy prey to the antithetical; and he may mean no more than that nobody could be as mad as Pentheus without the influence of drugs.[2] But that does not dispose of the question, for, as Verrall says, 'it is not easy to see, from a dramatic point of view, why the point should be brought in, unless it bears in some way upon the story'. And first it must be noted that the use of the words 'mad' and 'drugs' immediately relates Pentheus to Dionysus and his worship. Teiresias, indeed, has forgotten (or disregarded) the fact that he has recently sounded the praises of 'madness'. Doubtless, if he had been taxed, he would have said that a man must be mad in the right way, with the madness which is the higher *sophrosyne*—mad, that is, like the Bacchanals, who preach moderation in the next choral ode. When he speaks of drugs, he may have forgotten the 'drug' of Dionysus altogether. We cannot so easily do so. Clearly this remark of Teiresias, however little or much he meant by it, is related to the subsequent fate of Pentheus. For Pentheus falls under the influence of Dionysus and ultimately appears before us in a state which may justly be described as drugged. If Pentheus's madness is his refusal to worship Dionysus, then for him to be drugged and dressed in the outward appurtenances of a devotee is an ironic parody of a Dionysiac cure. But that stage is not yet. In what sense then can his madness—his stubborn resistance to the god—be said to be caused by drugs? If that is all his madness means, there is no answer, and the words of Teiresias are vain abuse. In fact, however, they contain an important clue to the interpretation of Pentheus's character.

Pentheus resists the worship of Dionysus. 'But', says Professor Murray, 'Pentheus is the wrong man for such a protest.' He is the

[1] ὃν not οὗς is a nice point: Teiresias will not admit that Pentheus has been laughing at him.

[2] Compare the reaction of the Argive elders to Clytemnestra (Aesch. *Ag.* 1407 sqq.).

wrong man, for the protest against the religion of drugs and frenzy can only rightly be made by one who is himself calm and rational. Teiresias might have made it, but judged it more politic not to do so. Pentheus makes it; and the situation is heavy with irony. For Pentheus has too much in common with those whom he is attacking; the persecutor is—in spite of himself—a disciple. We cannot limit the manifestation of Dionysus to the behaviour of his organised adherents; anything that leads to the pursuit of instinct through unstable emotion and unrestrained violence is the work of his power. We cannot limit his drugs to wine, or even to the music and dances and infectious contagion that act upon his *thiasoi*. May not the lust for power and praise be equally the source of a Dionysiac frenzy? With this Pentheus is intoxicated, and it will not be long before he gives us concrete proof of it.

To the prophet's speech the Chorus-leader, Cadmus and Pentheus in turn respond. She praises him for his *sophrosyne*, anticipating thereby the paradox of the following ode; a little out of character, she asserts that he has shown reverence for Dionysus without dishonouring Phoebus (328 sq.). For Euripides saw in Teiresias the prototype of the statesmanship of Delphi which had in very truth performed that feat.

Cadmus is heartened by his mentor's words to address his formidable grandson, though he hardly does so in the most tactful way. 'My son, Teiresias has given you good advice. Stay where we are, not beyond the bounds of tradition. For now you are all in the air, and your wit is without wisdom' (330 sqq.).[1] Teiresias himself might have said it. But Cadmus is rash enough to add a reason. 'For even if this god, as you say, does not exist, you should say he does! Tell a creditable lie to that effect, that Semele may be thought to have borne a god and we—the whole family—may gain honour.' Why, then, is Pentheus a fool? Because he is working against the best interests of the family. What was to be suspected before is now made explicit; now we know how much genuine piety lies behind Cadmus's championship of the new god. With Cadmus family comes first, and it is characteristic that he now cites in warning the exemplary fate of Actaeon, that other grandson of his who had fallen foul of Artemis and been torn to death by his own

[1] νόμων (331) looks back to 201 and forward to 891 (see pp. 111 sqq.). With πέτῃ (332) compare 214. οἴκει (331) prepares the family interest of 333 sq.

hounds.[1] 'Let that not be your fate', he adds; 'come, let me wreathe your head with ivy. Along with us give honour to the god.'[2] As he speaks he goes up to Pentheus and tries to put the garland on his head. Nothing could be more irritating.

Yet something more than irritation dictates the outburst that follows.[3] 'Do not touch me', cries Pentheus; 'go and play the Bacchanal, but do not wipe off your folly upon me.' Cadmus he knows is a fool; Teiresias is not, but he shall pay for Cadmus's folly. 'But this your instructor in foolishness I will punish. Go, someone, quickly—go to his seat where he watches birds, lever it up and overturn it; mix everything together topsy-turvy and cast his holy ribbands to the winds and tempests. For that is the way that I can hurt him most' (343–51). There are two things to be said about this outburst. First, Pentheus again shows some insight into the lowlier aspects of the prophet's character. Something of a ritualist, the latter is proud of his seat of augury (famous in Greek tragedy) and all its paraphernalia. The last words of Pentheus are incontrovertible, and are borne out by the subsequent behaviour of Teiresias. Secondly, such a paroxysm of ungoverned rage is reprehensible. It is more than that, it is behaviour comparable to that of the king's antagonists. When worshippers of Dionysus are opposed, then there is an outbreak of violence. It happens with our Bacchanals upon the mountains, when they fall upon flocks and villages; it is symbolised by the earthquake which follows the imprisonment of Dionysus.[4] In Pentheus reside the same explosive forces of blind emotionalism that are in his opponents. Yet observe how petty the catastrophe that he causes, how rash he is to compete in violence. For he works in isolation, and a solitary Bacchanal is anomalous and incomplete. To the perfection of Dionysiac technique the group is essential, and the

[1] See p. 26 n. 4.

[2] The repetition of μεθ' ἡμῶν (331, 342) is significant. Pentheus must 'stand in' with the family.

[3] 'His violent horror of such contact is a fine psychological stroke; something in him knows already the fascination and the mortal peril which the new rites hold for him' (Dodds, p. 109).

[4] Nor is it, I think, coincidence that an identical expression links together these three passages (349, 602, 741, 753). 'Topsy-turvy' is the Greek ἄνω κάτω, an expression which, if not uncommon, is sufficiently arresting to be recalled by repetition. (Among the tragedians there appear to be two instances in Aeschylus, none in Sophocles, and in Euripides seven apart from the *Bacchae*.)

thiasos will return him the sack of whole villages for the desecration of a chapter-house.

But Pentheus has not yet finished; nor in his anger with Cadmus and Teiresias does he forget the main cause of his predicament, but orders a hunt to be made for the 'womanish stranger, who is introducing his new-fangled disease for women and defiling their beds', that he may be brought bound for execution (352–7). In this way we are prepared for the encounter of the following scene. But at the same time we are taken back to his opening sentences. For just as his long first speech was rounded off by a return to the sexual theme, so is his part in the whole scene; and last impressions once more confirm the first. Surely, if Euripides meant us to accept Pentheus as chaste-minded, he has gone an odd way about it.

Teiresias has the last word; and it is an angry one. Gone for a moment is all the blandness, as he cries: 'Wicked man, you do not know what you are saying. Now you are mad indeed; though before you were out of your senses.' For he is in a slight difficulty; he had already called him mad (326), more in sorrow than in anger, and now, at some loss to dignity, he has to take the word back to use again.[1] But a Teiresias soon recovers himself. 'Let us go, Cadmus, and pray for him, wild though he is,[2] and for the city, that the god work no harm.' Now to pray for your enemies is (if you are the right person and do it in the right spirit) sublime. But hardly if you are this Teiresias and have just spoken the preceding lines.[3] 'Follow me with your ivy staff, and try to hold me up, as I will you. It would be shame for two old men to fall; but be it as it may. For the Bacchic god, the son of Zeus, must needs be served' (363–6). A high-sounding line. For Pentheus has shaken his self-confidence a little, and again he is preoccupied with his dignity. Perhaps the couple actually stumble as they begin to move. 'But beware that Pentheus

[1] Helped out by a change of tense, from μαίνῃ to μέμηνας (of a permanent state of derangement: *v.* Dodds, who aptly quotes Menander, *Epit.* 494).

[2] ἀγρίου (361). Compare 228 (θηράσομαι), 352 (ἐξιχνεύσατε). This important metaphor is getting into its stride before the entry of the beast-god (cf. 434 sqq.).

[3] And hardly if you frame your prayer in the suggestive way that he does this (the positive δρᾶν takes all the emphasis), and slip an angry epithet into the middle. On this passage I agree with Wilamowitz rather than with Dodds. Wilamowitz (says Dodds) disliked priests; but then Euripides disliked prophets.

bring not sorrow upon your house, Cadmus. It is not prophecy, but facts that make me say so. A fool ever talks like a fool.'[1] Thus personal pique in the end drives Teiresias into a frank 'unofficial' comment.

Not prophecy, but common-sense, but worldly wisdom: it is an appropriate final touch to this brilliant satirical picture of a shrewd ecclesiastic, not too scrupulous or too sincere, who gives his adherence to an emotional religion on politic grounds.[2] Thus Teiresias leaves the stage, not to reappear. Indeed, there is no place for him in the drama that follows, where, in the gathering tension and ultimate disaster, his suave rationality would be out of place. Or else we might say that there is henceforward room for only one calm, controlled and rational personage, and that will be the god, to whom Teiresias, leaving the play, bequeathes as a legacy his *sophia* and his *sophrosyne*. But, though he leaves the play so early Teiresias has, in another sense, the last word. He had prophesied that Dionysus would be great in Greece and would be worshipped with torches and dancing even on the crags of Delphi. Perhaps, here also, it was the word of rational insight rather than of inspired prophecy. At all events it came true, and a Dionysiac cult, ordered and controlled by the policy of generations of Teiresiases, was established alongside that of Apollo and brought fresh popularity to his shrine. Thus the 'wisdom' of Teiresias has the verdict of history.

But the posthumous verdict of history means nothing to its victims. Teiresias, on his departure, takes with him Cadmus; and Cadmus, less fortunate, is destined to return after he has made his pathetic second journey 'to the mountain' (1225) to collect the torn fragments of his grandson's body and follow his mad daughter back to Thebes. It is the same Cadmus that returns, with the same naïve preoccupation with his family pride, now shattered. But by then, much has happened, and the sympathy of the audience has shifted and is made to shift by the dramatist's treatment of his characters; thus, it is a more sympathetic Cadmus that returns to lead Agave with tenderness and skill back to sanity. In his earlier scene, however,

[1] The pun on the king's name (Πενθεύς—πένθος) cannot be reproduced in translation. With μῶρα—μῶρος he returns to the theme of 266 sqq., and also sounds the key-note for the following ode. Note that this Teiresias, unlike the Teiresias of *Oedipus Tyrannus*, appears to have no detailed foreknowledge of his ruler's fate.

[2] See Verrall, *op. cit.* p. 152.

there is little dignity, if much humour and some pathos in his presentation. He is one of a pair, and not the dominant partner. With Teiresias he represents the reaction of worldly wisdom to the impact of ecstasy, and regard for family interests in the one answers the wider 'ecclesiastical' considerations of the other. Both are in strong contrast with Pentheus.

Such sympathy as we have for Pentheus at this stage—and surely it is not intended to be much—is largely derived from that contrast. Do we feel for him in his irritation; do we applaud his instinctive aversion from the appeal of Cadmus and the sophistries of Teiresias; do we prefer his young, impetuous, unthinking opposition to the calculated attitudes of his elders? Perhaps, for he is sincere after a fashion. Yet it is not with a sincerity that can fathom its own motives, and he is betrayed by enemies from within. To regard Pentheus merely as the central figure of a drama, hero or villain, whose personal attractiveness or unattractiveness matters for his own sake, is to misread the part. He belongs to a wider pattern, of which he is a subordinate, if important, element—a pattern which reveals by similarity and contrast the operations of Dionysus in the world of men. Pentheus appears as the persecutor of Dionysus and his followers; Teiresias is their advocate. But, to the discerning eye, Teiresias has little in common with them, Pentheus all too much. He thinks he is rational and prudent, but really, like them, he is at the mercy of irrational impulse, and, like them, he expresses himself through violence. But in his isolation he is no match for them. No force that he commands can compete with theirs, while his unrealised sexual impulses and the lust for power—traitors within his own heart—will deliver him, bound and helpless, into the hands of his enemies.

CHAPTER V

THE PEACE OF THE BACCHANALS

The last note of the scene we have just been considering was 'folly'. There is wisdom and folly, madness and sanity. Teiresias is wise and sane, Pentheus a fool and mad: the former (we must presume) to accept, the latter to deny, Dionysus and his worship. Does this mean that in the religion of Dionysus lie true wisdom and sanity? Yet, in so far as the Entrance Song has given us insight into Bacchic excitement, Teiresias has little in common with Bacchanals, Pentheus too much. Further, madness is an equivocal term, which has been applied in praise to the devotees, in dispraise to Pentheus. Evidently there is madness and madness; so also there are two kinds of sanity, two kinds, perhaps, of wisdom and folly.

The song that follows deals lyrically with the same topics, and in it the Bacchanals expound a mode of sanity and wisdom which finds favour with them. Its tone and content are, however, in a way surprising. Bacchanals would seem to have little in common with Teiresias; yet it is from him that they now take their cue, praising Dionysus upon the same grounds, railing at the madness of Pentheus and commending moderation. Moreover, these Asiatics make use not only of the personifications of Greek religion, but of the commonplaces of Greek thought; and the ideals that they present are such as Greece in general and democratic Athens in particular could largely accept. There is a double paradox in these Maenad preachers of *sophrosyne*, these Asiatic Hellenists.

Each half of the paradox is partly explicable from the dramatic situation. Pentheus has laid himself open to attack upon these lines; and by advocating moderation and quietness the Bacchanals win sympathy against him, put themselves (by Hellenic standards) in the right and him in the wrong. Again, if the Asiatic missionaries wish to commend themselves to Greece, how better can they do it than by revealing kinship between their religion and Greek ideas? Yet the paradoxes remain paradoxical. For how far can the antithesis in ideals and conduct between Pentheus and the Bacchanals be maintained? And is there after all no novelty in what the latter have brought to Greece? In point of fact we know from the Entrance

Song that there is an element of frenzy and cruelty in Bacchic worship that never emerges from this ode at all.

What then are we to say? That this is propaganda, and disingenuous at that? To say so is to misunderstand the nature of Bacchanals. To conceal what they here conceal would be disingenuous, were it not characteristic of them to be wholly absorbed in one mood to the complete exclusion of another, were the mood in which they are now absorbed not a genuine feature of their experience. What was said in connection with the Entrance Song about the nature of the lyric poetry holds good here also.[1] From the point of view of the singers, the song is a sincere expression of an emotional sequence and of certain associated ideas. As for the poet, his purpose is indeed to present and render attractive one aspect of Dionysiac religion, namely its peace and joy. With what result we can consider when the ode has been analysed in detail.

Strophe 1. The tone of this stanza derives immediately from the predicament of the Bacchanals. Their Entrance Song had been an act of quiet worship, performed in (what was for them) a normal frame of mind. Now they sing under the stress of indignation at the blasphemy of Pentheus and a sense of danger from his threats. The primary purpose of the first stanza is therefore restorative; and they appeal to the goddess of Holiness (ʽΟσία), who symbolises their consecrated state and is their ground of confidence. 'Holiness, queen among the gods, Holiness, who passest over the earth on golden wing, dost thou hear these words of Pentheus? Dost thou hear his unholy insolence (ὕβριν) against Bromius, against the son of Semele, the god who is first among the Blessed Ones at the fair-garlanded delights (εὐφροσύναις)?' Holiness—their own holiness—they contrast with the *hubris* of Pentheus. But *hubris* rouses echoes. Pentheus had spoken of the *hubris* of the Stranger (247); and *tu quoques* (a staple feature of the play) are weak arguments. More striking, the combination of *hubris* and 'holiness' in one phrase is not new. In their earlier song they themselves had called upon Thebes to be 'holy in handling the hubristic wands'.[2] Pentheus's *hubris* is unholy: is there then a holy *hubris* also? Evidently there is *hubris* and *hubris*, just as there is madness and madness, though how they differ in quality, only the play can show. For the point is not

[1] See pp. 38 sq.

[2] 113: ἀμφὶ δὲ...ὁσιοῦσθε. See pp. 34 sq.

developed here; we pass instead to a recital of the glories and gifts of Dionysus—detail piled rhetorically on detail[1]—with which at once they vent their indignation and reassure themselves. 'These are his powers: to make of the company (θιασεύειν) in the dance, to smile at the sound of the flute, to give ease from care, when the sparkling juice of the grape enters into the banquet of the gods and in the ivy-garlanded feasts the bowl casts sleep over men' (370–85).[2]

It is now clear in what aspect Dionysus is to appear in this ode; it is as a god of joy—of joy through wine and feast and music. Not only is it well suited to the end of their reassurance, it is also closely linked to the content of the preceding scene. Teiresias laid the emphasis upon Dionysus as god of wine, and the lyrical phrases of the Chorus closely recall the prosaic eulogy of the prophet; as he foresaw a Hellenised god, so are we given here a god who may appeal to Hellas and find his place easily among the Greek gods.[3] Fierce ecstasy retreats before mild *euphrosyne*; all is joyous, carefree, and devoid of reproach. Yet when Teiresias praised the god for the power of his drug, rational criticism did not lag far behind; perhaps therefore even this lyric may be invaded by the memory that intoxication is but a temporary respite from care, that the bowl that brings sleep is no moderate potation, that the sleep it brings is the heavy stupor of drunkenness.[4]

Antistrophe 1. Now their thought returns to Pentheus, but is cast in the form of general reflections of a strikingly Hellenic character: in fact (without using the word) they preach a doctrine of *sophrosyne*. 'Of unbridled tongues and lawless folly the end is

[1] τὸν Βρόμιον, τὸν Σεμέλας, τὸν κτλ. Note the repeated article.

[2] ἐν δαιτὶ θεῶν: the feast of Theodaisia was celebrated in honour of Dionysus in a number of Greek communities (Farnell, *Cults*, v, p. 198). ἐν ἀνδράσι: in contrast with θεῶν; because respectable Greek women did not attend dinner parties; as a kind of counterblast to 261 (hence the repetition of γάνος).

[3] In particular, he is 'the genial wine-god of the Attic festivals' (Dodds, p. 112). Note the emphasis on μάκαρες, θεοί, and Dionysus's part with them.

εὐφροσύναις (377): the word is used with conscious reference to its etymology and, for the purposes of this ode, displaces σωφροσύνη as the abstract of φρονεῖν (390) and εὖ φρονεῖν (196), the antithesis of ἀφροσύνη (387).

[4] This may indeed be one reason why the poet first introduced this particular theme in an atmosphere that tended to invite, rather than inhibit, criticism.

misfortune. But the life of quietness and good sense abides unshaken and keeps houses in unity. Far away though they dwell in the ether, the heavenly ones keep watch on the deeds of men' (387 sqq.). For the unrestraint of Pentheus they (like Teiresias) prophesy a bad end; and their prophecy is justified. With him they contrast their own ideal of quietness (ἡσυχία). Upon the quality of this quietness, this peace, there will be more to be said, though even here it links itself naturally with the care-dispelling drugs of Dionysus and the sleep that his brimming bowl casts over the minds of men. Its immediate reference is negative; it is the antithesis of the restlessness of Pentheus and therefore *prima facie* commendable. For Pentheus is the busybody, the πολυπράγμων, whose restless interference shatters the communities—state and household—that he sought to unite.[1] And he will suffer punishment. Later indeed the manner of this punishment will be disclosed in its full horror. But no precise hint of its nature is allowed to disturb the serenity, the generality, the Hellenism of this ode; the personal vengeance of Dionysus hides behind the conventional Greek belief in divine watchfulness.

They continue: τὸ σοφὸν δ' οὐ σοφία. 'What passes for wisdom is no true wisdom'; or (using the twofold association of σοφία) 'cleverness is no wisdom'. Clearly this rejection of *sophia* is relevant to the preceding scene, where wisdom and folly were themes, no less than sanity and madness. The first part of this stanza is directed against Pentheus, and in a sense it may be said that he had claimed 'wisdom' by implication in accusing Cadmus of folly (344): at any rate he is treated by Teiresias and by Cadmus as the representative of a false wisdom (268, 312, 332).[2] But the principal association of *sophia* in the preceding scene is with Teiresias, to whom it is attributed by Cadmus, while his own rejection of it does not ring true. Some scholars have maintained that the Chorus here consciously reject the cleverness of Teiresias. This is hardly so: their conscious attitude is rather represented by the praise they have already tendered him (328 sq.); they welcome him as an advocate and do not look below the surface of his words. But the advocacy of Teiresias was founded

[1] Cf. 1308. Does not the word δώματα, however, come oddly from Bacchanals, who care nothing in fact for house, home, or civilised life in general? Cf. pp. 96 sq.

[2] φρονεῖν is the word, with its suggestion of sound practical good sense (and its side-glance at σωφροσύνη); σοφία is kept for the intellectuals (including Dionysus)—and the Bacchanals.

upon a reasonable consideration of circumstances, and this they must reject if they are to be true to their own nature. There is thus a kind of triangular relationship between Bacchanals, Pentheus and Teiresias; and the lyric in fact, though not in the conscious intention of the singers, involves a repudiation of the calculating rationality of Teiresias no less than of the unrestraint which with Pentheus passes for sound judgement. Wisdom indeed the Bacchanals claim, but put a characteristic interpretation on the word. To the question what their own wisdom is they will give an answer in the last stanza, though it will not yet be a complete answer.

'Cleverness is no wisdom, and more than mortal thoughts mean a brief life. Wherefore a man may pursue great things and miss what is at his hand. These are the ways of mad and ill-counselled men in my view' (395–401).[1] The ideas are still for the most part Greek commonplaces—the danger of presumption, the ideal of moderation, sanity and good counsel; and the stanza ends upon the note with which it began. Two comments suggest themselves at this stage. First, the singers, though they generalise, have Pentheus in their minds; and as a criticism of him their words are justified. He is restless, immoderate, even in some degree 'megalomaniac' (μεγάλα διώκων), though it is only in the uninhibited Pentheus of a later scene that we see how far his lust for power and praise extends. In sharp contrast to him the Bacchanals place themselves and their 'life of quietness'. Now, towards the end of the last chapter, it was suggested that Pentheus, persecutor of Bacchanals, himself has Dionysiac characteristics, so that the contrast between them is far from being as perfect as both parties think. But if what the Bacchanals here claim for themselves is true (and it is in some measure true), then the similarity also is incomplete. The Bacchanals know peace (of a kind) and have their own methods of obtaining it; but Pentheus is born neither to have peace himself nor to allow it to others. Both Teiresias and the Bacchanals have in their respective ways found

[1] 396: τό τε μὴ θνητὰ φρονεῖν βραχὺς αἰών. See Dodds, *ad loc*. The grouping of words is virtually settled by the converse statement at 1004 (βροτείως ἔχειν ἄλυπος βίος) and by the preceding references to δυστυχία and to watchful deities. 398: the natural meaning of φέρειν τὰ παρόντα may be 'to put up with things as they are', but here the context (and particularly the following stanza) demands a more positive sense, the winning of actual advantage in the present; τίς...φέροι (Tyrwhitt, Headlam, Dodds) is therefore unacceptable.

a harmony of life, he through reason, they through the rejection of it. But Pentheus makes the worst of both worlds.

The second comment also concerns the relationship of Pentheus and the Bacchanals. Pentheus was called mad by the eminently sane Teiresias; now the charge is (by implication) repeated—but by Maenads. It is a paradox, already anticipated by the prophet, a riddle which can be put in two forms. How can the Bacchanals be at once the antithesis and the spiritual kin of Pentheus? How do these apostles of joy and peace and Hellenic moderation come by the title of Maenads?[1] The present ode will not tell us: at least it will not tell us the whole truth. Its function is not to solve the riddle, but to propound it.

Strophe 2. With an apparently abrupt transition, the singers turn to express a longing for Cyprus, island of Aphrodite, and for all places where Bacchic worship is not forbidden. The connection of thought is closer than it might seem; it is twofold. The indignation that inspired the last stanza was in part a personal reaction to the ban placed by Pentheus upon their worship in Thebes. Further, their yearning is not (as in the Entrance Song) after their native Asia, but after places specifically associated with love and with music, with the Graces and with Desire. For they had sung of peace and implied that it was to be won from 'present things' (τὰ παρόντα). Are not the pleasures of Aphrodite and the Muses pre-eminent among these?

'Would that I might come to Cyprus, island of Aphrodite, where dwell the Loves who bewitch the hearts of mortals, to Paphos and the island which streams of the barbarian river with its hundred mouths make fruitful without rain. Where the Muses have their home in Pieria, fairest of all, on the sacred slope of Olympus, thither take me, Bromius, Bromius, thou god who leadest the Bacchanals with the cry of Evoe. There are the Graces, there is Desire, and there for Bacchanals is it lawful to perform their rites' (402–15).[2] It has caused scandal that the Bacchanals here salute Aphrodite and Desire, confirming, it would seem, the worst suspicions of Pentheus. Yet, when the Messenger from the mountain reports the chaste conduct of the Theban women, these suspicions are exposed and the Bacchanals enjoy a moral triumph. This triumph (which is, surely,

[1] On the Maenadism of the Chorus, see pp. 153 sqq.

[2] The problem of 406 (Paphos and the Nile) is unsolved; see Dodds, *ad loc.* I translate, without any confidence in its correctness, Schoene's Πάφον θ' ἂν θ'.

temporary) has a certain function in the drama and in the exposition of Euripides's thought, which will need comment at a later stage.[1] Here it must suffice to say that it would have been impossible to exclude the element of sex from an account of orgiastic religion without leaving it incomplete, impossible (and this is more particularly relevant to the present context) to exclude love from the company of present pleasures. But it is introduced here (as all else in this ode) in an atmosphere of decorous peace, associated with the charm of poetry, and set amid Hellenic divinities and holy sites—Aphrodite and Paphos, the Muses and Olympus; the Loves are decorative attendants upon a poetised Aphrodite, and Desire the pretty child of the vase-paintings. If this is what the 'orgies' of Bacchanals connote, then Hellas has little to fear from the religion of Dionysus.[2]

Antistrophe 2. 'There for Bacchanals is it lawful to perform their rites.' But the ultimate sanction for their conduct is the approval of Dionysus, who himself rejoices in their festivities and loves peace as they do. Thus the last stanza of the ode returns to the theme of the first. But, if it looks backward, it looks forward also: it is an immediate preparation for the forthcoming entry of Dionysus himself.

'The god, the son of Zeus, rejoices in feasts, and loves Peace, the giver of prosperity, the goddess who nurtures the young. And in equal measure to the prosperous and to the lowly has he given to have the griefless delight of wine. But he hates him who cares not for these things—to live the life of blessedness by day and through nights of joy. Wisdom is it to keep the heart and mind aloof from men of excess: what the mass of ordinary men (τὸ πλῆθος τὸ φαυλότερον) believes and practises, that would I accept' (416–33).[3] The praise of Dionysus as a god of joy and revelry is resumed from the first stanza, but with it the content of the second is interwoven. Peace, that Dionysus loves, recalls the life of Quietness that the Bacchanals pursue. There the restless rejector of this way of life was warned of the watching eye of heaven; now 'Dionysus *hates* him who cares not for such things'. Wine is the banisher of care, here as

[1] See p. 90.

[2] As little as from Solon fr. 20 (ἔργα δὲ Κυπρογενοῦς νῦν μοι φίλα καὶ Διονύσου καὶ Μουσέων, ἃ τίθησ' ἀνδράσιν εὐφροσύνας), or from the passages of Aristophanes aptly quoted by Dodds (*Birds* 1320, *Peace* 456, *Ach.* 989). On vase-paintings showing Πόθος in Dionysiac scenes, see Dodds on 414.

[3] Reading in 427 σοφὸν ἀπέχειν (Wilamowitz) or σοφὰ δ' ἀπέχειν (Dindorf).

in the first stanza;[1] but here the notion is amplified—it is a gift given alike to rich and poor, for among the pains from which it gives escape are economic hardships. So wine is a leveller of class; and we are reminded of the disclaimer of all ambition in the second stanza. Finally, the Bacchanals, who had there rejected *sophia* in the accepted sense, now give the content of the wisdom which they prefer to it. It is 'to keep the heart and mind aloof from men of excess'. They are thinking primarily of Pentheus and his violence.[2] But, lest we should take the phrase so narrowly, it is immediately generalised and a fresh paradox introduced. Whatever the mass of ordinary men believes and practises, that will they accept—that will they count wisdom. Wine then (and wine is but the type of all Dionysiac drugs) is a leveller both of class and of intellect; Dionysus is a democrat.[3]

The function of this ode is to present and to render attractive with the grace of lyric poetry one aspect of Dionysiac religion, namely, its joyous peace. It is that aspect of it which might appear most congenial to the Hellenic world; and this fact has its immediate dramatic relevance. More than that, it is an aspect under which Dionysus makes a universal appeal to the hearts of men. There is another side to his worship. We know this already from the Entrance Song and we shall know it better later. In the present ode it is suppressed or concealed, and for obvious dramatic ends. But perhaps even the fairest presentation of this religion may imply its own criticism.

Peace is a great word. The peace of God is perhaps the ultimate aspiration of man; and, in so far as the Bacchanals desire to possess their souls in quietness, they claim to be judged by high spiritual standards. Peace also in a narrower sense is a thing universally desirable: 'peace, giver of prosperity, the goddess that nurtures the young'. Euripides wrote these words towards the end of a long and futile war that had impoverished all Greece and slain its youth in thousands. It was a war that had been waged by Pentheuses on

[1] For this must, I think, be the meaning of ἄλυπον in the context.

[2] περισσῶν παρὰ φωτῶν (429). The last word perhaps acts as a link with the second stanza (401).

[3] And this was indeed part of his original appeal (Dodds, p. 121). σοφός)(φαῦλος is a common antithesis in Euripides, as elsewhere in Greek literature: hence the paradox. ἐνόμισε (431) looks back to ἀνόμου (387), to 331 and 201 sqq.

either side, men of crude patriotism and personal ambition, firm believers in the efficacy of violence; and the end of their 'unbridled tongues and lawless folly' had been the disruption of communities, disaster for themselves and for others. A god who loved peace and whose worshippers led a life of quietness might well find favour with Euripides and his war-worn audience.[1] But 'peace', like 'wisdom' and 'sanity', is a word to play with; and what stands as peace must be judged by its quality and by its fruits. The peace of the Bacchanals is bought at a price which must be and is paid.

The price they pay is the rejections that they make in order to secure it; and it is these very rejections that determine its quality. In the first place, they reject reality, which they will forget sooner than face; in the modern jargon, they are 'escapists'. Teiresias and Chorus alike praise wine because it gives relief from care. And it does indeed remove the consciousness of evils; but it cannot remove their causes, and as a method of dealing with them is efficacious only in so far as intoxication can be rendered continuous.[2] In particular, wine will bring forgetfulness of economic inequality, but at the expense of foregoing any attempt to end it.[3] To do so, indeed to remove any kind of evil, necessitates hard effort, to which Bacchanals prefer the 'sweet toil' of Dionysus. They reject individualism: their joys and ecstasies come from the *thiasos*, and their ideas are shared in common. Along with individualism they reject the intellect and the higher sensibilities.[4] Their standard is the convention and practice of the crowd; and the man who will not accept this standard, they, like Dionysus, hate. And this must mean not only the violent interfering Pentheus, but anyone who is περισσὸς φώς, any individual who stands out and refuses to adopt the standard of the majority. Against him rises the cry that he is cultivating 'more than mortal thoughts', and he is condemned and threatened with a vengeance from on high, because he will not share the tastes and the abandonments of the mass. He is 'lawless' (ἄνομος), for he will not accept customary legislation; he is 'extravagant', 'peculiar', 'odd' (περισσός), because he will not conform to conventions. Thus does

[1] See Dodds, p. 115.

[2] This is illustrated by the experience of Agave: see p. 115.

[3] Note ὄλβιον (421), following ὀλβοδότειραν (419). Peace may bring prosperity, but in it there will still be ὄλβιοι and χείρονες.

[4] The philosophy of the Bacchanals in this ode is indeed practically identical with that of the drunken Heracles in *Alc.* 788–802.

the generalised 'wisdom' that concludes the ode move away from a narrow relevance to Pentheus towards a broad and fundamental application.

Such are the renunciations that produce the peace of the Bacchanals, which is also their wisdom. But this peace has its undoubted attractions, and there are moods in which any one might feel that the price for it is worth paying—if this were the whole of the price, and if what it bought was peace perpetual. But in fact peace is only one phase of the emotional life of Bacchanals. The other phase is a fury and violence that make a mockery of their pretensions to sanity and moderation. And the same causes that lead to the peace—the rejection of intellect, the surrender to momentary impulse—lead also to the fury, so that it can be said with truth that part of the price they pay for their kind of peace is their kind of violence.

In this ode the latter is deliberately concealed. Only one hint emerges from its 'censored' version of Dionysiac religion that the whole truth has not been told. It comes in the form of one of those calculated discords, dear to the art of Euripides. The son of Zeus (the last stanza tells us) rejoices in the feast, loves Peace, gives the gift of joy through wine; but he *hates*.... Into the atmosphere of peace and joy breaks the harsh word. It is passed in a moment, and we return to 'the life of blessedness by day and through nights of joy'. But the serenity has been disturbed; and the remote divine watchers of an earlier stanza have become a god who hates. How will this hatred manifest itself? How will this god take vengeance upon the man of violence and excess and bring him to his end of misfortune?

His method will, in point of fact, itself be violent and excessive; it will, moreover, be carried out by one set of Bacchanals and applauded by another with a furious emotion which is the choric counterpart of the *sparagmos*. The present ode cannot be regarded in isolation; it must be taken in relation to what has preceded and to what is to follow. It must be taken in relation to the Entrance Song. For we already know more of Bacchic rites than is suggested by the discretions of this ode, enough to bring out the paradox inherent in Maenads who praise sobriety and fling accusations of madness. Of the hunt, of the tearing of the living prey and the eating of raw flesh, there is here not a word. But our knowledge of those things, previously acquired, invites us to amplify the sole hint of hatred and vengeance and prepares us in some measure, if inadequately, for the horrible form that vengeance takes. When Agave returns from the mountain carrying the head of Pentheus, she is full of the pride of the chase. 'Soon the Cadmeans', she begins (1194); and the Chorus break in—'Yes, and your son, Pentheus'; Agave accepts and continues: 'will praise his mother'. For she has taken a prey, in shape like a lion. 'A prodigious prey', sing the Chorus; 'and caught prodigiously', rejoins Agave.[1] But the words are περισσάν, περισσῶς, and have an appropriateness that underlies their superficial meaning. For the prey is Pentheus, the man of excess; and the manner of his taking is an answering excess of cruel violence.

Περισσός is not the only word taken from this ode that recurs in an important context. If one of its leading themes is the rejection by the Bacchanals of excess, another is their rejection of conventional cleverness, the wisdom of the intellect, and their substitution for it of a wisdom of their own. The themes are related; for cleverness they regard as a form of excess, and what they count wisdom is the pursuit of immediate pleasure in the life of quietness. Such at least is the implication of this ode. But, just as their rejection of excess is to be belied by what the Theban Bacchanals do and they themselves acclaim, so, with the change of circumstances, the content of their 'wisdom' will be strikingly modified. For there are for them other immediate and pleasurable ends, besides feasting and song and love, to be wholeheartedly and unthinkingly pursued. In a later ode—an ode, moreover, in which the main doctrines of the present chorus are re-emphasised—there occurs a brief verse, which is stressed by repetition. 'What is wisdom? Or what gift from the gods is fairer in the sight of men than to hold the hand of mastery over the heads of enemies? Whatever is fair is ever dear.'[2] This then also is part of the wisdom of the Bacchanals: frenzied vengeance as well as drugged peace.

The presentation of Dionysiac religion in this ode is thus incomplete; the seductive charm and impression of Hellenic sanity, if not entirely illusory, need qualification. For there are two aspects to the experience and behaviour of Bacchanals, sharply contrasted and yet complementary, since both are products of the same forces and the same approach to life; and (for reasons that have been discussed) only one of them is presented here. Elsewhere in the play they appear in combination. Already they have been juxtaposed in the Entrance Song, a far more complete, more concrete account than the

[1] See p. 137.

[2] 877–81 = 897–901. See pp. 107 sqq.

present ode, whose omissions it enables the audience in some measure to detect. More lucid commentary is to come later from the mountain in two Messenger speeches, both of which will describe the same Dionysiac process—the sudden shift of emotion and activity from peace to fury.

Meanwhile, however, the poet does not leave his audience without guidance. It may be said in brief that the essential omission of this ode is the theme of hunting. If that is so, the first remark of the Theban soldier, who now appears leading the captive Dionysus, breaks in like an accusing voice. 'Pentheus, we are here and have caught the prey after which you sent us.' Dionysus is the prey, Pentheus the hunter. In the Bacchic, in the natural, world the distinction is immaterial, the roles reversible. From now onward they are in effect reversed.

CHAPTER VI

THE GOD AND THE KING

We have reached a dramatic moment. Though nearly a third part of the play has gone by, the two chief personages, the god and his persecutor, have not yet confronted one another. Pentheus has appeared in a scene of which he shared the interest with Teiresias and (in a lesser degree) with Cadmus, though it was enough to give us a picture of the man: well-intentioned, but proud, hot-tempered, impulsive, with a repressed sensuality and a leaning towards violent methods. Of the god we know more—and less. From the Prologue we gained a somewhat enigmatic impression of an immortal, calm and beautiful, but actuated by personal motives. The mythological figure of the Prologue stands, however, in sharp contrast with the living god whom the Bacchanals worship, who is embodied in the attractive person of their leader. It is thus in a mood of some doubt that we await his appearance, a doubt enhanced by the manner of its immediate preparation; for, at the end of the last chorus, 'the god, the son of Zeus', was presented to us not merely as the lover of festivity and peace, and benefactor of the human race with his gift of wine, but as the hater of his enemies. Now the god enters, in the charge of Theban soldiers. But at first he is silent; it is a soldier who speaks, and his speech (434–50) falls into two parts.[1]

'Pentheus, we are here and have caught the prey after which you sent us, nor was our enterprise in vain. But we found this beast tame; he drew not back his foot in flight, and willingly gave up his hands; he was not pale, nor did he change the vinous colour of his cheeks, but with a smile told us both to bind and to lead him captive, and he waited, making my task easy. And in shame I said: "Stranger, it is not of my own will that I take you, but at the command of Pentheus who sent me out."' The relevance of this picture to the preceding choral ode is clear enough. As the leading theme of the ode was peace, so here the god is mild and peaceable; as befits a god who rejoices in the feast, his countenance is flushed; he smiles, and we remember that among his attributes is 'to smile at the sound of the pipe' (380); finally, as his followers base their wisdom upon the standards of the common man, here is such a one who feels the charm of the god and,

[1] See also pp. 7 sq.

unlike Pentheus, pays him reverence.[1] But, as in the ode, so here there is a discordant note. The ode told us, in passing and without emphasis, that the god could hate; the soldier compares the god to a beast. For him the metaphor is only a joke, but for the audience it must be disquieting; for they know that in some sense the god *is* a beast, they are reminded of something that the song had concealed. They remember also that the god is now in the presence of his adversary, who is both his personal enemy of the Prologue and the 'man of excess' whom upon general principle he hates. The peace may be, must be, the ominous calm that precedes a storm; and a smile may mean many things.

Abruptly, the soldier turns to the other half of his message, and foreboding is no longer dependent on vague hint and remote reference. 'But the Bacchanals that you imprisoned, that you seized and set in bonds in the common prison—they are loosed and gone to the glades, where they leap and call upon Bromius their god. Of themselves were the fetters loosed from their feet, and the bolts let the doors open without touch of mortal hand. Full of many wonders has this man come here to Thebes. But the rest is your concern.' Now of wonder and miracle the last chorus was as innocent as of beasts and hunting. But here the 'tame beast' of a stranger is also a miracle-worker; and, though the miracle now worked is not in itself particularly violent, and is directed against Pentheus's authority rather than himself, at least it suggests its author's destructive power, at least it modifies the impression of the song. In fact it supplies, in a manner still far from explicit, the element there missing; and the juxtaposition here of the smiling god and his disturbing miracle is a forerunner of those complementary scenes of peace and violence that the Messenger speeches will describe.

The opening phase, then, of this scene is closely connected with the preceding ode. It has a concern with the deeper issues of the play and the fundamental character of Dionysiac religion; and in it the god appears in the beauty, peace and cheerfulness of the song, though with a hint of hostility and a potentiality of violence. When the god speaks, there is a certain change of tone.

The character and bearing of Dionysus in this and the following scenes with Pentheus[2] have been examined in an earlier chapter. They

[1] 440 may look back to 66. He makes the soldier's work easy, as one who can, if he choose, banish pain and effort—a persistent theme.

441 (δι' αἰδοῦς): contrast 263.

[2] Dodds (p. 124) has a valuable note on the structure of these scenes.

are enigmatic in the earlier stages, just as the Prologue is enigmatic, but the riddle is gradually resolved and the sympathy of the audience, which tends at first to be with the god, swings away as his design is unfolded. Throughout the play, however, his stable characteristics are a cleverness (σοφία) and control (σωφροσύνη) that stand in sharp contrast with the folly and impulsiveness of his opponent. But no less do they diverge from the ideals of his followers as expressed in the recent chorus. His *sophia* is the conventional cleverness—of the sophist, of the intriguer—that they must reject; his *sophrosyne* is not that which ensures the peaceful enjoyment of momentary pleasures, but the capacity to plan and execute a long-sighted design. This design proves to be one of unexampled cruelty and violence; yet the author of it is to the end unruffled. It was suggested that this manner of characterising Dionysus may in part be explicable by the poet's intention to satirise a mythological figure: the god is thus given human traits which develop unpleasantly—not only a vindictive temper, but an irritating power of repartee, a capacity for being in the right, whatever he says, an expertness at the game of cat and mouse. His concern with Pentheus is not to save a soul, but to establish an ascendancy.[1] Nevertheless, these traits do not entirely detract from his impressiveness; and, though he has personal motives, there is a kind of detachment about him. For Pentheus is not only encountering a personal adversary too clever for him, but also an impersonal power too strong for him; and the calm control and effortless superiority that mark off the god from his followers are wholly appropriate if we regard him as the embodiment of a relentless force; he stands outside the events of which he is the cause, above, or below, the actual human Bacchanals who are his agents.

Pentheus's policy of drastic action has apparently succeeded; the important arrest has been made, and he has come out of the palace to inspect the prisoner. But in his servant's report bad news was mixed with good: if the leader has been caught, the followers have escaped, and in disconcerting circumstances. How will Pentheus react to this? Unfortunately the text of his first words is corrupt. If we adopt a plausible emendation, they run as follows: 'Let go his hands. For now that he is in the net, he is not swift enough to escape me.' Has Pentheus then not heard how the prisoner made no attempt at flight? And is it not surprising that he makes no reference whatever to the second half of the soldier's speech? Unless such a comment is lost or concealed, or unless we suppose that the incident appears to

[1] See p. 20.

him trivial (a strange assumption, when his authority has been so outraged), there is only one explanation: he has never heard the soldier's words at all, so intent has he been upon the figure of the captive.[1]

Interpreters of the play are not agreed about the stage at which Pentheus comes under the influence of the god. His advocates tend to postpone this stage as late as possible. Nor indeed could it be maintained that in the present scene his will is to any appreciable extent surrendered to his opponent. His interest in him, however, is undeniable, and borders upon fascination. We saw in the preceding scene how vividly he had pictured the supposed orgies on the mountain, how closely he had noted the sensuous details of the Stranger's description. It is now with an unrealised envy and desire that he looks upon him face to face; and from the conventional taunts he casts at his luxurious appearance emerges something other than contempt.

'So! In body you are not unshapely, stranger—at least for women's pleasure, which is why you came to Thebes. Your hair is long—no wrestler's hair, it ripples down your cheeks, full of allurement. You have a fair skin—carefully tended out of the sun's rays and in the shade, where with your prettiness you pursue Aphrodite. First then tell me of what birth you are' (453–60). Thus Pentheus savours the details of the description not unappreciatively, adding to each, however, a sarcastic comment in terms of the general Hellenic prejudice and the particular gross suspicions that obsess his mind. The comments are his self-justification for the length at which he dwells upon the subject, but they are not the cause of it. In fact the sinner is supplanting the sin in his interest; and the series of questions he now proceeds to ask is no mere dramatic convenience, but the product of a genuine curiosity.

On this curiosity the god plays skilfully. Of what birth is he? He is from Tmolus; Lydia is his native land. Whence come these rites he brings to Greece? From Dionysus, son of Zeus. Zeus? The very

[1] Except perhaps for ἄγραν and θήρ, which suggest ἐν ἄρκυσιν to him: it is in any case the metaphor of his own choice (228, 352).

On the textual problem of 451 see Dodds *ad loc.* If μαίνεσθε (attractive in itself) is to be retained, Verrall's suggestion of a lacuna (μαίνεσθε... ⟨μεθέσθε⟩) is the most plausible. But that Pentheus should ignore the miraculous story is perhaps in keeping with his later indifference to the palace-miracle: cf. 639 (τί ποτ' ἄρ' ἐκ τούτων ἐρεῖ;) and what he *does* say. See p. 86.

same Zeus that was joined to Semele. Pentheus lets pass the controversial point, in his anxiety to hear about the rites; and Dionysus by withholding information stimulates his desire to learn. 'They are secrets that the uninitiated may not know.' 'It is not permitted you to hear, yet are they worth knowing' (472, 474). The reply of Pentheus to this is interesting: 'That was a good trick to make me want to hear.' Pentheus is shrewd enough in his way; he can realise that the Stranger is trying to trick him and can detect an evasion (479) and a sophistry (489). He has in fact the lowly practical shrewdness that a ruler must develop in dealing with men, and is quick enough at detecting motives that are upon his own plane. Yet he continues to ask questions, for the warning insight is too weak for the emotion that drives him on. So it is now and will continue to be till it is too late.

Pentheus continues to ask questions, and his curiosity is now directed towards the character of the god. 'You say you saw the god clear: of what sort was he?' The question of the character and aspect of this god goes deeper than the superficial irony; and the immediate answer— 'of what sort he wished; *I* did not order it'— is not only evasive and provocative, but profound, in that it points to the Protean forms of the god's self-manifestation. To Pentheus it is merely an evasion, and he accuses his opponent of talking specious nonsense. The retort is that he is a fool (ἀμαθεῖ) and cannot understand the wisdom of the wise, the cleverness of the clever (480). His incapacity to understand, his ἀμαθία, will be shown still more clearly. A little later (500 sq.) Dionysus will speak—ironically—of the close presence of the god, and Pentheus will reply, 'Where is he? He is not visible to *my* eyes';[1] for Pentheus has not the insight to recognise the god—far less the god within him. Immediately, by continuing his interrogation, he shows how he underestimates his adversary's cleverness.

'Did you bring your god here first?' 'All the barbarians are dancing these rites.' 'It is because they have much less sense than the Greeks.' 'In this rather they show good sense; but their ways (νόμοι) are different' (481–4). Again Pentheus shows his limitations and an insular prejudice,[2] and the god's answer is perfect. Customs

[1] The passage is full of words of sight and seeing (469, 470, 477, 500, 501, 502). On the significance of this see p. 165.

[2] Cf. 779. That Dionysus here introduces the important motive of custom, convention, law (νόμος), and himself implies its relativity is interesting, but not immediately relevant; see however p. 112 n. 1.

differ: and Pentheus is written down as untravelled and uneducated. To Pentheus anything that is not in accordance with national custom, whether it be the outward appearance of the Stranger or the actions of his followers, is suspect; and his suspicions tend to follow a well-beaten track. The next question is not unexpected.

'These ceremonies—do you perform them by night or in the day?' 'By night, mostly; there is awesomeness about the darkness.' 'For women there is trickery and corruption.' 'Even in daytime can one contrive a shameful deed.' 'You must be punished for your wicked sophistries.'[1] 'And you for your stupidity (ἀμαθίας) and your impiety towards the god' (485–90). Dionysus's answer to the charge of immorality is not unlike that of Teiresias (314 sqq.). It is the same half-truth, and Pentheus has the shrewdness to realise that he is being fobbed off with something unsatisfactory. But if Dionysus is specious, Pentheus himself is crude. To his morbid imagination the whole movement is a cloak for sexual indulgence. He is incapable of any further effort of imagination; and to the beauty and attractiveness of a way of life which pursues self-oblivion in ecstatic excitement he is quite insensitive; he is ἀμαθής. Yet upon his crude assumptions he is prepared to punish without adequate evidence. He allows his public action to be dictated by his private character and thereby puts himself in the wrong.

The interrogation has ended with the idea that was in the mind of Pentheus when he began it: there is no more for him to ask. Meanwhile Dionysus has led him through a crescendo of ill-temper to the limits of his patience. Now it is the god's turn to ask a question: 'Tell me what I must suffer. What is the terrible thing you will inflict on me?' (492). On each point of the proposed punishment—the cutting of the hair, the removal of the thyrsus, the imprisonment[2]—he makes a confident and ironic comment; for Dionysus, as he says, is close at hand, but Pentheus has not eyes to see him, for he is impious. 'Seize him,' cries Pentheus, 'he scorns me and Thebes.' 'I say "bind me not"—I who am master of my senses say it to you who have lost yours.'[3] 'And I say "bind", who have more authority than you.' But in this direct conflict of orders and authorities we can feel no

[1] 489: σοφισμάτων may possibly refer, not to his subtlety in argument, but to the device of holding rites by night; however, in view of 491 this is less likely.

[2] 'Stage business with the Stranger's side curls and with his thyrsus' (Dodds).

[3] 504: σωφρονῶν οὐ σώφροσιν.

confidence in the superiority of the king. The calm of Dionysus is as ominous as the king's lack of calm, of self-knowledge, of *sophrosyne*. 'You know not what your life is', says Dionysus, 'nor what you are doing, nor who you are' (506).[1] It is true: Pentheus has none of the self-knowledge that is necessary for self-control; he cannot recognise the springs of his own actions and, in particular, that element of irrationality and violence in himself which he shares with those he is persecuting. It is these things that will betray him, and that deprive his claim to authority of any real foundation.

Dionysus makes a statement: 'you know not who you are'. But Pentheus takes it as a question and answers it. As he interprets it, it is not unlike the first question he himself had put to Dionysus (460). Thus the wheel has come full circle, and the interrogator become the interrogated. Dionysus had evaded the question (though he knew the answer); Pentheus gives a superficial answer. 'I am Pentheus, Agave's son; Echion was my father.' The tone of this remark is elusive. It has been suggested (and it may be true) that it is the remark of a bewildered Pentheus, confronted by something bigger than himself and seeking reassurance as the ground gives beneath his feet. At least the mere fact that he feels that an answer is demanded is a sign of something less than absolute confidence, and the answer he gives, with its pride of ancestry, is calculated to reassure. It may also remind the audience that Pentheus is son of the woman who is even now leading the Bacchanals upon Cithaeron. Concerning Echion the coming chorus will have something to tell. The very name Pentheus, says Dionysus (echoing the pun of Teiresias), is ill-omened; not less suggestive is his ancestry.[2]

The scene now moves rapidly to an end. Pentheus orders the Stranger to be shut up in the dark stables; there he may dance, if he will. Then as he turns to the Bacchanals of the Chorus, there is (inevitably) a side-reference to their supposed misdoings. 'These women you have brought with you as your accomplices in guilt, I will either sell into slavery, or stopping their hands from this thump and thud of the drum I will keep them as handmaidens at the loom' (511–14).[3] The Stranger replies with calm confidence, with an

[1] On the difficulties of this line see Dodds; the general sense is clear—the ignorance of Pentheus which embraces his own nature and status.

[2] *V. infra* p. 79.

[3] From which it is clear that they accompany the closing lines of the scene upon their kettle-drums. From 508 onwards (Dodds), or perhaps from 506, if we adopt the reading ὃ τείσεις.

accusation of *hubris* and a threat of vengeance—the vengeance of Dionysus; and on a note of superficial irony, god and king leave the stage.

The ode that follows arises immediately out of the closing remarks of Pentheus, and the emotion that informs it is the personal fear of the Bacchanals; for he has threatened to deprive them of their liberty, to drag them back from the 'sweet toil' of Dionysus to the humdrum domestic tasks of women and so rob them of their joy and their pride.[1]

In the *strophe* they call upon Dirce, the famous spring, taking it, we might say, as the representative power of nature in Thebes and appealing to it over the head of Pentheus. 'Daughter of Achelous, queen Dirce, blessed among maidens, for thou didst once receive in thy springs the babe of Zeus, when out of the immortal fire Zeus his begetter snatched him to put him in his thigh, and cried: "Come, Dithyrambus, enter into this my male womb; I reveal thee to Thebes, O Bacchic One, that she call thee by this name." But thou, blessed Dirce, dost thrust me away when I hold my garlanded communions in thy land. Why dost thou reject me? Why dost thou shun me? The time will come—by the clustering delight of the vine of Dionysus—the time will come that thou shalt have regard for Bromius' (519–36). There is a poignancy about this appeal, and a logic also in the reference to the double birth. The odd proceeding is enveloped in a queer kind of dignity, though it was a foetus brought prematurely to the light of day that was washed in Dirce's waters.[2] As in the Entrance Song, however, the indiscriminate piety of the singers embraces the whole legend and derives strength from it, so that the stanza ends upon a note of confidence, and they can proceed in the next to the abuse of their adversary. The emotional sequence is in fact very similar to that of the last ode. Shaken, they must first restore themselves; and this they do—in the earlier ode by a meditation upon the gifts of Bromius, and here by a loving recital of his holy names, Dithyrambus, Bacchius, Bromius.[3]

[1] Cf. 118, 1035, 1236.

[2] The word translated 'babe' is βρέφος. Commonly used of a new-born child, in Homeric usage (and perhaps by etymology) it means 'the child in the womb, the embryo'. Whether it could in itself, in a suitable context, carry that significance for a fifth-century audience is not clear; instances seem to be lacking between Homer and the first century A.D.

[3] Four names within ten lines.

The *antistrophe* consists of an explosion of violent hatred against Pentheus as persecutor and an appeal for the direct intervention of the god. 'Such anger, such anger does the child of earth reveal, he who is bred from the snake of old, Pentheus, whom earthly Echion begat—a wild monster, not a mortal man, but like a bloody giant to strive against gods: who will soon set me who am Bromius's in the toils, and already he holds my group-fellow within his palace, hidden in a dark prison. Seest thou this, son of Zeus, Dionysus, thy preachers wrestling with oppression? Come, lord, shaking thy golden thyrsus, down from Olympus, and check the outrage (ὕβριν) of the man of blood' (537–55).[1]

It is indeed natural that in their anger they should look for something that can be turned to the disparagement of Pentheus, and they find it in his sonship to Echion, one of the warriors whom Cadmus had raised from the dragon's teeth. They reflect that about this origin there is something monstrous to which his conduct is a counterpart: like the Giants he is 'earth-born', and like them he is cruel, violent, inhuman, and an adversary of the gods. It is surprising what emphasis Euripides places upon this circumstance both here and later,[2] and his motive for doing so is at first sight by no means clear. It amounts to giving Pentheus a mythological aspect, corresponding to that of his opponent. Yet Pentheus is a character so obviously and so fully human that it appears to be something of an intrusion. So far as Pentheus himself is concerned, it seems that Euripides has been content to leave it vague, as a dark and sinister element in his heredity, complementary perhaps to the emotionalism he inherits from his mother.[3] But it is to be noted that the attack upon him on the ground of his origin comes from the Bacchanals, here and in the songs that

[1] 554: 'Ολύμπου (Kirchhoff). The opening words of this stanza (οἷαν οἷαν ὀργάν) are bracketed by many editors, perhaps rightly (see Dodds). It is, however, strange that an interpolator should have written in a metre which is correct but far from obvious (molossi for ionics). But the amended text is admirable, since the two revelations are contrasted (ἀναφαίνω 528, ἀναφαίνει 538). Just as Dionysus is manifested throughout the play, so does Pentheus manifest the dark potentialities of his character.

[2] Cf. 995 sq., 1025 sq., 1155, 1274 sqq.

[3] See Appendix. The symbolism of the Snake in the *Phoenissae* appears to be similar: *v.* 657 sqq., 818 sqq., 931 sqq. The breed of the Snake is Θήβαις κάλλιστον ὄνειδος (821): κάλλιστον, because the Theban aristocracy are proud to claim descent from the Sown Men; ὄνειδος, because all its associations are with blood and cruelty (657 sq., 672 sqq., 937 sqq.).

belong immediately before and after the account of his death (995 sq., 1155). This is the significant fact, and it is one of central importance to the play.

Consider the charge brought against Pentheus in this stanza. In general, it is that he is sub-human, or super-human in a repulsive way, like some evil kind of divinity. In particular, he is charged with ferocity, blood and violence (ἀγριωπόν, φόνιον, ὕβριν). But is this a charge that Dionysus and his followers should bring? He is charged with being inhuman. But does not their own claim to humanity stand or fall with his? These qualities in him they attribute to his origin from a snake.[1] But the snake is an avatar of Dionysus, in whose honour they wear snakes in their hair (101 sqq.) and as girdles (698, 768); later, they will pray that he may appear in the form of a snake (1019). Can those whose contacts with the animal world are so close rightly bring a charge of sub-humanity? Are they not in fact abusing Pentheus for the possession of Dionysiac traits of character?

In making them do so, the poet's intention would appear to be twofold. On the one hand, he hints—and at this stage in the play it is only a hint—at the violence and cruelty which are potential in the Dionysiac way of life, whose closeness to nature carries with it more than the beauty of nature's peaceful aspects. It escapes the Bacchanals that they sing of the ferocity of Pentheus with an emotion equally fierce, which will later exult in action far more cruel; and this guileless concentration upon the emotion of the moment to the exclusion of self-knowledge is characteristic of them. None the less their words have a true application to Pentheus, who is also the prey of his emotions and is led by them to corresponding bestiality and violence; he also is devoid of self-knowledge, as he persecutes those with whom he has a close spiritual kinship. We may return to the stanza under consideration.

It is this monster that has ventured to threaten with bonds 'her who is Bromius's', as the proud phrase goes, that has already laid hands upon her group-fellow—and we remember the intensity of emotion with which the Bacchanals sang of him in the Entrance Song. Their pride, their liberty, their affections, all are attacked, and they

[1] And from the earth. Dionysus himself had chthonic associations (cf. Farnell, *Cults*, v, pp. 178 sq.) more or less obscure and overlaid, of which Euripides may have been aware. (On his relationship to the Eleusinian deities see *ibid.* III, pp. 146 sqq.)

call upon the god to rescue his missionaries, coming in majesty from Olympus to chastise the insolence of Pentheus. Olympus, as the mountain on which Zeus held his court and which the giants tried unsuccessfully to storm, is the symbol of Dionysus's assured and established divinity.

The summit of Olympus may have been visible to Euripides as he wrote these lines. And Olympus has associations, not merely with the Hellenic pantheon, but with the semi-civilised Macedonia that lay upon its northern slopes, with the district of Pieria and with the wild worship of Dionysus.[1] Of this Olympus the chorus will sing in the *epode*, and the transition is skilfully contrived. To pray to a god and, in ignorance of where he may be, to address yourself in succession to his favourite haunts is a convention of ancient prayer. So now, it is perhaps on Nysa, 'nurse of beasts', that Dionysus leads the *thiasoi*, thyrsus in hand, or on the Corycian crags. 'Yet perchance it is in the thick-wooded coverts of Olympus, where Orpheus once played his lute and gathered the trees with his music, gathered the wild beasts. Blessed art thou, O Pieria!' Where Nysa may be and where Corycia matter little; we have passed through them from an Olympus where a vigilant and avenging Olympian dwells to an Olympus of trees and beasts where Dionysus leads the *thiasoi*, his association with the animal world resumed.[2] This association is ambiguous; but here the poet has chosen the aspect of love and peace, and has blended with it the theme of music (Pieria was the birthplace of the Muses) and the lovely legend of Orpheus.[3]

'Blessed art thou, O Pieria! Evius honours thee, and shall visit thee to dance with Bacchic rites, and across the swift-flowing Axius shall lead the whirling Maenads, and across father Lydias, giver of prosperous happiness to mortals, of whom I have heard tell that he makes fertile with his fair waters a land of good horses' (565–75). Axius was the chief river of Southern Macedonia, Lydias the stream that flowed past the royal capital; on the name of the former

[1] See Dodds, pp. 119 sq.

[2] Hence θηροτρόφον (556), immediately following the Antistrophe in which the Chorus have attributed animality to Pentheus.

[3] Though his hearers may—indeed must—remember that this legend had a less lovely pendant and that Orpheus was torn to pieces in the rites of Dionysus, like the beasts over which he had such power, or like Pentheus. Compare the transient discord in the second choral ode, which this stanza resembles, though with the addition of the 'beast' theme, the presence of which takes us a step nearer to the full truth.

Euripides seems to make a pun (Ἄξιος, ἄξει); the tension drops. For the poet is now paying a compliment to the land and the king whose guest he is. If such a tribute was demanded, it could not have been more happily introduced, nor could social and artistic tact be more skilfully reconciled. For the Chorus has sung itself out of its fears; and a lull at this point makes the voice of the unseen Dionysus break in with all the more effect.

The 'palace-miracle' follows, on which something has already been said in earlier chapters.[1] In considering this episode, which, regarded as a piece of action, is curiously detached from the rest of the play, it is essential to hold fast to the symbolical interpretation. The imprisonment of Dionysus has been carefully prepared: by the binding and loosing of the Bacchanals, by the repeated threats of Pentheus both before and after the capture of the Stranger.[2] Moreover we have been prepared to expect some act of wonder in connection with it: by the mysterious escape of the Bacchanals, by the bearing of the captive 'magician', by the irony of certain phrases—'Imprison him in the stables near by', says Pentheus, 'that he may look upon murky darkness. There dance your dances!' (509 sqq.). Is it not a dangerous command, for may not Dionysus obey? In all these ways we are led to expect a manifestation of power; we expect a wonder, and a wonder occurs, as occur it must. For the universal Dionysus of whom Euripides wrote can be imprisoned in the dark, but not for long; and the inevitable explosion is symbolised in the play by a catastrophe to the palace of Pentheus.

The scene falls into two parts. At the end of the choral ode, a divine voice is heard calling upon the Bacchanals—it is the son of Semele, the son of Zeus. The voice[3] then calls upon the spirit of Earthquake to shake the solid ground. The Chorus, in great excitement, exclaim that soon the halls of Pentheus will be shaken to pieces and collapse, for Dionysus is in the house; after which they see the stone architraves gape at the joints. Once more the unearthly

[1] See pp. 8, 20. It is further discussed in the Appendix.

[2] 226 sqq., 443 sqq.; 239, 355 sqq., 451 sq., 497, 509 sqq. Cf. Weinreich, *Genethliakon für W. Schmid*, pp. 282 sqq.

[3] I agree with Dodds, against Grube, that 585 and 594 sq. are spoken by the god. The change to dactylic metre is probably significant. See Dodds (p. 140) also on the distribution of lines between individual members of the Chorus.

imperative: 'Kindle the bright flame of the lightning: consume, consume the palace of Pentheus.' And the Chorus see fire blaze up around the tomb of Semele hard by. They cast themselves to the ground and await what further catastrophe may come (600 sqq.).

Clearly the scene is conditioned by the practice and resources of the Attic stage, upon which Drury Lane effects, even if they were desirable, could not be produced. No real catastrophe is seen by the spectators, who must be content, wholly or mainly, with the words and obvious emotion of the Chorus, but upon whom the symbolical significance of earthquake and fire will not be lost. Similarly, the practice of the Greek theatre requires that the audience should depend upon a Messenger for an account of sensational events. This function the Stranger now enters to perform.

The story which he has to tell (and which he tells in the rapid melodramatic trochaic rhythm) has an atmosphere of its own, suited to the god's current role of wonder-worker, lighter and less impressive than the unseen voice and the lyrical responses of the Chorus. After he has comforted the Bacchanals, they ask how he gained his freedom. 'I saved myself', he replies, 'easily and without trouble.' Indeed he was never bound, for Pentheus, thinking to bind him, was mocked.[1] He had wasted all his efforts trying to bind a bull which he found in the stalls. Then came the Bacchic god who shook the palace and lighted a fire in his mother's tomb. Pentheus thought the palace was on fire and organised a fire-brigade. Then he seized a sword and rushed after his escaped prisoner, but Bromius created a phantom in the courtyard which Pentheus pursued till he was tired. The Bacchic god, for further measure, razed the buildings to the ground! And now the footsteps of Pentheus are heard. What will he say? The Stranger is ready for him.

The tone is light as the detail is vague, not merely because of the conditions of the Greek theatre or the current role of the god, but for a more fundamental reason of dramatic construction. The function of the palace-miracle is not quite what would appear from a straightforward prose account of the events involved, nor were these events contrived as final and catastrophic evidence to convince the unbeliever. Indeed, if the miracles at this stage were too overwhelming, they would make what follows an anti-climax; they would anticipate the complete epiphany of Dionysus; they would, moreover, render in-

[1] καθύβρισα (616): an interim reply to the *hubris* of the man of blood (555). See p. 146 n. 2 (on 1347).

comprehensible the psychology of Pentheus. When he emerges from the palace, his one thought is of the Stranger who has escaped him, with none to spare for the earthquake of which that Stranger has just spoken in such uncompromising terms. This is plausible only on two grounds: if his obsession with the person of Dionysus is already considerable, and if he has come less from a scene of real cataclysm than from a nightmare of terrors and phantoms and futile struggles in the dark. The dramatic interest of the play largely turns upon the struggle of wills between Dionysus and Pentheus. Now this struggle has hardly begun, and the last thing that Euripides (or the god) intended was that it should be terminated so soon, and upon the plane of miracle. The defeat of Pentheus must and will be a defeat of character; and to this defeat the palace-miracle is but a prelude of an intentionally vague description, foreshadowing indeed the ultimate catastrophe, but itself impalpable and phantasmagoric. It is a shadowy drama played in darkness, before both contestants come out into the light of day to resume the contest.[1]

If, therefore, neither Pentheus nor any of the characters subsequently refers to the wrecking of the palace, it is not a tactful reticence for the sake of the stage manager, nor is it the accusing finger of rationalism. Characters in Greek plays (as Professor Dodds points out) do not waste time in saying what is dramatically irrelevant, and the palace-miracle, regarded as an actual event, ceases to have any dramatic relevance as soon as the narrative is over. It is the symbolism which counts and which is of lasting effect.

Of the symbolism of the bull which Pentheus binds something has already been said.[2] It is right that it should be a bull, for the bull is a representative of Dionysus—of Dionysus as animal and particularly as sexual animal; and in binding it with effort and strain Pentheus is performing the futile task of constraining the animal Dionysus within himself. This symbolism is not, however, private to Pentheus. Though its primary application is to him, it tells us something of general significance about Dionysus, namely that force, without understanding, is futile in dealing with what he represents. The broader symbolism of the episode as a whole teaches the same lesson. Dionysus is treated with violence; he is confined in the dark, and the result is catastrophe, fire and earthquake. Consider the words with

[1] Which may be the point of the repeated προνώπιος ('in front, outside'), first of Pentheus (639), then of the Stranger (645).

[2] See p. 8.

which the Chorus usher in the god. 'Cast your trembling bodies to the ground, ye Maenads. For the lord, the son of Zeus, is coming upon this palace, turning it upside down' (600 sqq.). Ἄνω κάτω: it is an exhibition of destructive violence that finds parallels, first in the weak, petulant vengeance of Pentheus upon Teiresias, then in the wholesale devastation wrought by the Bacchanals upon the mountain.[1] Those are incidents upon the plane of real life, this an incident upon the plane of mythology and miracle. All in their different ways look forward to the ultimate disaster, which it is the function of the palace-miracle to foreshadow in symbol. And the details of the symbolism—earthquake, lightning, and fire—are extraordinarily apt.

They are apt because they are drawn from the phenomena of nature. Now Dionysiac religion is in close touch with nature, and it derives a large part of its attractiveness from that contact. Its worship takes place in the solitude of mountains, in company only with the animal and vegetable creations, which seem, as we shall see, in mystic fashion to share in the ecstasy of the worshippers; even the very ground produces wine, milk and honey for their use. They are in touch with nature—in one of her aspects. But her face is not always smiling. Living in a temperate land, where to-day few districts do not show to some degree the civilising hand of man, we tend, perhaps inevitably, to equate nature with the peace and beauty which she sometimes manifests; and our poets of nature have encouraged us to do so.[2] But in history and over the earth at large this is not the sole, it is not even the predominant, aspect of man's physical environment. Not only has he had perpetually to struggle against her normal inclemencies and excesses, but he has been at the mercy of her outbreaks of cataclysmic violence: earthquake, volcano, flood and fire. All these are as truly part of nature as flowers and woods, as milk and honey. The latter are the accompaniments of Bacchic worship, and fitting symbols of its quiet beauty. But it seems impossible to claim kinship with nature in her peace and to disown it in her fury. And, in fact, the Bacchanals reveal their affinities as much by the one as by the other, passing from peace to fury with transitions as sudden as nature's own. Such a transition is vividly described in the first Messenger speech, which immediately follows this scene; such another in the speech that tells of the final

[1] See pp. 55, 97 n. 1.

[2] Mr Aldous Huxley has an interesting essay on this topic: 'Wordsworth in the Tropics', in *Do what you will*, pp. 113 sqq.

defeat and death of Pentheus, when an effort to suppress by violent means the cult of nature is frustrated by an outbreak of natural violence. Here that effort and that defeat are foreshadowed in symbol by the imprisonment of Dionysus and the consequent earthquake and fire. Earthquake and fire show nature in a mood that is violent, destructive, ruthless and incalculable; and in this lies their aptness as symbols. For these are precisely the characteristics of furious Bacchanals living the natural life.

The episode of the palace-miracle or miracles anticipates upon a plane which is not entirely realistic the ultimate defeat of Pentheus, and during the course of it he displays those characteristics which we have already seen in him and which will lead to his undoing. But if in the open he had maintained the semblance of control, in the darkness within he was at the mercy of the mocking god. 'How excited he is', said Cadmus at the first entry of his grandson; and it is still the just comment, as we see him in a succession of brief pictures, past almost as soon as they appear: straining every nerve to bind the bull; dashing to and fro, giving orders, organising a vain attempt to extinguish an imaginary fire;[1] then, as a fresh idea strikes him, with a rapid shift of interest worthy of his opponents, dropping his task to pursue a phantom Stranger, stabbing the air, till he sinks exhausted and the sword drops from his hand.

The Pentheus who emerges from the palace is quieter, more normal, essentially unchanged from the Pentheus who committed Dionysus to prison. 'What will he say after this', asks the god; and the answer is that he will say nothing of anything except the escape of his prisoner. A sign undoubtedly of the hold that the prisoner has upon his imagination and emotions;[2] but a sign also of the plane upon which the immediately preceding events have taken place.

It is the same Pentheus and the same Dionysus, and their battle continues upon the same terms. Dionysus is still clever and controlled; still subtly provocative ('Did I not say, or did you not hear me say, that one would loose me?'); still ironic ('You will find me waiting, I shall not run away').[3] Pentheus is still the outraged autocrat, believing in fetters and compulsion (643). He is astounded

[1] Vain, because the palace was not on fire; vain, because the fire that Dionysus lights cannot be put out with water.

[2] Compare his reception of the soldier's message (p. 73).

[3] 649, 659.

at the boldness of his escaped prisoner (645, 648), and his first instinct is still to shut him in: 'I bid close every turret in our circuit' (653). 'What of that?' replies Dionysus. 'Cannot gods pass even over walls?' 'You are clever, clever', cries Pentheus, 'except where you need cleverness.' 'Where most I need it, there I am most clever', comes the reply. It is the old wrangle, but it is not immediately brought to a conclusion upon the stage. For at this point there enters a herdsman from the mountain with news for Pentheus. 'Listen to him', says Dionysus, 'and take his words to heart.'[1] And he is right; for there is little that need be known about the religion of Dionysus that is not contained in the speech that follows.[2]

[1] 657: μάθε. Cf. ἀμαθεῖ (480), ἀμαθίας (490).

[2] Note also that Pentheus is still curious (650); and I suspect, though I cannot prove, that the lacuna which follows or precedes 652 (see Dodds *ad loc.*) contained evidence that he is still prurient.

CHAPTER VII

BACCHANALS UPON THE MOUNTAIN

The contest between Dionysus and Pentheus in the dark interior of the palace is over. Strange and fantastic and detached from the main sweep of the action, it was rich in symbolism and foreboded the ultimate defeat of Pentheus. At the end of it the two contestants appear once more in the light of day and in front of the palace, virtually unchanged in character and bearing; and we expect the contest to be resumed before our eyes as a battle of wills. That is indeed to come; but it is postponed while in a speech of some hundred lines a Messenger carries us away from Thebes to the mountain where its women are worshipping Dionysus.

For this unexpected stroke Euripides had more than one reason of dramatic art. On its 'evidential' value for Pentheus we need not perhaps lay too much stress: Euripides is not building up a case against the obstinate unbeliever, who, if he will not 'believe' after the palace-miracle, will surely be convinced by nothing. Its psychological effect upon him is, however, crucial and twofold. It diverts the main course of his anger away from the Stranger in the direction of the Bacchanals; it stimulates, not only his indignation, but his curiosity and makes him fall an even readier victim to the plot of Dionysus. Its effect upon the audience is equally important. By giving them insight into the behaviour of Bacchanals, it prepares them for a second and similar narrative and illuminates the intervening scenes with a sinister light. So do Bacchanals treat disturbers of their worship; so will they treat Pentheus.

The immediate transition is effected, one might say, by the word σοφός, four times repeated in two lines (655 sq.). It is an important word, perhaps the most important in the play, and it may mean many things. Here in the mouths of Pentheus and of Dionysus it has a connotation of conventional cleverness and quickness of wit. It is a contest between god and king in respect of this quality which is now interrupted; but the commentary upon *sophia* is not. For if there is a *sophia* of the mythological Dionysus, there is also a *sophia* of his followers, and the two are by no means identical. It will be remembered that in the second choral ode the Bacchanals abjured conventional cleverness and substituted for it a wisdom of their own, which consisted primarily in the avoidance of excess (a simple and characteristically Hellenic principle) and in the life of quietness amid the pursuit of immediate pleasures. The whole ode in which this ideal finds expression is permeated with an atmosphere of peace and moderation. It is a partial and, so to say, edited version of Dionysiac religion. Its discretions are, however, to some extent betrayed by the Entrance Song that preceded it and is still fresh in the recollection of the audience. Through that vivid picture of wild, hunting Bacchanals, rejoicing in the tearing of the prey and the raw-flesh-eating, the absent element is supplied, the Bacchanals seen in their fury as well as in their peace. In the Entrance Song this contrast emerges even from the uniform lyricism of the singing Bacchanals. It is the function of the present Messenger speech to bring out that contrast still more lucidly in an objective narrative, and thereby to provide by a fully concrete picture of Dionysiac practice and psychology a commentary upon the nature of Dionysiac 'wisdom'.[1] This speech is the centre-piece of the play's design; and, for displaying the poet's insight into the religion of Dionysus, it is perhaps its most important feature. To it there will be little to add; and the further course of the drama is simply the working out of its implications in the lives of the characters. Thus the second Messenger speech in the main repeats its aesthetic pattern, but now with a terrible personal application.

The main narrative is prefaced by brief dialogue between the Messenger and the king. 'Pentheus, master of this Theban land', begins the former, and, though the presence of Dionysus makes the word 'master' sound a trifle ridiculous, the Herdsman clearly stands

[1] A link with the Entrance Song may be provided by 664 sq., in which the Herdsman describes the Bacchanals as ποτνιάδες. What is the force of the epithet? Two passages, both from recent plays of Euripides, fix the reference to the mad mares of Glaucus who tore their master in pieces at Potniae, a township between Thebes and Cithaeron. *Or.* 316 sqq. (δρομάδες...ποτνιάδες θεαί, ἀβάκχευτον αἳ θίασον ἐλάχετε), which describes the Erinyes, is not in itself conclusive, but *Phoen.* 1124 sq. (ποτνιάδες...πῶλοι δρομάδες) may be thought to settle the meaning of δρομάδες in the former passage (if *Or.* 45 does not). In the *Bacchae* (where οἴστροισι also fits) the reference (i) is locally appropriate; (ii) hints at a *sparagmos*; (iii) is related to the closing metaphor of the Entrance Song where the Bacchanals are compared to horses: κῶλον ἐξηκόντισαν (665) providing a verbal link with κῶλον ἄγει (167). The charming frisking creatures may also be hostile and destructive.

in considerable awe of Pentheus and will not begin until his own safety is guaranteed. 'I want to know', he says, 'whether I am to speak freely of what happened there or to curb my tongue. For I fear the quickness of your temper, master, your sharpness to wrath and all too royal habit' (668–71). This is disarming, and Pentheus can hardly fail to reassure him, though he adds an ingenious reason for his restraint. 'Speak', he says, 'you shall in no case suffer anything from me. It is not with the righteous that one should be wrath, but the more shocking (δεινότερα) are the things you say about the Bacchanals, the more shall I bring to justice this man who has taught our women such tricks' (672–6). The Herdsman had promised that his tale was one of strange (δεινά) deeds, more than wonderful (667). Pentheus reads into the words his own suspicions; he knows that the tale he is to hear will be not merely strange, but shocking. Beneath the severity of his official tones we can detect an eager curiosity. Strange things, shocking things, are what he wants to hear.

The Herdsman begins his tale: 'The pasturing herds of cattle were just climbing up to the hill-country, when the sun sent forth his rays to warm the earth. And I saw three bands of women-worshippers, one led by Autonoe, the second by your mother Agave, the third by Ino. They were all asleep, bodies relaxed, some resting their backs on greenery of the pine, others with their heads laid at random on oak-leaves on the ground—chastely, not, as you say, drunken with wine and with the sound of the pipe, and pursuing Cypris lonely in the wood' (677–88).[1] It was no doubt as great a surprise, as great a disappointment, to him as it would have been to Pentheus.

In this way we are given a kind of negative prelude to the positive account of the Bacchanals' behaviour. Whatever they may subsequently do, the Bacchanals, on the testimony of the Herdsman, are chaste; and so prominent have been the prurient suspicions of Pentheus that this information can hardly fail of an effect. Pentheus is discredited, his opponents enjoy a moral triumph. To some critics it has seemed that hereby the poet expressly dissociates himself from accusations of this character and vindicates the religion of Dionysus from the charge of immorality.[2] This is perhaps an unnecessarily simple view to take.

[1] θηρᾶν (688): the metaphor is kept in circulation. ὡς σὺ φῇς (686): how did he know? It does not matter.

[2] As also by the replies of Teiresias and the god (314 sqq., 488): see pp. 52, 76.

The last thing that Euripides wished to do was to present the issue in terms of sex or unduly to distract the attention of his male audience with that notorious red-herring.[1] The importance of sex in the *Bacchae* is for the part it plays in the psychology of Pentheus. Thus it is largely irrelevant, dramatically, whether orgiastic religion is commonly (and was in Greece) associated with sexual extravagance. It is not entirely irrelevant, for the Bacchanals of the Chorus sang yearningly of the island of Aphrodite, of the Loves and of Desire. In suitable abstractions, no doubt; but the love that ranks with wine and music among present pleasures is not abstract. Moreover, the Messenger himself, the witness to the chastity of Bacchanals, concludes his speech, as we shall see, by asserting the dependence of Cypris on the Dionysiac gift of wine.

That is what the Messenger in his heart of hearts believed, and doubtless it was common belief. And doubtless it was made a ground of attack upon the religion of Dionysus by those who looked askance at it.[2] But to emphasise this aspect of orgiastic religion is to distort as well as to distract. Sexual excitement is but one drug among many that Dionysus has to bestow; and to base disapproval solely or mainly upon this count may be to display the mentality of a Pentheus. Euripides will exhibit the dangers of an emotional creed upon a far wider scale. So the Bacchanals are vindicated against Pentheus. How much then is their 'moral triumph' worth? They are chaste; they are σώφρονες. But, as Teiresias said, in a shrewd judgement which is as true of religions as of individuals: 'what must be considered is whether *sophrosyne* is part of their nature in all respects and always' (315 sq.). By the end of the Messenger's speech we know that it is consistent with the *sophrosyne* of Bacchanals, when provoked, to rend wild animals in pieces, wound men and wreck villages. Further, all this is a mere foreshadowing of their future action when, led by his mother, they will tear and kill Pentheus himself. In face of this, the importance of their chastity or unchastity would seem to pale, and their vindication on that score only emphasises by contrast their vulnerability on the other.

The Messenger continues: 'And your mother stood up in the midst of the Bacchanals and cried to them that they should rouse

[1] Chaeremon (fr. 14) saw and seized the chance that Euripides had let slip!

[2] It was the contemporary charge against immigrant oriental cults (see Dodds, *Maenadism*, pp. 174 sq., and p. 151 below).

their bodies out of sleep, as soon as she heard the lowing of the horned cattle. And they, casting deep sleep from their eyes, sprang upright, a marvel of good order to behold, young and old and virgins yet unwed' (689–94). There is something characteristic in this awakening of the Bacchanals. They spring to complete wakefulness, whole-hearted and uncompromising as the deep sleep from which they are roused. 'And first they let down their hair over their shoulders and pulled up their fawnskins where the fastening bands had been loosed, and girded the dappled hides with snakes which licked their cheeks.[1] And some held in their arms roes or wolf-cubs of the wilds and gave them their white milk—all those whose breasts were still full, because they had recently given birth and had left their babies' (695–702). The suckling of animals by women, as that of human young by animals, is a common theme of folk-lore; and here indeed it may also have a ritual significance.[2] But with a shade of emphasis the poet has made it reveal an aspect of the Dionysiac life. In the Greek a considerable stress falls upon the concluding words of the quotation and thus upon the abandonment by these Bacchanal mothers of their babies still unweaned, for whose needs they no longer care. They have in fact forgotten them; and, in the wild natural life they are now leading, they find it proper to give their milk to the young of wild animals. There is a beauty in this and a symbol of mystic communion, but also surely a touch of inhumanity that jars, breaking for a moment the lyrical flow of the narrative. Even in their peace these Bacchanals are at odds with civilised life.[3]

'And they put on garlands of ivy and oak and flowering bryony. One took her thyrsus and struck upon the rock, and there leapt forth from it a dewy stream of water; another thrust her wand into the level ground, and there the god sent up a fountain of wine; and, had

[1] λιχμῶσιν γένυν (698): see Dodds. The words *may* mean merely that the snakes 'protruded their tongues as if licking their own jaws'. But I think the repetition of the cheek-licking at 768 is deliberate: the second time they lick *blood*. It brings out both the contrast of moods and the return to the earlier mood. See p. 98.

For a modern parallel to the handling of snakes in orgiastic worship, see *Picture Post* of 31 December 1938 (and Dodds, *Maenadism*, p. 163).

[2] See Dodds on 699–702.

[3] ἀγρίους (700) is stressed in order to bring out the contrast with βρέφη λιπούσαις. The relationship of mother and child counts for nothing with the Bacchanals, which has its relevance for the future action of Agave.

any a desire for a white draught, they scraped away the earth with their finger-tips and had abundant jets of milk; and from the ivied thyrsi dripped sweet streams of honey' (702–11). So closes the first scene, of quiet preparation and refreshment; and in the main it defies comment. Nor is there in it (except for the suckling of the animals) any novelty for one who has heard or read the earlier portions of the play. The correspondence between the narrative and the Entrance Song is in fact close and detailed, as to snakes and fawnskins, garlands of ivy oak and bryony, and the miraculous flow of wine, milk and honey. Those yearning imaginations of the Chorus are now ratified and reinforced by an objective account of an actual scene of worship.

'Had you been present and seen these sights', says the Messenger, 'you would have pursued with prayer the god you now abuse.' But the herdsmen did not pray. Like typical Greeks they held a debate, and an irreverent townsman[1] appealing to their self-interest persuaded them to curry favour with the king by 'hunting' Agave—a sinister metaphor in a Dionysiac context. Accordingly they laid their ambuscade. The episode serves as a pause between the peaceful preparations of the Bacchanals and their move to action. 'We hid ourselves in ambush in a leafy thicket; and they at the appointed hour began to bestir the thyrsus in their Bacchic worship, calling on Bromius, the son of Zeus, as Lord of Cries. And the whole mountain shared in their worship, and the wild beasts; and there was nothing that was not stirred by their motion' (722–7).

In the sublime and simple poetry of the last sentence the peaceful beauty of Dionysiac worship reaches its climax. The shift to the fierce and cruel comes immediately and swiftly. It is precipitated by the crude violence of the narrator who, as the dancing Agave comes near him, springs out to catch her. '"But", she cried, "O, coursing hounds of mine, we are hunted by these men. Follow me, follow me, with your thyrsi as weapons in your hands"' (731–3).

The scene of blood and violence that follows, harshly as it clashes with the previous harmonies, does not however find the audience

[1] It is not surprising that the Messenger, after the event, disparages him, and I doubt if the feelings of Euripides are much committed either way. Dodds quotes *Or.* 902 sqq. for his dislike of the ἀγοραῖος ἀνήρ, but it will be observed that there the speaker is a violent partisan, himself a countryman (866) and client of the Pelopidae (869 sq.), whom the townsman attacks; the peasant proprietor, whom the speaker sees as the salt of the earth (920), proceeds to commend the matricide—and the conservatives (930) applauded.

entirely unprepared. If the ivy-crowns and milk and honey of the preparatory phase were reminiscent of the final stanza of the Entrance Song, not less so are the leaping and dancing of their incipient worship (148); and, associated with them there, woven into the context of Bacchic ritual, were the hunting, tearing and eating of the prey. Here peace and fury are, as it were, sorted out and separated; but a link between them is provided by the word 'beasts' (727). The animal world, with which the Bacchanals have already in the earlier phase asserted kinship by suckling does and wolf-cubs, now seems to join in their worship. But the life of animal nature is not one solely, or principally, of peace and beauty; animals have teeth and claws, and use them upon one another; they hunt and are hunted. So the Bacchanals must (and do) accept this further implication of their animal status. They, too, are hunted, as animals are hunted, and when they turn the tables upon their pursuers and become the hunters they merely exchange one animal role for another. The word that Agave uses to summon up her companions is significant: they are *hounds*, animals which possess a keen instinct for the chase, and which hunt in a pack.[1]

The activities of the enraged Bacchanals fall into two parts, sharply distinguished from one another; first, they fall upon the herds and mete out to them the vengeance that the herdsmen have escaped by flight; then, in the full swing of their ecstasy, they pass on down the mountain to the fertile plains below, where they attack the dwellings of men.

'So we took to flight and escaped tearing (σπαραγμόν) by the Bacchanals, while they attacked with unweaponed hands the cattle at pasture on the grass. And you might have seen one drag apart[2] in her hands a bellowing heifer with swollen udders; others tore and rent full-grown cows. You might have seen ribs or cloven feet cast in wild confusion, and blood-stained fragments hung dripping upon the pines. Bulls, proud creatures hitherto with wrath mounting in their horns, stumbled to earth, dragged down by multitudinous maiden hands; and their covering of flesh was torn apart quicker than you could have closed your royal eyes' (734–47).

[1] For κύνες cf. 338, 977. The fact that hounds are employed and set on by a huntsman (here Dionysus) may also advance the parallel. The relationship of Dionysiac religion to animal life is further discussed in connection with the next choral ode; see pp. 107 sq.

[2] 738: ἕλκουσαν...δίχα (Reiske).

Such is the immediate impact of the narrative that reflection comes lamely upon the trail of excitement. But when it comes, it reveals a fascinating set of relations within the basic pattern of 'peace into fury'. This fury is precipitated by the action of men; it is not, however, upon the human intruders that the Bacchanals wreak their vengeance, but upon the harmless cattle. Thus the same women who a short time before were suckling animals are now tearing animals limb from limb.[1] In this emotional inconsistency lies something typical of the Bacchic mind, which, abjuring conscious intellectual control, is absorbed by the emotion and swayed by the impulse of the moment. Now in human beings, possessed of powers of reason and reflection, this is (ideally speaking) an inconsistency and a paradox.[2] It is not so in animals, whose relations to one another embrace peaceful companionship and internecine strife on equal terms. Thus, in so far as the Bacchanals accept animal status, there is nothing surprising about their action.

The fury is, in one aspect, an act of vengeance, in which they accept beasts as substitutes for men. But in one aspect only; for it is to be observed that in allowing their anger to be diverted from the men to the flocks they have simply passed to their familiar rite of tearing or *sparagmos*. The occasion is indeed abnormal, being an outrage upon their privacy; but their act is one which we know from the lips of Bacchanals to be a regular component of their ecstasies. The cruelty and the sheer physical ugliness involved is no mere product, then, of a coarse interference, but a result to which, if on a lesser scale, their uninterrupted rites might well have led. It is true that the beasts on which they now fall are not their normal prey of goat or fawn; they are domestic cattle, and, as such, standing in a close relationship to human civilisation, may act as suitable proxies for their human owners. But included among the victims are bulls; and, lest we should forget that the bull is a Dionysiac animal, they are expressly qualified as ὑβρισταί (violent, cruel, wanton, proud) and full of wrath. These mettlesome animals are pulled down and torn in pieces by the hands of young girls; the aesthetic contrast is vivid

[1] And, incidentally (742), befouling those pines that have been the object of lyrical emotions.

[2] Though less paradoxical in reality than in the ideal; nor need we go to the Dionysiac reactions of the fickle mob to find a parallel. The English country gentleman will tend an injured bird, not in order to ensure his future sport, but because he genuinely loves birds.

(ταῦροι, νεανίδων) and the operation an index of what Dionysus can effect in his worshippers. But besides the contrast there is a similarity, if pride, wrath and violence are also qualities of the Bacchanals.

Pentheus too is not forgotten. In this episode the Bacchanals take beasts for men; first they give their milk to wild creatures, instead of to their own babies, then they avenge the outrage of the herdsmen upon the herds, passing thereby to their customary rite of *sparagmos*. But, later, again interrupted, they will take man for beast, and, half aware, half unaware, of the substitution that has taken place, will make Pentheus the centre of a similar rite.[1] Thus, Pentheus is the unwitting auditor of an oblique prophecy of his own fate and, when he is addressed directly, the cruel irony is heightened. 'You might have seen', says the Messenger twice (737, 740). Indeed he will see something only too similar, while he still can see. For the words with which this section of the story closes are sinister, they suggest the closing of his eyes in death.[2]

This direct reference to Pentheus, and to Pentheus as king, serves, perhaps, as a transition to the second half of the narrative. For, though his future fate is grimly connected with the Bacchanals' treatment of the beasts, he is at present the ruler of a civilised community with which they are at odds. What follows will show them in their dealings, not with beasts, but with civilised man.

'They went on, like birds upborne by their own speed, over the plains stretched below, which, by the waters of Asopus, yield rich corn-crops to the Thebans, and upon Hysiae and Erythrae, settlements in the lower foothills of Cithaeron, they fell like enemies and scattered everything in wild confusion' (748–54). Dionysus has brought his religion to the cities of Greece; and from the first it has been a question how such a religion could possibly comport with an ordered human society. Teiresias believed that it could be made possible, but clearly he reckoned upon the power of tradition to modify and control it; when it had left the hands of him and his like it would be an orderly and discreet thing. In the ode that followed

[1] On the sacramental aspect of *sparagmos* and the relationship between Pentheus and Dionysus, see p. 156 n. 1.

[2] 'Quicker than you could have closed your royal eyes' (747). For the Herdsman this is merely the tactful embellishment of a proverbial expression (Thomson, *Oresteia*, II, p. 6, on *Ag.* 27). Note also the irony of 712, 760, 764.

the Teiresias scene the Bacchanals gave a rendering of their religion that was, or appeared to be, consistent with the ideals of Hellas. But this song did not tell the whole truth; and it was left for the present speech to disclose the quality of the religion in its full concreteness and to clarify its relation to normal human society. It is itself a social phenomenon. Its participants operate in groups, and the conduct of these groups is, as the Messenger says, a marvel of orderliness. They are homogeneous groups, for they are based on a community of thought, emotion and aim. And their aims are simple, straightforward, limited; limited by the absorption in the present which they share with the animals whose packs they emulate. But civilised life must take thought of the past and of the future, which mean nothing to Bacchanals; and it must to some extent subordinate the present to the future. It involves labour which is often irksome, and stable affections that are often bonds. Thus the abandonment by the Bacchanals of their own young children and the lavishing of their milk upon wild creatures is a revolt from the constraints of civilised life, no less than the leaving of their looms and shuttles. Now, in the sweep of their ecstasy, they fall upon the villages 'like enemies' (752); for in truth they are enemies of organised human society. Their place is the mountain and their food comes to them without effort; the plains below where men have laboured to subordinate nature, to grow corn (750) and live in ordered settlements (752), are alien to them. In order to build up such settlements and to develop agriculture men have subordinated the pursuit of instant pleasure by day and night, have taken thought and have harnessed ambition; and those who do such things Dionysus hates, and the Bacchanals with him.

Therefore they set upon the villages and wreck them, scattering and turning everything 'upside down'.[1] 'They snatched children from their homes. All that they put upon their shoulders stayed there without ties and never fell to the dark earth, neither bronze nor iron; they carried fire upon their hair, and it did not burn them. The men, in anger at the raid of the Bacchanals, ran to arms. Whereupon was this strange sight to be seen, my king. Their pointed spears drew no blood, but these, shooting their thyrsi from their hands, dealt wounds

[1] ἄνω τε καὶ κάτω (753), deliberately repeated after 741. An equivalent expression has already been used of the desecration of Teiresias's seat of augury (349) and of the palace-earthquake (602). On the relation between these passages see p. 55.

and turned them to flight—yes, women routed men—not without some god's aid.[1] Then back they went to the place whence they had started out, to the very springs the god had sent up for them; and they washed off the blood, and snakes wiped clean with their tongues the drops upon their cheeks' (754–68).

The episode ends as rapidly as it began, with a sudden and complete change of mood, with a return to the magic fountains and the snakes.[2] We may suppose that the Maenads lost all memory of the conflict as easily as they wiped away its bloody traces.

But the Messenger cannot let the matter rest here; he has given the evidence, he must draw his own conclusion from it. 'This god then, master, whoever he may be, receive into this city; for he is great' (769 sq.). Son of Semele, son of Zeus (as they say), or whoever he may be, accept him, for he has proved his power. But the phrase may have a further implication: 'of whatever sort he be', wild, destructive, anti-social, accept him and receive him into the city. Is it possible? Or has the Messenger himself brought the proof of its impossibility?

Dionysus is a great and powerful god; that he has seen, and upon that bases his conclusion. But not on that alone. 'For he is great', the man continues, 'in many ways, but this above all they say of him, as I hear tell, that he has given to mortals the vine which puts an end to grief. And if there is no wine there is no love nor any other pleasant thing left among men' (770–4). In content and in style this is bathos. The speech has taken us twice to a sublime level. Both the peace and the fury of the Bacchanals were sublime and in the communication of them the poetry transcended its vehicle. But this is a level upon which the Herdsman cannot live. We have seen with his eyes, now we must think with his mind; and the poet has deliberately made his thoughts the last impression of this episode which we receive.

Not, as Verrall thought, in order that the Herdsman's partiality should prejudice him as a witness. The point resides rather in the character of the bathos itself. The narrative has dealt with women dedicated to ecstasy, cut off from, and hostile to, any normal human society. But they and their fellows claim that the religion of Dionysus is universal and demands universal obedience; and the Bacchanals of the Chorus have given it a kind of theoretical basis, resting it upon

[1] A man's comment!

[2] On the licking snakes see p. 92 n. 1. The point of the suspected αὐτάς (766) may be to emphasise their return to the peaceful phase.

the abnegation of intellect and ambition and the acceptance of popular standards. What 'the mass of common men' accepts and practises, that do they accept. Here, in the Herdsman, is a representative of the common man, and this is what the religion of Dionysus means to him. He may admire and wonder at the apparent chastity and sobriety of the Bacchanals, but his very wonder shows the nature of his expectations and the crudity of his mind. Now the chastity or unchastity, sobriety or insobriety, of the Bacchanals Euripides purposely subordinates to wider issues. Yet now we are reminded that to a common man Dionysus meant an escape through wine (the most obvious of Dionysiac drugs) into the enjoyment of facile pleasures. Thus the Herdsman's final comment is at once a cruder reaffirmation of the doctrine of Teiresias and the second choral ode, and a counterpoise to the sublimity and high poetry of his own narrative.[1]

The anti-climax here is closely comparable to that which followed the Entrance Song. The latter ended upon a note of ecstatic excitement struck by great lyric poetry and was immediately followed by a drop to the level of Cadmus and Teiresias in a scene of prosaic satire. In each case a touchstone of common life is applied to lyrical exaltation. In the present instance, indeed, the sublimities are not merely followed, but introduced (and interrupted) by the coarsely normal.[2] They are introduced by Pentheus and his suspicions; and when the Herdsman reverts at the end to his proper person, it is a reversion to Pentheus's own level of morality and sensibility. The speech has been addressed to Pentheus: but what can he have made of it? Dionysus bade him take it to heart: but what difference will a passage that contains so much insight into Dionysiac religion have made to the persecuting king? But perhaps the dice were loaded against Pentheus by the Herdsman's final comment.

[1] With 772 compare 280 sq., 381; and with 773 sq. compare 283, a similarly sweeping statement.

[2] Introduced by 674 sqq. (see p. 90); interrupted by 714–23.

CHAPTER VIII

THE HUNT

The first Messenger speech describes the behaviour of Bacchanals toward their interrupters: they fall upon animals and rend them in pieces; they attack men and, women though they are, rout them. These are the two stages of their fury; and the fate of Pentheus, as described in the second Messenger speech, will combine aspects of them both—like an animal he will be torn asunder, and, a man, he will be vanquished by women. But first he must be delivered helpless into their hands. For, though the kill is reserved for the Bacchanals, it is Dionysus who hunts Pentheus down.

The Herdsman's narrative may be to the audience premonitory of Pentheus's end, but Pentheus takes no such warning from it. He greets it with an outburst of furious anger. Everything for the moment is lost in the insult put upon his race, his royalty, and upon his sex. 'Now close at hand kindles like fire the outrage of the Bacchanals, a great reproach in the eyes of Greece.[1] This is no time to hesitate. Go to the Electran gate. Bid all the shieldbearers and them that ride swift-footed horses muster, and all who poise targes and twang the strings of bows, for we will take the field against the Bacchanals. For this is really beyond bearing, if at the hands of women we must suffer what we do suffer' (778–86).

The response of Pentheus to the news he has heard is to call out his troops, and it is characteristic. To mobilise the entire armed forces of Thebes against unarmed women is, on a realistic consideration, a means out of all proportion to the end desired, and the excess of it is characteristic of Pentheus. But the recent narrative closed with a picture of men running to arms and yet unable to withstand the superior force of the Bacchanals. As actual fact, the rout of a few villagers after such a fashion is not impossible; as symbol, it is profound truth. For if the palace-miracle was designed to show the futility of bonds in dealing with Dionysus and his votaries, the scene upon the mountain shows the equal futility of direct violence. Yet Pentheus learns from neither incident. To the former he responds by locking the gates (653), to the latter by announcing an armed expedition.

[1] On the aptness of the metaphor see p. 85.

It is not, however, excess of anger alone that prompts this parade of force. The highly 'poetic' phrases of the edict[1] are no mere enigma of Euripidean diction. They are there to serve a purpose beyond that of a mobilisation order. They are there to bolster up the confidence of Pentheus, who is not merely angry, but frightened and insecure; and this emotional recital of the forces under his command is used by Pentheus, king and general, as a kind of incantation.[2] Thus not only does he meet force with force, but counters one intoxicating emotion with another; for an army on the march, an army with banners, is a Dionysiac drug, and not least for the general who commands it.

But Dionysus has other plans. The scene which follows has already been reviewed in an earlier chapter,[3] where we saw how the god, maintaining the calm, the subtlety and the smile of previous scenes, brings the king gradually under his domination. Now we must trace the stages by which the latter succumbs to the onslaught of a superior will. 'You pay no attention to my words', says Dionysus; and the remark is both true and untrue. It is true that Pentheus learns neither from experience nor from advice; but he may be brought to obedience by subtler methods. The advice that Dionysus now gives, which is to be quiet and abandon the use of force against the god (789 sq.), is good advice, which he knows will be rejected; but he also knows that he can direct the restless activity of Pentheus into other channels. Rejected the advice is, with an angry shout and a threat.[4] Dionysus returns with an exhortation which is hardly conciliatory: 'I should sacrifice to him rather than kick in wrath against the goad; for you are mortal, he is a god' (794 sq.). 'Sacrifice I will', rejoins Pentheus, 'making lavish slaughter of women, as indeed I am entitled,[5] in the glens of Cithaeron' (796 sq.). So terrible a thing does he propose, so terrible is it to

[1] All the more striking for the humble colloquialism which follows them. On οὐ γὰρ ἀλλά (785) see Dodds *ad loc.* and Denniston, *The Greek Particles*, p. 31.

[2] Comparable to the lyrical restoratives of the shaken Bacchanals (see p. 60 and p. 78).

[3] See pp. 21 sq.

[4] The threat ('or I will put you in prison again') is all but comic.

[5] 796: ἄξιος (Wilamowitz). I take this as referring not to the god, but to Pentheus: i.e. ἄξιός εἰμι θῦσαι. Like φόνον θῆλυν, where the adjective may be objective (as Pentheus intends) or subjective, ἄξιος is ambiguous (ἄξιός εἰμι φονευθῆναι). On the further development of this theme see pp. 143 sq.

claim justification for it, that we feel his anger to be already trembling upon the verge of insanity. His experiences in the stables, the Herdsman's narrative, the dialectical pinpricks of the Stranger, have not after all failed of their cumulative effect. In answer Dionysus prophesies flight and ignominy for the vaunted army. 'There is no dealing with this Stranger with whom I am at grips, for neither in bonds nor out of them will he keep silence.'[1] Pentheus is exasperated; but his anger has nevertheless been diverted from the Stranger to the Bacchanals, and he cannot but listen. 'Come, sir, it is still possible to arrange the matter happily.' 'How? By serving my own slaves?' 'I will bring the women here without use of arms.' It is a plot, says Pentheus; but he still listens. 'A plot? If I am willing to *save* you by my arts?'[2] It is a plot, Pentheus repeats; and orders his armour.

The struggle has reached a crisis. For Pentheus, who feels the force against him (and within him), feels also, however dimly, that he must escape while escape is still possible, while the power to resist remains. It is a crisis, and demands from Dionysus new weapons. At this point our text gives to him the exclamation ἆ. It is indeed hard to fix the significance of a single vowel, but of the several connotations which this exclamation may bear in Greek drama, that of protest seems most appropriate here. 'Ah!', says Dionysus, perhaps with an intense stare and a grasping of Pentheus's hands, as he begins to exert some kind of psychic power over his victim.[3] At all events, the exclamation marks a change in their relationship and the beginning of a process, however we may describe it, which will end in the complete domination of the will of Pentheus.

For to argue (with Verrall) that Pentheus retains entire control of himself till the end of the scene is to neglect half the indications of the ensuing dialogue. The first question and answer are conclusive. A question is shot at Pentheus: 'Would you like to see them as they

[1] An inadequate translation of οὔτε πάσχων οὔτε δρῶν (801). Superficially δρῶν is a weightless antithesis to πάσχων, but the word may be an unconscious admission that the initiative is passing to the Stranger.

[2] On the sincerity of Dionysus's offer see p. 21. As I understand it, τέχναις (806) rankles—and was intended to rankle—after δόλιον... μηχανᾷ. Note that Pentheus is now pure tyrant and speaks of his subjects as slaves (803).

[3] See Dodds *ad loc.* and the stage direction in Lucas's translation ('suddenly changing his tone, and from this moment dominating his victim').

sit together on the mountains?' An answer comes back pat; and it is the true answer. 'Indeed I would, and would give a countless weight of gold for it!' This is, as Professor Dodds remarks, the answer of a maniac. 'What?' replies Dionysus, 'have you fallen into great love of it?'[1] For so sure of himself is he that he can play with Pentheus, touching the dangerous word 'love' and feigning a shocked surprise. The dominating will relaxes, inhibition returns, and Pentheus tries to correct his slip. 'I should of course be sorry to see them drunk.'[2] Thus Pentheus 'rationalises', as a psychologist might put it, his unconscious desire as a painful duty. 'Yet you would gladly see a sight that would be bitter to you?' The ironic comment is lost on Pentheus, for his mind is now filled with a picture—the picture of himself spying upon the Bacchanals. 'Be sure I should—sitting noiselessly beneath the pines.' Herdsman or no herdsman, he has no doubt of what he will then see.

Now it is a question of ways and means; and the Stranger is no longer an enemy, but a wise counsellor. 'Even if you go in secret, they will track you down.' We can imagine how Pentheus would have answered this even a few moments ago. But his vivid imagination and the persuasive Stranger (ultimately are they not the same force?) have control of him; and his own scheme of secrecy has lost him the right to indignation. 'Then I'll go openly: that was well said.'

A rapid question and answer reveal the king's impatience to be gone (819 sq.);[3] and Dionysus can safely reveal his plan. 'Then put on a dress of linen.' 'What? Am I to rank as woman instead of man?' 'Lest they kill you, if you are seen there as a man.' 'That is another good suggestion; how wise (σοφός) you have been all along!' (821–4).[4] And this is said in all sincerity by the man who had jeered sarcastically at the Stranger's cleverness. What reply, we may again ask, would a Pentheus fully himself have made to such a suggestion? He would have seen threats and insults, where this Pentheus sees a salutary caution; he would have raged, where this Pentheus mildly expostulates. When the Stranger ascribes his wisdom to Dionysus (825), Pentheus lets it pass and only asks for details.

[1] 813: τί δ'; εἰς ἔρωτα (Lucas). [2] 814: λυπρῶς μέν (Bruhn).

[3] Possibly in 820 the true text is τοῦ χρόνου δ' οὔ σοι φθονῶ—a hasty attempt to deny the impatience the first half of the line betrays.

[4] Contrast 655.

'I will take you into the palace and dress you.' 'In what dress? In *woman's* dress? I am ashamed.' The blend of emotions is nice: Pentheus jibs again—yet is clearly fascinated by the proposal. 'You no longer desire the spectacle of the Maenads', says Dionysus. When it is so put, the attraction is irresistible. Pentheus, in his indecision and to gain time, puts again a question to which he already knows the answer: '*What* dress do you speak of putting on me?' Dionysus replies with the full details—a flowing wig, long robes to the feet, a head-dress, a thyrsus and a fawnskin. Pentheus attends with interest, only to have another moment of revulsion: 'I could not put on woman's dress.' 'But you will cause bloodshed, if you join battle with the Bacchanals.' 'You are right; first I must go and reconnoitre.' Half aware that his project comports ill with the king and general of Thebes, he is enabled by Dionysus's mention of a battle once more to 'rationalise' his desire, which now becomes a military task; Paul Pry becomes a commander engaged in personal reconnaissance.[1] 'That is certainly wiser', says the god ambiguously, 'than to hunt evil with evil' (839).[2]

Pentheus, despite his earlier revulsion, is on the point of accepting the plan. But, not yet entirely blind to the ridiculous, he asks how he may pass through the city without being seen by his subjects. Dionysus promises (and we soon know that it is a false promise) to lead him secretly by deserted ways. 'Anything', says Pentheus to himself, 'is better than for the Bacchanals to mock me'—anything, even woman's dress and the risk of being seen in it. Then, to the Stranger: 'We will go into the palace and...I will deliberate upon my decision' (843). Here the anacoluthic construction of the Greek, a dual participle followed by a singular verb, reveals the divided mind of Pentheus. The dual implies acceptance of the plan of Dionysus; second thoughts reserve (with a touch of desperation?) the decision for Pentheus himself. Dionysus affects indifference; and indeed he is prepared to meet any eventuality (844). 'I will go in', says Pentheus; 'either I will march out under arms or I will take your counsel'; and with these words he enters the palace. The decision is not yet made, his will is still free; and, though we may suspect that this is a last and futile effort to retain that freedom, the

[1] κατασκοπήν (838): cf. 916 (κατάσκοπος). The words have clear military associations (*v.* L.S. *s.vv.*).

[2] A variation on the proverbial κακῷ κακὸν ἰᾶσθαι, but with a suggestive change of metaphor. See also p. 112 n. 1.

suspense that the balanced propositions indicate is dramatically effective.

Dionysus remains behind, and delivers a speech which has already been considered in another context.[1] In it the mythological aspect predominates, as the god reveals his fiendish plan to take Pentheus in mockery through the streets of Thebes to be slain at his own mother's hands. This horror, now first disclosed, resolves the enigma of the bearing and character of the god. On Pentheus no fresh light is thrown. 'Dionysus', cries the Stranger, 'now is it for thee to act—for thou art not far away. Let us take vengeance upon him. And first drive him out of his wits and put in him an inconstant frenzy; for never in his senses will he consent to put on woman's dress, but with wits distraught he will put it on' (849–53). The author of madness implies that Pentheus is still sane, still in command of his will, and that without the intervention of the god his decision will be against the god's plan. But the god is dramatising himself and the situation. Dionysus has been close at hand, Dionysus has been acting upon Pentheus, since king and god first met upon the stage; and, whatever the latter may here imply, Pentheus, the arrogant blusterer of the earlier scenes,[2] is already half-way to insanity. But to put the whole process of dissolution upon the stage would have been tedious and perhaps unconvincing, whereas the sudden irruption of a helpless giggling Pentheus dressed as a Bacchanal is a striking, if horrible, dramatic effect. Therefore the actors retire, and the Chorus sings an ode, which must now be examined in detail, for its relevance to the scenes that precede and follow is both intimate and subtle. 'He shall learn', says the god in his closing words, 'that Dionysus, son of Zeus, is very god most terrible, yet most kindly to mortals.' Most terrible, most kindly: on this theme the Chorus of Bacchanals will play a significant variation.[3]

As in the second ode, the foreground is occupied with simple lyrical emotions or the statements of faith. The Bacchanals express their sense of relief in the beautiful simile of the escaped fawn; they turn swiftly to the theme of vengeance; they repeat their creed; they

[1] See p. 22.

[2] Cf. 856. Note that he has already shown himself ἐλαφρός (851) by his rapid changes of plan (816, 818, 824).

[3] The postponement of ἀνθρώποισι seems to emphasise the second part of the antithesis, in preparation for the choral ode.

return to vengeance; they sing once more of escape and of the happiness which their creed brings them. Full of a simple and symmetrical lyricism, it seems, despite superficial points of contact, to take us far from the gruesome drama that it interrupts. In the background, however, lies a complex structure of ideas, a complex set of aesthetic relations, binding it intimately to the development of that drama.

Strophe. Their last song had breathed a keen sense of personal danger; the emotion with which this opens is one of personal relief, for they now have good hope that Dionysus will win and the future of their Bacchic worship be assured. 'Shall I then yet set down my white foot in ecstasy in the night-long dances, flinging back my head in the clear dewy air? Like a fawn that plays amid the green joys of a meadow—when she has escaped the terrifying hunt, away from her watchers and over the woven nets, while the huntsman shouts and urges on his coursing hounds. With toil of swift running, storm-swift, she leaps along the water-meadow, rejoicing in places empty of men and in the branches of the leafy, shady wood' (862–76).

It is appropriate that the Bacchanal in her liberation from a great peril should compare herself to a woodland creature escaped from the huntsman. 'We are hunted', cried Agave, when the herdsmen broke ambush; and she was calling to women who had proved their kinship with animals by suckling young roes. This stanza is a vignette of animal life. It will be observed that it is designed in three parts, of which the last repeats the first. At the beginning and at the end we have the liberated fawn playing in meadowland and woodland; the core of the stanza is the picture of that same fawn frightened and hemmed in by a pack of hounds. The three divisions of the stanza represent three phases of emotion; and each has its characteristic word. That of the first is 'joys'; the transition to the second is marked by the stressed discord of 'terrifying'; the final phase brings back a word of joy.[1] Joy and terror in alternation make up the life

[1] ἡδοναῖς (867); φοβεράν (868); ἡδομένα (874). With the first and last, compare 66, 135, 165 (the keynote of the Entrance Song).

873–4: the interpretation is uncertain. In the translation above Hermann's ἀελλάς is adopted. μόχθοις then belongs to the third phase, recalling the πόνος ἡδύς of the Bacchanals (66), but suggesting also the fearful agony of pursuit which the fawn has just undergone and so acting as an aesthetic link with the second phase. Dodds, accepting the traditional

of the fawn, and she passes easily and completely from one to the other, for she lives in the present. So to live is the creed also of the Bacchanals, but their relationship to the fawn and to the animal world is, as we shall see, complex.

To the first stanza is appended a kind of Refrain or Coda (*ephymnion*), which is repeated after the *antistrophe*. 'What is wisdom? Or what gift from the gods is fairer in the sight of men than to hold the hand of mastery over the head of enemies? That which is fair is ever dear' (877–81).[1] And in the following stanza their subject (though they do not mention him) is the sin and punishment of Pentheus. Thus the connection of the Refrain with what follows is clear enough: but is not the transition from the joy of the liberated fawn to the glorification of vengeance inexplicably abrupt?

Now the hunted fawn has no thought of vengeance or power to secure it. It is different with the Bacchanals, of whom she is the temporary symbol; and, when they compare themselves to fawns, it is well to remember that their relationship to such animals is somewhat ambiguous. They suckle their young, they wear their skins, they *are* fawns: yet, before they can put on these skins to wear, they have killed the living creature.[2] If the Bacchanal is an animal, she is a hunting, as well as a hunted, animal. 'We are hunted', cried Agave; but she cried it (paradoxically) to her 'coursing hounds', who then turned upon their pursuers. Can the reference to hounds in the simile of the fawn fail to stir this memory? In the figure of the huntsman hallooing on his hounds can we not perhaps recognise the god himself? For the scene upon Cithaeron is a microcosm of the drama as a whole; and there also the twofold aspect of the hunt is continually before us. Pentheus hunted the Theban Bacchanals (228), as his soldiers hunted the Stranger (434). But the tables are now turned; Pentheus is the prey, Dionysus and the Bacchanals are

text, takes μόχθοις of the painful effort of the first dash for freedom, ὠκυδρόμοις ἀέλλαις of the subsequent spurts 'which pass from painfulness to pleasure as she outpaces the hunt'. This interpretation is subtle and may well be right.

[1] See Dodds *ad loc.* for criticisms of various divergent interpretations of these lines.

[2] Photius, *s.v.* νεβρίζειν· ἢ νεβροῦ δέρμα φορεῖν ἢ διασπᾶν νεβρούς (though doubtless σπαραγμός did not leave a very serviceable skin). Compare their equally ambiguous relationship to snakes: e.g. Galen, *de antidot.* 1, 6, xiv, 45K: οἱ τῷ Διονύσῳ βακχεύοντες εἰώθασι διασπᾶν τὰς ἐχίδνας.

the hunters.[1] Thus even in the picture of the hunted fawn is implicit, by contrast, the vengeance to which they immediately turn.

This vengeance they claim to be fair or honourable and, by implication, wise. As to its wisdom, something has been said in an earlier chapter.[2] For wisdom has already been a theme of the Bacchanal singers in the second choral ode, where they rejected the conventional associations of the term, placing their own wisdom in quietude, in the avoidance of excess and the pursuit of immediate pleasures. The connection between these two odes is close, and they both employ (as we shall see) the same general ideas, so that it is not surprising that the theme of wisdom recurs in the present context. Not only, however, are the circumstances entirely different (then they were bidding for support in a hostile environment, now they feel that they themselves have 'the upper hand'), but the intervening scenes have cast further light upon the psychology and behaviour of Bacchanals. Their wisdom is to live for the day, as the fawn does; and the preceding stanza has shown how that involves her in strife and terror as well as in joy. The Bacchanals, like the fawn, are hunted, but need not be, like her, defenceless. The Theban Bacchanals upon the mountain had retaliated with crude violence. Such was their momentary impulse, to gratify which was as much a part of the 'wisdom' of Bacchanals as to seek the quieter pleasures of the second choral ode. And now, by the very act of singing this Refrain, the Bacchanals of the Chorus identify themselves in retrospect with the attack upon the herds and villages, and in prospect (as they will do with ever-increasing passion) with the slaughter of Pentheus.

Further, the vengeance is καλόν: it is an honourable thing and one to thank the gods for. Such at least is the common judgement of men, the accepted standard of morality.[3] It was not the standard of Euripides (or of Socrates); nor, for that matter, will the Messenger who brings the news of Pentheus's death find it καλόν that the Bacchanals should exult over the fate of their enemy (1040). For it is less shocking that vengeance in general should thus be glorified than that this glorification should immediately follow the disclosure of the nature of this particular vengeance. We are thus prepared for

[1] 817, 848 (cf. 839); 977 (Λύσσας κύνες); 1146 (τὸν ξυγκύναγον).

[2] See p. 69.

[3] ἐν βροτοῖς (878): see Dodds. The word καλός is constantly used in the plays of Euripides of the standards of honour and fair dealing which are accepted by the characters, and often with a controversial note.

the way in which the Chorus greet that news and receive Agave. Then the word καλός will be taken up and by constant repetition be made a savage commentary not only upon the god who has brought about this deed, but upon the devotees who can so welcome it.

For 'that which is fair is ever dear'. The closing line of the Refrain is a proverbial expression. According to legend, a version of it was sung by the Muses and the Graces at the wedding of Cadmus, and it is indeed ironical that the Chorus should now use it to justify the murder of Cadmus's grandson. What precisely the Muses and the Graces meant on that famous occasion we cannot be sure, but its meaning here is clear enough: to this privilege of vengeance men cling and, in the view of the Chorus, rightly so. What Euripides has done, therefore, in this Refrain is to put into the mouths of the Bacchanals an equation of the wise, the fair and the dear, and of all these qualities with the desire and act of vengeance.[1] These equations are based on proverbs; they are traditional wisdom; they are the popular standard of the common man, which the Bacchanals accept. The ground is now prepared for the re-statement of their creed in the following stanza.[2]

Antistrophe. This stanza treats of divine punishment and of the sin that calls it down. Pentheus is in the minds of the singers, but the terms employed are as vague and general as in the second ode. 'Slow to move is the divine might, yet is it sure; and it chastises those mortals who hold in honour obstinate folly and, in the madness of their thoughts, will not glorify the gods. In their subtlety they cover up the unhastening stride of time, as they hunt down the impious man' (882–90).

The second stanza of the second ode is at once recalled.[3] 'Far off though they dwell in the ether the heavenly ones look upon the

[1] Moreover, revenge is φίλον to them, a source of satisfaction no less than the innocent pleasures of the *strophe* (ἡδοναῖς, ἡδομένα of the fawn). Compare also φιλεῖ (419) in the second choral ode. Even the oblique reference to the Muses and the Graces may serve as a link with the earlier ode, over which they were presiding deities.

[2] An illuminating parallel is provided by the attitude of Alcmene in the *Heracleidae*: 881 (παρ' ἡμῖν μὲν γὰρ οὐ σοφὸν τόδε, | ἐχθροὺς λαβόντα μὴ ἀποτείσασθαι δίκην); 963 (εἴργει δὲ δὴ τίς τόνδε μὴ θνῄσκειν νόμος;); 965 (ἐχθροὺς τοιούσδ' οὐ καλὸν κτανεῖν;). To her the murder of Eurystheus is wise, honourable and in accordance with νόμος (*v. infra*).

[3] See pp. 61 sqq.

affairs of mortals.' They look, and they have power to punish, even if the punishment is slow in coming. Between the two passages there are these differences, that now the singers see their faith in process of justification, and that now the audience know the means that the divine vengeance is to employ.[1] The sin to be punished is described in familiar terms which include the paradoxical accusation of insanity by Maenads. The word ἀγνωμοσύναν is particularly appropriate to the sinner they have in mind, for among its meanings is that hardness of heart, that lack of sensibility which we have seen to characterise Pentheus. In their thoughts, however, the idea of arrogant folly, of obstinate pride is foremost—'the unbridled mouth and lawless folly' of the 'man of excess'.[2] The second half of the stanza is in effect a commentary upon the word.

'For it is never right to think or to practise what outsteps the laws (τῶν νόμων). It costs but little to believe that it is with the divine—whatsoever the divine may be—that power lies, and that what has been accepted (νόμιμον) through long ages is eternal and grounded in nature' (890–6).[3] The obscure generalities of this passage demand a commentary; and a commentary is in part provided by the earlier ode, where the same doctrines are given a simpler and less concentrated expression. There men were enjoined to shun 'more than mortal thoughts' and 'the pursuit of great ends'; to accept, as the Bacchanals accept, 'whatever the mass of ordinary men believes and practises'.[4] The lines now under discussion are in the main a re-statement of that teaching, but a re-statement after an interval, during which we have learnt more than we knew then about the nature and behaviour of Bacchanals. Between the two choruses lies, in particular, the Herdsman's speech with its account of the infuriate vengeance of the Theban women. Both the tone and the content of the earlier ode suggested that the rejection of 'great things' was merely the rejection of the vain arrogance of a Pentheus, and that the acceptance of a

[1] The key-metaphor (890), embedded in the stanza, links the abstract divine justice with its agencies.

[2] The close parallel with 386–401 seems to establish the meaning of ἀγνωμοσύνη as 'folly' rather than 'ruthlessness'. It corresponds to ἀφροσύνη (γνώμη = φρένες), just as σὺν μαινομένᾳ δόξᾳ (887) corresponds to μαινομένων (399). See also n. 4.

[3] Accepting Dodds's interpretation of this sentence.

[4] 396 sqq., 430 sqq. ἐνόμισε χρῆταί τε (431) corresponds to γιγνώσκειν καὶ μελετᾶν (892), but the notion of ἐνόμισε also recurs in νόμων, νόμιμον (891, 895): *v. infra.*

humble code of belief and conduct was merely the acceptance of a quiet life of simple pleasures, together with the worship of the god who provided them. Now we know (what we could even then suspect) that the renunciation of rational control is as likely to lead to violence as to peace; and we have just learnt from the Bacchanals of the Chorus that among the popular standards they accept is that which justifies a cruel revenge. The god who demands and facilitates this type of conduct is not merely the giver of the vine, the inspirer of love and of song: self-forgetfulness in a passionate communal hatred is equally among his drugs. This god the singers here acknowledge in a phrase which the poet has chosen carefully. 'The divine, whatsoever the divine may in the event (ἄρα) be, has power.' But in what sense are we to take 'the divine (τὸ δαιμόνιον)'? Of whatever is really sovereign in the universe?[1] Or of the daemonic Dionysus and his manifestations? The force, the dangerous force, of the latter is beyond question; but to assume, as they assume, that this force must be acknowledged as sovereign and obeyed uncritically is to beg the question. So to acknowledge and obey is indeed the easiest course; but, if easy, it may be also (in their own word) 'cheap' (κούφα δαπάνα). The effort of thought and criticism is eliminated; the individual transcends his own weakness in the acceptance of a tradition, which at the same time enables him to gratify his simplest and strongest impulses. For is the tradition ultimately anything but the codification of these impulses?

Νόμος—'practice, custom, convention, tradition, law' (it fluctuates among these senses)—is one of the important words of the play. At first the references are vague, and a little puzzling. The Chorus sing the hymns 'that have been ever customary' (71); they brand Pentheus as 'lawless' (387), after Cadmus has urged him not to step 'outside the laws' (331). Similarly, the prophet Teiresias, in his politic defence of the new religion, appealed to 'the traditions of our fathers, coeval with time', which are impregnable against reason and cleverness (201 sqq.). But Teiresias was in fact a clever man and something of a rationalist; and, if he was also a traditionalist, he was so with a difference. Yet if, in the case of Teiresias, the reference to tradition is vitiated as a serious defence of religion by his rationalism (and indeed by the whole satirical treatment of his character), in the case of the Chorus it is vitiated by the context of revenge. What then

[1] 'The indeterminate formulation is an expression of religious humility in face of the unknowable' (Dodds, p. 179).

does νόμος mean to them? What are the laws and customs that Pentheus, in opposing a new and revolutionary religion, has defied?

But this novelty Euripides is always willing to forget. For the truth is that the religion of Dionysus never was new; and the laws which its adherents accept and whose transgression they hate and punish are those laws of impulsive, irrational conduct that nature has laid down for them. This is now made clear for the first time, when, following and amplifying the reference to divinity, they assert that 'what has been accepted (νόμιμον) through long ages is eternal and grounded in nature' (φύσει). The phrase is full of interest in several ways. It seems to assume, if it does not expressly state, that long custom must remain an abiding law;[1] and so it makes of the accepted convention that same bar to progress or to elevation that has been observed to follow from the levelling doctrine of the earlier ode: what was there called 'more than mortal thoughts' is here stigmatised as 'beyond the laws'. Now, however, a notion fresh to the play is introduced in support of that assumption—the notion of nature, or natural growth.

The antithesis between nature (φύσις) and law or convention (νόμος) pervades the thought of the sophistic period; and it was an antithesis which had in some way or other to be resolved. Callicles, for instance, in Plato's *Gorgias* resolved it by rejecting conventional moral standards and conventional religion and elevating 'nature' into a 'law'—the νόμος τῆς φύσεως. Plato himself, and Aristotle after him, solved the problem on different lines: according to them the antithesis disappears when the terms are properly understood, for law or custom rests upon nature.[2] Clearly, the effect of any resolution of this antinomy depends upon the sense given to 'nature'. For Plato the nature of man included the potentiality of virtue and social life, and reason was an element, and should be the sovereign element, in human 'nature'. Callicles had in mind the powers of the exceptional individual, directed by ruthless intelligence. To the Bacchanals

[1] Dionysus, admittedly, confuses the issue by referring (484) to the relativity of νόμοι. It was in fact the discovery of diverse *mœurs* in Greek and barbarian communities which, as much as anything, led to the moral relativity of the sophistic period. But then Dionysus is something of a sophist. Nor is this the only occasion on which the intellectual god blows the gaff upon his votaries. σοφώτερον γοῦν, he says (839), ἢ κακοῖς θηρᾶν κακά—a wise reflection which runs as counter to their practice as to that of Pentheus.

[2] See Dodds on 895 sq.

'nature' can, in the context of the play and of the ode, mean only the natural tendency to act upon irrational impulse in the herd. If Callicles rejects conventional religion as an obstacle, the Bacchanals accept Dionysiac religion as an aid. If Plato recognises the social element in human nature, so do the Bacchanals, but their society is the *thiasos*, Plato's the city-state. It is the laws which the herd accepts and dictates which the Bacchanals recognise as eternal and as having an unchallengeable basis in nature; and for them, unlike Plato, man is most himself when he is most like the animals, living for the day, catching the pleasures of the day, hunting and being hunted. In this life lies 'wisdom'; and so the Refrain is repeated, and the *antistrophe* is remorselessly enclosed in a context of violence. Nothing could then be clearer than the relevance of repeating the Bacchanals' democratic creed at this point. Wisdom in the second choral ode and wisdom here have the same roots in the unthinking acceptance of popular, of natural standards; but what seemed in the earlier passage to issue solely in peace and quietness is now seen to lead equally to violence and cruelty. 'What is wisdom? Or what gift from the gods is fairer in the sight of men than to hold the hand of mastery over the head of enemies? That which is fair is ever dear' (897–901).

The structure of ideas in this song is now becoming manifest: let us recapitulate. The *strophe*, which is primarily concerned with escape, approaches (but does not touch) the theme of vengeance through the simile of the hunted fawn. For the hounds of that hunt recall the paradox of the hunted hounds upon Cithaeron, the hunted Bacchanals who turned so suddenly into hunters. Thus the transition in the Refrain to the idea of vengeance is only superficially abrupt. The Refrain in its turn prepares for the *antistrophe* by presenting revenge in terms of popular morality. The *antistrophe* opens with the vengeance (or punishment) of heaven, but by using the metaphor of the hunt reminds us of its human agents. The second half of the stanza, contrasting with the sinner the state of mind of the believer, reiterates from an earlier ode the 'wisdom' of the Bacchanals. For it is in fact their uncritical acceptance of natural impulse, sanctified by tradition under the guise of law, that now issues in a longing for cruel revenge and makes them find it wise, fair and dear. The Refrain, repeated at the end of the *antistrophe*, establishes an inescapable relationship between revenge and the basic tenets of their piety.

Epode. In the closing stanza the symmetry of the ode is completed by a return to the theme of escape which dominated the *strophe*; but interwoven with it are ideas akin to those of the *antistrophe* and derived, like them, from the thought of the second ode.

'Happy is he who has escaped storm upon the sea and has found harbour; happy is he who has passed beyond toils' (902–5). It is a return to the theme of escape, but with a different tone and emphasis. The first stanza dealt, by a simile from the life of animals, with the material removal of a threatened danger: the strain of the *epode* is that of mystical religion, and in it escape takes on a wider and more general content. With the sinner of the *antistrophe* is now contrasted the εὐδαίμων, he who has piously accepted the god and his religion and has received the promised benefits.[1] And what greater benefit does Dionysus confer than that of escape? Escape from toils and troubles (πόνοι, μόχθοι), and the substitution for them of 'griefless delight' (423) or that toil in the god's service which is no toil (66 sq.). From the material escape that the *strophe* celebrated we have passed, through the generalisations of the *antistrophe*, to that escape in the wider sense that is fundamental to Dionysiac experience, for it is made possible only by the drugs (of whatever sort) that Dionysus provides, which enable men to forget their sorrows by living in the moment. In this happy moment all men, rich and poor, great and small, can live with equal content; for, in the words of the second chorus, 'in equal measure to the prosperous and to the lowly has he given to have the griefless delight of wine' (421 sqq.). Our stanza, then, continues in similar terms:

'In various ways does one surpass another in prosperity and power. Moreover, thousands have a thousand different hopes. Some of them end in prosperity for mortals, some come to failure. The man whose life is happy (εὐδαίμων) in the day, him do I count blessed' (μακαρίζω) (905–11).

Dionysus is a leveller, the enemy of effort and ambition; and

[1] εὐδαίμων (902, 911) is used with conscious reference to δαιμόνιον (894), for the 'happy' man is he who stands in right relation to the divine power. I cannot accept Fraenkel's interpretation of this stanza (*v.* Dodds on 902–11), if it implies that the εὐδαιμονίαι of 902–5 are rejected or disparaged. Their relation to Dionysiac religion is discussed in the text. With them are contrasted the struggle for wealth and power and the restless ambition (ἐλπίδες), which do not confer εὐδαιμονία, but are rather types of what the Bacchanals escape from to enjoy, like the fawn, 'happiness in the day'.

to worship him is to take out a policy of insurance against disappointment. The future is uncertain; and hopes, though they may be fulfilled, may fail (and fail more often than they are fulfilled). Therefore live for the day, of which alone and of its pleasures you can be sure. The doctrine is as attractive as the lyric is beautiful. And yet it is one that few human beings accept consistently and continuously. For it is attended by disadvantages, and the happiness it promises is not obtained without a price.

The Bacchanals are at this moment happy, just as the fawn was happy 'playing amid the grassy joys of the meadow'. Yet, a short time before, the fawn, in danger of her life, had been equally absorbed in the emotion of terror. With animals it is like this. Largely without memory, they live in the present; and it is perhaps this fact alone that makes the life of the hunted tolerable. To such a condition the Bacchanals also aspire. But for human beings, in whom memory and anticipation are lively, to say nothing of their capacity, such as it may be, for rational thought, it is not easy to attain in its perfection. To that end a discipline and a way of life are necessary; and such the religion of Dionysus provides. Drugs are helpful; and Dionysus has these also at his disposal, not only the crude intoxicants that come from without but the absorbing passions from within. Yet even so the results may be incomplete and impermanent. Circumstances may withhold the drug, the passion may decrease in intensity or work itself out, and the subject awakes to find that the forgotten or evaded sorrows are still present or even that the actions of her intoxicated state have involved her in fresh sorrow. We may think of Agave.

'O blessed is he (μάκαρ)...', began the hymn in the Entrance Song. With 'Him I count blessed' (μακαρίζω) ends the present ode. But the word does not disappear from the play. Since it is evidently a word of Dionysiac religion, it is not surprising to find it on the lips of Agave. 'A blessed prey' (1171), she says, holding up the head of Pentheus. 'Blessed, blessed are you in my achievement' (1242 sq.), she cries to Cadmus; and, in particular, 'Blessed Agave!' 'So am I called in the *thiasoi*' (1180). Can we separate the μακαρισμός, the blessing of Agave from the μακαρισμός of these choral odes? Only if her plight resulted from different precepts leading to a different course of action.[1] But Agave, when possessed by the god, acted in full conformity with the Dionysiac creed and, in so doing, executed

[1] On the relation of the two sets of Bacchanals see pp. 153 sqq.

the revenge for which the Bacchanals of the Chorus now scream and over which they will gloat.

Now at last we can see with full clarity the relevance of this ode to the situation in which it is placed. When the Bacchanal way of life was first expounded in the second chorus, it was in a studied and seductive context of peace and joy. Now it reappears interwoven with the theme of vengeance and illuminated both by the Herdsman's narrative of destructive violence and by an intimation of still more terrible events in train to happen. And these events are a logical outcome of the Bacchic creed; for they result from the abnegation of intelligent control, from the unthinking acceptance of a traditional standard, and from the pursuit, uncompromising and uncritical, of momentary impulse and the pleasure it offers. That the impulse which now reigns is one of ferocity and violence is partly the result of circumstances, since the instinct of self-preservation has been aroused in both sets of Bacchanals by the threats of Pentheus or the interference of his agents. Even apart from that, however, such fury forms part, we know, of their normal rites; and, from whatever instincts in the psychologists' catalogues they may spring, impulses to hunt and to destroy are inherent in the human personality. They are impulses which men share with the animal world, and the Bacchanals gratify them as readily as do animals. Indeed, the kinship of the Bacchanals with animals is a constant motif of the play. The simile of the fawn in the *strophe* is there to remind us of it; and though (with the exception of one metaphorical word) the theme is then dropped, the whole ode is in effect a commentary upon the animal life and the aspiration of human beings towards it. How completely and satisfactorily and permanently can it be lived by them? Part of that question will be answered when Agave returns to sanity.[1] Upon part of it the ode implies its own comment. In hunting, the Bacchanal is assimilating herself to the animals; but in hunting with a conscious and vindictive hatred, is she not importing into the practices, impersonally cruel, of animal life a characteristically human 'beastliness'? She may ape the absorption of animals in momentary impulse, but she cannot attain it in its saving purity. The odious Dionysus of the following scene is a not inadequate interpreter of her emotions.

Dionysus enters alone, speaking to Pentheus within. 'You who are anxious to see what is not yours to see, who are hastening on an

[1] See Chapter x.

errand where no haste is due, Pentheus, come out in front of the palace: show yourself, I tell you, dressed up as a woman, a Maenad, a Bacchanal—you spy upon your mother and her troop!' Then, as Pentheus appears: 'Well, to all appearance you are one of Cadmus's daughters!' It matters little whether Pentheus hears these cruel words or not: the mocking allusion to his military reconnaissance, the reference to his disguise in which every word tells (woman, mad-woman, devotee of Dionysus). It matters little now what Dionysus says, for Pentheus is past understanding; and in the scene that follows he pursues his own trains of fuddled thought, while Dionysus directs 'asides' to an appreciative audience. The first words of Pentheus reveal his new condition.

'Look! I seem to see two suns, a twofold Thebes with seven-gated citadel!' (918 sq.). What then has happened to Pentheus? Since double-vision is (and presumably was then) a symptom of alcoholic intoxication, Euripides would appear to have gone out of his way to suggest to the audience that Pentheus is drunk. The detective eye of Verrall saw in this a 'rationalistic' explanation of the whole situation: the Stranger has drugged Pentheus with a crude physical drug. Those who cannot accept his uncompromising rationalism must not, however, evade the issue; nor can they deny the suggestion of intoxication. It is, after all, perfectly appropriate. Dionysus is the god who has given men wine, and this gift of his has been praised at intervals throughout the play. It has been praised by different people: by Teiresias, by the Chorus, and by the Herdsman—and for different reasons; as the source of forgetfulness and of sensual pleasures. To reduce the relationship between Pentheus and Dionysus here to that of a drunkard and the man who has plied him with drinks is altogether too simple, too literal. Yet Pentheus is certainly in some sense the victim of the drugs of Dionysus; and the very crudity of drunkenness makes it the more savage a symbol of his degradation.

But the double-vision is not the only illusion under which Pentheus labours. 'And you seem to go before me as a bull, with horns grown out upon your head. Why? Were you a beast all the time? You have certainly taken on bull's shape' (920–2).[1] To which Dionysus replies; 'The god attends us; once hostile, now he

[1] Dodds makes the attractive suggestion that Pentheus sees two figures, one the Stranger in his wonted shape beside him, the other the Stranger's double—save for the horns—which beckons him onwards.

is in league with us; now you see what you should see' (923 sq.). Behind the superficial irony lies the profounder truth. For Pentheus, turned in appearance and behaviour into a devotee, now sees in his true nature the god whom the Bacchanals hymn as 'bull-horned' and pray to reveal himself as bull (or lion or snake). And this revelation comes at the moment when all ambiguity in the conduct of Dionysus is over, his full savagery apparent.[1]

Pentheus's attention is as unstable as a kitten's, or a drunken man's. He is no longer interested in the bull-headed god; he has not been listening to the Stranger's words; he has been trying to gauge the effect of his own costume, by which he is as fascinated as a child by its fancy-dress. 'Well, how do I look? Do I not carry myself like Ino or like Agave, yes, like my mother Agave?' (925 sq.). On the painful episode that follows we need not dwell. It was the purpose of Dionysus to make Pentheus ridiculous, and he achieves it.[2] 'As I look at you', he says, 'I seem to see their very selves'; then steps back for a critical examination. A lock is out of place; he will set it straight. 'There', says Pentheus, 'you arrange me—I am altogether in your hands.'[3] The girdle is loose, the dress falls unevenly over the ankles. Dionysus gives the necessary touch, saying: 'You will, to be sure, count me the first among your friends—when you see the Bacchanals chaste against all expectation'. But Pentheus is not yet ready for this theme, he is absorbed in a problem of Bacchic etiquette. 'Shall I look more like a Bacchanal with the thyrsus in my right hand or thus in my left?' 'Raise it in the right', says Dionysus, 'in time with the right foot. I commend your change of heart', he adds, as Pentheus shifts the thyrsus from left hand to right, and in attempting the preposterous gesture stumbles or falls.[4]

[1] On the animal aspect of Dionysus see pp. 29 sq. On words of seeing see pp. 164 sqq.: here we have them at 912, 914, 918, 924 (*bis*), 925, 927 (*bis*).

[2] 'The stage business with Pentheus's costume (925–44) is the counterpart of the stage business with the Stranger's costume at 493–7; for the outrage then done to his person the Stranger now takes a fantastic revenge on the pretext of playing the valet' (Dodds, p. 181).

[3] 934: ἀνακείμεσθα suggests 'dedication'.

[4] This is admittedly not certain, since we do not know the postures of the Bacchic dance. 944: μεθέστηκας φρενῶν is ambiguous; you may change your former φρένες for better (947 sq.) or you may take leave of φρένες altogether (850).

Equipped, Pentheus seeks an outlet for the powers he feels within him. 'Should I be able to carry on my shoulders the glens of Cithaeron, Bacchanals and all?' 'You could, if you would', is the answer (for faith can move mountains); 'your heart before was not sound, but now it is—as it should be'. As usual there is a point beyond the obvious irony. The heart and wits of Pentheus were not sound before; Teiresias knew that (326 sq.). Are they now so much changed? Has anything happened to Pentheus more than the releasing by wine, by drugs, by hypnotism, in short by Dionysus, of the inhibitions which concealed his true desires?

Pentheus pursues the project: shall he use levers? Or (better still) uproot the mountain by sheer strength of shoulder, arm, and hand?[1] But Dionysus refuses to be drawn into a detailed discussion. 'Ah! do not destroy the sanctuaries of the Nymphs and the seats of Pan where he plays his pipes.' The appeal to sentiment has often frustrated the violent intentions of a drunken man; and so it is with Pentheus.[2] 'You are right; it is not by strength that women must be conquered; I will hide myself in the pines.' 'You will find such hiding as find you should, since you go as a crafty spy upon the Maenads.' The first line is lost on Pentheus; the second reminds him of all he hopes to see. 'Look! It is my fancy that they are caught in the sweet nets of their beds of love, like birds in the bushes' (957 sq.). There is no denying the prurience of Pentheus now; and his emotion and his imagination find expression in a poetic simile. Yet the same figure occurs as a metaphor in the first speech of Pentheus (223). Was the picture in fact any less vivid to his imagination then than now? Has anything changed except that the avowal of his interest is franker? 'That is the very reason', says Dionysus, 'why you are going out to watch.' Of course it is: no scandal, no need for a spy or a watcher. But Dionysus knows, and has known all along, what Pentheus was really going out to see.

Now all is ready for the *exeunt*; and Pentheus, who had desired a secret departure (840), himself demands publicity. 'Take me through the midst of the land of Thebes, for I alone am man enough to dare this deed.' So speaks this man in woman's clothes; and Dionysus picks up his words: 'Alone, alone, do you toil on behalf of this city'.[3]

[1] Compare the feat of Agave (1125 sqq.). Later she too shows amid her insanity a similar capacity for the rational discussion of details (1212 sqq.—see p. 137).

[2] Cf. Méautis, *L'Acropole*, III (1928), p. 163.

[3] Cf. 195 sq.

And alone he soon will be among his enemies. The god now compares the coming struggle to an athletic contest, to which Pentheus will go, like a contestant to the games, and will return with a victor's triumph.[1] 'Therefore there await you the contests that are your destiny. Follow me; I will go to give you safe conduct. But another shall bring you thence.' *Pentheus:* 'My mother!' *Dionysus:* 'Manifest for all to see.' *Pentheus:* 'It is for that I go!' *Dionysus:* 'You will come carried home....' *Pentheus:* 'You pamper me!' *Dionysus:* 'In your mother's arms.' *Pentheus:* 'This is sheer luxury to which you force me!' *Dionysus:* 'Yes, such luxury.' *Pentheus:* 'As my acts deserve' (964–70).

Pentheus assumes that he is to return in glory and in luxury. Ἁβρότης, τρυφᾶν: they are words with which Greeks stigmatise the effeminacy of the Orient. Yet this contemptuous Hellene accepts them, hardly under protest, and regards them simply as his due. And so is revealed the ultimate value of his *sophrosyne*. It is revealed as the superficial covering of a lust for power and glory; and, when the conventional inhibitions are relaxed, this lust appears as naked and as unashamed as that other, that physical lust, its fellow-traitor in the soul of Pentheus.

[1] See pp. 24 sq.

CHAPTER IX

THE KILL

Pentheus precedes Dionysus off the stage. The god remains to utter a final jeering comment, which sets the tone of the following scenes. 'Terrible are you, terrible, and to terrible experiences are you going, whereby you will win a fame that soars to heaven. Stretch out your hands, Agave, and you her sisters, Cadmus's daughters. Here I bring the young man to a great contest, wherein the victory shall be with me and Bromius. The rest the event will show' (971–6).[1]

Pentheus and Dionysus have now left the scene, the former not to return alive, the latter to return only as a conventional figure, shorn of the dynamic vigour of his human disguise. The action passes to Cithaeron, and is described to us, in the Greek fashion, in a Messenger's speech. This speech is preceded and followed by choral songs, the first being a frenzied cry for vengeance, the second a brief exultation; and our interest is divided between the narrative itself and the reception of it by the Bacchanals, who alone of the principals of the drama are before our eyes between the exit of Dionysus and the entrance of Agave.

A distinction was drawn in an earlier chapter between the Dionysus of the play and his followers.[2] It was suggested that, while he is in the main a simplified figure of mythology, they are the real representatives of his religion in its full concreteness, both in its attractive and in its repulsive aspects. This distinction, however, loses its importance in the closing stages of the play, after the god has been revealed to Pentheus in his bestial form and has left the stage. The vengeance of the mythological Dionysus blends with the vengeance of his outraged adherents, the revelation of his godhead with the revelation of the potentialities of his religion. It follows that all those artistic means which Euripides employs to render his epiphany odious, and, in particular, that intricate patterning of certain themes—justice, honour, victory—which was examined in the earlier chapter,[3] are equally relevant in their satire to the self-revelation of the

[1] The description of Pentheus as τὸν νεανίαν (974) may be designed to elicit the sympathy of the audience for him at this stage (D. W. Lucas *ap.* Dodds, p. 186). 971: δεινός ironically of Pentheus (cf. 856); but Dionysus is δεινότατος (861) and will inflict δεινὰ πάθη (cf. 1374, 1377).

[2] See p. 29.

[3] See pp. 23 sqq.

Bacchanals. The theme of justice, for instance, is prominent in the ode which they now sing, but the mood is one of concentrated fury and vindictiveness. The clash is emphasised by the formal structure.

For in form this ode repeats the pattern of its predecessor and exhibits the same symmetry. A first stanza, which summons the bestial agents of vengeance to attack a bestial victim, is followed by a Refrain, which calls upon the divine Justice to punish the impious. The second stanza is yet another re-statement of the Bacchic creed of piety, and is followed by a repetition of the Refrain: Justice upon the impious. The third stanza, calling upon the god to appear in bestial form, returns to the key of the first.

Strophe. 'On, swift hounds of Frenzy, on to the mountain, where the daughters of Cadmus hold their congregation. Rouse them to fury against him disguised in woman's dress, who spies upon the Maenads in his frenzy. His mother first will see him watching from some smooth rock or pinnacle; and she will cry to the Maenads: "Who is this, my Bacchanals, that has come to the mountain, to the mountain, tracking the Cadmean mountain-rangers? Who can have borne him? For not of women's blood is he sprung, but is the breed of a lioness or of the Libyan Gorgons"' (977–90).[1]

The imagination of the Chorus, gloating in anticipation over the coming scene, is incompletely prescient;[2] and it may be noted that it is fed in part upon the Herdsman's narrative. In fact it will be the god and not Agave who calls to the Bacchanals. But they remember how she rallied her followers to retaliate upon the ambuscade. 'My coursing hounds', she cried then, and now those hounds reappear, but with a slight change of role; now they have become the 'swift hounds of Frenzy' that are to madden the women—till they become themselves the hounds that drag down the human prey. But, though Agave's cry exists only in the imagination of the Chorus, its content reflects accurately her state of mind, and her denial of the humanity of Pentheus is prophetic of the illusion which will lead her to take him for an animal, for a *lion*.

[1] 982: πρώτα (Dindorf). σκόλοπος (983) is an unsolved puzzle (see Dodds), probably a rock-pinnacle or (perhaps better, in view of the ensuing narrative) a pointed fir-tree. ἐς ὄρος (986): cf. 116, 165 and Dodds, *Maenadism*, p. 156 n. 4—a ritual rallying-cry.

[2] Or inaccurately clairvoyant, if we regard the events of which they sing as even now in the process of happening. Cf. Wassermann, *op. cit.* p. 280, quoted by Dodds, p. 187.

The sub-humanity of Pentheus was indeed the theme of one of the Chorus's earlier tirades, and it will recur in the Refrain. But here Euripides has skilfully contrived to convey at the same time the sub-humanity of Agave. 'Who can have borne him?' With venomous irony the Chorus put these words into the mouth of his mother. No woman, is the answer, but a lioness or a Gorgon. And it is true now, for to all intents Agave has ceased to be a woman, and become a beast, a monster; and a monster aptly chosen, for Gorgons, like Bacchanals, have snakes in their hair or at their girdles. If Pentheus is brutish, he will be met with even cruder brutality; if he is frenzied, the hounds of pure essential Frenzy will take on human embodiment and hunt him down.[1] It is no novelty in this play to find the same items on both sides of the balance-sheet.

Refrain. 'Let Justice come, manifest and sword in hand, stabbing through the throat and killing the godless, the lawless, the unjust man, earth-born of Echion's breed' (991–6). Though the emotion is so simple, almost every word in this brief verse invites comment. Every one, for instance, of the abusive epithets which they load upon Pentheus has significant connections. He is an earth-born monster. The charge is linked not only to the oblique forecast of Agave's loss of humanity in the preceding stanza, but to the invocation of a sub-human god in the *epode.* He is godless. But Pentheus is now full of the god and transformed by a crude animality which he shares with his opponents. He is lawless. And indeed his 'lawless folly' was stigmatised in the second choral ode, but since then the word has taken on a richer content. He is lawless because he opposes their laws, which are natural laws. (Though, again, is it not possible that he is really acting upon them?) Finally, he is unjust, unrighteous, a wrong-doer who must be brought to justice. So they bid Justice come, manifest and sword in hand. She will indeed be manifested; and it will appear that, as their laws are 'natural' laws, so their justice is a 'natural' justice, which consists in the right of the attacked to retaliate in kind, the right of taking a ruthless vengeance on your enemies.[2]

Antistrophe. The second stanza begins in tremendous anger and

[1] Λύσσας (977), λυσσώδη (981).

[2] 992: φανερός, ξιφηφόρος. Justice will become 'manifest' in the most literal sense when Pentheus's head is displayed to view (1175). Nor will this be severed cleanly by a sword, so that the conventional epithet ξιφηφόρος (perhaps Orphic) is in effect a calculated euphemism.

hatred, but passes, like the *antistrophe* of the preceding ode, from the sinner to the saved and the way of salvation. (Unfortunately, the text of this stanza is seriously corrupted, and the translation which follows depends largely on conjecture.) 'Whosoever with unjust will and lawless wrath, concerning thy mysteries, god of Bacchanals, and thy mother's, sets out with mad craft and distracted spirit to master the invincible with violence, his purposes does death chasten; but the unequivocal service of the gods, as befits mortality, means a life without pain.' If we look back to the second stanza of the second ode we find a similar train of thought (386 sqq.): the lawless madness of Pentheus leads to ruin, the way of peace to security; more than mortal thoughts mean a brief life; cleverness is no wisdom. So now they continue: 'I grudge not the wise their wisdom. My joy is in hunting after those other things which are great and manifest, and they lead man's life towards honour: namely, to be holy and reverent day-long and through the night, and dismissing all customs that are without the pale of justice to honour the gods' (997–1010).

Detailed discussion of a conjectural text is better relegated to a footnote.[1] Nevertheless the main lines of the stanza remain firm. The sinner and enemy is loaded with abuse amid a profusion of epithets, and the accusations are, as usual, double-edged: he is mad, he is violent—but in the fury of their indignation, are they so sane themselves? With him and his threatened end they contrast the believer: modest, disclaiming cleverness, yet pursuing (it is the sinister metaphor of the hunt) great things. There is an apparent contradiction here of the doctrine of the second ode, where they sang that 'a man may pursue great things and miss what is at his hand'.

[1] My translation is based upon the suggestions of Dodds, who discusses the difficulties exhaustively. In 1002 both θάνατος and ἀπροφάσιστος (or a cognate) have strong claims to retention, the former because there should be some reference to the fate of Pentheus (more than the implications of τἀνίκατον) to contrast with the ἄλυπος βίος of his opponents, the latter because its normal sense of 'unhesitating, whole-hearted' is eminently Dionysiac. But the words cannot belong together. Hence the virtue of Dodds's text at this point. The analogy of 386 sqq. supports the interpretation of 997–1001 as a *generic* relative clause: 'bad men come to a bad end'. Another cardinal point is that χαίρω θηρεύουσα (1006) must look forward to τάδ' ἕτερα, not back to τὸ σοφόν (the sense of 1005 being fixed by 395). Part of the effect resides in the sense which the words can bear in isolation; 'I love hunting', with its reference backwards to the *strophe* and forward to the *epode*.

But it is not of restless ambition that they are thinking now. As there is wisdom and wisdom, so is there greatness and greatness; and what they count great is the pious service of their god. But the word would hardly have been used, if what that service now entailed was the calm cultivation of peaceful pleasures and not a resounding vengeance. The great and manifest things of their pursuit are in fact the 'great and manifest things' that Agave will claim to have wrought 'by this day's hunting' (1198 sq.), in which she will rejoice as they do.[1] Further, that 'honour' or glory (τὰ καλά) towards which their life is now being directed is the vengeance which they greeted in the last ode as fair and dear to them, and which will be hymned by them as a 'glorious contest' (1163), winning for Dionysus the title of 'glorious victor' (1147). Finally, they round off the stanza and prepare the Refrain by returning to the concepts of law and justice, of which they are the exponents, against which Pentheus offends.

Refrain. 'Let Justice come, manifest and sword in hand, stabbing through the throat and killing the godless, the lawless, the unjust man, earth-born of Echion's breed' (1011–16).

For the third time the Bacchanals have expounded the basis of their faith and practice: in the *antistrophes* of the second choral ode, in the *antistrophe* of the fourth, and again in this *antistrophe.* There is little variation in content, as they contrast the mad, lawless sinner with their own modest recognition of human status, their acceptance of 'law' or 'convention', their pursuit of certain pious ends. The context of the second ode was quiet, with the emphasis on peaceful pleasures. In the fourth ode it became apparent, partly from the development of the action, partly through the formal device of embracing the 'creed' in a repeated Refrain, that the ends which they pursue are furious as well as peaceful, and that among the νόμοι or conventions which they accept is revenge, which they find wise and honourable and desirable. That point has been established, and that significance will therefore attach to their references to wisdom (negative), honour and joy in the present ode. Here too Euripides uses the same formal device of a repeated Refrain embracing the statement of belief, but to slightly different effect. The theme of this

[1] γέγηθα (1198), after χαίρω has been picked up by 1033, 1040. With μεγάλα φανερά τε (1006) and μεγάλα καὶ φανερά (1199) compare 1031 (θεὸς φαίνῃ μέγας): the events are such because they reveal the greatness of the god. φανερά also reappears as φάνηθι (1017).

Refrain, like that of the preceding ode, is the vengeance.[1] There it was represented as a heaven-sent privilege, honoured and welcomed by men; here it is the abstract divine Justice itself. Before the first occurrence of the Refrain comes the *strophe*, which deals with the bestiality of the agents of the divine punishment; after its second occurrence comes the *epode*, which deals with the bestiality of the god himself. The symmetry is complete; so is the commentary upon the divine justice and the preparation for the narrative which is to follow.

Epode. 'Manifest thyself as bull or as many-headed snake to view or as a flaming lion to behold. Come, beast Bacchus, over the beast-hunter of the Bacchanals cast with smiling countenance the noose of death when he has fallen among the herd of Maenads' (1017–23).[2] The apparent clumsiness of summoning, first Justice, then the god, to manifestation conceals a characteristic piece of Euripidean art. For if justice means nothing but the victory of the god, there is in fact but one appeal; and the manifestation of both god and justice will be made through the actions of his human followers. But how different in tone are, first, the austere abstraction of a specious morality, secondly, a god amoral and ferocious as the animals whose form he takes. For there are two strands of thought leading from the *antistrophe* and Refrain to meet in the *epode*. First, the Chorus are reverent and honour the gods; Pentheus is 'godless'. What is the god whom the Chorus worship and Pentheus dishonours? Again, Pentheus is a sub-human monster (born surely not of woman, but of a lioness or a snake-wreathed Gorgon). What is his opponent? The answer to both questions is the same. The god, Pentheus's opponent, is one who can fitly take the shape of a bull (in which shape Pentheus has already seen him), of a snake (and a snake was Pentheus's mythical ancestor),[3] or of a lion (and Pentheus will be taken for a lion by his lioness mother). If Pentheus has gone hunting beasts, a beast shall be waiting for him—a beast and a herd

[1] With which it is interlocked at each end by the repetition of identical or similar words. ἄθεον, ἄνομον, ἄδικον (995) are picked up, in reverse order, by ἀδίκῳ, παρανόμῳ, σὰ ὄργια. νόμιμα, δίκας, θεούς (1009 sq.) lead, through δίκα, into the repetition of ἄθεον, ἄνομον, ἄδικον (1015).

[2] 1020: θὴρ θηραγρέτᾳ (Tyrrell).

[3] Cf. the almost immediate reference to it at 1026. Note the appropriateness of πολύκρανος, for the god's revelation will come through a mob of snake-bearing women.

of beasts (ἀγέλαν).[1] The irony of it will be pleasant to Dionysus, and he will smile, not for the first time. Now at last the meaning of that enigmatic smile with which the 'gentle beast' surrendered to his captors (439) is made clear.

Into this atmosphere of bestiality comes a normal human being, and restores to the play something that has been absent while distraught king, scheming god, and vindictive Bacchanals have held the stage. Simple, loyal and sympathetic, the servant who now comes with news from Cithaeron both serves as a touchstone for the quality of the others and by his very humanity lays a foundation for the human tragedy of the restored Agave.

He begins, in the conventional style of messengers of ill, by apostrophising the royal house in its misfortune. 'House that once was known for prosperity throughout Hellas—house of the old Sidonian who sowed in the land the earth-born crop of the snake, I mourn for you, slave though I am.' His words at once establish that divergence of sympathy between the narrator and his immediate audience which characterises the entire scene. 'Have you news from the Bacchanals?' cries the Chorus-leader. 'Pentheus is dead.' 'Lord Bromius', sings the Bacchanal in triumph, 'thou art manifested as a great god!' The Messenger is shocked. 'Do you rejoice at the evil fortune of my masters, lady?' This tasteless exultation in disaster is something outside his experience.[2] The Bacchanal disregards him, but provides with her next words the kind of explanation he can understand: 'I, a stranger, sing Evoe in my barbaric strains; no longer do I cower in fear of bonds.' This is sense to his Greek soul, and stirs his indignation. 'Do you count Thebes so unmanned....' But she sweeps him aside:[3] 'It is Dionysus, Dionysus and not Thebes, that has the mastery over me.' These are the old clashes between Greece and Asia, between the wild worship and the city-state; and her words must have roused every inherent prejudice in the Greek

[1] The god is a beast, the Maenads are beasts (ἀγέλαν); and Pentheus is a beast, for, apart from other indications, θηραγρέτᾳ in this context is ambiguous: 'hunter of beasts' or 'beast-hunter'.

[2] They react very like Medea to the news of a vengeance of roughly equal brutality: cf. *Med.* 1121 sqq., and note especially κάλλιστον (1127) and χαίρεις (1131). See also *Hec.* 1257 sq. For a decent Greek reaction (on the part of an Egyptian) see *Hel.* 1197 (οὐδέν τι χαίρω).

[3] Actually the end of the Messenger's sentence may be lost through defect of the text (see Dodds *ad loc.*).

man, which makes his response the more remarkable. 'I do not blame you,' he says,[1] 'yet to rejoice over evils wrought, ladies, is an ignoble thing' (1039 sq.). His sympathy for their situation makes the revolt of his decent instincts the more impressive. It is ignoble: οὐ καλόν. They know better. Revenge is an honourable thing which they hold dear. Certainly they rejoice, and will rejoice in every detail of the coming narrative. 'Tell me, recount, by what death did he die, the unrighteous man in his unrighteous enterprise?' (1041 sq.). Did Justice come, at their command, manifest and sword in hand?

The Messenger begins his speech. 'When we had left the homesteads of this Theban land and passed the river Asopus, we struck into the hill-country of Cithaeron—Pentheus and I (for I was in attendance on my master) and the stranger who was the escort of our mission' (1043–7).[2] It opens like the Herdsman's speech, with the ascent of the mountain slopes. There is a more significant parallel, however, in the mention of those dwellings of men that lay beneath Cithaeron by the river Asopus (749). Past them goes Pentheus to meet the fate that has already been foreshadowed by their fate—past them and beyond ordered civilisation to a wild place where only the writ of Dionysus runs. The narrative continues with brilliant economy and suggestiveness.

'First we sat in a grassy valley, keeping silence of foot and tongue, that we might see and be unseen ourselves. There lay a ravine, steep-sided, watered with streams and shady with pines, where sat the Maenads, their hands occupied in pleasant toils. Some of them were restoring a thyrsus that had lost its crown of ivy locks; others, like fillies that have left behind the painted yokes, were singing in antiphony a song of Bacchus' (1048–57). Maenads they are called, but seem little to deserve the title. The work of the one party is almost domestic; the others are singing such a hymn, we may suppose, as the Entrance Song.[3] This was not what Pentheus came to see—and

[1] συγγνωστὰ μέν σοι (1039): it is 'understandable'. Contrast the ἀγνωμοσύνη, the ἀμαθία of Pentheus; and compare the Chorus in the *Heracleidae* (981) in face of a somewhat similar situation (see p. 109 n. 2).

[2] πομπὸς θεωρίας: cf. 965. The latter word suggests not only the role of Pentheus as 'spectator', but (ironically) an official deputation sent by a state to a religious function, as it might be to the games (cf. p. 24).

[3] With which πῶλοι (1056) perhaps establishes a connection (cf. 166). Compare also ἐν τερπνοῖς πόνοις (1053) with πόνον ἡδύν (66). On 1054 sq. Dodds points out that a thyrsus which has lost its ivy has ceased to be a thyrsus; hence ἐκλελοιπότα.

he does not see it. 'But hapless Pentheus, not seeing the throng of women, spoke thus: "Stranger, where we are, my eyes cannot reach these spurious Maenads. But on the banks, if I climbed into a stately pine, I could see properly the Maenads' scandalous deeds"' (1058–62).

The Stranger now performs his last wonder. He takes the tip of a pine and bends it 'down, down, down' to the ground in the arc of a circle.[1] Placing the king in its branches, he releases it gently. Thus Pentheus is raised to eminence, riding on the tree. Thus Pentheus does not so much see the Maenads as be seen by them (1075).[2]

The narrative continues: 'For just as he was becoming visible sitting aloft, the stranger was no longer to be seen, but a voice from the sky—it was Dionysus, one must suppose—cried out: "Young women, I bring the man who is making mock of you, of me and of my rites. Punish him!"[3] As he spoke the words, a flash of awful fire stood between heaven and earth. And the air went still, and the woody glade held its leaves in stillness, nor could you have heard the cry of any beast' (1076–85). It is a turning-point in the action; and nature is still with expectation. Nor is this the first time that she has participated sympathetically in the drama. We are at once reminded of a similar passage in the Herdsman's speech, where nature, animate and inanimate, seemed to share, as here in stillness, there in movement: 'the whole mountain shared in their worship, and the beasts, and there was nothing that was not stirred by their motion' (726 sq.). But the present description has an effect which is all its own. The flash of lightning and the utter quietness when even the birds stop singing, these are the prelude to a storm; and the storm soon breaks.[4]

[1] The difficulties of 1066 sq. have recently been elucidated by L. R. Palmer (*Eranos*, XLIV (1946), pp. 59 sqq.).

[2] At this point we may note the large number of words of sight or seeing in this passage (1050 *bis*, 1058, 1060, 1062, 1063, 1075 *bis*, 1076, 1077). See pp. 164 sqq. οὐράνιον (1064) and ἐστηρίζετο (1073) together pick up οὐρανῷ στηρίζον (972) to ironical effect.

[3] νεάνιδες (1079): for their varied ages compare 694. But ἐπιλελήσμεθ' ἡδέως κτλ. (188)—a functioning Bacchanal is *ex hypothesi* young. γέλων τιθέμενον (1081): cf. 272, 286; thus the punishment fits the crime, and mutual ridicule takes its place in the pattern of the play.

[4] Perhaps the parallelism of the two narratives goes farther still. Both begin with the arrival of the profane. In both cases the Bacchanals are found at peace, 'a marvel of good order' (in the latter the description is brief—that point has been made, the peculiar beauty of this mood established). In both cases there follows a descent to intrigue—and that

Nature was still, both wood and beast; but the Bacchanals had not heard clearly, though they stood up and looked around. Then the voice spoke again, and this time they recognised 'the bidding of the Bacchic god' and sped forward with the swiftness of doves. 'And through the torrent bed and over the boulders they leapt, maddened with the inspiration of the god. When they saw my master sitting in the pine, first they mounted a crag that towered up opposite and cast stones at him with all their might; and he was shot at with branches of pine. Others cast their thyrsi at Pentheus, a cruel targeting. But they effected nothing. Too high for all their eagerness sat the poor wretch, helplessly trapped. Lastly, they rent down[1] boughs of oak, and tried to heave up the roots with levers not of iron. But, when they failed to make the goal of their labours, Agave spoke: "Come, stand round in a circle and catch hold of the stem, my Maenads, that we may capture this riding beast and he may not tell of the god's secret dances"' (1093–1109).

Agave's speech is of great psychological interest because of the mental confusion it reveals. They must seize, she says, 'the rider' (τὸν ἀμβάτην)—and the word picks up a metaphor already used to describe Pentheus in the tree (1072). 'The beast', she adds; and, being the first evidence of her illusion, it is quite unexpected. Still, the whole phrase (τὸν ἀμβάτην θῆρα) is apt enough and suggests some panther or wild-cat crouching on a branch. The real paradox comes at the end. Though it is a beast, it is yet capable of revealing mysteries; Pentheus is at once an animal and a human spy. Such a doubling of parts is familiar in dreams; and it is the condition of dreaming, where logic is in abeyance and symbolism reigns, that gives the clue to Agave's state of mind. Under the influence of the god, she has passed back behind the threshold of rational thought into the primitive world of imagery. And there she meets her son on equal terms. For he too, under similar influence, had confused the symbol with the thing and seen Dionysus horned like a bull.[2]

in the latter the intriguer is the god has its own satirical relevance. Then, ushered in by the participation of nature, comes, in both cases, an outbreak of natural violence. The metaphor at 1090 recalls a similar stage in the earlier narrative (748).

[1] συγκεραυνοῦσαι (1103). The other extant occurrences of this word are both in what may be called Bacchic contexts (Archilochus fr. 77; Cratinus fr. 187), and Dodds seems right in recognising it as 'an element of the special Dionysiac vocabulary on which Euripides draws repeatedly in this play'.

[2] Dodds argues that θῆρα (1108) is 'a fleeting fancy, perhaps no more

Both mother and son are under the spell of a dream-like illusion; and to both of them will come a time of waking, but it will come first to Pentheus. 'And they put multitudinous hands to the pine and uprooted it from the earth; and, headlong to the ground from his lofty seat, with countless cries, fell Pentheus. For he understood that he was near to doom' (1109–13).[1] It is the shock that brings him to his senses, which is psychologically correct. Yet it is an added horror in a horrible episode that not even the clear realisation of his impending death is spared him.

'His mother first as priestess inaugurated the slaying and fell upon him.[2] And he cast away the headband from his hair, that wretched Agave might recognise and not slay him; and he spoke, touching her cheek: "It is I, mother, your son Pentheus, whom you bore in Echion's house. Pity me, mother, and do not for my offences kill your son"' (1114–21).

Thus the 'atheist' recants; and what the palace-miracle and the hearsay of wonders could not do, the imminence of death has done; it has convinced Pentheus of the god-head of Dionysus. Yet perhaps the theological aspect should not be overstressed. For the real interest of his last words lies elsewhere, in the relationship of mother and son, in the futile appeal of the sane to the mad.[3]

'But she, foaming at the mouth and rolling wild eyes, her wits all astray, was possessed of the Bacchic god; and he persuaded her not.' The scene which follows is described with gruesome realism, exceeding, perhaps, what seems to-day permissible; and we may spare ourselves a detailed contemplation of the dismemberment of Pentheus by the whole band of Bacchanals led by Agave and her sisters. It is the scene which the rending of the cattle foreshadowed, but for which nothing can really prepare us. To the Bacchanals what

than a metaphor', though one that later (1141) becomes a fixed delusion. It seems more appropriate, however, that Agave should see Pentheus as an animal from the start (cf. 985 sqq.).

[1] 1112 sq.: the juxtaposition of οἰμώγμασιν Πενθεύς is perhaps intended to recall the etymological prophecies of Teiresias (367) and Dionysus (508).

[2] προσπίτνει (1115): commonly of an affectionate embrace (cf. 1163 sq.).

[3] 1120 sq.: 'the offence of an individual cannot justify the violation of the blood-tie' (Dodds). It is possible, however, that the contrast of personal adjectives (ταῖς ἐμαῖς...παῖδα σόν) implies more than this. If with these words Pentheus regards Agave and the awfulness for her of what she is doing, then he enjoys a moment of moral victory in defeat and the gross evil of the scene is mitigated by a gleam of humanity.

is it? The answer is that it is a mixed thing, confused as the aspect in which Pentheus appeared to Agave. He appeared as a beast; and in hunting and rending this beast they are carrying out a normal rite of *sparagmos* under the laws of their being as Bacchanals; the frenzied effort that the process demands is a 'sweet toil', in the violence of which they delight out of pure love of violence; it was not 'by strength' that Agave tore out the shoulder of Pentheus, but 'the god gave his gift of ease to her hands' (1128). But Pentheus also appeared as a human spy, a trespasser on their secrecy and a threat to their security; and upon him they avenge themselves as women actuated by a malignant hatred, born of fear. The motives are blended in them as intricately as are reality and fantasy in the vision of Agave.

So Pentheus's body was scattered among the rocks and trees.[1] But his head Agave had taken, and 'fixing it upon the point of her thyrsus she carries it, as though it were that of a mountain lion, through the midst of Cithaeron, leaving her sisters with the bands of Maenads. And, exulting in her luckless prey, she is coming within these walls, calling on the Bacchic god as "fellow-hunter", "fellow craftsman of the prey", "fair victor"—but her prize of victory is tears!' (1141–7).[2] Now the stage is set for the arrival of Agave with her trophy. She will arrive alone, as the exigencies of the drama demand; but also, by separating herself from her companions, she has put herself in the conditions that make her return to sanity possible.

The Messenger is comprehensibly anxious to be gone before she comes. But first he, like his predecessor, must (according to convention) round off his speech with a reflection. There are in fact two immediate comments upon this narrative. There is the triumph-song of the Bacchanals, which is hideous, but expected. The comment of the Messenger himself is of subtler interest. He is moved to speak as follows: 'To be sane and to reverence the gods is the noblest—yes, and I think also the wisest—thing mortals can possess and pursue.' As a generalised comment, the words fit the character of the man, himself sane and honourable. Superficially it is a counsel of acceptance,

[1] See p. 95 n. 1.

[2] 1147: ᾧ (Reiske). See Dodds for criticisms of other readings and interpretations. The real victor is Dionysus; the κῶμος is the celebration (1167) of the 'unconquerable' (1001), to which the Chorus receive Agave as σύγκωμος (1172). Agave thinks she is the victor (cf. 1239), fellow-victor with the god, but the victory which she has won for him or in his service (ᾧ) means but a prize of tears for her.

like that of the first Messenger, though quite how it is related in the speaker's mind to the exultant bearing of the devotees, which he found οὐ καλόν, we cannot be sure. But through his words Euripides takes us back to the reiterated statements of the Bacchic creed. Sanity and piety they had claimed as the distinguishing marks of their religion, as honourable and wise in their eyes, as the standards which they accept. In the fourth choral ode this creed was associated inexorably with the threat of violence and the popular valuation of revenge. Now, after the full horror of their revenge has been disclosed, the poet returns to these themes. Here is the sanity, the piety, the honour and the wisdom of Bacchanals.[1]

The Messenger has said that sanity and reverence for the gods is most honourable and most wise; and the Bacchanals of the Chorus do not demur, for they know what these things mean; they know that wisdom and honour reside in (among other things) violence and revenge. Accordingly they sing: 'Let us lift our feet for the Bacchic god; let us lift our voices for the fate of Pentheus, offspring of the snake, who took on woman's garb and the blessed thyrsus-wand, accoutrements of death, and had a bull to lead him on the way of fate. Cadmean Bacchanals! A famous hymn of victory have you made—to end in wailing and in tears. Fair is the contest—to clasp a child with a hand dripping with his blood!' (1153–64).[2]

Their song falls into two parts, in the first of which they exult over the fate of Pentheus. They greet the success of the intrigue in phrases that recall its earlier stages, the robing of Pentheus for death (857) and his vision of the bull-headed god (920). The bestial origin of Pentheus has been a staple feature of their abuse; here 'snake' and 'bull' in combination suggest the reciprocal bestiality that relates the two opponents. In the second half they turn to their fellow-Bacchanals. They pick up Agave's cry of 'fair-victor', together with the Messenger's bitter comment that tears were *her* prize of victory. For the attitude of these Asiatic Bacchanals (1168) to their Cadmean

[1] And the standards which they accept, for τοῖσι χρωμένοις (1152, and χρῆμα, if we accept P's reading) recalls 431 (ἐνόμισε χρῆταί τε = γιγνώσκειν καὶ μελετᾶν, 892).

[2] 1157: ὁπλισμὸν Ἅιδα (Wilamowitz). The elements in the last sentence are clear enough, their grammatical combination uncertain (*v.* Dodds *ad loc.*). χέρ' αἵματι στάζουσαν (Wilamowitz) περιβαλεῖν τέκνῳ (Kirchhoff) is perhaps supported by *Med.* 1253 sq. (φοινίαν τέκνοις προσβαλεῖν χέρ' αὐτοκτόνον).

sisters (1160) is not a simple one, because the Bacchic status of the latter is not simple. It is the same power that works in them, and to the same ends. They are the instruments of the god's vengeance upon Pentheus, which the Chorus applaud, and to which they can apply the term 'honourable' or 'glorious' in all sincerity, since 'to hold the hand of mastery over the head of foes' is to them an honourable thing.[1] At the same time they use it with cruel irony. For Agave and her companions, true Bacchanals though they may be in their behaviour, are, in the terms of the story, Bacchanals against their will, who are themselves punished for their previous blasphemy by becoming the instruments of the punishment of Pentheus;[2] and, when normality returns, as it will, they will bitterly regret what they have done. It is a famous victory; but Agave's is to be an unenviable fame.[3] It is a glorious contest indeed that means placing bloody hands upon—a child.

'Child' is Agave's cue. The Chorus see her approaching and prepare to receive, to constitute themselves, the revelling band that celebrates the victor's triumph.

[1] καλός, though used in the play primarily of social standards, retains some aesthetic reference, and at 1163 (for instance) implies the sheer physical ugliness of the proceeding.

[2] See further p. 153 n. 3.

[3] Ambiguous as the lifting-up of Pentheus (966 sqq.).

CHAPTER X

A BACCHANAL WAKES

Of the themes whose intricate patterning in the closing stages of the play has already been investigated, there are two which dominate the interval between Agave's entry and her restoration to sanity. There is the theme of *epiphany*. For the divine manifestation, which was promised in the Prologue and has been taking place in some sense and degree at every stage in the action, has now entered a new and literal phase. The glorified appearance of Dionysus is not yet; but, when Agave carries in the head of Pentheus, the vengeance with which the god establishes his divinity can be seen with the eyes, and words of sight and seeing abound in the text. Only Agave cannot see, or sees amiss, and the disparate visions of her and of the Bacchanals (later, of Cadmus) add piquancy to the episode. There is the theme of *hunting*. 'Hunt', 'beast', 'prey'; the words fall insistently on the ear from the lips of Agave and of the Chorus. But, particularly, it is Agave who is obsessed with this theme, triumphant in the pride of a successful huntress. The Chorus also triumphs, and in the outcome of the same hunt, but their triumph has a wider scope; it includes Agave and relishes her delusions. Thus, there are not only rival visions, but also, corresponding to them, rival exultations of victory.

'Bacchanals of Asia', begins Agave. Blind to their hostility, she sees in them friends and fellow-worshippers, upon whose moral support and approbation she can depend now that she has left her own band; and, until the arrival of Cadmus brings her into contact with a normal human being, there is no hope of her restoration to sanity. 'Bacchanals of Asia!' 'Why do you call upon me?' 'I bring from the mountain a new-cut curling thing to the palace, a blessed prey.'[1] It is the head of Pentheus, the visible symbol of the vengeance the Bacchanals have acclaimed in song. But seeing is another matter,

[1] Whether θήραν (1171) is taken in the sense of 'hunting' or 'prey' (in which sense perhaps we should read θήραμα), the thing which Agave carries and describes as ἕλικα is the head of Pentheus, which elsewhere she imagines to be the head of a lion. But the head has been fixed upon the end of a thyrsus in place of the normal bunch of ivy leaves. Ivy tendril, human hair and lion's mane are all confused in her mind and represented by the one word ἕλιξ (applicable to a great variety of curled or spiral objects: *v.* L.S.).

and it has been held that in this scene even the Chorus is stirred to pity. Their answer now is small support for that belief. 'I see', they reply, 'and will accept you as a fellow-reveller.'

Agave continues her proud narrative. 'Without snares I seized him, this young whelp of a wild lion, as you may see.' 'In what lonely place?' 'It was Cithaeron...' 'Cithaeron?' '...that wrought his death.' 'Who struck the blow?' 'Mine first was that privilege.' 'Blessed Agave!' 'So am I called among the worshippers.' 'Who else?' 'It was Cadmus...' 'Cadmus?' '...whose daughters (but after me, after me!) laid hands upon this beast. A lucky hunt was this' (1168–83).[1]

In the absence of the music and the dance-movements the antiphony is bleak, but the loneliness of Agave and the devilish play of the Bacchanals emerge clearly from their leading questions and ironic pretence of ignorance. Now she holds the head out towards them and bids them 'partake of the feast'.[2] They reject the offer. With ironical deference? With contempt? With disgust? Uncertainty of text and punctuation obscure the tone, but it can hardly be one of pity. Certainly, if Euripides meant his audience to suppose that the Bacchanals feel pity for Agave, he has given singularly little indication to counteract the cruel and gratuitous irony which they employ.[3] It is, however, all the same to the bemused Agave, who continues: 'Young is the bull and but recently has down grown on his cheek beneath his crest of delicate hair.'[4] 'Yes', reply the Bacchanals, 'the hair makes very clear his likeness to a beast of the wild.' 'The Bacchic

[1] 1180 is divided (with P) between the Chorus and Agave; and similarly 1196.

[2] Which is the sequel (*a*) to a sacrifice (1114, 1246), (*b*) to a hunt. See p. 25.

[3] E.g. at 1172 and 1195 ('and your son Pentheus'). At 1184 τί; μετέχω, τλᾶμον; (so Murray after Hartung and Wilamowitz) may well express revulsion and disgust. But neither τλᾶμον here nor τάλαινα at 1200 need imply pity. These words are primarily an objective description of a condition of wretchedness, to which may be added an emotion of disgust, of indignation or (commonly) of pity in the mind of the speaker. *Or.* 526 is an example of τάλας, *Andr.* 348, *El.* 404 of τλήμων (all in the vocative) without a connotation of pity. At 1200, if the Bacchanals feel pity, they should not in the same breath bid Agave display her trophy to the citizens. See also p. 144 n. 1.

[4] See Dodds on the difficulties of 1185–7. Since it is doubtful in the extreme whether μόσχος here can mean lion's whelp, we must suppose that Agave's illusion has temporarily shifted (cf. p. 135 n. 1): a young bull is not merely a typical victim of *sparagmos*, but also a more suitable dish for a sacrificial feast.

god', continues Agave, 'was the skilled huntsman who set the Maenads skilfully on to this beast.' 'For our lord is a hunter.' 'You commend me?' 'I commend you.' 'And soon will the Cadmeans...' 'Yes, and Pentheus, your son...!' '...will commend his mother.' 'For she has taken a prey...' 'This prey in shape like a lion.' 'A prodigious prey!' 'And caught prodigiously!' 'Do you exult?' 'I rejoice, for I have wrought great things, great and manifest, by this hunting' (1184–99).

The threads run through the play and are sorted without difficulty: the 'wisdom' of Dionysus; the hunting god; the manifestation by this deed of his greatness; the excessive vengeance (for such is the ambiguity of περισσάν, περισσῶς) taken upon the man of excess. But, in particular, it is the lyric statements of Bacchic orthodoxy that are recalled at this climax of horror. Dionysus is σοφός, not merely as skilful huntsman or as the god who conducted so cleverly the intrigue against Pentheus, but because revenge itself is part of the 'wisdom' of his worship. The great and manifest accomplishments of Agave recall the great and manifest ends of Dionysiac piety and are the logical consequence of that devotion to an animal god which is symbolised by the reiterated metaphor of the hunt. 'Do you commend me?' asks Agave. They cannot in truth do otherwise, if they are faithful to their creed.

Now lyric gives place to spoken dialogue, in preparation for the entry of Cadmus. The Chorus-leader bids Agave display her 'spoil of victory' to the citizens, and Agave is only too willing to obey. 'Ye dwellers in the fair-towered city of the Theban land, come that you may see this prey, the beast which we daughters of Cadmus have hunted down—not with the thonged javelins of Thessaly, not with nets, but with the sharpness of our own white hands. Why then should men boast while they get them useless weapons from the spear-maker? When we with hands alone caught him and tore his beast's limbs apart' (1202–10).[1] The inherent horror of the deed is enhanced by insistence upon the mode of its execution, by the reference to white hands. It is enhanced also by the awful semblance of rationality with which Agave generalises her experience.[2]

[1] 1210: θηρός is deliberately postponed so that τόνδε can suggest Pentheus; τόνδε and θηρός thus represent the two discrepant parts of Agave's consciousness.

[2] Similarly, the suggestion which she now makes for the affixing of the head to the entablature is horribly appropriate, since lion-head ornaments were employed in Greek architecture.

'Where is my aged father? Let him draw near. And my son Pentheus, where is he? Let him take and set against the house a wooden ladder that he may ascend and nail this head to the triglyphs —this lion's head that I bring home from the hunt' (1211–15).

Where is Cadmus? Where is Pentheus? The questions are easily answered. Pentheus's head is held in her arms, and Cadmus now enters, followed by attendants carrying the *disjecta membra* of the body. It is a Cadmus old and tired and sorrowful. How different an entry from his first, when age was forgotten and fatigue denied! Now he comes after 'toil of endless search' bringing the body which he had found scattered in the glens of Cithaeron. He tells his story simply. 'I heard news of my daughters' terrible deeds when I was already returned within the town walls, with old Teiresias, from the Bacchanals. Back I turned to the mountain and now bring my son who died by the Maenads' hands.' Now comes a fine touch which, with its truth to Cadmus and to age, relieves for a moment the tension of the scene. 'And there I saw Autonoe who bore Actaeon to Aristaeus....' He cannot help it; he must point out, allusively and with a shake of the head, that his warning (337 sqq.) has been justified, that one grandson has shared the fate of another. Autonoe and Ino are still mad, still in the woodland, but Agave is here and will soon be sane. 'But she, they told me, Agave, was coming hither with dancing feet—and the tale was true. For I see her, and it is no happy sight.'

Agave's greeting shows how well she knows her father and his family pride.[1] 'Father', she says, 'now may you make your greatest boast, that you of all mortals have begotten daughters by far the best —all of us, but me above all who, leaving loom and shuttle, have passed to greater things—to hunting beasts with my hands.' So speaks the Bacchanal, who has abandoned the humdrum tasks of domestic life (118) for the nobler service of the god (1006, 1198). She offers the gruesome prize, visible in her arms, to her father for the adornment of his palace and concludes: 'Exulting in my prey, summon your friends to a feast, for you are blessed, blessed, in that I have wrought such things.'[2]

[1] κομπάσαι (1233) at the beginning, γαυρούμενος (1241) at the end of her speech.

[2] μακάριος (1242 sq.): see p. 115. ἐξειργασμένων (1243), in combination with μείζονα (1237), recalls 1199—the element φανερά being supplied by ὡς ὁρᾷς (1238; cf. 1244 ἰδεῖν).

'O grief immeasurable', replies Cadmus, 'not to be looked upon —for it is death that you have wrought with your unhappy hands. A fair sacrifice have you offered to the gods that you summon all Thebes along with me to the feast. Alas for woes—yours first of all, then mine. How has the god destroyed us, with due cause and yet excessively. Bromius the lord has destroyed us—our own kin!'[1] On this acceptance of the god's right to punish, combined with a vague revolt of conscience against his methods, something has already been said.[2] The mild soul of Cadmus is perplexed, but serious questioning is not for him. He is overwhelmed by his daughter's sorrows and his own. And, if he puts hers first (and he will soon devote himself tenderly to her case), the full pathos of his own situation comes out in his last words. He has built his life and his pride around his family, and out of family pride has embraced the cause of Semele and the worship of her son: now it is Semele's son that has brought his pride to naught, and broken his life. 'Our own kin':[3] it is the pathos of Cadmus that even in the midst of horror we cannot help smiling at him.

Dimly in the mist of her insanity Agave feels that her triumph has met a disappointing reception. She had called upon her father and her son (1211 sq.). Her father responds only with words of gloom, which she ascribes to the churlishness of age (1251 sq.), while her son is absent. It is because he is no hunter.[4] If he would emulate his mother and win fame among the Thebans in the chase! But he is only capable of fighting against the gods. He needs a grandfather's admonitions.[5] But where is he? 'Who will call him hither into my sight that he may see me in my happiness?' (1257 sq.).

The insistence throughout this episode upon the words of sight and seeing has already been remarked; and it serves more than one end. Partly, it is linked with the theme of the god's epiphany. Is proof demanded of his divinity? Then it shall be given, visible to the eyes of all, in the bloody head of Pentheus. But there is also a

[1] πένθος (1244): the fulfilment of 367, 508. καλόν (1246): see p. 24 n. 2.

[2] See p. 26.

[3] οἰκεῖος γεγώς (1250): more literally, 'born a member of my house'—a commentary, from Cadmus's point of view, on ἄγαν.

[4] εὔθηρος (1253), θηρῶν (1255). For the irony compare e.g. 228.

[5] νουθετητέος: (*a*) he has already been admonished by him with no success; (*b*) it is Agave who needs and will receive restoration to sense (νοῦς) at Cadmus's hands (cf. ἔννους 1270).

commentary upon sight and blindness, upon clarity and illusion, which will later be shown to have far-reaching importance for the interpretation of the play.[1] Agave points again and again to the visible token of her exploits (1175, 1199, 1238), yet she alone is blind to what she in fact has done, and the irony of her last words lies in the twofold fact that, though Pentheus is there, his eyes are sightless and hers cannot see him as he is. His eyes are sightless, and he cannot see her *happiness*. For that is the spiritual counterpart of her material illusion. 'No happy sight' Cadmus had called it (1232), but the word has connections farther back than that. For happiness (εὐδαιμονία), which consists in right relationship to a divine power and makes a man blessed (μάκαρ) in the eyes of others, is the promise of Dionysus to his worshippers. 'Blessed is he who has the happiness...' began the hymn in the Entrance Song (72); and with 'The man whose life is happy in the day him do I count blessed', ended the fourth choral ode (910 sq.). Agave, who has already accepted the title of 'blessed', now claims 'happiness' in the midst of the horror to which Dionysus has brought her.[2]

Yet Agave is happy—while her illusion lasts. To Cadmus remains the task of destroying that illusion. He expresses the dilemma inherent in her situation. 'Alas! If you come to clear knowledge of what you have done, your grief will be terrible; but if you abide to the end in that state in which you are, though not fortunate, in your mind you will escape misfortune' (1259–62). But is it of the nature of Dionysiac ecstasy to last for ever? Cadmus knows that a time of awakening must come and with great tenderness tries to make the transition as gentle as it can be.

Agave might brush away, half-comprehended, Cadmus's earlier speeches, but the reiteration of grief and misfortune in his recent words must penetrate even her confused mind. 'What is there here', she asks, 'that is not nobly (καλῶς) done? What is there for grief?' 'First let your eye rest upon this sky.' 'So! Why do you bid me gaze upon it?' 'Is it still the same, or has it changed for you?' 'It is brighter than before and more translucent.' Thus, as her vague, cloudy, drunken vision begins to clarify, she sees the bright light of day.

Cadmus continues: 'And is your soul still full of this excitement?'

[1] See pp. 164 sqq.

[2] μάκαιρα, μακάριος (1171, 1180, 1242). Note that εὐδαίμονα is the last word of her complete insanity.

'I do not know what you mean by that...but I am becoming somehow...sensible (ἔννους) and changing from my former mood.'[1] Reason is returning, and with its return comes forgetfulness (1272) of the preceding illusion. To restore her lost memory Cadmus invokes the aid of association. To whom was she married? To Echion. Who was the son she bore him? Pentheus. Whose face is that in her arms? Now this is too close to the truth. 'A lion's', she says quickly, seeking to retreat into her illusion. But it is too late, and she hesitates. 'A lion's—at least so said the hunting women.' At last she can dissociate herself from the *thiasos*.

'Look properly; looking is but a brief effort.' 'Ah! What do I see? What prize is this I carry in my hands?' 'Look closely upon it, and understand more clearly.' She must see with the eyes (note again the reiterated words of seeing) and with the mind: the moment of understanding has in the end come to her as it came to Pentheus (1113). 'I see my greatest sorrow. Woe is me!' She sees, not a lion, but the head of Pentheus.

'My greatest sorrow.' But this is not true;[2] she has worse to learn. 'Who killed him?' she asks. 'How came it into my hands?' But she has a presage of the answer, even before Cadmus gives it. 'You killed him, and your sisters.' 'Where did he die? Was it at home? Where was it?' 'It was where once Actaeon was torn to pieces by his hounds.'[3] It was on Cithaeron. But Agave's memory is a blank, she can account neither for Pentheus's presence there nor for her own, and Cadmus must tell her that she was once a Bacchanal and Maenad (1293, 1295). 'It was Dionysus that made our ruin; now I understand.' We may doubt, however, whether Agave yet realises fully what has happened, whether the impact of the news is more than intellectual. She can reason, she can make deductions, and what she deduces is the real existence and the power of Dionysus which she had denied. No comment, neither humble acceptance, like that of Cadmus,[4] nor bitter criticism. Later, no doubt, sweeping emotion came, but from this point onwards the text is incomplete. There is

[1] ἔννους (1270) takes the stress. 'She speaks very slowly and simply: we shudder as we watch her beginning a new life' (Wilamowitz). On the amnesia which follows, and in general on the psychological insight displayed by Euripides in this scene, see Dodds's notes.

[2] For similar irony cf. *Hipp.* 817 sq.

[3] It is natural and pathetic that Cadmus should choose this way of referring to Cithaeron; cf. p. 54.

[4] 1297: θεὸν γὰρ οὐχ ἡγεῖσθέ νιν; cf. 1325 sq.

at least one large lacuna, perhaps two.[1] Not only have we lost the entrance *ex machina* of Dionysus and the bulk of his formal opening speech, but, as we learn from ancient testimony, Agave had a lament over the torn fragments of her son's body. If the passages generally quoted from the twelfth-century *Christus Patiens* derive from this speech, we may well believe that the pity of an ancient audience was stirred, but may doubt at the same time if we have lost much that would have commended itself to our more squeamish taste. It is not certain whether this speech fell here or, as is more probable, in the large lacuna that includes the epiphany of Dionysus. However this may be, all that now remains before the remnant of the closing scene is a speech of some length from Cadmus. It is an important speech, for it serves as an epitaph for Pentheus.

It is introduced by a query from Agave: 'What part had Pentheus in my madness?'[2] The answer comes obvious enough. 'Like you he proved himself to be, not reverencing the god; who has therefore joined all together in a common ruin, both you and him, with result to destroy our house and me myself, who, having no son for child, have seen this fruit of your womb most shamefully and cruelly put to death' (1301–7). For Cadmus, having tenderly served Agave, may now turn to his own plight. The comprehensive, indiscriminate (and, therefore, typically Dionysiac) vengeance of Dionysus has struck as hardly upon the loyal Cadmus as upon any of the offenders. His family, which was his life, is destroyed; and had Dionysus been a moral god, we might have said that he had weighed the interested piety of Cadmus in the balance and found it wanting.[3] It is at least a cruel kind of justice that Cadmus should pay for his simple guile with the loss of the stake he was playing for. In the speech that follows, thoughts of family and position are combined with a more personal emotion towards Pentheus, in whom he has lost at once the mainstay of his house and an affectionate, protective grandson who took the place for him of the son he never had. 'He was the light of the house. O my child, it was you, my

[1] See Dodds, p. 218 and, on the contents of the large lacuna, p. 220.

[2] ἀφροσύνης (1301): the word is used with reference to Pentheus at 387. On the 'likeness' (1302) between mother and son something further is said in the Appendix, p. 181.

[3] It is, of course, possible that Dionysus said something to this effect in the missing part of his speech, but whether we regard him as a Greek god or as a natural force it is conformity rather than sincerity which he requires.

daughter's son, that held my palace together and were an awe unto the city; and, seeing you, no one would insult the old man, for you would have exacted condign punishment. But now I shall be dishonoured, and an exile from my home. I, Cadmus the great, who sowed the race of Thebans and reaped fair harvest. Most beloved of men (for though you are no more, my child, with me you will still count among my loved ones), never again will you touch my beard, call me grandfather, and embrace me, child, saying, "Who wrongs you, sir, who dishonours you, who troubles you and grieves your heart? Tell me and I will punish him who wrongs you, father." But now...' (1308–23).[1]

This speech tells us nothing that is strictly new about either grandfather or grandson, but by taking us inside the palace and behind the time of the play's action tells it with a different emphasis, swinging the pendulum of sympathy towards the victims of the god. We knew that Cadmus was the ruin of a once famous man, a pathetic contrast in the actual figure he presents to the fame to which he clings. We knew that he could prove an embarrassment to Pentheus, who would try with genuine affection to protect him from himself or others. Most characteristic is the blend of gentleness and harshness in Pentheus, a son's gentleness to Cadmus, the harshness of a young autocrat. The old man he will cherish and protect, but, if this involves the punishment of an offender, he will mete it out with satisfaction, for he is a terror to the city (1310), and the bonds with which he holds the state together are those of fear. This is the Pentheus whose 'quickness to wrath and all too royal temper' the Herdsman feared, the Pentheus who ordered the desecration of Teiresias's sanctuary, the Pentheus also who planned to go out against the Bacchanals and kill them, 'as he had every right to do'.[2] This was what condign punishment, 'punishment just and merited' (δίκη ἀξία) meant to Pentheus on that occasion. In a few moments the expression is picked up by the Chorus.

Cadmus ends his speech: 'But now wretched am I, and wretched you, pitiable your mother and her sisters. If there is anyone who scorns the gods, let him look upon this man's fate—and believe in them.' What will the faithful reply? 'For your part, Cadmus, I grieve, but your daughter's son has justice such as he deserves, though it brings grief to you' (1327 sq.). This, the last comment upon the fate of

[1] συνεῖχες (1308): cf. 392.

[2] 796 (ὥσπερ ἄξιος). See p. 101 n. 5.

Pentheus that our text has preserved, demands and rewards attention. The ironical use of the word 'justice' in the later stages of the play has already been noted;[1] it seems, indeed, a curious word to apply to this brutal revenge, employing the most hideous means and working indiscriminately upon the 'just' and upon the 'unjust'. But justice it appears to the Bacchanal Chorus, and rightly upon their interpretation of the term. For justice to them is 'natural' justice, which is in fact indistinguishable from the victory of the stronger animal; and that it should not discriminate is only in keeping with their cult of nature and abnegation of rational control: neither do the blind forces of nature discriminate in their operation. Yet, hollow as the word sounds, there is a kind of ironical justice in the fate of Pentheus, as in that of Cadmus. It is meted to him with the measure with which he metes to others. Stern justicer himself, he conceives justice as the infliction of violent penalties upon those who outrage his pride, and, when he too is provoked, his idea of the appropriate punishment expands to outrageous excess (796). Pentheus and his enemies are fighting on the same terms and in the same spirit; and it is the tragedy of Pentheus (if indeed we may use the word) that he chose to fight them with their own weapons of unbridled passion and violence, and in these he is hopelessly outmatched. 'My deeds deserve it' (ἀξίων μὲν ἅπτομαι, 970) are his last words upon the stage. What he imagined himself to deserve was the luxurious triumph Dionysus appeared to prophesy for him; what he found was the terrible fate that those riddling words really signified. And that fate, since it is the logical outcome of his motives and his actions, can be described, in a sense, as 'justice' and as 'deserved', as δίκη ἀξία.

The mutilation of the text has left the appearance of Dionysus with a suitable, if fortuitous, introduction. 'If there is anyone', says Cadmus, 'who scorns the gods, let him look upon this man's fate and believe in them.' For Dionysus, who has been manifesting himself throughout the play, adduces the death of Pentheus as the ultimate proof of his divinity. There is nothing more to show, and the literal epiphany of a god in glory, which now takes place *ex machina*, is spectacular, but empty.

[1] See p. 23 and p. 122. It will be noted that the sympathies of the Chorus follow the 'party-line': no pity for Pentheus, but pity for the orthodox Cadmus (σόν, σός, σοί); Agave is not mentioned.

For the first part of the god's speech we must depend upon the testimony of the Greek Argument. 'Dionysus appears and, after certain general exhortations, reveals to each one his fortune.' The nature of those general exhortations we can perhaps guess from the tone of what is left. As to the prophecies, there is reason to suppose that he foretold the destruction of Thebes by the Argives; it is certain from what follows that he ordained the exile of Agave and her sisters; what he said to Cadmus has been preserved. Cadmus will be turned into a snake, together with his wife Harmonia, daughter of Ares; driving with her a cattle-drawn chariot, he will lead barbarians in a great host to the sack of many cities, till finally they plunder the oracle of Loxias and have a disastrous return, from which Ares will save Cadmus and Harmonia and establish them alive in the Land of the Blessed.

It is a rigmarole of odd mythology, which can in fact be sorted out with the help of Herodotus and other writers. There were divergent accounts in legend of the fate of Cadmus, and it is not clear what led Euripides to employ this particular version. Part of his intention was, perhaps, a faint ridicule of the mythology itself; therefore the quaint details are set out as matter of fact, yet incongruous in their association with the human, prosaic Cadmus. It is, moreover, a frequent characteristic of such scenes in Euripides (where gods pronounce *ex machina*) that they offer, upon divine authority, a solution which is either inadequate or irrevelant.[1] So here Cadmus is promised 'blessedness' at the last, but in some vague mythical future life, so utterly remote from the actual Cadmus of the drama and his present sufferings that he himself feels the hollowness of the boon (1361 sq.).

Dry, pedantic, unreal, these prophecies are felt as an intrusion upon the human sufferers;[2] but it is not further prolonged. Dionysus rounds off his speech with a moral. 'This say I, Dionysus, son of no mortal father, but of Zeus. If you had known sanity, when you would not, you would have had the child of Zeus for ally and been happy.' There is a brief dialogue between Cadmus and the

[1] Especially is this the case in satirical plays such as the *Orestes* (e.g. 1653 sq.: a nice introduction) and *Electra* (e.g. 1290 sq.: 'now go and be happy'), but satire is an element in the *Bacchae* also. Contrast *Andr.* 1253–62, which, by the absence of the ridiculous and the presence of the poetic, provides a standard by which we can judge the present speech of Dionysus.

[2] Cf. Verrall, *op. cit.* pp. 142 sq.

god.[1] 'Dionysus, we beseech thee, we have sinned.' 'Too late have you recognised me; when you should, you knew me not.' 'We realise it; yet your visitation is excessive.' 'For I, a god born, was outraged (ὑβριζόμην) by you.' 'Gods should not be like in temper to mortals.' 'Long ago did Zeus, my father, decree these things.' As before (1249 sq.), Cadmus admits the god's right to punish, yet is moved to protest against the excessive nature of the punishment. (This is a strange lesson in *sophrosyne* to give to mortals.) And Dionysus, who has justified his action upon the principle of retaliation (1347),[2] turns off the protest by referring the responsibility to Zeus. Coming from the personal Dionysus it is a lame defence which evades the issue. But Dionysus is more than a personal god, and Zeus more than his mythical progenitor. The appeal to Zeus is an appeal to ultimate mystery, to a world-structure in which the forces Dionysus represents are an inescapable element. With that there is no quarrelling, and Agave recognises that this word is final. Addressing her father (does she ever address the god?), 'Alas!' she says, 'it is decided—our miserable exile'. Finally, with the words, 'Why then do you delay what is inevitable?' Dionysus leaves the stage.[3] Unsympathetic and impatient, if the words fit the person of this mythological god, they fit also the representative of blind forces: there is no stopping to reason with a thunderbolt or an earthquake.

The stage is left to the stricken mortals, and at first both are preoccupied with their own sorrows. Cadmus has turned over in

[1] Elmsley transferred 1344, 1346, 1348 to Agave, and has been widely followed. The ascription to Cadmus is not, however, ruled out by the confession of sin, since it is quite in keeping for him to identify himself with his family. And is it really inappropriate for Dionysus to include him in the condemnation as he has been included in the punishment? We cannot settle this point, since the mutilation of the text has left us no certain clue to the attitude of Agave towards the god. It is dramatically effective for Agave to ignore the god, but this may not have been the effect that the dramatist intended. There remains the possibility that Cadmus spoke 1344 and 1346 (which recalls 1249), but Agave 1348 (which goes farther in protest). So Lucas; and this too is dramatically effective, but equally uncertain. See also p. 166.

[2] The return of ὕβρις for ὕβρις was allowed by popular morality (cf. Gorgias fr. 6: ὑβρισταὶ εἰς τοὺς ὑβρίζοντας) and practised by such as Eteocles and Polyneikes (*Phoen.* 620); no less by the Olympian gods, by Aphrodite (cf. *Hipp.* 445 sq., 474 sq.), by Dionysus—and by Hera (9), so that the play begins and ends with ἀθάνατος ὕβρις.

[3] See p. 147 n. 3.

his mind the curious fate awaiting him. It is characteristic what rankles: 'Unhappy am I! To *barbarians* I shall go, an old man and a sojourner.' It is a sadly symmetrical end to the career of Cadmus, who had come from the barbarians of Asia to be a sojourner in Greece, where he had won fame and founded a great city. Now all that he built up is gone for nothing: his city is to be sacked, his royal house is shattered, he himself is to become a wanderer again and, most bitter of all, to lead a barbarian host against 'the altars and tombs' of that Greece where he had become a hero. This is the real blow. The metamorphosis, that has no relevance to the actual Cadmus, is dismissed in a line. The promise of ultimate blessedness, equally irrelevant, he disregards, or regards only as a refusal of natural death and the peace that there at least he might have hoped to find.[1]

Agave is to lose both her father and her native land. She tries to cling to him in terror of her coming loneliness: 'Whither shall I turn, an exile from my country?' 'I know not, child; small help is your father.' The metre changes and a musical accompaniment begins, as Agave bids farewell to house and city. Then her thoughts turn to her father[2] and his to her, and they forget themselves in mutual consolation. 'I grieve for you, father.' 'And I for you, child; and I weep for your sisters.' 'Cruelly has lord Dionysus brought this outrage upon your house.' She knows her father, and where his heart is; and his reply is in keeping: 'Yes, for he suffered cruelly at your hands, having his name without honour in Thebes.' It was a sad mistake, but it was not Cadmus's.[3] They exchange farewells, and Cadmus leaves the stage to Agave.

'Lead me, my companions, where I may find my sisters, my poor fellow-exiles. And may I come where neither loathsome Cithaeron may see me, nor I behold Cithaeron, and where no dedicated thyrsus

[1] 1360 sqq. παύσομαι κακῶν, ἥσυχος: peace and an end of pain are the boasted gifts of Dionysus. For Cadmus and the πόνος-μόχθος motif, cf. 187 sqq. (the illusion), 1218 (the reality).

[2] Who has, in a speech now mutilated (1371), referred for the last time, directly or indirectly, to the Actaeon theme.

[3] I have followed Hermann in ascribing 1377 sq. to Cadmus (with ἔπασχεν for ἔπασχον). If Dionysus speaks these lines, we must suppose either that he has waited in silence (which seems inartistic) or that he is heard as a voice 'off' (which seems more Shakespearian than Euripidean). His disappearance before the end of the scene is not specially motived as that of Artemis in the *Hippolytus*, but Euripides had learnt from that play the effectiveness of leaving the stage to the human sufferers.

can remind. Let other Bacchanals have thought for them.' The mountain that has been the sinister background of the play looms up to the last. Mountain and thyrsus she bequeathes to other Bacchanals. There would be no lack of them in matter of historical fact to worship on Cithaeron, no lack either of women and men to follow the religion of Dionysus with its joys and furies.

While Agave and her companions leave the stage in sad procession, the Chorus, as they themselves file out, bring the play to a close with that comment upon the strange variety and unexpected issues of human life with which Euripides chose to end a number of his plays. 'Many shapes are there of divinity, and many things do the gods ordain beyond our expectation; things that were thought are not accomplished, and for the unthought-of god finds a way. Such was the event of this action.'

CHAPTER XI

EURIPIDES AND DIONYSUS (2)

'Many shapes are there of divinity' (τῶν δαιμονίων). Tag though it may be, it is an appropriate enough conclusion to a play in which a Protean god has manifested himself so variously. The lines that follow, expressing and accepting the mystery of human destiny, have a calm dignity. Their naïvety, however, disqualifies them as the poet's final comment upon the play's action. Ultimately there may be mystery, but the mind of man can read some of its riddles, and to those who have become familiar with the shapes of this particular Daimon the events he brings about may not be so unexpected after all.

Having reviewed the play in detail, we can now return to the discussions of the opening chapter. The *Bacchae* has exercised its modern interpreters because it has been felt uncertain how Euripides stood towards the theme he treated. Doubtless, it is the first function of the dramatist to write an effective play, of the poet to write poetry which stimulates, delights and enlarges the imagination; and the *Bacchae* has enthralled thousands who have never greatly cared to determine its author's attitude to its subject. Yet when a great artist at the height of his creative power treats a theme of wide scope and universal interest, it would be strange if the treatment did not in some way reveal the conscious opinions of the writer. They may not be obvious, for they will be embodied in the structure of the work of art; they are not likely to be dogmatic, for width of sympathy does not tend to dogma.

Our problem then is not an imaginary one. It is important, however, that it should be rightly stated. What is the play about? Broadly, it is about the religion of Dionysus and the behaviour of his votaries. Such is the obvious and also the correct answer, provided that we do not put too narrow an interpretation upon the terms. For the *Bacchae* has sometimes been approached as though its sole or main concern was with the contemporary cults of Dionysus in Greece or Macedonia, and as though the sole or main questions to be answered were these: did Euripides approve or disapprove these cults, did he wish to commend them to his audience or the reverse? Before the wide applications to all human life that our examination of the play has disclosed, such questions surely pale into relative insignificance. Even within the narrow context they imply, they may be somewhat misleading.

Of the details of Dionysiac cult in fifth-century Greece our knowledge is limited to miscellaneous information which gives us little or no insight into its quality.[1] A primitive ecstatic worship had entered the country some centuries earlier, and we should wish to know, not merely how far details of ritual, but how far its original character had survived. There is a danger, no doubt, of exaggerating the extent to which the immigrant cult had been tempered and hellenised, on the false assumption that civilisation advances with perfect uniformity and logic. The process must, moreover, have varied considerably from one part of the Greek world to another. We can well believe (though the evidence is slight) that in Asia Minor, cheek by jowl with the wild worship of Cybele, the Great Mother, and of Sabazius, the rites of Dionysus were themselves wild. From Crete we hear of the rending and eating of a bull, but there the worship of Dionysus had been engrafted upon the orgiastic cult of another great mother-goddess; and Crete was remote from the main centres of Greek culture. However, on the Greek mainland also and in the Aegean islands a mention of Maenads or Lenae, a cult of Bakchos or Bakchios, suggest here and there a worship that had once at least been ecstatic. Even at Thebes, even at Delphi, there were rites of wild women (Maenads at Thebes, Thyiads at Delphi), conducted upon the mountains at night by torchlight. In particular the rite of Delphi, prophesied by Teiresias in this play, had caught the imagination of the Greek poets and is described in famous passages of Sophocles and Aristophanes. But we know few details; and that, for instance, at both Thebes and Delphi there was in historical times the dismemberment of a sacred animal is a matter of uncertain, if probable, inference. On the other hand we do know that in either case the celebrant women were public functionaries, that their activities were under the control of authority (at Delphi of Apollo's oracle) and limited to fixed festivals occurring in the winter of alternate years.[2] A rite so constituted may have been a rich experience for the performers, but it can hardly be said to have served an important social function, when these performers were a small company of consecrated women. Was it for this that Dionysus

[1] See Farnell, *Cults*, v, pp. 85–344, esp. pp. 150 sqq.

[2] See Nilsson, *op. cit.* pp. 208 sq.

brought his worship to Thebes? Was it this that Euripides desired to praise and propagate or to resist? Euripides, moreover, though at a dozen points he shows his knowledge of the trieteric festivals, was an Athenian and writing for Athenians;[1] and nowhere, it seems, had the ecstatic tradition more completely disappeared. Once Attica too had had its wild women, as the very name of the Lenaean festival testifies; but in historical times, apart from a mission of Attic Thyiades sent regularly to assist in the Delphic rite, ecstasy had disappeared from the Athenian cult of Dionysus; his festivals were either rude and grotesque or sober and magnificent; the women of Athens carried baskets not thyrsi in his service.[2] To discourage Dionysiac enthusiasm, in the strict sense, at Athens was therefore a needless task, to encourage it a vain one; and neither task could Euripides have expected to achieve by displaying to his fellow-citizens something so remote from their own cult as is the content of the *Bacchae*.

If anything within their own experience was recalled by the play, it was more likely the oriental cults which made an appearance in Athens in the latter half of the fifth century: cults of Cybele, of Bendis, and especially of Sabazius, a close congener of the original Dionysus. These worships of orgiastic type, introduced by the growing foreign population of slaves and metics, seem to have made some headway among the Athenians, predisposed by the stress and strain of war, and to have stirred up a degree of controversy. The evidence has recently been reviewed by Professor Dodds,[3] who points out that 'the coming of Sabazius was in essentials a re-enactment in modern dress of the theme of the *Bacchae*', and suggests with plausibility that the contemporary controversy would have been in the minds of poet and audience alike, particularly during the debate between Pentheus and Teiresias. Orgiastic cult had thus become once more in some degree an issue, and an issue which may well have stimulated the poet's thought about such phenomena and the audience's interest in them.

[1] Even if the *Bacchae* was performed in Macedonia (which is uncertain), there can be no doubt that Euripides intended it for the Attic stage. See Nihard, *op. cit.* pp. 31 sqq.

[2] 'Only the Lenaea may perhaps have kept something of the original fervour which its name betokens' (Dodds, p. xix). But the evidence is disputed.

[3] *Maenadism*, pp. 171 sqq.

It is indeed possible that this was a more important influence upon Euripides than his Macedonian visit. The fact that the *Bacchae* was written, or at least completed,[1] in Macedonia may have its significance, but it must not be given the wrong emphasis. Plutarch[2] tells us that the cult of Dionysus had long flourished there, and his account of the behaviour of Olympias has features that recall our play. Beyond this we know nothing. We are, however, perhaps entitled to use our fuller information about the aboriginal Thracian cult and to infer that Macedonia, a near neighbour and only partly civilised, had retained more of the ecstatic self-abandonment than had Greece proper. It did not, however, need Macedonia to create in the poet an interest in religious phenomena of this kind. 'Pure has my life been since the day when I became an initiate of Idaean Zeus and herdsman of night-wandering Zagreus, and having accomplished the raw feasts and held torches aloft to the Mountain Mother, yea torches of the Kuretes, was raised to the holy estate and called Bakchos.'[3] This passage does not come from the *Bacchae*; it is a fragment of the *Cretans*, and the *Cretans* is probably an early play. Over such matters the mind of Euripides had brooded for a generation, and his thought upon them was the mature reflection of a lifetime rather than an old man's momentary discovery. Moreover, it is at least unlikely that he could have seen much, though he may have heard something, of a female cult at which he could not have been present with impunity. The change of environment may, as has often been suggested, have stimulated and refreshed his poetic gift. It was then a lucky chance for us that took him to Macedonia, but it did not create, though it may have enhanced, the poetry and drama of the *Bacchae*.

The *Bacchae* is, however, concerned with more than an ecstatic religious cult. If there was a topical interest in the treatment of such a cult, this is far from exhausting the content of the play. There is a wider theme, which is emotionalism as a factor in human life, both political and individual; and myth and cult in combination provided

[1] We do not know how quickly Euripides worked, but the conception and execution of a work upon the scale of the *Bacchae* may well have covered years rather than months. There are many features in the *Phoenissae* and the *Orestes*, the immediately preceding plays, which may suggest that Euripides was already meditating the greater play which followed.

[2] *Alex.* 2.

[3] Transl. Guthrie, *Orpheus and Greek Religion*, p. 111, *q.v.*

Euripides with unsurpassable symbols for the poetic expression of this theme. Treated as symbol, extended in scope and given that generality which they can so easily carry, Dionysus and his worship have wide applications to the life of civilised communities even in circumstances other than those of overt breakdown or relapse; and it is in these wide applications that the moral and intellectual value of the play lies, and lay for the contemporaries of Euripides no less than for ourselves.

The impact of the *Bacchae* may thus be said to radiate, like that of a pebble cast into water, in widening circles. The play has an immediate relevance to the worship of Dionysus in Greece, being a priceless document for the history of Greek religion. At the next remove it is relevant to all emotional forms of religion in all ages, and particularly to those which manifest the power of the group. But similar manifestations occur in connection with objects not specifically religious, and so the scope of the play is widened to include the phenomena of group emotion in all social and political life. Finally, though the association of individuals may lead to an enhancement of emotion its power over the isolated individual is still the work of Dionysus: Pentheus is unknowingly his servant no less than the Maenad devotees. With these various planes of reference in mind, we can summarise the Dionysiac phenomena that have been observed in our study of the play,[1] but first it is necessary to return to a question which was raised in the first chapter and which is crucial to the interpretation.[2]

These Dionysiac phenomena are exhibited for the most part (naturally enough) by the portrayal of Bacchanals. Of these there are two sets—the Asiatic band that follows Dionysus, and the Theban women whom he has 'driven mad' to Mount Cithaeron. There is one obvious difference between the two sets: the former serve Dionysus by choice, the latter perforce and as a 'punishment' for earlier impiety (for which reason, as we have seen, the former hate the latter and rejoice in their disaster).[3] It has been argued that this

[1] Nature also has its Dionysiac aspects, which are introduced by means of the palace-miracle and the Messenger speeches.

[2] See p. 12.

[3] If indeed it is correct to state that they were made Bacchanals as a 'punishment'. 114–19 regards them as the first-fruits of Theban participation in the cult. Their punishment may reside rather in the fact that they were the instruments of the punishment of Pentheus.

difference is fundamental and that Euripides intends to contrast the belief and conduct of the truly blessed Bacchanals of the Chorus, who are in right relation to the god, with the diseased Maenadism of the Theban women. Such a play could have been written. But did Euripides write it? Only the Bacchanals of the Chorus can answer this question for us.

One thing is clear, that it is dangerous to defy this god, to suppress the force which he represents. The Theban women, like Pentheus, had defied him, and we may assume that, like Pentheus, they had been full of a suppressed emotionalism. The warning is salutary: it is the lesson of the palace-miracle no less than of the first Messenger speech. But was it the precepts of the Chorus that would have saved them, if they had listened in time? Superficially yes, for the Chorus preach moderation. Yet if the preceding analyses of their songs are not in error, the poet has been at pains to show that an extremity of violence is implicit in their creed as much as peace and moderation. Is it true, or did Euripides think it was true, psychologically and sociologically, that people are rendered immune from the extremes of Maenadism by abjuring intellect, concentrating on immediate satisfactions and accepting whatever the mass of ordinary men believes and practises? Or does the play not rather demonstrate that the suppression of emotion and the exclusive cult of emotion may lead sooner or later to the same results?

For, if the Theban Bacchanals represent the suppression of emotion, the Asiatic Bacchanals represent, not a moderate regular cult of Dionysus, like the trieteric festivals of historical times, but rather the incursion of Bacchism, disturbing, violent and uncompromising. They are Asiatics, and stand for orgiastic cult in its aboriginal purity. But as the Chorus of a Greek tragedy, whose traditional function it is to illuminate the action, their circumstances neither demand nor allow displays of physical violence. Yet violent they become to the point of mania in their emotional reaction to Pentheus, with a lyric violence which is the counterpart of the physical activity to which his interference leads the Theban Maenads.[1] Moreover, while the latter were still in the peaceful phase of Dionysiac activity, there was latent or half-concealed in the Entrance Song of the Chorus the violence which was later to be revealed upon Cithaeron. For the combination of peace and fury, which is afterwards made explicit in the great Messenger speeches, and indeed in

[1] Cf. Wassermann, *op. cit.* p. 280.

their own later songs, was already implied; and from the *sparagmos* and *omophagia* of the Entrance Song to the killing of Pentheus and the 'feast' of Agave is a genuine dramatic crescendo,[1] which is also a progressive revelation of the god.

If, then, the Chorus sing in odes of great beauty of rites which they make to sound not only attractive but harmless, whereas the Theban women perform deeds of horror upon the mountain, this difference has a dramatic explanation; and the drama reveals, as it develops, a similarity more significant than the difference. Thus the Theban Bacchanals act, the Asiatic Bacchanals explain how it is that they come so to act. Both reveal the nature of Dionysus and his religion; and, since the revelations are complementary and mutually consistent, we are entitled to use them together to answer the questions that will now be put. What are Bacchanals like and how do they behave?

They are women, organised in groups under a male leader.[2] That they are women is partly an accident of legend, partly a reality of cult. Though Greece knew Bakchoi as well as Bakchai, the ecstatic cult of Dionysus was mostly, it seems, in the hands of women; and this corresponds to wider experience. For though men too are susceptible to group emotion in religion, women have tended in all ages to outrival them in the degree of their enthusiasm; in particular, the spectacle of a band of female devotees under an adored male leader, moved by a nice blend of religious and sexual emotion, is one of universal interest. The group is bound together by loyalty to the leader, but also by outward symbols: by a common dress, consisting of fawnskin, headdress and wand, and by a common rallying-cry of Evoe—by a uniform and a slogan.

Thus constituted and equipped, how do they act? They go to the mountains, where, remote from normal life, and in close touch with nature and the animals, they perform secret rites. Of these the central feature is a dance, accompanied by music of oboes and tambourines. Decorously it may begin, but its movements grow wilder and wilder, the Maenad's head is thrown back in ecstasy, her eyes roll or squint, her mouth foams, she has earned her name, she is a Mad Woman. In this dance the limitations of self are laid aside and the dancer feels at one with the god, with her fellows and with all nature. But the intensity of emotion aroused must find some

[1] First a goat, then a number of larger animals, then a man.

[2] For the Stranger seems to be the ἔξαρχος of the Theban Bacchanals also (cf. 63). In his absence Agave naturally takes the lead.

outlet, and the dance may turn into a hunt. A wild creature, a goat, a fawn or a bull, is pursued, pulled to the ground, torn limb from limb (*sparagmos*), and eaten raw (*omophagia*).[1] Then the ecstasy passes and the Maenads return to peaceful activities. For not all the time of their sojourn on the mountain is spent in the orgiastic dance. Before and after it everything is 'a marvel of good order': they sing hymns ritual and contemplative to the god; they dandle young animals, even suckle them; they busy themselves with quiet, almost domestic tasks; they refresh themselves with the god's gifts of wine, milk and honey, miraculously produced at their desire; they sleep. So enigmatic a combination are their activities.

To explain the enigma it is necessary to consider their aims and their characteristic states of mind. And, while their activities, at least upon a literal consideration, may seem special to a particular historical cult,[2] their aims are of more general reference. They can be stated in this way: to serve the god and to receive his gifts. His service entails purity, which means (in this context) scrupulous observance of ritual acts and avoidance of contact with the profane; and it ensures 'happiness' (εὐδαιμονία), his crowning and comprehensive gift which makes them 'blessed' (μάκαρες) in their own eyes and in those of the beholder. But 'happiness' is a vague term without further definition, and the 'happiness' which consists in right relation to a Daimon must be relative to the particular Daimon concerned. The Dionysiac happiness or blessedness, as revealed in this play, has a negative and a positive aspect. Negatively, it is a liberation: from the trammels and duties of civilised life (and so has a particular attraction for women in any age when their life is dull and their instincts repressed), from the limitations and responsibilities of individuality, from the burden of self-knowledge, from

[1] Anthropologists tell us that the omophagy was a sacrament in which the worshippers partook of the god, as embodied in the sacrificial animal, and that Pentheus was in origin a kind of double of Dionysus, to whom human victims seem to have been offered in primitive times. Euripides can hardly have been aware of either of these things. If he was, he excluded them from his play. Pentheus, to whose fate all references to the *sparagmos* look forward, was not destined to be eaten; and the only hint of omophagy after the Entrance Song (139) is the imaginary banquet of Agave (1184). Pentheus, moreover, stands to Dionysus in a more subtle relation than that of identity (*v. infra*).

[2] Though admitting parallels of the greatest interest from diverse times and places (see Dodds, *Maenadism*, and Introduction to his edition).

the effort of thought and from care for the past or the future. It is an escape from all these things into a mindless joy in the present, which is the positive aspect of their blessedness. This joy may derive from their peaceful activities, from the feast, from sleep, from hymn-singing, from milk, wine and honey, from the oaks and pines among which they move; it may equally derive from the wild ecstatic dance. It may derive from the ritual act of suckling animals; it may equally derive from the ritual act of hunting them down and tearing them in pieces.

Into their characteristic states of mind the description of their activities and their aims has already given us some insight. Having separated themselves from others to worship the god, they are intensely conscious of their separateness, to the point of spiritual pride. Their devotion to their god is boundless, so is their faith in him; and this devotion and faith cannot be easily disentangled from their devotion to and faith in their leader. They feel a sense of release from the burdens and cares of normal life; they do not realise that they have exchanged one form of bondage for another, or, if they do, they glory in it, for the service of Dionysus the god himself makes easy with his drugs. They experience extremes of satisfactory emotion, passing quickly from one to another, from peace to fury and back to peace. How is the clash of moods tolerated, the inconsistency of conduct compassed? Bacchanals are whole-hearted in all their moods and actions, in sleep as in waking, in peace as in fury. They can be whole-hearted, because reflective thought with its concern for past and future, cause and effect, is banished and their whole attention concentrated upon the present. To inhibit completely the human faculty of 'looking before and after' is not an altogether easy task, and perhaps no Bacchanals do so over long periods with entire success.[1] It is not easy without a technique directed towards that end; it is not easy without drugs. But their whole organisation and activities provide such a technique, and the drugs at their disposal are manifold. There is wine; and, since the notorious effects of wine—to release, to excite, to stupefy, to create oblivion and concentrate attention—correspond to various phases of their experience, wine is well regarded as the distinctive gift of Dionysus. There is music, there is love-making (Dionysiac gifts of the Muses and of Aphrodite); above all, there is the wild dance, whose move-

[1] This (legend apart) is the lesson of Agave's awakening. But she did not return to rationality—become ἔννους—till she had left the *thiasoi.*

ments have an almost hypnotic effect upon the dancer. The mutual stimulus of the group has something of the effect of a drug; emotion is more easily shared than thought, and the member thankfully merges her own personality in the collective ecstasy. By one method and another emotional tension is heightened; state succeeds to state; and, since there is little memory and no conscious comparison, successive states may clash and the Bacchanal feel no inconsistency, but entertain them all alike for their value as present pleasure. For one thing remains fast, like a pedal point beneath moving discords, a continuous satisfaction, a fundamental peace of mind, which is retained amid the wildest manifestations and is that 'happiness in the day' which they count blessed.

But this does not exhaust the list of emotions felt by Bacchanals in the play. There are others; and they belong, strictly speaking, not to the cult but to the legend. Within the enclosed circle of the cult the worshippers experience entire satisfaction, and the wider social value of their experience is irrelevant. But the Bacchanals of the Chorus are not in isolation. They are attempting to introduce their worship into a civilised community, to which the Dionysiac in its pure form is inimical.[1] In consequence they are persecuted; and in consequence they feel the emotion of fear. This fear is a product of the legend, since the Bacchanals of an established cult have no cause to be afraid; it is far, however, from being irrelevant to the modes of thought and way of life of Bacchanals. When their fears have been relieved, the Chorus compare themselves to a fawn which has been terrified by the huntsman and his dogs, but has escaped once more into joy. The aptness of the comparison has been discussed at length in an earlier chapter.[2] For Bacchanals in their concentration upon present emotion aspire to the condition of animals. Like animals they hunt; but, like animals, they are liable to be hunted. Absorption in the present entails this disadvantage, that when adverse circumstances and painful emotions inevitably arise, they are felt with characteristic intensity.

The response of the Bacchanals to fear is human rather than animal. They combat it with the psychological weapons at their command—with faith and with the spiritual pride which is its by-product. They hate the object of their fear with a personal and vindictive hatred, and their exultation over their enemy's downfall

[1] This is symbolised by the attack on the villages: see pp. 96 sq.

[2] See pp. 106 sqq.

is infused with a malice absent from the triumphant animal. Being human, they seek to hide the naked struggle for existence proper to the jungle beneath pretentious claims to law and justice. Their hatred is directed immediately against Pentheus the persecutor. But Euripides takes advantage of the choral odes to extend its reference. Servants of a jealous god who hates those who will not accept his religion, this hatred they share;[1] and it reaches as far beyond the immediate context as that religion itself transcends the limitations of a particular cult. In effect, then, they hate those who are unlike themselves and will not share in their rejections—of thought, of effort, of aspiration, of individualism. They hate those who will not accept the standards of the mass upon which their claims to law and justice are based.[2]

It is by the implications of the choruses that the wider scope of their hatred is revealed. For in the main their adversary and victim is Pentheus; and Pentheus, so far from being their antithesis, himself exhibits Dionysiac phenomena. It is true that the herd or group gratifies the instinct to associate and, at the same time, provides an enhancement of other instinctive emotions as well as an organisation for leading the emotional life with greater efficiency. But clearly this life can be led without that particular stimulus and under conditions of relative isolation. Bacchanals differ from other human beings in degree, not in kind. It is part—and an important part—of the function of Pentheus to show how an individual of powerful instincts and intense emotion may resemble Bacchanals in his mental states and in his actions.

From the first Pentheus is represented as unstable and excitable, a man of quick temper and violent reactions. As the play develops, we learn of two particular instinctive appetites that are strong in him—the sexual impulse and the lust for power.[3] Now, were he a perfect Bacchanal, he would proceed to the straightforward gratification of these desires. As it is, the sexual impulse is repressed, and therefore the more dangerous, like a stream imperfectly dammed; the desire for power and glory is indeed partially gratified, but not

[1] See p. 67. It is an apparent paradox that Dionysus, who loves peace (419), is also a hating god (424). But the paradox disappears when the relation of Dionysus and his followers to the animal world is borne in mind. 'He is the principle of animal life, ταῦρος and ταυροφάγος, the hunted and the hunter' (Dodds, p. xvii).

[2] See pp. 112 sq., 123.

[3] For φιλοτιμία as a form of μανία, cf. *Phoen.* 531–5.

acknowledged. It is not until a process comparable to hypnotism is accomplished upon him that he drops all pretence and frankly reveals his underlying motives. He falls an easy victim to the fascinating personality of the god-stranger, and the ease of the god's victory is an index of the extent to which Pentheus was already his unconscious follower, already familiar (as even Teiresias perhaps realised) with his drugs.[1]

Despite all resemblance, however, Pentheus is clearly no perfect Bacchanal; and the difference also is significant. There is a difference of circumstance, a difference of technique. The Bacchanals are associated with others of like mind and, disclaiming personal ambition, sink their separate selves in a kind of common personality. Pentheus seeks the glorification of his individual person. Again, the Bacchanals have chosen the environment that fits them; Pentheus is living in a civilised or partly civilised community, which at once gives him the opportunities for self-aggrandisement and commands him to obey a code of self-restraint. Thus, while they surrender whole-heartedly to their emotions, he either fights against his or refuses to avow them, and thereby misses the inner harmony and peace of mind that they (at whatever price) have attained. Moreover, an isolated individual, he commands less force than the Bacchanals, united in the group, and so his Dionysiac manifestations pale before theirs.[2] Yet he competes with them in violence.

This is the irony of the career of Pentheus, that he makes the worst of two worlds, neither a reasonable man nor a successful Bacchanal. It might be called a tragedy that a man not without worth should be brought to a disastrous end by fatal weaknesses. Yet tragedy does not seem the right word nor Pentheus to be of the stature of tragic heroes; and any attempt to make such a hero of him is bound in one way or another to distort the character as revealed by the text of the play. He is drawn with understanding and, for dramatic purposes, there is a swing of sympathy towards him in the closing scenes, but it is the relentless analysis of weakness that is the salient feature of the portrait. Nor does Pentheus, like a tragic hero, take the centre of the stage. It is true that the action of the play is the progress of his downfall, which we watch with growing horror, felt more, however, for the things done than for the fact that they are done to

[1] 326 sq. Hence the irony of describing Pentheus, at any stage of the play, as ἄθεος, ἀβάκχευτος, etc.

[2] See p. 55.

Pentheus. Hardly even in his first scene is he the dominant figure; it is a scene, not of tragedy but of satire, and Teiresias claims it. Always after that Pentheus is accompanied by the enigmatic person of the god-stranger, who commands an equal or major share of our attention, while in the foreground stand continually the Bacchanal Chorus, enigmatic as the god and even more vivid. The play is rightly known, not as *Pentheus*, but as the *Bacchae*; and the personal career of Pentheus, 'tragic' only in the cheapened sense, is part, if an integral part, of a wider theme. Were he too fine, too interesting, were he truly tragic, the Bacchanal context would become a background to his fate. As it is, we can regard him with enough detachment to see how he belongs himself to the Bacchic pattern.

The problem propounded at the beginning of this chapter has been modified in its content. If the play is about the religion of Dionysus, it is only slightly concerned with the contemporary cult. The dramatist has taken the primitive Dionysiac legend and discovered in it universal significance and symbols of the blind working of emotion in human societies and individuals; and, if the incidents of the legend allowed him to show men and women acting under the influence of this force which is Dionysus, he was enabled by the choral convention of Attic tragedy further to analyse their states of mind and expose the fundamental assumptions that underlie their way of life. The problem is modified in its content: it still remains unsolved. How does Euripides stand towards Dionysus and his religion?

Now of Dionysiac cult in the narrower sense, or of orgiastic cult in general, we might ask whether the poet approved or disapproved of it. The wider scale dwarfs such a question in such terms: one does not 'approve' of the smiling face of nature and 'disapprove' of a forest fire or the Mississippi in flood. Just as physical nature is powerful and dangerous, so are the natural forces of emotion—so powerful and so dangerous that human life is often wrecked among them. This power must be acknowledged, and by some it may be accepted, like fire and flood, with pious resignation. Indeed the protest even of an individual of genius may seem futile. Yet, particularly outside the Christian tradition, there have been poets and thinkers who have felt resentment at the conditions of humanity. It was suggested in an earlier chapter that the satire which, in this play as in others of Euripides, attends the manifestations of divinity upon the stage derives not merely, perhaps not mainly, from the reforming moralist but from the sensitive humanist confronted with the human predicament.

Acceptance may be humble or resentful; but that is not the end of the matter. The analogy of physical forces is again helpful. Man has proved his power to deal with fire and flood, averting their dangers or even employing them in his useful service. So too he can deal, and has dealt with all too variable success, with the psychological forces in himself and his societies. How should we treat Dionysus? Should we fight against him like Pentheus or worship him in complete abandonment like the Chorus of Bacchanals? Had Euripides formed a judgement upon this question also, and did he express it in his play?

Euripides was a keen observer of humanity, and his experience of the vivid political life of Greece had culminated in a ferocious and devastating war. He had also lived during one of the great creative periods of the human intellect and imagination. He was, moreover, an old man when he wrote the *Bacchae*, and old men should be wise. What is the wisdom of Euripides in this matter? We may be justified in putting the question in this way, since 'wisdom' (σοφία) and 'wise' (σοφός) are important words in the play. A claim to wisdom is advanced at one time or another by many of the characters: there is a *sophia* of Dionysus, a *sophia* of the Bacchanals, a *sophia* of Teiresias (which he disclaims while exercising it); there is perhaps even (since he hurls charges of folly) a *sophia* of Pentheus. Is it possible to discover what Euripides also counted *sophon*? It may not be easy.

There are two easy ways of tackling the question, and both must be regarded with suspicion. One of them is arbitrarily to select passages from the play (by preference from the choruses), to isolate them and say that here the poet is speaking in his own person. Now it would be rash to assert that nothing that he puts into the mouths of his characters coincides with his own opinions. But we should be chary of assuming this in any instance unless the passage in question stands out undramatically from its context; and, if our examination of the play is valid, it has revealed a closely-knit and self-consistent work of dramatic art, every detail of which is relevant to the progress of the action, the states of mind of the characters, their philosophy of life and the hidden springs of their motives. The other easy way is to assume that Euripides identifies himself so completely with one or other party in the play that their 'wisdom' is identical with his. But this assumption of simple partisanship is difficult to maintain. For with whom can he identify himself? With the unstable Pentheus, groping in the dark? With the cruel intriguer god? With the ingenious self-satisfied 'modernist' Teiresias? With the Bacchanals who tear a man in pieces or the Bacchanals who gloat over the deed? It is surely part of the difficulty in deducing the *sophia* of Euripides from the play that it deals (and had to deal) with a disastrous action. Pentheus, Cadmus, Dionysus, the Bacchanals—all act according to their lights, and the outcome is the pitiable events we witness. The shallow morality of Pentheus, the cool cleverness of the Stranger, the 'wisdom' that the Bacchanals find in self-abandonment to their emotions, all lead to the same appalling end. Teiresias indeed has for his politic counsels a kind of long-term justification. It would indeed come about that the religion of Dionysus (in the narrower sense) was accepted in Greece and its turbulence controlled, and this result must have been achieved, in part at least, by the judicious policies of his successors. But, if the future belongs to Teiresias, he cannot help the present crisis, and rightly he leaves the action of the play at an early stage.

If the wisdom of the characters is weighed and found wanting, it does not follow that the wisdom of Euripides is to be found within the play. But if it is there, the poet will have used methods of art to communicate it to his audience. Now the function of certain recurrent motifs in the construction of the play has emerged clearly enough from our earlier examination. None is more persistent or more important than that of 'manifestation' or 'epiphany'. The play is opened with the god's announcement that he will manifest his deity to mortals, to Pentheus and to Thebes; the play closes with the appearance of that same god in glory; and all that lies between has been in some sense a manifestation of the god in some guise to someone.

The epiphany of Dionysus has already been treated in an earlier chapter, but from a limited point of view. Dionysus was a major god of the Greeks and received worship from them; and to him as an object of worship, as in other plays to other gods, Euripides seems to adopt an attitude which is critical and satirical. In particular he prepares and accompanies the final epiphany of the god with such discordant themes that its glory becomes a mockery. How far it is the 'mythological', how far the 'real' deity[1] that evokes this treat-

[1] See p. 17.

ment may be a matter of debate. But the epiphany of the 'real' deity is made not merely or mainly through the personal god upon the stage (who is so limited in his dramatic presentation that no really profound revelation can come from him), but through the happenings he causes and the persons he inspires. To whom, then, is this epiphany vouchsafed?

Let us come closer to the Greek text. The means by which the poet emphasises his significant themes is, partly at least, a verbal technique. A word or group of cognates and synonyms is constantly repeated and thrown into relief at salient points of the play.[1] Such is the employment of φανερός ('manifest'), φαίνεσθαι ('be manifested'), and similar words. The god's announcement in the Prologue of his self-revelation (ἐμφανής 22, φανέντα 42, ἐνδείξομαι 47) is picked up at the climax of the play. The death of Pentheus is prepared by a summons to justice to come 'manifest' (φανερός 991, 1011), is hailed by the Chorus as a manifestation of their god's greatness (θεὸς φαίνῃ μέγας 1031). But it has been the work of human hands: therefore first the Bacchanals of the Chorus claim that the ends they pursue are 'great and manifest' (1006 sq.), then Agave picks up the phrase and applies it to the achievement of her hunt (1198). The god, his nature and his works, are manifest, are clear, are φανερά: they can be *seen*.

To φανερός, φαίνεσθαι, we can add a group of words of sight and seeing—ὁρᾶν, ὄψις, and their synonyms. The accumulation of such words in the scene that follows Agave's entrance has already been noticed. It seems to serve two purposes. It insists upon a particular aspect of the god's epiphany, which is now literally visible in Agave's hands and is not a pleasant sight to see (ὄψιν οὐκ εὐδαίμονα 1232). It is also relevant to her own deluded vision, as she calls on all to see what she mis-sees herself. Mis-sees or misinterprets, for her illusion is of the mind rather than of the outward eye.

'Look upon it (the head)', says her father 'and understand more clearly' (σαφέστερον μάθε 1281). 'It was Dionysus that destroyed

[1] Cf. the treatment of ὕβρις, ὑβρίζειν: γέλως, γελᾶν: σωφροσύνη with its opposite μανία (and their kindred and synonyms); νόμος, νόμιμος, νομίζειν; καλός; the group of θήρ, θηρᾶν, ἄγρα, ἀγρευέιν; σοφία and σοφός. The technique is familiar to students of Aeschylus; it is less prominent, at least less dependent on the repeated word, in Sophocles (but see T. B. L. Webster, *op. cit.* p. 185; and Kitto, p. 174, on the *Electra*); it is revived by Euripides in certain of his plays; cf. Sheppard, *C.Q.* x (1916), p. 72, on the *Hercules Furens.*

us: now I understand' (μανθάνω), says Agave a few lines later (1296); and we can add 'understand' (μανθάνειν) to the significant words in this category. 'This city must learn to understand' (ἐκμαθεῖν), said Dionysus in the Prologue (39); later he reproaches Pentheus for his ἀμαθία, his lack of understanding (480, 490); finally at the close of the play he tells his victims: 'too late have you understood me (ἐμάθετε), and, when you should, you knew me not' (1345).

Throughout the play Dionysus is manifesting himself, to the eyes and to the understanding: the theme is fundamental. Yet who within the play sees and understands him as he really is? Does Pentheus?

Let us recall the first scene in which Pentheus and the Stranger are confronted. The former's curiosity is aroused and he asks questions. 'You say you saw the god clear (ὁρᾶν σαφῶς): of what sort was he?' (477). The answer is evasive, but significant: 'Of what sort he would —*I* did not order it.' The initiate cannot command his revelation of this god of many forms; yet in fact the form in which the god appears will depend upon the nature and capacities of the subject. What does Pentheus see? A troubler of his kingdom (and that he surely is); an irritating sophist who challenges his authority; a beautiful young man whom he suspects and envies.[1] The presence of the 'god' he does not divine: 'Where is he?' he replies, when the Stranger refers ironically to his close proximity; 'he is not visible (φανερός) to my eyes.' The god who is close to him and whom he will never recognise is the god within him, the Dionysiac forces of sensual and egotistic emotion that actuate him. This he understands as little as he understands the working of Dionysus upon the women of Thebes, thinking their worship a mere pretext for sexual promiscuity. He is ἀμαθής: crude, insensitive, devoid of understanding. Later he suffers, like Agave, from gross physical illusion; and it is noteworthy that his entrance in this state is, like hers, accompanied by an accumulation of words of sight and seeing.[2] In this state he goes to the mountain. Not till the last moment did his vision clear so that he could 'understand (ἐμάνθανεν) that he was near his doom' (1113). He understood his physical danger; of greater insight there was, and

[1] The sensual appearance of the Stranger is precisely the form in which Dionysus should and could reveal himself to the suppressed sensuality of Pentheus (453 sqq.).

[2] See p. 118 n. 1. Note, however, that the illusion of both includes a symbolical revelation: to Pentheus of the animal in the god, to Agave of the animal in Pentheus.

could be, nothing, nor should we read too much into his ultimate admission of error.

But Pentheus is ἀμαθής, and lack of insight (except on the lowliest levels) is characteristic of him. He can see Dionysus externally as sensualist and as competitor for power, for these things he does understand; beyond this, it is through him rather than to him that the god reveals himself. Others may see more clearly. Does the second human principal? Does Agave?

Agave is a Bacchanal, but a special case among the Bacchanals, at once member of a band and an individual character of the play. Like Pentheus, she serves to illustrate, only from another angle, the relation of Dionysus to the individual life. At first, swept away in a collective enthusiasm, she is blind and in the ecstasy of the moment unwittingly destroys what is dearest to her and glories in it. It is this state of illusion, comparable to that of Pentheus, which is presented with cruel insistence at her entry. But she has now returned to conditions where clear vision is possible, and under her father's treatment she becomes ἔννους or rational. Her father bids her 'look and understand'. But how clear her vision became, how much mental insight she gained into what had happened, the mutilation of the text does not permit us to determine. Her one speech of profound emotion is lost; lines in which she may have addressed the god are of doubtful attribution.[1] Her one certain comment is as follows: 'It was Dionysus that destroyed us: now I understand.' But does this imply a deeper understanding of the works and nature of Dionysus than the confession of sin on the dying lips of Pentheus? It seems hardly probable: more we cannot say.

Similarly, all the other characters, greater and lesser, have their partial and incomplete vision of Dionysus. Teiresias can view him objectively, but is temperamentally incapable of any deeper insight; he has the politician's view of what can be done with him, of how he can, by judicious treatment, be turned into something other than he is. Cadmus's view is equally external; he sees him as an asset to his family. When the catastrophe comes and the indiscriminate working of Dionysiac force has dashed down the edifice of his pride, he is left in confusion of mind, torn between protest and submission.

So also with the minor characters. The Soldier sees in Dionysus a gracious and smiling prisoner, and, if he is also the worker of strange and violent wonders, no sense of discrepancy arises in his

[1] See p. 146 n. 1.

mind. The Herdsman sees him as the source of sensual pleasures. The second Messenger has better opportunity than any of seeing the devastation he can cause, but ends his speech with the expressions of conventional piety.

The characters then, according to their capacities, differ in the degree of their understanding of Dionysus, but in none of them is it clear or profound. Perhaps it is otherwise with his devoted followers, the Bacchanals of the Chorus. Now it is true that in their songs we find a lucid revelation of their god. Yet that lucidity hardly derives from lucid minds in the singers, and our examination, if it is valid, has shown how often the full significance of the words sung escapes the singers and aesthetic and moral discords pass unnoticed by them. They are partisans. They know Dionysus indeed as the author and sharer of their joys, their peace and their frenzy, but how he works in the world they cannot see, for their view is deliberately restricted to the appetite and emotion of the moment; they are blind, like the blind forces of nature they so closely resemble.

Dionysus is manifest; but who sees him? There can only be one answer to this question. It is Euripides who sees Dionysus clearly and has presented him in the play, not partially through the eyes of the human beings involved in it, who are in the midst of forces they do not understand and blunder into fatal events, but through the play as a whole, which is the product and expression of his own surpassing insight into the nature and works of Dionysus. He has presented him through his treatment of the action and the characters, making those short-sighted agents the vehicle of a revelation denied to themselves; he has presented him above all in the choral commentary, using the creeds and polemics of a fanatical band to imply a lucid understanding of fanaticism.

We have asked what was the 'wisdom' of Euripides, and we have perhaps found a partially valid answer. It was a legitimate question on more than one ground. Euripides wrote for an age preoccupied with the idea of *sophia*; for over a generation sophists had been claiming to teach it in every department of life, and we may believe that the word σοφός, 'wise' or 'clever', was as constantly upon the lips of intelligent Athenians as it is on those of Euripidean characters. So, in making this idea an emphatic—and controversial—element in his play, Euripides must have provoked in his audience the query as to what he himself considered σοφόν. Nor was there anything surprising in the association of *sophia* with a poet and his poetry.

The first and obvious meaning of the word in this connection is that of craftsmanship or skill: it was so that Pindar used it of his own poetry, and Aristophanes in the *Frogs* seems in general to mean much the same when he speaks of Aeschylus and Euripides as 'wise poets' in competition. The *sophia* of Euripides is thus exemplified in his poetry, in his drama; it is the quality that brings them to success; and, if we regard a play simply as an effective construction of effective lyrics and dialogue and narrative, then his *sophia* is simply his technical ability. But a play of the calibre of the *Bacchae* involves something more—a relationship to, and an interpretation of, its subject-matter. We must therefore correspondingly enlarge the conception of the *sophia* which shaped the play, defining it as that combination of intelligence and sensitive sympathy which enabled the poet to grasp the phenomena with which he was dealing and to embody them in a work of art. The play is more than an exhibition of technical skill, it is a revelation; and it is the *sophia* of Euripides, regarded as insight and understanding, that has made this revelation possible.

The poet's *sophia*, as we have so far considered it, is a personal quality. Its possession is consistent with complete detachment and complete indifference to the human predicament. To the Greeks at least such an attitude would have seemed incomprehensible. When 'Dionysus' in the *Frogs* makes the final test of the competing poets one not of art, but of political wisdom, we must doubtless beware of pressing the evidence of a comic (and topical) poet too far. Nevertheless, there is an undeniable vein of didacticism in Greek poetry, and, in particular, the solemn circumstances of the Attic stage encouraged the Athenians to think of their dramatists as performing a function both religious and political. If a poet was 'wise', σοφός was a term, not only of craft, but of practical and political life. Ancient critics often press the didactic element in poetry to an extreme, nor should we rashly attribute to the poets the naïvety of their interpreters. The purposes of art are manifold, and its relationship to life perplexing; and this is no place to prosecute the debate upon its social function. It is assumed, however, that insight is one characteristic of art, and that one of the functions of the creative artist is to illuminate the nature of things. It would be strange if this illumination cast no light at all upon the practical conduct of life.

The *Bacchae* indeed implies a practical problem. That problem is, most widely stated, how to deal with the forces of emotion, particularly as they are generated in the associations of human beings. Euripides has envisaged this problem with clarity: has he also made a contribution of wisdom towards its solution? It is important to bear in mind the limitations under which he wrote. The particular dramatic form that the problem was given depended on the conditions of the Greek stage and the *data* of Greek legend. In one respect the legend was of the utmost service, for in the Bacchanals the dramatist found (as it were) the pure essence of emotionalism and in their way of life a technique of surpassing efficiency for leading the emotional life. At the same time it involves a degree of abstraction and simplification which is absent from concrete historical situations. This disruptive force comes into contact with an ordered human society, but the effects of it are only selectively shown. The women take to the mountains; the chief executive of the state, who is responsible for dealing with the situation, reveals his own unstable emotionalism; disaster follows. It is no part of the play, for instance, to show the reactions of the male population to this force. Nor is there opportunity to study the ultimate effects upon the community of its incursion: the knot is arbitrarily untied, as so often in Euripides, when the poet has said what he wished to say.

In point of fact, a movement upon the scale of that in the *Bacchae* has a past and a future which can only be hinted at within the framework of a Greek play. It is astounding how much Euripides has contrived to include. The movement may be in part fortuitous, arising from migration and the clash of cultures; and the Greece-Asia contrast is an indication of this. If, when it arrives, it meets with immediate success, this is probably a sign that all has not been well with the existing social life, apparently so stable; in the case of Thebes the circumscribed life of its women, symbolised by their looms and shuttles, had pent up in them emotion that longed to be liberated (which is the psychological interpretation of the legend of punishment). It falls to Pentheus to deal with it; but he too suffers from the society in which he lives, which is competitive, which places a high value upon power, and yet demands *sophrosyne* even from its rulers. The result is explosive emotion in him also, which quite disqualifies him for his task. This task a genius might have accomplished, but in what manner the play does not and cannot tell us. The solution that Greece ultimately found is represented in the play by Teiresias, but this does not mean that if Teiresias had been in charge all would have been well. The Greek solution must in actual fact have come about over a long period of experiment and occasional disaster, and have resulted not only from the politic wisdom of individuals but from the complicated interplay of many factors: national character, pre-existing social conditions, the tendency of movements to peter out in diminishing returns. What the play can and does show is a broad generalisation.

For the disaster in which it ends is the joint product of the magnitude of the forces released and of the absence of any kind of understanding on the part of those who had to deal with them. Yet insight and understanding are essential if human beings are to have a chance against the blind forces in and around them. If they begin to understand, then and not till then can they begin to control them. So we return to the 'wisdom' of Euripides, to discover that the personal quality of *sophia* which enabled him to write his play and the contribution of *sophia* which he makes in it are, in the last analysis, one and the same thing. Insight made the play; and it is the play's service that it can at once call attention to the necessity of insight and, within its own effective limits, provide it.

CHAPTER XII

EURIPIDES AND DIONYSUS (3)

At the end of the preceding chapter the problem of the *Bacchae* was discussed in terms of society and as a practical issue of politics in the widest sense. This approach is legitimate, not merely because of the tradition of Greek drama or even because of the interest which Euripides, like Shakespeare, so often displays in the social and political setting of his plays, but because the play itself presents the coming of Dionysus as a political problem. Pentheus, who had to face this problem, is not made the centre of a tragic individual conflict; and the very detachment with which he is treated perhaps in itself entitles us to place the political issue in the forefront. The issue is of course far wider in scope than the impact of a cult, and the implied conclusion is valid in the wider as in the narrower context.

This conclusion does not take the form of a policy or prescription, which it was not the function of the poet to provide. Euripides did not write the play in order to advise the Athenian government how they should deal with the cult of Sabazius or Bendis or with any other political problem which involved the forces of emotion. Nor need we suppose that, after observing for a lifetime the working of emotion in individuals and in communities, he was sanguine of the possibility of applying reason and understanding to human affairs.[1] Yet the conclusion to which the play tends—that insight is necessary for the avoidance of disaster—is the more helpful because insight is itself provided by the poet in the play. It is a conclusion equally valid if we regard the personal aspects of the subject-matter; and indeed the mass phenomena can be analysed, though not exhaustively, into individual problems.

It is from this point of view that the *Bacchae* has more often been approached, and with good reason. The play deals largely with the quality, value and implications of Dionysiac experience, which, when organised and consequently enhanced, creates a political problem, but which exists as an element in individual human experience. In particular, the songs of the Bacchanals are often capable of carrying

[1] He had recently, in the *Phoenissae*, made Jocasta the somewhat incongruous spokesman of σοφία (e.g. 453, 460, 530, 569 sq., 584), to demonstrate the weakness of σοφοὶ λόγοι (1259) in the face of passion.

a personal reference. The beauty, the emotion, the whole way of life seem to challenge and evoke a personal response.

In the preceding chapter, psychological forces were compared to natural phenomena which can be tamed and harnessed. But there is this difference. In dealing with fire or flood man is controlling, or trying to control, external forces, whereas in psychological matters the intellect which should control and the emotional force to be controlled are part of one and the same complex personality; and the judgement of an individual upon Dionysus may depend not merely upon his observation of society but upon an idiosyncrasy which is attracted or repelled by the Dionysiac technique for the gratification of emotion. Thus, when it is agreed that Euripides saw the social danger of Dionysiac emotion—a danger that could only be averted by clear-sighted understanding—we may still ask what was his own individual and personal response to Dionysus. Did he hanker after the Dionysiac experience? Did he, as has often been suggested, turn to its contemplation in revolt against the arid intellectualism of his urban contemporaries? Is this why the choruses of the *Bacchae* are so evocative and so moving?

The foothold of the literary critic is always precarious: we are here on exceptionally uncertain ground. One thing perhaps can be agreed, that Euripides, the intellectual poet, the critic of accepted standards, the dramatist whose plays won more notoriety than prizes, had followed the hard path and may have found it hard. There are passages in a number of earlier plays which may reflect the personal bitterness of one who had met the usual reward of a critical and unconventional mind;[1] and when, in this play, the Chorus sings its warning against the cleverness which is no true wisdom, against thoughts that are not fit for mortals and the pursuit of ambitious ends, appropriate as these sentiments are to the immediate context of the play, it may be that the poet had, among other things, his own career in mind. For Euripides had consistently in the realm of thought pursued a *sophia* that seemed pernicious to the common man with an intellectual ambition that seemed overweening and extravagant (περισσόν). It may be that the very contemplation of mindless ease brought him an enhanced sense of his own agonies and his deprivation of modes of escape which were open to others but not to him.

These things may be true, but we should be chary of assuming them too confidently or overstressing their significance for the

[1] E.g. *Med.* 294 sqq.

interpretation of the play. It is indeed rash to conjecture what mental conflicts or harmonies prevailed behind the austere bearing which tradition ascribes to Euripides. By his plays, and only by his plays, is he known to us, and before we attribute to him, on the evidence of the *Bacchae*, a hankering after Dionysiac experience, a *Sehnsucht*, the futile emotion of an inharmonious mind,[1] we should be clear what we are doing.

Certainly, the mere fact that Euripides was enabled by the imaginative sympathy of an artist to express the peaceful aspects of the Bacchic life in poetry of such compelling power and beauty does not entitle us to assume that he yearned after that life. The critic, if he is to avoid the worst pitfalls of subjectivism, must adopt a self-denying ordinance in these matters; he must be slow to ascribe to a dramatic poet the sentiments expressed by the characters of the drama, unless these sentiments are patently undramatic. The hunting-ground for the undramatic pronouncement, in the *Bacchae* as in other plays, has of course been the choral odes; and it can be justly pointed out that the philosophical lucidity displayed in them is, in a sense, undramatic or at least conventional, like the actual presence of the Chorus. What critics have sometimes missed is that these abstractions, formally 'undramatic' though they may be, without exception reveal a state of the singers' minds or else make explicit the assumptions that underlie their way of life. And though in this process a commentary is often implied which cannot *ex hypothesi* emanate from the singers, this commentary is implied, not stated; the method is essentially aesthetic, by juxtaposition and contrast putting the utterances of the singers into wider (and dramatic) relations, of past and future, of cause and effect, than the relatively simple (and essentially lyrical) moods of Bacchanals admit. But it need never be assumed that the poet has moved out of the dramatic context of his play. Within this dramatic context it was necessary for him to gain sympathy for the Bacchanals—to render their activities and their philosophy attractive—and, being a great dramatic artist, he did so with entire success. No less consummately did he express their furious and revengeful mood.

Before we ascribe to Euripides a hankering for the Bacchic life, we must have better reason than his success in the prime function of a dramatist. We must, moreover, ask and answer the following

[1] Or even assume, with Wilamowitz (*Herakles*, I, p. 133), that he had been haunted by 'wild spirits'.

question. If Euripides hankered, after what precisely did he hanker? Was it simply after the quietism of the Bacchanals that he yearned, exasperated by the restless political activity of Athens, or exhausted by his own self-questionings? But the play does not deal with people who are quiet and stay quiet: it deals with the indissoluble union of peace and fury in the life of the Bacchanals. Was it then after the emotional intensity of their whole life that he hankered, contrasting it with the arid intellectualism (if that be the phrase) of an argumentative generation—intellect and arguments which had been expressed not least in his own theatre? There is a conflict between reason and emotion. If Euripides had failed to resolve this conflict in himself, perhaps he looked with frustrated longing towards the standard-bearers of emotion. Yet the play is not, in simple terms, concerned with the conflict of reason and emotion in the individual person.

In fact, one of the difficulties of discussing the play from the personal angle is that Euripides has not written it from that angle. We see, indeed, the effects of Dionysus upon Pentheus, upon Agave, and upon the minor characters, but nowhere do we see a tragic conflict between reason and emotion. Pentheus is no Phaedra; he is all emotion, though the emotion is partly dammed by convention and prejudice. The part of Agave is mutilated, but can hardly have exemplified such a conflict in the circumstances of her stage-appearance. It is doubtless true, and seemed true to Euripides, that reason and emotion, which co-exist in the human personality, must be harmonised and that neither can be neglected with impunity. But this is not the immediate issue and moral of the *Bacchae*, though it may be implied. Euripides might indeed have written a play upon these lines, and did in the *Hippolytus* write a play upon a comparable subject, in which the element of tragedy lies in the fact that there are two goddesses, each claiming service, whose claims are incompatible.

In the *Bacchae*, however, there is one god only, Dionysus, first and last: like Aphrodite and Artemis, a god of exclusive claims; but, unlike them, with an exclusive hearing for those claims. He is the god, not of emotion—there are many gods of emotion—but of an ecstasy which can only be obtained by the extreme and uncompromising cult of emotion. He demands the absolute worship which is given to him by the band of Asiatic fanatics, and it may be doubted whether he would be content with the lukewarm tributes of modern scholars. This Dionysiac gift of ecstasy, at whatever price it may be bought, has its own unique quality and attraction. But was it after ecstasy that Euripides hankered?

It is worth considering the elements which give attractiveness to the life of Bacchanals as portrayed by Euripides in this play. There is emotion itself; there is peace, quietude and contentment; there is nature; there is the group, with its comfort and support. In the context of Dionysiac religion, we have seen what these things mean and what they involve. But a vote against the exclusive claims of Dionysus is not a vote against emotion, peace, nature and the group, though it is a refusal—because of the price which has to be paid—to accept the enhanced intensity in the experience of all these things which Dionysus may give.

The value of emotion, as such, is not really an issue of the play. There is indeed one instance in Greek literature of an artist (and essentially a dramatic artist) who was led by the conflict of reason and emotion in himself and in society into a strong hostility towards emotion. Since Plato expressed this hostility, paradoxically, in moving art, it is not inconceivable that Euripides should have written an exciting play with the object of deprecating emotion; and the achievement of such a paradox might well have been attended by disharmony and by a yearning after the very experiences which he had rejected. But the play gives no ground for ascribing such an attitude to Euripides. Indeed what the suppression of emotion may lead to is made all too evident. Again, there are two 'intellectual' characters in the play. There is Dionysus himself, whose calm logic displays the heartlessness of the god, the heartlessness of the force. There is Teiresias, but he is treated satirically, and neither as a manifest rationalist nor as the incongruous champion of enthusiasm can his authority survive the shafts of irony. Euripides himself has an appreciative insight into the qualities of emotions, not a merely objective understanding of their effects. He pleads for insight in deprecation, not of emotion, but of the blind cult of emotions without consideration of their consequences or discrimination of their qualities.

The Bacchanals are shown in moods of quiet enjoyment, and they praise peace in their songs; the essence of their peace is contentment with the moment and a life self-justified in the present. It is the very persuasiveness of such passages that has tempted critics to say that Euripides is 'on the side' of the Bacchanals or that he hankered after their way of life. For quiet contentment is a desirable thing and must be known in the present or not at all. When the Bacchanals sing of a peace that gives prosperity and allows young men to live, the appeal of this to a war-harassed generation is obvious.[1] Nor was a contentment which is a common gift to high and low a negligible ideal to a Greece torn by the struggle of rich and poor. Yet in what does the peace of the Bacchanals consist? The gift of which they sing is the Lethean gift of wine; the source of their contentment is oblivion; the life of quietness which they praise is capable of changing in a moment into hideous fury.

The Bacchanals of the Chorus praise peace; the Theban Bacchanals pursue it by fleeing from the city to the woods and mountains and entering into communion with nature, animate and inanimate. Here again there are passages of compelling beauty which describe the environment of their worship and the participation in it of beast and mountain. Nor perhaps would Euripides, who (according to tradition) used to retreat from the dust and crowds of Athens to a sea-cave on Salamis, have denied the truth that Virgil and Wordsworth taught, that such communion is possible to man and is a source of inward peace. But nature is diverse and Bacchanals undiscriminating. Their revolt from 'civilisation' is too complete. They move with the blind hostility of natural forces; they embrace the internecine cruelty of hunting animals; and, if in their peace they suckled wild creatures, in their fury they tear them and befoul the grass and trees with blood.[2]

Bacchanals associate in bands, which are knit by close ties of sentiment and aim. The instinct to associate is deeply rooted in human nature, and may be a valuable source of strength and stimulus, even to a poet. It may also be a cause of envy in the solitary, since humanity is too weak for complete individualism. We know too little of Euripides, who had his friends like other men, to say how heavily the burden of individualism lay upon him. Still less can we assert that some hypothetical poverty of social life led him to hanker after group-emotion, raised to the point of ecstasy by the worship of Dionysus. For, when Aristotle said that the solitary man must be either a beast or a god, he forgot perhaps that there were social groups which could make a man both at once. To the *thiasos* of Dionysus everything is surrendered, including the intellect and the individuality; while it enables the individual to transcend his limitations, it is

[1] See p. 66.
[2] See p. 95 n. 1.

indifferent to the direction of that transcendence; it allows the lowest to set its easy and uncritical standard.

For it is part of the wisdom of the Bacchanals to accept 'whatever the mass of ordinary men believes and practises'. They are traditionalists who hold that 'what has been accepted through long ages is eternal and grounded in nature'.[1] For the adherents of a new religion to base its defence upon tradition is perhaps a formal inconsistency. Similarly, by his reference to the 'ordinary man' and popular standards, Euripides might seem to have strained in some degree the limits of his theme. For what is the common ground between the emotionalist and the traditionalist, the revolutionary and the conservative? Broadly, what they share is the intolerance of criticism and the rejection of the intellect. It has been held that it is Euripides who pays tribute to the value of tradition and who strains his context to express a sense of kinship with the common man.[2] But is the context really violated by these themes or does it rather illuminate them?

Tradition is not something which can be called good or bad *in vacuo*, since it contains both what is valuable and what is harmful to human progress. The common man is Protean; courageous, loyal and full of an instinctive wisdom; cruel and treacherous; violent, patient, generous, and crassly stupid. There were the shepherds who kept watch over their flocks by night, and there was the mob that shouted for Barabbas. In the *Bacchae* itself the common man ranges from the crudity of the first Messenger to the sensibility of the second.[3] We must ask, therefore, what characteristics of the common man are relevant to the context of the play. The answer must surely lie in those characteristics which he exhibits when acting in the mass (πλῆθος), for it is then that he resembles the Bacchanals, and it is the mass, not the individual, that they commend. The answer must lie in those characteristics which he exhibits when he follows accepted tradition blindly and uncritically, with a massive emotional response. These traditions may be merely the codification of instinct, but they

[1] 430 sqq.; 895 sq. (see pp. 111 sq.).

[2] Murray, *Essays and Addresses*, p. 84; Dodds, p. 123.

[3] In other plays of Euripides the role of the common man is as various as the dramatic situations demand. The Nurse in the *Hippolytus* is loyal and affectionate, but the intervention of her lowly traditional morality is disastrous. Best of them is perhaps the Peasant in the *Electra*, a decent, sensitive man, but one who shared the social assumptions upon which the Pelopidae battened. (On another αὐτουργός, see p. 93 n. 1.)

bear the title of νόμοι and borrow the dignity of civilised Law; they are greeted as καλά, as setting the standard of honour. One such tradition is so greeted in the play and provides the primary context for all references to popular and traditional standards. This is that revenge over one's enemies than which there is no gift of the gods 'more honourable in the sight of men'. This tradition, though rejected by Euripides and by the finer spirits of his age, was, and was to remain, as characteristic of the mass of common men as it is appropriate to the psychology of Bacchanals. Indeed, all history is full of the Dionysiac reaction of the crowd. Euripides, who hated demagogy and 'power politics', did not halt in his dramatic stride to pay a tribute to their tools and victims. Nor did he betray a lifetime spent in the criticism of traditional standards and conventional cruelties.

This, then, is the subject of the play: the Dionysiac group and its disastrous potentialities; the natural life and the way in which it may dehumanise the men and women who lead it; the drugged peace which alternates with furious violence; the exclusive and undiscriminating cult of emotion. To this context everything the play contains is relevant, and nothing is left over to be explained upon some other basis. Was it after these things, then, that Euripides hankered? The play itself gives little ground for asserting it. These were in any case types of experience barred to him by his own nature, and by the very fact that he could write the play and the actual lyrics which have prompted the belief in his nostalgic yearnings. To write it was a necessity of his nature, but it meant not only entering imaginatively into the emotions of Bacchanals, but standing outside them with firm rational control and clear-sighted vision.

Euripides saw Dionysus clearly and whole, both in his beauty and in his great danger, and presented him as he saw him. The entire play is concentrated to an extraordinary degree upon this single, if various, subject. Though we are shown the effects of Dionysus upon certain individuals, there is no conflict except the contradiction in the nature of the god,[1] no tragedy except the tragic condition of humanity exposed to this contradiction. For, if Euripides wrote a play which showed Dionysus first as beautiful and then as cruel, this was not mere subservience to a given plot or to obvious dramatic effect, but he so shaped the play as to focus attention upon the cruelty and to demonstrate the inexorable interdependence of the cruelty and the beauty. Euripides recognised Dionysus for the danger that he

[1] Grube, pp. 399 sq.

was, publicly in the societies of men, when he works at full strength through the group, and privately in the lives of individuals. The worship of such a god he could not commend; and the anthropomorphic god upon the stage is treated with a satire which is essentially consistent with the treatment accorded to his subtler manifestations throughout the length and breadth of the play. Euripides recognised, but hated Dionysus. He recognised his power, and saw that there was only one weapon to employ against him, which was to understand him and to propagate understanding of him.

It is what Euripides says in his play that matters, and not his private psychological problems. As we have seen, it is rash to draw conclusions about these problems from the text, and the manipulation of choral odes for this purpose is an easy game. Let us play it for once, remembering that in the creation of this masterpiece Euripides was experiencing the supreme tension and excitement of artistic achievement. 'I grudge not the wise their wisdom', sing the Bacchanals; and their words may conceivably reflect certain moods of bitterness in the poet. But when they continue: 'I rejoice in hunting after these other things great and manifest', it may well have been in his mind that he too was a hunter and knew the joys of the chase; that the objects of his pursuit were great ends, though rejected by the singers, and were as manifest to him as they were hidden from them. For it was understanding itself that he pursued and its expression in art.

APPENDIX

EURIPIDES THE RATIONALIST

In Chapter 1 Verrall's interpretation of the play was mentioned and dismissed. To Verrall (and to Norwood, who anticipated Verrall in applying the latter's general principles to the *Bacchae*) it was a primary purpose of Euripides to discredit the received religion by providing a rationalistic explanation of ostensibly miraculous events.[1] This view was dismissed on the ground that, if the attention of the audience is concentrated upon the question of natural *versus* supernatural causation, it will be distracted from the poetic and symbolic value of the events described. This is the conclusive argument against Verrall, but many errors and improbabilities, more or less damaging to his thesis, have been pointed out by various writers, to whom the reader is referred.[2]

It would be wrong to suppose that 'rationalism' of a kind plays no part in the drama of Euripides. The Greek was under no obligation to believe in every detail of the myth, and there were doubtless sceptics in the audience (just as there are sceptics in the plays themselves).[3] The 'rationalism' of Euripides, such as it is, is a corollary of his 'realism'. The general trend of his theatre was towards the normal conditions of contemporary life.[4] For the purposes of his plots he accepts supernatural assumptions, but his 'realistic' characters are not in general motivated by mythical considerations. This is normally a matter of tacit inference, and Euripides never goes to the trouble of providing an elaborate structure of natural causes in substitution of the supernatural. Sometimes, however, in dealing with the mythical antecedents of his characters, he will throw out a hint of scepticism. Where the tone of the play is relatively light, the intention may be partly to divert the audience, partly to put them in the right mood for a realistic treatment of the subject.[5] A more

[1] Norwood, *The Riddle of the Bacchae*; Verrall, *The Bacchants of Euripides*.

[2] E.g. C. Bailey in *C.R.* xxv (1911), pp. 143–5; Dodds, pp. xliv–xlvii; Grube, ch. iv *passim*; Kitto, pp. 380 sq.

[3] Menelaus at *Or.* 1556 sqq. is the Verrallian rationalist to the life. Compare the alternatives at *I.T.* 1166.

[4] Cf. Aristoph. *Frogs* 959.

[5] Cf. *Hel.* 17, 21 (on which see Kitto, p. 319); *Or.* 5, 8.

serious instance occurs in the *Hercules Furens*, where the divine paternity of the hero is essential to the mechanics of the plot, being the cause of Hera's jealous persecution; yet, at the climax of the play, Heracles himself in a noble utterance rejects the myth.[1] The inconsistency is largely formal, since behind the mythical superficies lies a human drama, in which the madness of Heracles is the product of his own character and way of life; if Hera symbolises the gratuitous malice of fate, superimposed upon these factors, the symbol can be thrown aside when it has served its purpose.

Similar movements of mind may be found in the *Bacchae* also. When Agave is asked by Cadmus to give her husband's name (1273), she replies: 'One of the Sown Men (so they say), Echion.'[2] 'The words sound', as Professor Dodds aptly remarks of the parenthesis, 'like an acknowledgement that the Sown Men, who grew from the dragon's teeth, belong to legend, not to the real world of human suffering in which this part of the action moves.' Otherwise, the mythological antecedents of Pentheus—for he too has a footing in the supernatural—are taken at their face-value, though perhaps regarded as a vaguely sinister contribution to his heredity (see p. 79). The very names of the Sown Men (Ground-man, Earth-man, Overweening and Monster, as well as Echion, the Snake-man) suggest that from his grim father's blood he may have derived a vein of ferocity, just as he may be supposed to have derived a tendency to emotionalism from his mother; and this joint heredity seems to be stressed at 507 and 1276. For Euripides knew that no human being can be fully understood apart from his heredity.[3] As

[1] Grube (p. 58) argues that *H.F.* 1341 sq. refer only to amours within the divine circle. But 1345 sq. (δεῖται γὰρ ὁ θεός...οὐδενός) applies equally to the amours of gods with mortals. Heracles is throughout puzzled by the question of his parentage and never gets it straight (1258, 1263). But in these words he brushes aside the whole mythological aspect of the play as an irrelevance (1340) and bases his decision on human values. Note συμφοραῖς (1349), τύχη (1357), and the combination Ἥρας τύχη (1393). There is no further reference to the gods, and the play ends with a purely human moral—the value of friendship (1425 sq.).

[2] The effect of similar expressions at 605, 629, 1078, is different, depending on the ironical fact that it *was* Dionysus.

[3] Similarly in the *Hippolytus* the stories of Pasiphae and Ariadne are not treated sceptically, but indicate a difficult heredity for Phaedra (337–43, 372). Hippolytus himself may owe his peculiar temperament to his Amazon mother and the circumstances of her union with Theseus (10, 307, 351, 581, 1082 sq.).

to the mysterious birth of Dionysus, 'rationalism' is left to the characters, to Semele's sisters (26 sqq.) and to Pentheus (245), who thought that Semele, having sinned with a mortal, had at the prompting of Cadmus ascribed the sin to Zeus. A plausible, but erroneous, explanation!

Miracles that form part of the action fall into a different category from mythological events precedent to the drama. Of the reported miracles in this play—the loosing of the Bacchanals and the various happenings upon Cithaeron—Verrall sought to show that they were presented on evidence deliberately made suspect by the poet. His attempt must be reckoned a failure, both for the slenderness of the indications he quotes, and because to look for them, if they were there, would to all but prosaic minds be a thankless if not impossible task in face of the poetic power and the wide range of thought which bear irresistibly in other directions. The so-called 'palace-miracle', which, if it occurs, occurs in the presence of the spectator, needs fuller consideration.

As has already been suggested in Chapter VI, the handling of this episode is conditioned by two factors:

(i) The convention and resources of the Attic stage did not provide more than a minimum of scenic illusion; and the Athenian spectator, seeing little or nothing happening before his eyes, would not suspect fraud, but would, like his Elizabethan counterpart, allow his imagination to be fed through the ear instead of the eye.

(ii) It was a dramatic necessity for Euripides to 'play down' the palace-miracle, since if it were too overwhelming, it would make what follows an anti-climax (see pp. 83 sq.).

For both these reasons, and perhaps for others, there is a vagueness, a phantasmagoric quality, about the whole episode (including the narrative of the Stranger) which has exercised some critics. And there are difficulties, if we should wish to plot the occurrences accurately by time and place. Earthquake is invoked, and the Chorus see the architraves of the palace-front gape apart. (It is doubtful if the audience see any such thing, though they doubtless hear a noise.) Fire is bidden to consume the house (δώματα) of Pentheus; what the Chorus see is an uprush of flame in the tomb of Semele. (And perhaps, but not certainly, the audience see it too.) From the last words of the Chorus before the Stranger enters it would appear that they expect the main effect to follow.[1] But he enters in the role of

[1] 602: ἔπεισι (fut.) governs the time of τιθείς.

Messenger. In the forefront of his account stands the story of the binding of the bull, symbolically so important (see pp. 9, 84), but an event which corresponds in time with the singing of the preceding ode. 'Meanwhile, Bacchus came and shook the palace and lit fire in his mother's tomb.' This corresponds to what the Chorus saw. 'When Pentheus saw it, thinking the palace was ablaze....' But the palace was not ablaze, and there was in fact no effect fully corresponding to the σύμφλεγε δώματα of the divine voice. To the shaking of the palace, which is mentioned by the Stranger at 606 (διατινάξαντος) and 623 (ἀνετίναξε), the Chorus are witnesses; but the mention of headlong collapse at 633 (δώματ' ἔρρηξεν χαμᾶζε) is introduced late in the narrative and in an oddly abrupt and incidental fashion. When and where did this happen? There is hardly time to ask before Pentheus returns to the stage.

These things cause no difficulty so long as we recognise the plane of reality upon which the whole incident takes place and that the sheer illusion which set Pentheus to bind a bull and pursue a phantom is little further removed from actuality than the earthquake and the fire.

It is interesting to compare the only comparable episode in Euripidean drama—the irruption of Lyssa in the *Hercules Furens*. Here too there is a suggestion of structural damage on a large scale, but the stage effects are governed by Attic convention. Here too we find the same difficulty in determining 'what actually happened'. Lyssa says (864 sq.): 'I will break down the halls and will assault the house, having first killed the children'—i.e. no such catastrophe before the murders. The events within the palace are (as in the *Bacchae*) accompanied by lyrics from the Chorus and then narrated by an eyewitness. The lyrics, which are factually vague (because the Chorus cannot see what is happening), are punctuated by cries from Amphitryon (within). We cannot relate these cries with precision to specific details in the following narrative, which implies a far longer interval between the first alarm and the last of the murders than there is between Amphitryon's ἰώ μοι μέλεος (887)[1] and the entry of the Messenger (911). By 900, however, the children are presumably dead, and the material catastrophe foretold by Lyssa is due, and is seemingly announced. ἰδοὺ ἰδού, θύελλα σείει δῶμα, συμπίπτει στέγη (904 sq.). But the ascription is uncertain. If the words are spoken by a choreute, he saw something which could not be

[1] This attribution is fairly certain.

adequately represented upon the Greek stage, but they may be spoken by Amphitryon within (so Wilamowitz). In any case, the sole visible relic of the catastrophe is the broken column to which Heracles is bound when he is revealed to the audience (1094 sqq.).[1] There is, however, a further complication. The bloodshed was, so the Messenger tells (1001 sqq.), cut short by the appearance of Pallas, who cast a stone into the breast of Heracles which 'put him to sleep'. It is clear that 906 sqq. also refer to this incident,[2] which is described as τάραγμα ταρτάρειον—a strong expression. Is it not then the action of Athena, not of Lyssa, which shakes the house and collapses the roof (905, 1007 sq.)? The truth seems to be that (as in the *Bacchae*) the poet has cultivated a deliberate vagueness. Noise and tumult are all that pass beyond the palace-front to the Chorus and the audience. What is to be attributed to the personal activity of Lyssa (who in any case works through Heracles), what to the manic fury of the possessed man, what to the violent but beneficent intervention of Athena—this is left in uncertainty. At the most we may say that there is some intentional misleading of the spectator: what appears at first to be the completion of Lyssa's work turns out to be the harsh kindness of Athena and so provides a ray of hope. For both Lyssa and Athena have their value as symbols: Lyssa of the madness of Heracles and its essential injustice, Athena of the power of friendship which, through the Athenian Theseus, will yet save him.

It remains to consider the theory of Verrall that the phenomena witnessed by the Chorus in the *Bacchae* were purely subjective. This cannot be dismissed as readily as most of his hypotheses. Whereas these generally impede the purposes of the drama, to represent the Bacchanals as victims of mass-hallucination would, on the contrary, subserve a fundamental purpose of the *Bacchae*, which is to exhibit the Dionysiac in the widest possible range. That a group animated by a single emotion is capable of auditory and visual hallucination seems to be a well-established fact. It is on the 'suggestibility' of the group that mass movements in religion and politics depend, and there is no

[1] Not only do the characters make no subsequent reference to a general collapse of the palace, but Amphitryon at 1056 is afraid that Heracles, if he wakes, will destroy it!

[2] ὦ Διὸς παῖ refers to Pallas, not to Heracles: this is conclusively argued by Wilamowitz. His ascription of the lines to the Chorus is less convincing. Why should they assume from 905 'the presence and activity of Athena'? After 864 they would more naturally put the disturbance to Lyssa's account. Murray follows Verrall in ascribing the lines to Heracles.

more powerful or more dangerous manifestation of the god who wills that his servants serve him in the *thiasos*.

The Bacchanals of the Chorus have been stimulated by the succession of fear, relief and adoration, before they hear the unearthly voice calling upon the spirit of Earthquake. This conception, once implanted in their minds, they accept with childlike faith in an atmosphere of worship (586–90). Then, and not till then, do they see—or ask one another if they have seen—what it has been suggested they will see. Similarly with the fire. The voice calls upon the lightning, and at once a choreute asks: 'Do you not see fire?' They fall down in an ecstasy of adoration, awaiting the appearance of the god. What did they see that was also visible to the audience? Perhaps nothing at all. It seems a distinct possibility (I rate it no higher) that Euripides—(*a*) given a miracle which he must, alike for the sake of tradition and for its symbolic value, introduce, but which he was bound, for dramatic reasons, to treat in an 'unreal' fashion; (*b*) given the conventions and conditions of the Attic stage, (*c*) given a chorus of emotionalists—intended so to write the scene as to suggest subjectivism. Not only would this add a brilliant and convincing feature to the total picture of Dionysiac psychology, but such a reaction on the part of the Chorus would be complementary to the illusions of Pentheus within the palace. Pentheus is a sinner and the Bacchanals 'saints', but I have argued elsewhere that he is in fact portrayed with Dionysiac characteristics and that his similarity to his opponents is part of the pattern of the play. It would, therefore, be appropriate for both him and them to display the same kind of reaction at the same juncture to the same manifestation of the god. This seems to be a possibility, no more. Against it is the complete absence of evidence that Euripides would have been aware of the phenomenon of collective hallucination.

SELECT INDEX

(The small figures refer to footnotes)